Praise for Mona Simpson's

Commitment

"A minimalist masterpiece. . . . In a story utterly devoid of car crashes, murders, abductions and explosions, Simpson bears down on the truly important questions about life—home, work, love and family. . . . *Commitment* makes the case in a quiet but insistent voice that our lives do matter, even if other people think they are broken."
—*The Washington Post*

"Vivid. . . . Excellent. . . . An absorbing, moving portrait of a Los Angeles family . . . as they navigate financial troubles, addiction and, centrally, mental illness. . . . [*Commitment* captures] the pain and joy and strangeness of being a person in a family."
—*Vanity Fair*

"*Commitment* manages to be both a model of the intricate network of familiar coordinates—love, money, art, work—and an intimate portrait of each individual caught, for better or worse, in its web. . . . Larger social, cultural, and emotional strains [are] sharply and movingly conveyed."
—*Minneapolis Star-Tribune*

"Simpson's latest is an astute tale of family trauma and resilience."
—*People*

"A heartbreaker. . . . Deeply felt. . . . Detailing the lives of a single mother who falls into a deep depression, and her three children, who suddenly must cope on their own."
—*Air Mail*

"The questions [Simpson] explores throughout *Commitment* are nuanced. How much are we in control of our own stories? How much of our lives do we spend chasing the security we think we knew as children, and how futile is that effort? . . . Simpson's affinity for [stories about American families] hasn't waned. Nor has her skill at exploring it in various modes." —*Alta Journal*

"A majestic novel, its vision and scope bringing to mind the work of Tolstoy, Stendhal, and Balzac." —Yiyun Li

"Simpson is a national treasure. *Commitment* is a sweeping family epic that took me from one American coast to another, through a difficult but unforgettable time period, and through the growing pains of three remarkable siblings. Simpson is so attuned to the family heart and oh dear Walter, Lina, and Donnie, have you forever moved mine." —Weike Wang

"A powerful family love story propelled by Simpson's profound understanding of people tested by that which could destroy them. In this beautifully written novel, the constant emotional and financial struggles make their hard-won triumphs, large and small, that much more glorious." —Amy Hempel

"A resonant novel about family and duty and the attendant struggles that come when a parent falls ill. The novel honors the spirit of fragile, imperfect mothers and the under-chronicled significance of friends in determining the lives of our children left on their own." —Justin Torres

Mona Simpson

Commitment

Mona Simpson is the bestselling author of *Anywhere But Here, The Lost Father, A Regular Guy, Off Keck Road, My Hollywood,* and *Casebook*. She has received a Whiting Award, a Hodder Fellowship at Princeton, an NEA Literature Fellowship, a Guggenheim Fellowship, a Lila Wallace–Reader's Digest Writers' Award, an American Academy of Arts and Letters Award in Literature, and the Mary McCarthy Prize in Short Fiction. *Off Keck Road* was a finalist for the PEN/Faulkner Award and won the Heartland Prize from the *Chicago Tribune*. She is the publisher of *The Paris Review* and is on the faculty at UCLA. She lives in Santa Monica, California.

Also by Mona Simpson

Anywhere But Here
The Lost Father
A Regular Guy
Off Keck Road
My Hollywood
Casebook

Commitment

MONA SIMPSON

VINTAGE BOOKS
A DIVISION OF PENGUIN RANDOM HOUSE LLC
NEW YORK

FIRST VINTAGE BOOKS EDITION 2024

The Library of Congress has cataloged the Knopf edition as follows:
Names: Simpson, Mona, author.
Title: Commitment / Mona Simpson.
Description: First edition. | New York: Alfred A. Knopf, 2023.
Identifiers: LCCN 2022023269 (print) | LCCN 2022023270 (ebook)
Subjects: GSAFD: Novels.
Classification: LCC PS3569.I5117 C66 2023 (print) |
LCC PS3569.I5117 (ebook) | DDC 813/.54—dc23
LC record available at https://lccn.loc.gov/2022023269
LC ebook record available at https://lccn.loc.gov/2022023270

Vintage Books Trade Paperback ISBN: 978-0-593-31296-4
eBook ISBN: 978-0-593-31928-4

Book design by Maria Carella

vintagebooks.com

Printed in the United States of America
10 9 8 7 6 5 4 3 2 1

FOR KEVIN THOMAS

Once there was a way to get back home.

Paul McCartney, "Golden Slumbers"

Book 1

Walter Aziz, America

1.

Walter arranged for a ride up to Berkeley with a girl he barely knew. He promised to bring only his stereo, his albums, and one suitcase. She reminded him that he was moving for the whole rest of his life. He didn't think so. He was already planning to return.

He had to go to college; he understood that. All his life his mother had spoken of her nursing degree in a reverent tone, sometimes fingering the coin around her neck, proud to be the first person in her family to graduate. But he thought of himself as a slender pin that kept the machinery of his family ticking.

The morning he was leaving forever, according to the girl, his family piled into the Chevrolet and his mom drove to her address. It belonged to a house with a wide, deep lawn in the Palisades, where a woman carried a picnic basket, followed by a compact man in slippers pushing a miniature refrigerator on a dolly. Two middle school boys—one on each side of an ice chest—stumbled out of the front door. The street was high above the ocean, but Walter could see the sharp-cut dark blue waves.

A wood-paneled Ford Country Squire waited in the driveway, with all its doors open.

In an upstairs window, the girl waved extravagantly when Walter stood up out of the car. Susan, her name was. She and Walter had attended four years of high school together. He had never actually thought about her before. He had a faint recollection of her at a table trying to sell him a ticket to a dance.

The red front door hung open to reveal a room with white walls and an old wooden statue. The arrangement was balanced, quiet-feeling, like in a museum. Music trickled out; something with flutes and violins. Vivaldi? Not quite Bach. Walter unloaded his stereo from the trunk.

His sister and brother crouched in the back seat, their heads close together. He wondered for the millionth time what they talked about.

His mom stood out of the car, too. "Thanks for taking Walter," she called to the other mother.

The other mother took her time to answer, dedicating herself to fitting the small refrigerator into the station wagon. "You're not driving up? *I* wouldn't miss it for anything."

Her certainty alarmed Walter. Women with that tone intimidated his mom, who abruptly sat back inside the car and stationed her hands at nine o'clock and three o'clock on the steering wheel.

Susan stood in the doorway now, short with short dark hair. This whole family was short and dark-haired. Walter, still holding his stereo, climbed back into the car.

"We can just drive up," his mother said.

"We don't have to. It's fine."

By then, the small, well-built father was jogging over in his slippers. He had on glasses and would probably have rather been sitting with the paper. But he had a conciliating smile, and Walter's mom did better with men. She rolled down the window, pushing the hair off her forehead. An hour later, they were driving up Highway 5, following the station wagon, where the compact man was keeping them, he'd promised, in his rearview mirror.

"This is it?" his mom asked, six hours later. She bent close to the steering wheel, inching down Telegraph Avenue. "It's not what I expected." Walter could imagine what she expected: doming gold-edged clouds. "It looks a little dumpy."

Walter saw what she meant. He'd read about hippies in *Time* and seen them on the evening news—Cronkite talking to a long-haired girl with violet granny glasses—but the people at Indian-print-covered tables on the sidewalk looked *old*. It had never occurred to him that hippies could be *old*. Now they passed a park, with shaggy trees looming in the distance.

"Look at him, poor thing," his mom said, gazing at a man carrying an ancient army backpack. "That's probably everything he owns."

Where his mom picked out a homeless pilgrim, Walter noticed a low, beautiful church, half-covered in wisteria. As usual with his mom, he saw it both ways, a kind of double bookkeeping. The station wagon stopped in front of dormitories, where students and parents pushed rough-looking orange wheelbarrows filled with suitcases. Hurrying. No one looked happy. "Do you want to get out?" his mom said.

She wasn't a confident parallel parker in the best of circumstances. His brother, Donnie, hauled Walter's suitcase from the trunk, leaving him only the light turntable and box of records. They met Susan in the courtyard, where girls with index card boxes looked up your name and gave you a key. They were both assigned to the seventh floor. Walter hoped her compact father would invite his family to join them for dinner. His mom needed something before the long drive home. Susan's mother had shamed her into this.

Music leaked from under doors. *Gasping at glimpses of gentle true spirit, he runs.* Walter had that album. The lifting melody made him a little excited to be here.

Walter's mom called "Thanks for keeping us in your mirror" down the corridor to Susan's family, who stood in a cluster with all her luggage. His mom envied wives. Even if she did derive satisfaction from her job, she had a long commute and came home every night tired. She sympathized with husbands and thought that wives had the better deal.

Walter learned, later, that Susan's mother also worked. She didn't have the graceful life his mom probably imagined. She turned out to be unhappy, too.

When Walter opened the door, his roommate bolted up in bed, quickly pulling a T-shirt on. He stuck out a hand, saying "Ken," but didn't get up, Walter assumed, because of his mother and sister. He probably didn't have on pants. As Walter looked around the bare room, he stopped at a horn in the corner, mostly hidden by a brown cover but showing one patch of gold.

His family stood uselessly, trapping his new roommate under the covers. Walter wished they would leave; the feeling of these two eras of his life overlapping was unbearable.

His sister, Lina, went down the hall to find a bathroom and Donnie began to hook up Walter's stereo.

"Should we all go grab a bite?" his mom asked, trying to be the way a mother should be.

"Cafeteria opens in an hour," Ken said.

"Walter, come here a minute." In the hallway, his mom lifted an envelope from her purse. "Put this somewhere safe." She was watching him, eyes wide, as he opened the envelope, thick with cash. "It took me a long time to save that."

Lina returned from the bathroom and whispered, "There were boys in there."

Donnie was underneath Walter's bed to plug in the extension cord for the stereo. Then the three of them left. Walter felt winded. He suddenly had an overwhelming desire to sleep.

Twice, Ken got up (he *was* wearing only boxers and a T-shirt) and looked out the window. "People in the cafeteria." Walter could see shapes moving through the glass walls.

"You hungry?" Walter asked.

"Yeah, but I don't feel like meeting new people. Having to talk."

He'd said exactly what Walter felt. They stayed in their room.

"Are you Chinese?" Walter asked an hour later.

"Yup. What are you?"

"Me? Nothing."

"You look like something. Mexican or something. And your name."

"My dad's from Afghanistan but I don't really know him. Now I *am* hungry," Walter said, but by then the cafeteria was dark and the hall had quieted.

"I have walnuts," Ken said, and pulled out a burlap sack from under his bed.

———

Long after midnight, the phone rang, vibrating the plywood desk, and Walter leapt and caught it. What if something happened on their drive home? But it was her; he heard them moving in the kitchen. A sob skipped up his throat. He was afraid his roommate heard. For a minute, he couldn't make words.

"We just walked in. Talk to you on Sunday," she said, because long distance was expensive, charged by the minute. Sundays, the national telephone company lowered its rates.

He and Ken never talked about that first night. Walter didn't know if Ken had slept through or heard him cry. But afterwards, it was as if they had always been close.

2.

Walter hadn't had a real friend before. He'd walked with certain guys through the halls of Pali High; he'd called them friends, but not one of them had ever seen his house, because he and his sister attended their high school illegally. Years ago, their mom had driven to Pacific Palisades from the Valley to do their wash Sunday mornings in a high-ceilinged, mostly empty Laundromat that played the classical music station. The Korean owners liked the three children who folded their own clothes and told Walter's mom about the lottery system that had allowed their own kids, now both UCLA graduates, into the Palisades district. She tried the lottery, failed twice, and, finally, smuggled them in using the address of a woman she'd met at an exercise class, who eventually stopped returning her calls. That woman must have still received mail from the high school; she could have turned them in. They'd had to lie low. Walter had complained about never being able to accept a ride home and his mom admitted the difficulty, calling it a trade-off. But Walter was legitimate now. He'd come to Berkeley the usual way, with better grades than the others from Pali.

Every Sunday, Ken wrote a letter to his parents that began *Dear Father and Mother*. Walter wasn't in the habit of writing letters, but he tried one.

I made a friend, he wrote. *We eat together every meal.* She would be glad to know. He scribbled a PS for his sister. *Carrie Appel— remember her, the Goddess? Guess who she rooms with?*

The goddess from Pali, who'd once come to school in a see-through gauze dress, a pile of hair pinned on top of her head, now shared a room with the average eighteen-year-old who'd worked on the decorations committee for dances Walter didn't attend. Susan.

Lina would know them both. She studied girls at Pali the way some guys watched the field during a game in play. While they'd followed the station wagon up the length of the state, she'd said she couldn't imagine Walter dating Susan, which was a preposterous thing to say. Walter didn't plan to date anyone. *Date* was a ridiculous word, more suitable for the edible sugary fruit. The Goddess was a goddess. He was a virgin, but that didn't top his list of concerns. Ken was too. Walter could tell.

At night in their beds, the two young men talked. Ken had grown up the Central Valley. His parents were immigrants, both doctors but not rich, not like American doctors here, he said. They thought he should become a doctor, too.

"I want to be a doctor," Walter said. "We can be doctors together."

Ken's father had made him join ROTC. He signed up for the marching band, but for that he had to play tuba instead of French horn. Ken's father had been an army medic and still marched as a reserve in the Fourth of July parade. Ken's birthday was February 24, the number picked first in the original lottery. Since President Nixon abolished deferments, students were classified 1-A, *available for service,* just like the rest of the American male population. They couldn't draft you, though, until you were twenty. And that would be 1974 and Nixon had promised a completely volunteer army by then. Ken's father believed him, but Ken thought a year was too close for comfort.

Walter had never worried about being drafted. No one he knew in high school worried personally either, though the fairness of abolishing student deferment had been a topic in his civics class.

Once, his mom had talked to someone from where she'd grown up and, afterwards, shook her head. "Another boy went overseas," she said. "I did the right thing getting you here." She believed the world worked differently for the rich, keeping them from danger. Now, listening, Walter questioned her assumption that graduating among the rich would extend him protections. Safety might require more direct payment. Otherwise, why would Ken be vulnerable? His parents were doctors, even if not as rich as the American ones.

"Does it matter much to you, being Chinese?"

"I don't know. I've never not been." Ken didn't speak any Chinese language, but he'd gone to China school Saturday mornings and understood a little Mandarin. "Does it matter to you not being anything?"

"I guess, like you, I've always been." When he was new at Pali, people had asked what he was. "They meant were we Christian or Jewish. I was nothing there, too." Then he told Ken his secret, about going to a school he didn't belong in.

He often paused at Susan and Carrie's doorway. He loved their room. Each of the dorm rooms had come with metal bed frames, metal wastebaskets, and plywood desks. Walter and Ken's remained exactly as they'd found it. But these two had set their beds at a ninety-degree angle so their heads nearly touched while they slept. They'd folded neat quilts over bedspreads. Their desks were side by side, with matching orange lamps. They had a small portable television, with an antenna. Walter hadn't been friends with them at Pali; friendship was his great discovery in college, more important than classes and than the job he'd found manning a food cart.

When they say coed dorm, he wrote, *they mean it, even the bathrooms. I never see girls in there. They must shower at dawn.*

He avoided the coed bathrooms, too. When he could, he used restrooms on campus, which were still labeled MEN and WOMEN.

As Walter stood, watching Nixon announce his electoral victory, Susan shook her head. "It's not right." Walter assumed she meant Nixon. "Nine days late."

"My allowance," Carrie explained. "My dad forgot to send the check."

Allowance. *Wow.*

"That money should be here on the first," Susan said. "Like clockwork."

"You need some dough?" Walter had money from his job. But the young women began a chorus of no-thank-yous, and it suddenly occurred to him that his offer felt dishonest. He didn't want to appear, as he must have at Pali, richer than he was. His mom was ashamed of their relative poverty. At Berkeley, he was awakening to the possibility of being unashamed. Clarity, he thought, made friendship possible. "I don't get allowance, but I work for the food service, so I've got some dough." He tossed two twenties onto Carrie's bed. The Goddess looked at him wet-eyed as she handed them back. She was the kind of person you felt you knew way better than you did, from all the times you'd imagined having sex with her.

3.

On the first day of Introduction to Chemistry, a middle-aged man shuffled to the podium and mumbled into the microphone. "Look to your left, then look to your right." A thousand students rustled in their seats. "Two of the three of you won't get into medical school. So I hope you're here for better reasons. There *are* other reasons to study inorganic chemistry."

Walter was not here for better reasons. Ken was on his left, and on his right, a thin girl with freckled arms was taking copious notes.

"Beauty, for example," the professor said.

Beauty!

Walter had seen failing bodies in the convalescent homes where his mom worked. But he didn't imagine pushing a syringe into papery skin when he thought of his future. He didn't think about what doctors actually did. He needed *some* profession. He'd once walked over a lawn to a classmate's house. (The boy's father, whom Walter had never met, was a cardiologist.) A recently groomed dog thumped its tail against the door, which opened to a spacious room of light and warm clutter. Walter wanted *that*.

Walter and Ken passed gray-haired women in avid conversation at the same café table where they'd recently tasted their first cappuccinos. A man standing outside the used bookstore turned to watch the sun slip into the bay and they stopped, too. Rags of fog blew over their heads. They felt that they owned the city, as much as anyone did, and also that Berkeley was too significant to ever be owned. They understood that they were anonymous freshmen at a state university who had not yet done anything to distinguish themselves. Walter wondered if there'd be tomato soup at dinner. He'd discovered he loved tomato soup with buttered saltines, the combination. He liked being one in a herd. After dinner, he and Ken trudged to the library. Sometimes the freckled girl, Melinda, drew them diagrams to explain the chemistry equations, and Ken looked stricken. Walter didn't understand the attraction; she was what his mom would call too thin. He'd seen her outside the dorm after a run, eating a head of iceberg lettuce cut in two.

One Friday, she said she was taking a bus to Palo Alto to see her high school boyfriend, and she returned Sunday in time for dinner and told Susan, Carrie, and everyone else at their end of the table that she and Tom—that was the boyfriend—had always wanted a whole night together. *A whole night,* Ken repeated as he and Walter walked to the dorm.

Walter tried to imagine sex. What he couldn't conjure was what he and Carrie would say to each other during the act. He also wondered how long the whole thing would take.

Three days later, Melinda was sitting cross-legged on Carrie's quilt.

"He's in the wrong," Susan was saying.

"I feel like he should *want* to call me, now more than ever." Melinda seemed to assume the whole dorm knew she'd lost her virginity. Maybe the whole dorm did. Poor Ken.

"You shouldn't put up with this." Susan turned. "Don't you agree, as a man?"

Walter had never before been asked for his opinion *as a man*. He was unsure. Susan understood the rules of private life. If there'd been a book, he'd have checked it out of the library. "Well, but what do you need him for?" he finally said.

The young women laughed. These people on the seventh floor and their problems were of central importance to him. Even his family receded; he hadn't thought about them for a day, even longer. He felt happier than he'd ever been.

In high school, Susan pointed out, Melinda and her boyfriend wouldn't have had a whole night. At the mention of high school, Walter told them that he'd gone to Pali illegally. In less than a minute, the secret of his life was out.

"Your mom shouldn't have put you in that position!" Susan said.

"She was trying to give her kids a better education," Carrie said.

"Maybe she couldn't afford to live in the district," Melinda ventured.

"For sure not." Walter felt socked. His mom had once been in an orphanage.

"What if she went to Mr. Nibley and told him, 'We don't live in district, but I want my kids to go to this school,'" Susan said.

"He could kick them out," Carrie said.

"Well, he *shouldn't*."

Walter's heartbeat stuttered. For the first time, Susan seemed dangerous. "My sister's still there. Please don't tell anyone."

"Probably every parent with a kid in an LAUSD school would rather have him at Pali." Carrie shrugged her slender shoulders. "They can't let in everyone. I'm glad you were there, though."

"This has to be our secret," he said.

"It's not what *should* happen, is all I'm saying," Susan said. "You shouldn't have to sneak around to get your kids a better life."

"I don't make the rules," Carrie said.

"I don't either," Susan said. "I wish I did."

"We all wish you did," Walter said.

Melinda and Ken started walking around campus together, talking in low voices. Ken still slept in his bed every night, but he had the look of someone carrying a crucial secret. There was nothing smug or proud in him, no air of triumph. He still addressed his parents *Dear Father and Mother*. Then, at a dance in the lobby, Melinda stood on platform shoes, wearing what looked like a belted leotard, so thin you could see every curve and bulge of her miniature body. When she danced, her hips moved in startling rhythms. She shouted at Walter over the music (*Your mama don't dance and your daddy don't rock and roll*) that she'd broken up. Ken cupped her elbow.

So this was sex. Walter wasn't sure he wanted it. Not with someone who twitched like that. He stood against the wall until a girl whose name he didn't know asked him to dance, then shuffled his feet and swung his arms, trying to look nonchalant. His sister and brother had told him to bend more. You're like a ruler dancing, Lina said.

Even so, another girl approached. He wasn't classically handsome, but he thought from a distance he could look, well, maybe dashing. He'd heard that word applied to tall, dark-haired men with average faces. Long hair helped. He would have looked worse with a Cary Grant cut, which eventually, when you grew up, everyone had to get.

4.

Lina Aziz didn't see the point of social life. Eventually, that would change, she assumed, the same way that someday she would have better clothes. Sixteen, a junior on the honors track with an after-school job, Lina didn't have time for fun. Her mother tried to push her to parties. She had ideas about what social life could do for her children; she'd worked to get them into the Palisades district, not only for their educations. But how would parties help? Did her mother think another sixteen-year-old could hire her? Obviously, she was at least a decade too young to get married. Even her mother understood that. Lina's present abstention didn't prevent her from noticing the social hierarchies, though; she was a vigilant observer of the moving politics of popularity. Not that she tried to enter those races; every lunch period she went to the clay room to avoid the annihilating pressure of the cafeteria or the tiered lawn where everyone ate. Her brother's aloofness had made him popular. Everything worked easily for Walter. He'd graduated second in his class. Still, his friends couldn't pull him along to their Ivy League colleges, which he'd claimed not to want anyway.

But Lina did. She wanted to go *back east,* as her two friends called the coast where they hadn't yet lived but imagined daily when they sat outside in the sheer California winter sun. Lina took her bike down the wild hill ride to the ice-cream parlor, where she scooped herself a sundae for dinner or made one of her signature shakes. At this time of her life, she could eat ice cream for supper and still wake up with a concave stomach, two inches from front to back. She considered this an asset. She liked her job because of the top ten radio music. She was learning the names of bands. The glum twenty-seven-year-old manager had taught her how to close up, count the cash, and deposit it in a zippered bag down a chute on the side of the bank. She arrived home after midnight, cash from the tip jar in her pocket, when everyone in the house was asleep, except the boarder, whose sitar music leaked out of her room. Lina covered every pimple on her face with acne cream, then went to bed. Her hours were accounted for.

So when Lauren Moses and Jess Jaffrey invited her to an antiwar rally, she said no.

"Do you have to work?" Lauren asked. Lina nodded. "You *are* against the war, though?"

"Sure." Lina didn't think much about Vietnam. It was easy enough to distrust the American government; from what Lina could tell, it hadn't helped her family. Once, years ago, a grandmother of whom she had no memory stapled her into a dress made with two posters saying NIXON'S THE ONE. She knew this from one of the three pictures she had of herself as a child. Her grandmother had been cruel to her mother when she was young; her mother had told them terrible stories, with a strange air, and missing parts. By the time of Nixon's second bid, her mother and her nurse-friend Julie had become Democrats, their allegiance tipped by a Paul Simon lyric.

"We'll stop and see you on the way." Lauren rarely gave up, from what Lina could tell. Both tracked for AP, Lauren and Jess had long been assured of their intelligence. It compensated, they tried to believe, for deficits in what they knew to be the more significant realm of looks. They were just then beginning to understand privilege. They'd confessed to Lina that they'd never had to worry about money. "I mean, there've been times when my dad told my mom to stop buying clothes for a while." Jess had shrugged.

Lina understood that they found her mysterious. She worked almost every night at an ice-cream parlor, and this was *junior year*, they'd said, when everything counted. Did her parents not know? They said "parents," though Lina had never mentioned a father. Once, the boarder, a woman too young to be Lina's mother, had dropped off a book for her at school. She didn't look like a housekeeper or a nanny. What housekeepers and nannies looked like to white high school girls in 1970s Los Angeles was Mexican. Lina's brother had worn jeans and Wallabees and walked through the school like a god. Lina was a good student who wore overalls that most days smelled of clay. In classes she kept quiet, but once in a while she looked up and said something startling, as when she'd said that Mrs. Dalloway was boring, although everyone knew Virginia Woolf was Mrs. Anjani's favorite author and Mrs. Anjani had cancer. A patch of her hair had fallen out.

"We'd been talking about Woolf's ability to depict the inner life," Mrs. Anjani said.

"The inner life of Clarissa Dalloway is pretty trivial. She's a rich, silly wife."

Lauren and Jess had been close for so many years they hardly felt to each other like another person. They'd long ago negotiated their small differences and rubbed away the edges with conversation. Jess had a concise mind, but Lauren was ardent, with a sense of fancy. They depended on and annoyed each other, discussed everything with patient boredom, but they didn't thrill one another at all. They needed something besides the pursuit of grades for college. Lina suspected that was where she came in.

Lauren had said once that Lina was beautiful, "not honors-track beautiful, but beautiful beautiful," like the girls who were crowned prom princesses and queens. It wasn't her clothes or style, either, which they could have respected or tried to copy, she'd gone on. Lina was beautiful in ways impossible not only to fake but also to achieve with teenage regimens of dieting or hair experimentation. Lina understood that she was beautiful, not from looking in the mirror (where she saw multiple flaws), but from a dozen years of the world's response, though she wouldn't have said that. We all know what we have. She had heavy hair, olive skin, and a beak-shaped nose with a bump that should have been a problem—it was for Lauren, whose cousins had all had nose jobs—but somehow, Lina's face held a symmetry. She was only five three, but her legs were long, her hips slender, her breasts not especially small. She had the rare body that looked good in torn 501s, which she wore when her overalls were in the wash. She was wearing them now, with her hair pulled back for scooping.

Even the guys working at the ice-cream shop had to have ponytails.

"Are these your friends?" her incredibly tall manager asked. He was a geek, with acne. At the edges of the social world themselves, Lina, Lauren, and Jess could easily recognize someone even worse off. "Do they want cones or cups?" he asked.

They said over the glass case that they were on their way to a protest. They hoped to talk Lina into coming.

"And what are they protesting?" he asked Lina, bending like a sunflower heavy on its stalk.

"Vietnam War," she said.

"My draft number is 292. Now you can figure out my birthday. Go. Here." With long fingers he extracted a twenty from the sundae dish that held tips. "I'll pay you to protest."

Lauren's mother nosed the black Buick through bumper-to-bumper traffic. She asked when she should pick them up eight times; Jess's fingers tapped, silently counting. Mrs. Moses tried so hard to befriend her daughter's friends that it was easy to loathe her. Though Lauren's family was rich, Mrs. Moses wore a housedress, with ankle socks and tie shoes, like the woman in that photograph from the Depression. Jess's mother followed fashion and cooked gourmet meals that her brothers refused to eat because they were morons.

Traffic slowed to a complete standstill coming into Beverly Hills. Cars were honking. Lauren said they could walk the rest of the way.

And then they were in the air, free. It was exhilarating to be outside; Lina was usually in the ice-cream store until midnight. She had bigger problems than Richard Nixon, she thought, threading through the crowd of older people; yet, amid screams of "One two three four, we don't want your fucking war!" she found herself buoyed by indeterminate waves of rage. "We're waiting," Lauren yelled to be heard over the crowd, "for Spiro Agnew!" Someone had brought crates of oranges to throw at the cars turning in to a hotel's semicircular driveway. Lina fell into a rhythm; her scooping arm moving automatically, she threw hard pitches that hit a black limousine once on a hubcap, another time squarely in the middle of the passenger window, citrus exploding on the glass. She loved screaming *fucking war*. The astringent smell hung in the air as a middle-aged cop with a belly opened a small notebook and asked their names.

"I think we might be getting arrested," Lauren said.

The man ducked their heads into the back of a squad car. "Not going to cuff you. I'm guessing this is your first pickup." By the time they stood in the spacious, clean booking station of the Beverly Hills jail, Lina was crying. Lauren used the telephone on the counter. The officer asked again for Lina's parents' names and telephone number. She crossed her arms and wouldn't tell.

Lauren and Jess looked at Lina—they were good girls, too, neither had taken a drag of marijuana or been seriously kissed, yet they'd both recited their names and numbers. "Your mom'll understand," Lauren said.

"You don't know her."

"It's a poli*t*ical protest, protected by the Constitution. It's not like stealing."

Lina still refused. She began to shake. Her face was a streaked mess behind the tangle of hair. Maybe I'm actually crazy, she thought. "Should have just stayed at work," she mumbled to herself.

The cop now addressed Lauren and Jess. "You all know her name. I need first and last. I could cite you with contempt."

"My mother is fragile." Suddenly clear, Lina lifted her head and spoke with harsh dignity. "She cries every day. If she doesn't get better, we'll have to move. If she can't do her job anymore." She wiped her nose on her sleeve. "May I please use your telephone?"

The policeman made a courtly gesture with his heavy arm toward the rotary phone.

"It's long distance, but I can pay you." Lina pulled the curled twenty from the tip jar out of her pocket.

"You don't have to pay," he said. "Dial nine first."

She listened to muffled rings. From the sound of Ken's voice, Lina assumed she'd woken him, and left a message with the number of the police station.

"What seems to be the problem, Officer?" Lauren's father pushed open the door. His head was square and his quality of attention responsive to stimuli no one else could see, what they would later think of as *on the spectrum*. But the respect he showed uncurled the man's posture like a plant receiving light and water. The policeman explained the exploded oranges, the cussing, and his opinion that girls should learn that civil dissent stopped short of thrown objects and disrespect for officers of the law. Mr. Moses listened, his face completely still. Then the two men inclined their heads. By the time Lauren's father and the officer looked up to watch the final play of a game on the television in the corner, Lauren whispered, "I think it's going to be all right." Mr. Moses signed a paper and, in a stiffer voice than he'd used with the cop, said, "Come on now, kids." The girls looked at each other. They could just walk out into the full night. Lauren gazed up at her father as if he were an astonishing being. Was he proud of her for getting arrested? That mother, Mrs. Moses, certainly wouldn't be. Lina preferred Lauren's father; this plucked a strange twinge of guilt.

She felt different, having cried in front of her friends, rinsed, the way she had been once after swimming all day in the ocean.

Mr. Moses matter-of-factly asked her for her address. Lina said, "I have to go to the ice-cream store where I work. I left my bike there."

"It might be closed by now," Lauren said.

"You don't want to get it tomorrow?" her father asked. "Your parents are probably wondering where you are."

But Lina insisted. When he parked in front of the store, the lights were still on inside; they could see the manager sitting in the back booth, probably counting the register the way she did, the stools already upended on the counter. He closed early some nights; Lina hadn't known he'd still be here, but she couldn't tell Lauren's dad where she lived. They could get kicked out of school if anyone knew. She could see her bike in back, against the freezer, but she sank into the deep leather seat. It was hard to push herself up. Lauren had told Lina that her father had argued a case in front of the Supreme Court. Lina had an impulse to ask if he would pay for her college.

They were all waiting. Lauren's father finally asked, "Why don't you grab your stuff. I'll take you home."

"My bike won't fit," she said. "I need it tomorrow to ride to school."

"Was what you said about your mother true?" Lauren asked. "Or were you just saying it so they wouldn't call her?"

"That's what she says. If it happens, I don't know if I can go to college." The car was silent, except for the sound of the heat. She'd done it then, she'd asked.

"Could we help, Dad?" Lauren asked, in the piping tone of Superman's daughter, if he'd had one.

"Come and talk to me if the time ever comes. Probably won't. Parents have bad days, too." He opened a tiny box built into the dashboard and extracted a business card. She put that in her pocket, then jumped out and pounded on the ice-cream store door.

Her tall manager opened it. Lauren and her dad drove off. She hadn't revealed where she lived.

5.

Walter managed his money. He'd opened a bank account with the nine hundred dollars his mom had given him. He'd had to take cash out for books, but with his paychecks from the food service, he'd replenished that and now his balance was over a thousand. He saw his friends every day. They gossiped about each other, but kindly. He maintained an A average in chemistry without ever really liking it. He'd not lost his virginity yet but he hoped to, maybe even with Carrie. He thought his life would keep on like this, going up and up.

One day in December, Walter found Ken slumped at his desk. In the thousand-person chemistry class, you had to turn in a stamped, self-addressed postcard for your grade, and Ken had gotten a C. Walter sprinted to the mailroom, for the first time in weeks. At the beginning of fall, he'd checked his box daily, but while other people received package slips, usually for tins of homemade cookies, Walter found cards from his mother, which left him unaccountably sad. *Love, Mom* was all she wrote. He let them pile up, in his box.

Now he moved the lock forward, back, and around until it clicked. He found his grade card. A-plus. *Okay.* He made a fist at the bank of numbered boxes. There was something luxurious about that plus. He was surprised he'd beaten Ken, but in another way, winning felt entirely natural. There were cards from his mom. He opened the last piece of mail, which had holes on one side of it, as envelopes generated by mainframe computers did then: $1,755, the paper said he owed for the dorm, meal plan, and fees. This new knowledge felt like a metal disk balanced upon the wet rounded organs in his chest.

He stashed the thin paper between the cards (*Love, Mom*) and ran up, two stairs at a time. His old anxiety, a slim gray man, sat back down on his customary chair. Susan and Carrie were giving him a ride home for the holidays. He'd have to ask his mom then.

"How'd you do," Ken asked.

"Okay. Good. I don't know what happened with you. Think it's some kind of mistake?"

"You and Melinda are just better at this."

Walter stashed the bill in the back of his drawer and lay on his bed while Ken called home. Ken's father and mother took turns on the telephone. No one seemed to raise a voice.

"I don't think there's any point," Ken said. He said those words again, his fingers moving in the air over the keys of his French horn.

"They want me to take Chem B," he said after he hung up.

"One grade won't make a difference. You can still get in."

"I'm no good at it," Ken said. "Melinda'll get in. I love her."

Walter had never loved anyone like that.

They were having sex, Walter knew, but he couldn't figure out where. Ken fell asleep in his bed every night. Now, though, they both lay awake. Neither wanted to leave Berkeley.

"People ask if I'm going home for the holidays," Walter said. "But here is home."

"I'll bring us walnuts," Ken said. "They're best now, just picked." His father, a doctor who worked for the Veterans' Hospital, owned a walnut farm. Walter remembered that Ken was Asian. (Normally, he didn't think of the two of them as different.) Did Chinese people have Christmas?

"We go over to friends'," Ken said. "They do Christmas. They're Chinese, too. What do you do on Christmas?"

Walter's mom usually waited to see where they were invited. He would have to talk to her about money. The hard metal disk balanced on the tip of his lung. He hoped his life here wouldn't end. He looked around the room, at the simple shapes in dim light: desk, chair, stereo, lamp. *College Life.* "Does it snow in Modesto?"

Ken nodded. It amazed Walter how different their lives were when they were themselves so much the same.

Walter had asked his mom if he should check the box that said FINANCIAL AID on his college application.

"That's all taken care of," she'd said. "The Afghans." Her face was certain but distant, closed. He'd heard about the Afghans all his life, though he'd never met one, except for his father.

Now, in the back seat of Susan's Saab, he tried to imagine a Kabul businessman writing a check. Where would he send it? To *Walter Aziz, America*? The Afghans had no address for him, he was pretty sure. They'd moved at least twice since the last time his father called. Walter had left the box unchecked. Why had he let himself slide under the billow of his mother's fantasy?

He'd been relegated to the back seat of the Saab because he was the only one without a license. Susan drove while Carrie flipped through the course catalogue.

"*Design 11: theories of representation; freehand drawing . . . in plan, section, elevation, axonometric, and perspective. Projects address concepts of order, scale, structure, rhythm, detail, culture, and landscape.*' Wonder what 'axonometric' means."

"I'd take it," Walter said.

"It's the same time as the poetry workshop," Carrie said. "But I probably won't get in."

Highway 5 was a limbo, neither school nor home. They took the turnoff for San Juan Bautista to see the Mission, where Hitchcock shot *Vertigo*, and Susan and Carrie switched places. They passed Castroville, the artichoke capital of the world. Green signs ticked by, assuring Walter that they were still hundreds of miles from Los Angeles. Susan pointed to Harris Ranch near the Coalinga Pass. "When I was a kid, you'd go to the field, pick a cow, and they'd cook it for you."

"That can't be right," Walter said.

Air from the open windows carried the stink of manure. The road unrolled through fields of almonds, then oranges, then strawberries, beads of water flying out of pipes. Carrie and Susan compared family holiday plans at the music center, Will Rogers, the Bel-Air Bay Club, and the Malibu Colony. Susan's family was throwing a Christmas Eve party for eighty people, including the housekeeper's family and the mailman. The freeway widened to nine lanes near the 405, a spot Walter forever after associated with tightness in his chest.

6.

Walter tried to see his family the way he had before, but they all seemed worse. Lina had decided Berkeley wasn't good enough for her. Donnie bounced a basketball against the wall for hours and their mom let him. "He needs to bounce," she said, as if that were normal.

They had no plans for Christmas. Susan had invited his family to their party, but he didn't tell his mom. Susan's mom could set her off again.

Walter asked his mom if she wanted to invite Julie, another nurse who lived alone. She had no kids that Walter knew of. His mom usually had a friend like Julie, come to think of it.

"Oh, she'd be thrilled. I bet she'd cook. You know she cooks."

Why did his mom assume her friend would be thrilled to cook for them? That she'd still be free, two days before Christmas? If Julie was a friend, she was a friend. At Berkeley, Walter had come to believe that friendship was sacred.

Julie arrived early Christmas morning when the others were still asleep. She brought five bags of food. Walter stepped outside barefoot, into the still, clear day, shooed her in, and carried the bags himself. Each leaf on the neighbor's persimmon tree had gone orange from the center out.

On holidays, they never seemed enough, by themselves. Maybe they should have gone last night to Susan's, even with that mother.

Julie talked, washing celery, while a turkey sat naked in a pan. She bent down to pick up a translucent onion husk. All day long her voice modulated within the same range. She dropped scraps of information, lacking peaks or endings. In a way, she was relaxing. "The Hoppers," she was saying, "Diane, you know, that's Nancy's family, you've met Nancy, they're driving to the desert." Walter waited for a punch line.

Neither he, Lina, nor Donnie had ever heard of Nancy Hopper.

"Well, what do you know," Walter finally said, and his brother and sister erupted in laughter, Donnie sitting on his hands. Even

Julie smiled. He could do that here, make fun of someone in front of her without it being mean. She swatted his arm and then started telling another non-story about a cousin in Michigan who loved rhubarb. Did they remember that the leaves were poisonous?

What do you know? The phrase could apply to almost anything.

Walter couldn't ask about money today.

They made pies while the turkey baked, Julie instructing them to roll the dough with an empty wine bottle from the boarder. Donnie turned out to be a genius peeler, skinning an apple in one coiled strip. Julie showed Lina how to lattice the crust while telling them that, every Christmas, she arranged the delivery of a home appliance to her brother's family. "This year the washer-dryer," she said. "Last year a color TV. They liked that." She paused. "Diane, I wonder where the Learjet is today. Now that Bonnie won't be cooking his Christmas."

"Who's Bonnie?" Walter said.

Their mom's eyes opened wider. "That's Learhoff's wife."

Lina took ice cream from the freezer. Everyone at the store stole ice cream, she said. It wasn't even stealing. "We're allowed to eat as much as we want."

"Do you carry it out in front of the manager?" Walter asked.

Julie left while it was still light.

Walter had to talk to his mom about the bill, but they were never alone. Finally, the morning he was leaving, he found her in the kitchen, his grade card in his back pocket. She smiled, a smile that made itself up while she beheld him. He was her joy, he knew. His departure saddened her. He pulled out the grade card and handed it to her. He had other As, but even his mom knew that this was the one that mattered. And the plus seemed an amulet. In the pale winter light, branches outside stretched bare and black. They'd never owned the places they lived. Walter had carried boxes into a series of apartments; they'd sanded floors, repainted, always fixing up rooms, until she found the bungalow. She'd wanted him to finish high school in a house. She'd gotten this far.

"The dorm sent me a bill." He unfolded the printout. She put on her reading glasses. They studied the paper.

"This is on top of tuition?"

"Still cheaper than other places. Way cheaper than the ones Lina's talking about."

She took off the glasses. "I've been worried because I haven't heard from them."

She meant the Afghans. "Mom, do you have anything in writing? Which Afghans said they would pay?"

"It was your grandfather. He promised me when I was pregnant with you."

When she was pregnant! He was eighteen years old. "Do you have his address or phone number?"

She had no numbers. No name except the surname, and she'd always said *Aziz is the Smith of Afghanistan.*

"When is the last time you heard from any of them?"

She looked helpless. Knowledge sifted into him: he should have applied for financial aid. There were no Afghans to support him. Walls were crumbling.

"Julie gave me money for each of you. For Christmas. I'll give you Lina's and Donnie's, too, so you can pay a little down."

His mind skidded. He could have screamed. But she was telling him her way. *A little down.* A curtsy, meant to show that she was trying. As if the University of California cared that they were trying!

He fled the room as she put the grade card on the refrigerator.

Susan honked; his mom ran out to press an envelope into his hand, which contained six clean hundred-dollar bills from Julie. Nice of her. He felt awful taking Lina's and Donnie's portions, but he had to pay that dorm bill.

He shared the back seat with leftovers, a whole pie in a bakery box. Heat from the Saab's vents circulated the smell of warm spice.

By the time they passed Bakersfield, blame began to shift in his body. His mom had made too few provisions, but on her salary she probably couldn't have done much more. He should've asked: Which Afghans? Where? Can I call them? He'd let himself wish upon a star. Now he was afraid to learn more. He'd believed his mom, not only about the Afghans. Securities he needed—the idea that he had abilities, for example, even greater than other people's—had been wound into him. She made the joining fabric of his life. He couldn't afford to pull that apart. She had once told him being his mom was the most important thing she'd ever done. He'd run out of the house. He was glad now he hadn't said more.

Carrie worked at a cassette with a bobby pin. Her arms were thin and tan, with a small, almost indecent bulge of muscle at the top.

"Anyone hungry?" Susan asked. "We have sandwiches."

He was in love with both of them. Carrie was the one he imagined in the night, but he needed Susan's daytime steadiness, too.

"My parents are splitting up again," Carrie said as she slid in the cassette. Joni.

"It's something they do," Susan explained to him, then turned to Carrie. "I think it upsets you more than it upsets them."

"Do you mind your parents being divorced?" Carrie asked.

He liked it when her questions landed on him.

"They've always been." His parents' divorce didn't matter to him at all, but maybe it was something that he and Carrie could have in common. "I'm hungry. But not for sandwiches."

"For pie," Carrie said. "Me, too."

Susan, the always organized, had forgotten utensils. "Well, what do you know," he said. Somehow this was hilarious. Walter broke the pie in half, then again. He handed Carrie a jagged quarter, still laughing. He ate one himself. Then a second. Each of their lives had a problem. His was money. He hoped he could stay in college. He didn't tell them this yet. It was too raw and terrifying.

And Susan already didn't like his mother.

7.

"You didn't ask for financial aid?"

"I didn't think I'd need it. But I do."

The woman clipped together papers, banging them into a stack. "Submit these with your parents' 1099 form."

Winter in Berkeley was colder than in LA. Ancient pines and redwood fringed the hills and dripped, releasing an astringent, lifting scent. The city seemed more beautiful than ever, now that he might have to leave.

He and Ken still trekked to the library after dinner. Melinda joined them there later; first she ran laps around a track at the School for the Deaf and the Blind. She and Ken walked home slowly, with their arms around each other.

Walter left by himself. He didn't mind solitary walks. Since Design 11, the course he'd signed up for just because Carrie had, he'd noticed the city in new ways. He recognized eras of housing stock and arteries of public transportation. At night, Berkeley smelled of jasmine and rosemary. In an upstairs window of a Craftsman building, a naked woman sat playing a harp. He stepped in and out of rooms of woodsmoke. Carrie had dropped Des 11 when she was accepted from the wait list into a poetry workshop, but by then Walter had discovered his passion. He reached the dorms now and kept walking. He passed the church he'd noticed his first day here, near People's Park. Someone had told him a famous architect named Julia Morgan had built it.

His mother had talked about college. She'd told him, solemnly, when he was a boy, that someday he would go and he was meant to understand that this experience would determine his life. He'd thought that another of his mother's whimsies, but he was beginning to understand.

Streets widened in the blocks below the Claremont Hotel, a white castle built in the teens. Life had not grown up haphazardly, he now saw, it had been made. Even tonight, this late in the story, in old cities around the world, people were redrawing it under desk lamps.

Maybe I can do that, he thought.

He passed a sign on a lamppost for a bicycle auction at the fire department. He wanted a bike. But he was broke.

Walter signed up for more shifts with the food service. He took over a cart from an engineering major at noon, on top of a hill by the Campanile. Business was slow, except for flurries at 12:50 and 1:50, when classes let out. He stood sketching a plan for a town commons—an assignment—on the top of the cart. He liked his teacher. Jan Tudor wasn't a regular professor; she was a working architect, refurbishing a derelict, once-grand department store in downtown Oakland when she wasn't teaching. Not old and not beautiful, she seemed always to be secretly laughing.

Rory, a football player who lived at end of his hall, bought an It's It from Walter. "Nice job, huh?"

Walter didn't particularly like it; working with food felt menial.

"You get to be outside." Rory stretched his muscled arms in the sun, cracking his knuckles, taking pleasure in even the small movements of his impressive body.

At two, when the Campanile stopped chiming and customers dispersed, Walter pushed the closet-sized cart downhill toward the loading dock, where it would be restocked. He held his sketch pad with his thumb on top of the right handlebar. The front wheel bumped over a rock and turned askew. The thing gained velocity. Walter yanked his wrist to rein it in, the pad flew, wheels veered to the left as the cart careened downhill. It was pulling him, but he still had some power if not to stop it at least to steer; he was trying not to knock anyone down as the metal box hurtled faster. He held on, jerking the handles to avoid people, and yelling so they'd get out of the way. He decided to swerve into the ravine. He was running full-out now and for a moment flashed to how much easier it would be if you were trying to mow people down rather than dodge them. He ran, his heart gonging, his pulse fast, drawn by the thing's speed and heft, heading for the creek until abruptly it stopped with a thud that knocked the cart backwards, slamming into him. He fell. Rory had gotten in front of the box with his roommate, Cub, who'd banked his side against it in a blocking tackle.

"Ought to have brakes," Cub said.

"Weighs four times what you do." Rory was laughing.

The cart was partway down the bank of the creek. They pushed the thing back up to level ground. Walter moved to take it from there, but Rory wouldn't release the handles; he steered it all the way to the loading dock, where Walter signed in, glad to be rid of it. He had to thank the two football players. He wished they hadn't seen him being pulled like a banner. He went back and found his sketch pad still there on the ground.

That night in the dining hall, guys he didn't know looked at him, then to each other, holding in laughter. The football team had heard. He hated his food service job.

He thought of that bike sale. He knew how to repair bikes. Maybe he'd go after all.

The place to pay tuition in the basement of Sproul Hall had barred windows like a pawnshop. He pushed a stack of hundred-dollar bills through a small tunnel to a woman on the other side. He'd added to the money from Julie.

The woman gave him a new statement reflecting his payment. He'd known he would still owe hundreds of dollars, but the bill had jumped. December's rent and food. He was using his mom's method, after all, paying down a little. That night, he typed his name, date of birth, social security number, and address on a financial aid form. He couldn't apply as independent; for that, you had to have filed tax returns for five years. The regular application required a parent's 1099.

He wrote to his mom, then crumpled the letter. He didn't want to rub it in that she couldn't pay. Finally, he walked down the hall. Light eked out below the girls' door. Susan, wearing a nightie, let him in. You wouldn't notice right away, but there was really nothing wrong with her body. Carrie sat on the bed, wrapped in a towel, bent over, stroking a tiny brush of red on her toenails.

"Could I borrow a piece of stationery?"

Carrie offered old postcards. A Berkeley oak tree, Shattuck Avenue with hand-tinted department stores. He picked a picture of the church by People's Park. Susan asked if he had stamps and, without waiting for his answer, gave him three.

Dear Mom, I'm applying for a scholarship and need your tax form 1099. Love, W.

Scholarship sounded as if he were eligible for some honor.

Before going to sleep, he imagined opening Carrie's towel, one end in each of his hands, and sticking his head in, her body giving off steam like a loaf of fresh bread.

The next day, when he relieved the engineering student of the cart, she smiled, looking at the ground. The news had made it all the way to engineering.

8.

Walter found his friends crowded around the TV in Carrie and Susan's room, the president's torso filling the screen.

I have asked for this radio and television time tonight for the purpose of announcing that we today have concluded an agreement to end the war and bring peace with honor . . .

He glanced at Ken; a danger Walter had never fully believed in was ending.

. . . at this moment in Washington and Hanoi . . .

Walter's skin lifted in goose bumps. He hadn't paid much attention to Vietnam, but he'd respected Ken's fears; they were public and honorable. Walter couldn't talk about his own terror without making his family sound worse than it was.

"I guess the draft's over," Ken said. "If there's no war."

"What about the POWs?" Rory said. "Our guys?"

"We've still got draft numbers," Cub said.

A peace that lasts. A peace that heals. The cease-fire will take effect at 2400 Greenwich Mean Time, January 27, 1973.

"Par-tay!" Rory said, lifting his large arm. Cub slapped his back. Walter didn't like these two in Susan and Carrie's room.

Walter found his way to the Piedmont Fire Station early Saturday morning. A man in a uniform shrieked up the metal door to reveal bikes on a cement floor next to a polished fire truck. While he browsed, a woman came in, asking for tricycles. She was young, but her hair was tangled and her bare legs looked more functional than pretty. The man stepped into a back room and returned with a tricycle in each hand. She gave him a ten-dollar bill and carried them off.

"How much are the bikes?" Walter asked.

"Depends. Some need work. Make me an offer."

Walter's heart sped. He'd fixed his sister's bike. "Five for twenty-five?"

The guy sucked his cigarette. "Give you all seven for thirty. We can both go home."

Walter made three trips, one bike in each hand, then rode the last, a five-speed Raleigh, made in England.

Carlos, the dorm janitor, let Walter store them in the basement. Sunday, Walter and Ken pounded out dents on two upended bikes, with Ken's transistor radio going. Ken tied a bandanna over his hair, which he'd let grow and had to rubber-band for ROTC. When a song came on that he liked, he set down the hammer and lifted his arms, swaying.

They decided to paint the bicycles white. One color would be cheaper. Berkeley Bikes, they'd call them.

Walter checked his mailbox every day. After three weeks, he called home.

"Mm-hmm. I'm looking for it," his mom said.

After another week he wrote his sister:

Make mom send her tax return. I need it. No joke. When you apply to college, check the box for financial aid. No matter what she says.

Susan and Carrie were rushing. Sororities didn't seem at all Berkeley, not Walter's Berkeley, anyway. The old Greek houses above campus had stood mostly empty since the sixties, he'd heard, and were starting to fill again. Even Melinda, who, at the beginning of the year, had set her hair in rollers, wore jeans now, and when she raised her hand in chemistry, Walter saw she'd stopped shaving under her arms.

He hadn't told anyone about the dorm bill, but he had the feeling Ken knew.

Lina called. The bank had written her, asking her to come into the branch. She'd thought she was in trouble. Maybe a sixteen-year-old wasn't supposed to deposit in the night slot. But two bankers brought her into a private room and showed her three checks with her name signed in what even they recognized was not her penmanship. Lina knew immediately that it was their mother's but didn't tell. They asked if she had all her checks. She looked; four had been ripped out from the back. Because one was still missing, they said they had to close her account.

"So it's closed," she said, and Walter heard the catch of a sob.

He had to leave for class in seven minutes. "What did she use your checks for?"

"Gas stations," Lina choked out.

He felt for their mom then, for the first time since his own fury about the mythic Afghans. "I guess she had to get to work. It isn't as if she's out buying fur coats."

"But parents *manage*!" Lina shrieked. "They don't use their kids' money to buy *gas*!"

What did she want from him?

"Most parents don't need to." Walter had gone days without thinking about any of them. His guilt pulsed with his sister gulping on the other end of the line. But did she have to cry so much?

"I can't wait to get out of here," she whispered.

She took things too personally. She told him then about getting arrested for throwing oranges at Henry Kissinger. "I called you from jail."

Walter had tried to return her call, but when Beverly Hills Police answered, he assumed it was a wrong number and hung up.

Now hearing she'd been in jail, he felt protective. He should be there.

"How much of your money did she spend?"

"Almost three hundred."

He remembered Lina riding her bike home from that ice-cream store late at night. He'd first learned how to make repairs on that bike.

"I can send you money," he said.

"Thank you," Lina whispered, and he heard the swoop of relief. It was the first time he felt the power of generosity—generosity, in this case, above his means. But Lina was young. He wanted her and Donnie to believe that the world was safer than it even maybe was. The shrill accusation left her voice. She sounded shy, grateful. He'd always suspected things would be better with money. Here was proof. He wrote a check for three hundred dollars, sketched the bungalow, its peach tree, and mailed it.

He needed to pile up money. He never wanted to get sent back to Go.

9.

Walter asked at the desk for books on bicycle repair. He'd found nothing in the card catalogue. "Try the public library. We don't"—the student pronounced his *t* with exaggeration—"stock repair manuals. Or any self-help, for that matter."

"'Cept Plato," Walter mumbled.

His Lit Core teacher had thrown a paperback *Phaedrus* at Rory, who'd fallen asleep in class. "Think of it as self-help," she'd said. "To teach you to live without illusions." So Friday, after his shift, Walter set out for the public library. He stopped in the eucalyptus grove to read on a stump. He loved the smell. He was reading Vitruvius's treatise from the first century. Jan Tudor had written *firmitas, utilitas, venustas* on the board: solid, useful, and delightful. Half-shred strips of bark curled up off the eucalyptus trunks and the air opened small folds in his lungs. Jan Tudor had called his dorm block Fascist architecture.

Corbusier wrote, *The styles are a lie.* But he'd also said, *Our own epoch is determining, day by day, its own style. Our eyes, unhappily, are unable yet to discern it.* What was the style of 1973? Walter didn't know if he'd like it. His favorite building was still the church by People's Park. His taste embarrassed him. He wanted to be a modernist.

The house is a machine for living, Corbusier wrote. *One can be proud of having a house as serviceable as a typewriter.* Walter and Ken's room was serviceable; they had what they needed and no more.

Space and light and order. Those are the things that men need just as much as they need bread or a place to sleep. Walter couldn't live on space and light and order; he needed his bed and cafeteria pass more. Corbusier would have, too.

In the distance, Walter saw Carrie, holding books to her chest. He stood and called her. The ground was spongy with fallen leaves. He'd been reading for the class she'd talked him into taking; he should probably thank her, he said, even though she'd bailed. "I love it. I don't consider this homework." It seemed inevitable that she'd led him to his passion.

"I would've taken it if it were any other time."

"So are you an English major now?"

"I want to be a poet. But my dad says as soon as I graduate, he's not paying my rent. My mom worked as a saleswoman at Bonwit Teller after college. Maybe I'll do that." *I'm not special, I know that,* she seemed to be saying. An enchantment. He wouldn't mind an ordinary life with her. He would know she was a treasure, even in a shop, disguised as a salesclerk.

She was on her way to her professor's house. Walter walked her there. In a few minutes, maybe, he would slip his arm under her hair and pull her toward him to whisper—but what? Whatever you said so that, from then on, you became a couple. He loved her, but he didn't know her well enough to say that.

Suddenly, rain clattered in the trees above them. Carrie opened a pretty blue-and-orange umbrella.

He blurted, stupidly, "I remember how you wanted to get into that poetry class."

"With some things, the best part is getting in. Cheerleading was like that. But this class is the most, I don't know, meaningful thing I've ever done. It's hard, though."

Walter felt that about architecture.

"My teacher's paralyzed. A football player carries her into class."

A football player! Walter remembered his disgrace. He hoped Rory hadn't told Carrie about him flying behind the food cart, calling attention to his underdeveloped muscles. His sister had called him Gandhi Legs.

The teacher's house was a 1930s cottage behind two ancient redwoods. People congregated here every Friday to read poems, Carrie told him. When the front door swung open, the professor called from her chair by the fireplace, "Come on in. Sit down."

Walter held up his hands. "I'm not a poet."

"Come in anyway, have a sandwich." She had a small, round head. Propped on a chair, she made a straight diagonal, unbent as a log. Walter noticed the room. Everything was where it should be.

"Tea or wine?" the professor asked. Carrie said wine and he said tea. A young woman served and the professor introduced them to a couple who owned a small press. Most people in the room looked middle-aged. Logs broke in the fireplace, opening flames and sifting ash. This was the first private home Walter had been inside in Berkeley.

A young man read a poem about dying. Walter didn't understand certain phrases; they were abstract and could have meant several different things. A man over forty, with a full beard, read a love poem. He told the younger writer, "I'm the one who should be thinking about death. You should be writing love poems."

After more poems that Walter could make neither hide nor hair of, the professor read one that she said was written by a seventeenth-century Japanese traveler.

Falling sick on a journey
My dream goes wandering
Over a field of dry grass

When the professor talked, you forgot she couldn't walk or probably even hold a teacup. Her hands were gnarled, the fingers bent over each other.

Walter stood up to find the bathroom, mostly to see the house. He admired the layout: a dining alcove opened to the living room, the fireplace in the center of the wall and casement windows. A simple, narrow kitchen that reminded him of the bungalow.

He should have said something to Carrie. He couldn't say *I love you*, but he could have said something. What, though? I want to date you? *Date* was an inadequate word. And they were friends. He didn't want to lose what he had. If he said the wrong thing, she might pity him and never be herself with him again. If only he knew his life would work out right, that he could feel about someone the way he felt about Carrie and live with her in a house like this, then everything would be bearable. But he didn't have the certainty of a good ending. Through a window shoved up in the professor's clean bathroom, he heard rain. By the toilet a steel bar had been installed. He wondered whether the professor could manage the bathroom by herself. He hoped she didn't need a football player to help with that.

He'd been down at the end of the hall where the football players wrote the names of girls they'd had sex with on the back of Rory and Cub's door. Walter had read the list quickly, relieved not to find Susan's or Carrie's name. Ken never spoke about sex, but his laughter seemed deeper. Could Walter be the only male virgin left in the dorm?

He should have said something to Carrie. The eucalyptus grove had been his chance.

Now Carrie was opening her spiral notebook. She took a gulp of wine, then read a poem called "People's Park" in a small voice. Her wrist trembled.

Her talent stunned him. People murmured when she finished. He felt lucky to know her.

But she looked at him with miserable eyes. "Was that okay?"

How could she wonder? "It was great. Can I have a copy?"

She ripped the page out of her notebook and gave him the paper with its confetti edge. Then she handed him her wineglass, to sip. They shared it back and forth, their fingers touching on the glass stem. A woman with a long gray braid read a poem with the refrain *for friends share everything*.

I like that, the man with the beard said. Walter did, too. *Friends share everything*.

Walter had to get to the library before it closed. He needed a repair manual. He put the poem inside Vitruvius and thanked the professor. She tilted her head to the left. It seemed the only mobile part of her. She asked him if he knew any athletes. Her helper, she said, was leaving for school year abroad.

Walter said he'd ask around. Had she not asked him because he didn't look strong enough? Should he have volunteered to carry her? He left, liking the idea that the people there would think of him and Carrie as a couple.

That night, Rory and Cub came to his room asking Walter if he wanted Rory's job at the film place in the museum. Rory didn't need Walter's job, but Cub could man the food cart and that might be good all around. They smiled. At the film place, you just took tickets; then you could study or do whatever. Go in and watch the movie if you wanted. The movies they showed were pretty weird, though. Rory just did his homework. But now, he was going to carry a crippled lady professor to her classes.

Carrie must have asked Rory. When did they talk? Walter hated the idea that she and Rory saw each other besides the times the whole floor crowded in front of Susan's television. Rory slouched against the doorjamb, quietly muscular.

When Walter gave notice at the food service, he could tell people were trying not to laugh. "I'm going to work at the Pacific Film Archive," he said.

"Well, that'll be real nice for you, now, won't it?" the supervisor said.

10.

Carlos helped Walter and Ken hang bike frames from a pipe on the basement ceiling. They had the thick manual from the public library, its laminated pages already smudged. Ken turned up the volume on his transistor for Bob Marley singing "Stir It Up." Ken could actually dance.

They sanded. They'd have to let the frames dry between coats, the book said. They dropped chains to soak in a bucket of linseed oil.

Ken turned up Stevie Wonder. "You know he's blind?"

Ken was teaching him. He told Walter the places where Brian Wilson used a bike bell, a dog barking, or the sound of a train. Lina had played "California Girls," but Walter had never considered the Beach Boys real music. According to Ken, *Pet Sounds* inspired *Sgt. Pepper*. And Bob Dylan once said that Wilson's left ear should be donated to the Smithsonian Museum.

"Why his left?" Walter asked.

"He was deaf in his right. His father hit him when he was a kid."

Ken turned out to be the better spray painter. His first coat was even; Walter's stippled with drips.

Carlos presented them with canvas full-body uniforms. Walter pulled one on over his clothes. It smelled like oil. He remembered the day in the eucalyptus grove when he'd wanted to kiss Carrie. What would she make of him now, a fingernail cracked, his hair full of grease? Even in America, even in California, there were still social classes. And his wasn't hers. He'd have to wait. She'd probably picked her sorority by now.

He and Ken took BART to Chinatown, where Ken bargained in his China-school Mandarin. They paid forty-five cents apiece for bicycle bells. "I'm impressed," Walter said. "You belong in two worlds; I only have one."

"They called me Doctor Son. Good guess."

Walter checked the mail every day, but nothing arrived. He thought of going home to ransack his mom's file cabinet, but it was a six-hour drive and no one was leaving in the middle of the quarter. Every week in April, he moved his alarm fifteen minutes earlier. He found Melinda in the cafeteria at six. For all he knew, she'd been sitting here since September, sipping coffee before dawn. She wore a man's watch on her flat wrist. "So now it's only us," she said. Ken had quit pre-med. He'd sat on his bed in full ROTC regalia, holding his French horn like a baby, telling his parents about his second C. After that, he'd slept fourteen hours. "Ken's just not a student, not that way," Melinda said. "For a long time, I thought he could be." She had the narrowest face. It held disappointment, acceptance, something else. She looked, for a moment, older.

Chemistry was a language Walter was still memorizing one word at a time. He could read building plans. *It's just bars and dots* was a joke among architecture students, a variation of *It's Greek to me.* A girl in class said, "It looks like Morse code!" But glancing at the frets and symbols on paper, Walter saw buildings swell into full dimension, the way those flat sponges grew once you added water. The bars and dots that looked like Morse code had been the Acropolis.

Walter heard Melinda giggle. "What?" he said.

She held up her notebook. She was laughing at an equation!

"If I didn't know you, I'd feel a lot better about my aptitude for science."

"Want me to look at your lab report?" she offered.

But Walter hadn't been working on his lab report. He'd spotted a flyer on a layered paper-covered corkboard outside Wurster Hall, the design building, announcing a contest. *Environmental design scholarship. Draw your dream campus.*

He had been sketching utopia, roads with bike lanes, creeks and buildings. *A scholarship*, he'd written to his mom. When he'd lied as a kid, saying he had a stomachache to stay home from school, he'd become sick. His dream campus had a lot of public greens. But he didn't draw long before coming up against the limits of design. You could draw beautiful buildings, parks, and good houses, but how would you make places to live for the people who maintained it all? For Carlos?

To render utopia, you first had to figure out a way to redistribute wealth.

"I'm not sure I like our generation." Susan was complaining about the guys who hung around their room, pursuing Carrie. Muscles around his heart constricted. He'd been an idiot to think his feelings original. Apparently, he was one of a drove. Susan said that Carrie could tell them no without actually saying it. "She's been doing it since she was fourteen." Walter had the awful premonition that Carrie had *already* said no to him and he hadn't even realized it.

On Sunday nights, the football players talked about the sex they'd had over the weekend. *Scuzzy,* Rory called a tiny girl he'd boned on the fifty-yard line. She'd had little stones around her mouth. Another guy complained that a girl farted. All the girls Cub popped were Black. He sorted his girls, though not his friends, by race. Walter asked what a mark meant, next to one of the names. "Bleeding," Rory said in a lower voice. "She stank." There seemed to be an ugliness to sex.

"Anyway," Susan said, "the sorority will give us a chance to dress up."

"Another reason not to join," Walter said. "I don't have a suit."

"You'd look good in a suit."

11.

Mrs. Em Ball, the Environmental Design librarian, carried a stack of books about Julia Morgan; Walter told her he'd thought Morgan designed his favorite building here—the church he'd seen his first day in Berkeley—but it turned out to be by Bernard Maybeck.

"Did you know Julia Morgan was his student?" she said. Maybeck had encouraged her to go to the Académie des Beaux-Arts in Paris, but they'd never had a woman before. She had to try three times before they let her in. She worked on Berkeley's Greek Theatre. Her boss bragged that he had an excellent draftsman whom he could pay almost nothing because she was a woman. She figured out a new way to use reinforced concrete. Still, reporters asked her about pillows and chintz, assuming she was the decorator. Almost all of the hundreds of buildings she designed were commissioned by women's clubs. "Oh, that Maybeck church you like, on Dwight Way? I grew up in that parish."

"Do you still go?"

"No, I left the church when I was twenty."

Walter didn't know Mrs. Ball well enough yet to ask why.

Walter brought his teacher sketches he'd made of a Julia Morgan building on campus, thinking she'd like them, being another lady architect.

Jan Tudor exhaled as if explaining things to him required patience. "Since Michelangelo, no one reinvented architecture until Corbusier. You have to *contend* with him. I've come to his way of seeing the old architecture; it's ornate, like a wedding cake. 'Look to American engineers,' he said, 'beware of American architects.'"

Walter had lived in concrete apartment buildings in LA. He wanted to own a house someday. Not a unit in an apartment block, not even one of Corbusier's scissors modules. If shingles were ornamental, they still made a building look like a home.

In May, Walter and Ken hauled the bikes up into the light. They offered one to Carlos, who refused it; he already had a bike. "Me, you know what I want? I want education. Someday I become engineer."

This was hard to think about. "What about your wife and kids?" Walter finally asked. "Would one of them want a bike?"

Carlos shook his head. "No, no, no thank you."

Susan and Carrie each bought three-speeds for eighty-five dollars. Walter had planned to ask sixty, but Susan said that was too little.

"New white bike, new white dress." Carrie sighed. "Springtime."

A line formed. Six people wanted bikes but they had only four left and a guy from the second floor said he'd been there first, so, yeah, hey, and Rory said, but he came like a minute after and he really really needed the big bike, he couldn't use a smaller one, and he'd pay more, he'd pay a hundred. The guy from the second floor said he'd pay a hundred twenty-five. People held out money.

"Tell you what," Walter said. "We were going to keep one for ourselves, but we won't. So five of you can have bikes now. Decide who'll pay the most. Whoever doesn't get one today goes on the wait list. We'll have more in a few months."

They earned over seven hundred dollars and the wait list had three names. Walter sprinted to the fire department to find out when they'd hold the next sale, the roll of twenties rubber-banded in his pocket. I can do this, he thought, blood ticking as he ran. He would buy his mom a house someday. No more landlords. There'd been one she'd loved, a cottage with five holes drilled in the roof for birds. Jan Tudor would call that "cute." But Walter's mom couldn't afford the rent and they'd kept looking—it was amazing how people allowed themselves to be sorted. Why didn't they fight to claim what they loved?

The next sale wasn't going to be until mid-June. Walter talked to Ken. "From now on, we'll split everything, but this time, can I reimburse myself for what I paid the fire department?"

Ken wouldn't take any money. "I don't even spend all my allowance." Walter knew then that Ken understood his secret.

Ken put on a record, handing Walter the jacket. Three guys in sweaters, singing "When You Wish Upon a Star." Dion & The Belmonts. Ken lifted the needle and put another LP on the stem. "Listen to this. It's the same chords as 'Surfer Girl.' Brian Wilson's first song." The categories were blurring; Walter wouldn't have considered either of these songs serious music, but Ken knew more than he did. He told Walter there was a lot of Bach underpinning the Beatles, and when he marked the places with a raised finger, Walter heard it, too.

With cash from the bikes, Walter paid down $1,175. He still owed over $2,000. He asked the woman in the cage, "What happens if I'm behind at the end of the year? Will they kick me out?"

She looked at him. "I really have no idea."

———

Walter considered hitching to LA to find his mom's 1099 form, but he'd never hitchhiked before. On a ride board, he found a guy who was driving as far as Bakersfield and said he'd take him if he didn't mind reading out loud from a book.

The guy drove up to the dorm in a Toyota with the seat all the way back because his legs were so long. "Book's there." He nodded to the foot space. The guy smoked, a kind of foreign cigarette, thin and dark with a strong smell. He was skinny, with bristly hair.

In the middle of life's journey, Walter read, *I found myself in a dark wood. . . .*

The guy was a comp lit major and he worked himself up talking about the book. He was driving home because his mom was having an operation. "She's getting her whole female part removed," he said, ticking ash out the window. After two hours, he said, "Okay, let's take a break from that one." By then, Walter loved what he'd been reading. The next book had a torn corner of notebook paper marking the page.

> *Do I dare*
> *Disturb the universe?*

Be my guest, Walter thought. This writer sounded like someone alive now, wildly smart and modern, wanting to pick a fight.

They passed the Bakersfield city limits in the late afternoon and drove to a new subdivision in the dusk. The land looked recently cleared; even with small lights over the garage doors, the country felt empty. The guy invited Walter in for a sandwich before taking him to the interstate to thumb a ride. The guy's mother was sitting at the kitchen table eating a steak with a silver line of gristle.

"My last meal," she said. "I can't have anything tomorrow before surgery." Then she stood up and made them bologna sandwiches.

"Tell you what," the guy said. "If you can read by the car light, I'll drive you down. I just want to be here in the morning. To take her in." Walter continued *The Inferno* and fell back into its enchantment. At the turnoff to the Pacific Coast Highway, the guy asked Walter what he'd read in freshman seminar.

Portrait of the Artist. Walter said he didn't like Stephen Dedalus. He seemed full of himself. Pretentious.

The guy shrugged. "Got me out of Bakersfield," he said.

When they pulled up to the bungalow, Walter invited him in but the guy wanted to head back. He took a Coke bottle from the floor of the car, unzipped his fly, and peed into it. Walter took the warm bottle—it seemed the decent thing to do—and poured it out by a persimmon tree at the corner. Maybe it would fertilize the roots.

12.

The sound of running water and the clatter of pots had awakened Donnie most of the days of his life. Good sounds he now remembered.

The first time his mother overslept, he heard a bang against the wall they shared, then exasperated muttering until she rushed to her car. He turned over in his bed, hugged his pillow, and fell back asleep. His sister would pound on his door ten minutes before they had to go. Three mornings later, his mother was still asleep when he and Lina left for school. When he returned that afternoon, she was still in bed. He knocked on her door and asked if she'd like some toast. The two of them had always been easy together. He made cinnamon toast, cut in fours, the way she did.

She sighed and said she wasn't feeling well, and the next day she stayed home again. She seemed tired and maybe sad, but herself.

After school, Donnie usually went to the computer lab, which was a room in the middle school with no windows and a mainframe that took up a wall. Most days he found Evan there, eating his lunch and laughing at jokes in a book. Evan could program while turning the pages. But today, since his mother didn't go to work, Donnie skipped the computer lab and went right home.

She got up, pushed a brush through one side of her hair, and followed him into the kitchen. He opened the back door and they sat at the table, each eating a bowl of cereal. Donnie was used to being home alone. Lina worked at the ice-cream store. Being with his mother in the afternoon felt like a strange vacation.

Her eyes greedily scanned the room—alighting on the cupboards she'd once painted, the old table, sanded down in the backyard then waxed, the dishes they'd bought for an amazing price at a yard sale, now arranged behind glass. She nodded, ticking them off to him—her accomplishments. Donnie understood that she was proud to have made a good home for them. They sat among their plain treasures with the back door open to the yard, where Walter's bike had once been stolen and never replaced and the ancient peach tree emitted its faint smell. Later, Donnie understood that she had been saying a slow goodbye to that worked-for, cherished place. But that afternoon, he wondered what program Evan was writing. They played a game on the computer, and when the string of numbers worked, the mainframe made a small blunt noise. Donnie felt that click shudder through his body. He collected those clicks.

After she'd been home a week, they ran out of milk and cereal, and Donnie skateboarded to the ice-cream store. Lina fished a ten out of her apron pocket. She'd saved eight hundred dollars, but that was for college. She hated spending, she said, because ten dollars would buy milk, cereal, and the boxes of macaroni and cheese they liked, but then they'd have to do it all over again.

"Do you think she'll go back to work soon?" Donnie asked.

"She has to or I don't know how we're going to pay for things."

They hadn't told Walter yet. They couldn't have said why. Walter was far away. That was part of it. He hadn't written to Lina since he'd sent three hundred dollars to make up for the stolen checks. Donnie had seen Lina cry when she'd opened that envelope. Mostly, it was because this still felt temporary—it had only been a week—and if, in a few days, their mother got up, washed her face, and drove to work as she always had, then they would have caused a blowup for nothing. Their mother wouldn't want Walter to know. She'd always showed her best side to him, her *college boy*. She was more herself with Donnie and Lina.

The next Friday evening, Julie arrived. Lina sat in the living room like a lady, one leg crossed over the other, talking to Julie while Donnie warned their mother, who didn't look happy.

"Oh, no. What's *she* doing here?" She sighed and pulled her knees up and in twenty minutes shuffled out to the couch by the bay window. As he turned on the light, Donnie noticed dust balls under the sofa. He'd never thought that vacuuming actually did anything. Now, he understood, he'd been wrong. From the kitchen, he and Lina heard their mother's voice and occasionally picked out her boss's name—Learhoff, she and Julie called him. Dr. Learhoff employed dozens of nurses and dispatched them to drive their own cars to convalescent hospitals he'd contracted with throughout Southern California. These women, newly minted with diplomas they'd struggled to obtain, happily handed over 60 percent of their earnings to this tall man who promised them security. That had been their opportunity. Years later, contemplating the business model, Donnie remembered this Friday in the seventies, when the two women laughed: a startling, beautiful sound. Donnie and Lina looked at each other and began to laugh, too.

All would be okay, they thought. She was still herself.

But she didn't go back to work. Her checkbook, with a brown leather cover, rested on her dresser. Lina walked in while she was sleeping and tore out three yellow checks.

Julie brought over hamantaschen. "They're half price after five. How's your mom feeling? It's been three weeks. If she's still sick, she needs to see a doctor."

Donnie liked her certainty. If their mother was sick, there would be a doctor's appointment and medicine to make her better. Lina somehow doubted this. Her mother cried too much. Her shoulders curled. Her face lost its order. What illness was that? Not one the world would count. Defeat, surrender: those were not illnesses, exactly; they were afflictions people blamed you for. Her mother stayed in bed now most of the day. But she had never been lazy. Many times in the past, Lina had fallen asleep to the sound of her mother vacuuming.

The bungalow had been built in 1911 and the walls were solid. Lina and Donnie could hear the women talking in the bedroom, but they couldn't make out distinct words.

Julie finally emerged. "She says she's seen a doctor, but I'm not sure I believe her."

Donnie shrugged. "When I get home after school, she's just getting up." He remembered her telling him about the furniture and the dishes. Cataloguing. As if she didn't want to forget anything.

"I'll talk to Learhoff about sick leave," Julie said.

Lina and Donnie both looked at her. Surprised. Grateful.

They filled the wire cart at Ralphs every week with boxes of macaroni and cheese and the cookies they liked, hanging the bags on Lina's handlebars. Lina signed her mother's yellow check without entering the date or the amount in the register, the way her mother faithfully had.

Julie arranged for extended sick leave, so every other week, their mother received a paycheck and Lina deposited it in the bank. Lina said she would call Walter, his number was there scribbled on the kitchen wall by the phone, but she put it off and off and then, one night when she rolled her bike in the back door, her overalls sour from melted specks of ice cream, Walter was sitting in the dark with his head in his hands.

"How long has she been like this?" he asked.

He'd found the house dusty, an empty macaroni box on the counter and his mother in bed. What Walter had always feared would happen if he left. Donnie said she'd stopped going to work. Walter waited up for his sister. But the answers Lina was giving him now that she was home were enragingly vague.

"She hasn't been working since February, I think. Julie talked Learhoff into sick pay."

"What does Julie say?"

Lina shrugged. "You should ask her."

He'd come home to find a single sheet of paper. Not this. He'd been planning to go back tomorrow. But could he now, with the bungalow in chaos? Light from the boarder's lava lamp pinked the walls.

The next morning, Walter sat on the floor before his mom's file cabinet. He found the folder with his report cards, small baggies with each of their baby teeth. There was a file labeled *Love Letters*, which he flipped past. He found cashed checks and a folder with her nurses' retirement statements, but no sign of taxes. Could she have just not paid?

When she awakened, he asked her about her tax returns.

"Maybe they're at work. I know I paid them. Do you want me to write a note?"

A note! Walter wanted to cry. "Are you going back to work?"

"Oh, sure," she said. "Pretty soon."

"What's wrong, Mom?"

She sat up in bed. "I don't know," she said, her face bunching. "I really don't know."

"Don't worry," Walter said, a hand on her back, feeling her small bones.

They ate dinner in the kitchen. Donnie made macaroni and cheese and tore open a package of bean sprouts. His mother picked at her food like a child, looking at her plate. Julie drove over later with a bakery cake.

"Her sick leave is just about up," Julie whispered. "I don't know how much longer I can push Learhoff. We may have to look into disability."

"She's right here," Donnie said. "We can include her."

Julie looked straight into their mother's face then, the way people did to the uncomprehending, and said, "Di, I've gotten as much as I can out of the old Learjet. Another month, then you have to come back. What do you say? Can we try for June?"

Donnie put his head on the table. "She can't go back yet, I don't think."

Walter helped her into her room. "Okay. You just stay home awhile and rest." But what was she resting from, exactly?

Donnie looked at Julie, really looked at her for the first time, and saw the oval of prettiness that was her face. He also noticed bare patches in her hair, the flat top of her head, all the peripheral things that must have made people miss that oval.

Donnie had thought about the moment Lina would tell Walter what had been happening; he'd imagined Walter listening exactly the way he was, intent, his head still. He'd expected it would be a relief to tell him, like giving over two suitcases. But now that Walter was here, it was hard to think of what he could do.

Julie drove Walter to the bus station downtown. A classic nurse, he thought, competent, a little dull, completely sane. When she stopped the car in front of the station, he stayed sitting. "Should I just drop out for now? I could get a job to keep the family going." He thought of Carrie. "I can always go back later."

"It would kill her if you left. Besides, whatever job you'd get without a degree . . ." She shook her head.

He slept with his head against the Greyhound window, arriving in Berkeley at midnight. After a long walk to the dorm, he found everyone in Susan and Carrie's room, passing around a joint held by a tweezer. Melinda sat on Ken's lap. He remembered Susan's rant about disliking their era. She was lying right in the middle of it now. He wanted air. The last thing he needed was to get high. That was for kids who had nets.

Alone in his room, he shoved the window up. He thought of his mom in the bungalow. He'd felt strange leaving, but everyone took it for granted—Julie did, even Lina, most of all his mom—so he thought he had to, that the right good thing was to make something of himself. The only person who longed for him to stay was his little brother, whose round face had beamed pleas at him. He thought of the house he would someday buy his mom, the same size as the bungalow but nicer, a simple design.

Years later, he interviewed a young woman and noticed, on her résumé, that she'd taken six years to finish her undergraduate degree. He asked why, thinking rehab, drugs, maybe—she wasn't thin enough for anorexia. She told him, with summoned dignity, that her mother died and she'd needed time.

A long-poised marble dropped into its slot.

He should have stayed. He could have returned to school later, another way. They should have been together.

The bungalow doorbell rang one Monday night in June and it was Julie, holding a cardboard box. She entered in a gust of cold evening air. "Learhoff replaced her. A new girl showed up this morning. Your mom's patients are all asking for her." Donnie had never heard Julie rattled like this—it frightened him. She'd collected their mom's belongings from the three hospitals where she worked. "How many years already? I think it's nine. You were just a pipsqueak when I met you," she said.

All those years fit into this box.

"Can she still go back?" Lina asked. "Or could he send her to a different hospital?"

"Probably he could. He's got so many contracts. Learhoff always liked her."

Donnie picked out items and put them on the table. A magenta uniform. Their mother had been one of the first to wear colored uniforms when the regulations changed. Donnie held up a one-pound weight. A rubber-banded stack of flashcards she'd shown him once, syllables with pictures that she'd used to teach stroke patients to talk again. He kept lifting things from the box. Lina was waiting for a picture of *them*. But there was nothing. She looked ashamed for having expected that. Julie came out of their mother's room.

"Do you have a family doctor who knows her?"

Lina said their mother had once taken her to an ear, nose, and throat specialist in a luxurious Beverly Hills office when her earache wouldn't go away. But they couldn't think of a doctor who would remember them.

"She's got to see somebody," Julie said. "This has just been too long."

13.

On the other side of her life, Lina sat with Lauren and Jess on the high school lawn during morning break, sipping coffee, which she'd learned to like with packets of powdered cream and Sweet'N Low, listening to their intricate dilemmas. Lauren had a twenty-five-year-old boyfriend, a law student who judged county debates, to whom she was incrementally relenting her virginity while the debate coach tried to dam the avalanche. Lina hoped they couldn't tell that she was listening with only the surface of her attention. She enjoyed the prettiness of their lives, their voices back and forth above and around like birds.

Her forty-six-year-old mother stayed home all day and no longer bathed. It wasn't only that she didn't rush to work anymore in a hectic flurry—the *tat tat tat* of heels—but Lina couldn't even *imagine* those mornings returning, not really. That life, with its money panics and disorder, now seemed an irrecoverable buzzing happiness. Her family was hurtling toward emergency, something larger than she could think in a straight sentence. Fortunately, her friends didn't notice that she didn't contribute to the conversation. Most people didn't, she'd observed. When they were talking about themselves, they assumed you were all in. You could drift. Lina was not all in.

When they offered to pick up Lina at her house Friday morning to drive to Malibu to watch surfers, she snapped to attention and made an excuse. But when they suggested a diner near school on Monday, she couldn't say no. They would just keep asking.

So at seven in the morning, Lauren was hassling her to order food. Every time they'd been in a restaurant together Lauren picked up the bill, but to be safe, Lina ordered only coffee. They talked about money in front of her, as an indirect argument for her to eat. There had never been a time, Lauren said, when she couldn't have ordered the most expensive thing on a menu. "I could've always had the steak."

Lina had eaten steak in a restaurant only once; sawing the meat with a serrated knife, she'd felt acutely conscious of its price. She hadn't liked the taste.

Later, she would think of Lauren's steak as an elegant way to define wealth. She would wish she'd gone to see the early-morning Pacific surfers. Mostly, she would regret not trying to explain more of the truth. But that day in the diner she'd just changed the humiliating subject, saying, "I don't like to eat in the morning." This wasn't true, but hearing herself say it and sipping the black, bitter coffee (the waiter hadn't yet brought the Sweet'N Low or creamer), Lina caught a glimpse of herself as a young woman in overalls with her hair pulled back who drank black coffee and had no breakfast.

But what about her mother? The question stopped Lina every time.

The worst had still not happened. Her mother was still there. All these months, her mother just stayed in her room. They were running out of money. Lina had seen pictures of asylums, but those were from long ago. Would they send her mother away? Shame snuck up on Lina from behind: Was she concerned for her mother, or herself? Lina had been shown an orphanage once, in the Central Valley town where her mother had grown up. But she and Donnie would never have to go into an orphanage, she thought. They had Walter.

And maybe her mother would still get better. Years ago, in an elementary school library, Lina had opened the *World Book Encyclopedia* to a three-inch color picture, under an entry for *Polaroid*. The photograph was of a girl covered with freckles, her red hair long, below her elbows. That glossy rectangle seemed a door for Lina to fall through. Lina's mother bought a cream to fade her freckles and marveled over her daughter's superior skin. When Lina was small, strangers had stopped them and said Lina was beautiful. More than once, they'd asked, Adopted? Lina's memories of these instances were of painful shyness; she hid behind her mother, shamefully pleased.

Only Lina found her mother beautiful. But there was proof in the *World Book Encyclopedia*.

Jess was talking about what Lauren would lose if she went all the way. To them, talking about sex was more personal than talking about money. Jess said what Lauren was afraid of losing had already been ceded. Lina enjoyed parsing these distinctions. Lina had a crush, too, on a senior who didn't know her name. Suddenly, though, the quiet had gone on too long. Both girls were staring at her.

"How is, how is your mom?" Lauren asked.

"She's fine." There was far too much to explain.

Lina still assumed the life Lauren and Jess talked about was meant for her, too, only later. She would be diverted just for a while. Her essential self would remain intact and qualified to merge back into the general stream of parties, boyfriends, and fun. She couldn't yet imagine the far-fetched possibility that she might change into someone who would no longer wish to join.

Lina swept the house now on Saturday mornings and Donnie mopped the floors. They had to be quiet because the boarder slept in. When Donnie knelt scrubbing the bathtub first with Comet, then with white cider vinegar, which the boarder requested, his mother drifted in and stood with a hand on the wall. "Thank you," she whispered.

Her last check from Learhoff had come. No doctor had been seen, and Julie had stopped harping on that. Their mother seemed to cry less and sleep more.

Walter called late one June night to ask Lina if he should come home. He could get a ride down and stay the summer, or longer. But he had no job or anything in LA. Up there he fixed bikes and worked at the movie place and now he'd been offered a job in a store, to sell suits on weekends. He'd found a room he could rent in a fraternity for cheap.

Lina was alone in the kitchen, her bare feet up on the table after a good shift at the ice-cream store. Branches outside swayed, fern-like in the dark. "You're asking me?" Her hand went to her chest. She felt important to be asked.

"Yeah, which do you think would be better?"

She didn't know so she guessed, the way she sometimes guessed at school, when she hadn't done the reading. She knew she'd hit the right answer because he said okay right away and got off the phone. She sat in the dark. That night, another scooper had asked her to a concert of Grand Funk Railroad.

Walter remembered the conversation differently. He'd told Lina about the jobs in Berkeley, his boss at the archive saying he could send back the film cans, mumbling, *I hate that shit,* the suit store with a HELP WANTED sign, and bikes he'd bought to refurbish. He'd asked her what she thought would be better: him or money.

"Maybe the money," she'd said quietly. "No offense."

He'd felt relieved and also ashamed that they didn't want him.

14.

"My father said when he was in college you'd never marry a girl who slept with you," Susan said, pulling a suitcase to her car. "And you'd never sleep with a girl you wanted to marry."

"That's no fun," Walter said. Susan's shoulders were square and she had nice skin; it must have been hard for her, always standing next to Carrie. They were both going to LA for the summer. Susan would intern in a senator's office, and Carrie had a writing job for a TV game show produced by a family friend.

Melinda had told Walter about cheap rooms in a fraternity. She'd moved into an attic with no closet, for forty dollars a month. For the same price, they gave Walter a corner room with wainscoting and a slant view of the bay. He asked to swap, but no women were allowed on his floor. The first minute in his room he felt lucky, but then he was just alone. He'd started that morning at the Princeton Shop. Mr. Barsani Senior showed him how to steam a suit. He could send money home. Still, if his mom didn't go back to work, it would never be enough. The next morning, he met Melinda in the frat-house kitchen, cluttered with pizza boxes.

"Let's get out of here," she said. "I'm going to let myself eat one doughnut a day."

This was a real friendship with a woman. When he looked at Melinda, he didn't picture her naked or think of running his finger along her clavicle, the way he did whenever he saw Carrie in a blouse.

The night the fraternity had a party, Melinda barricaded herself in the attic. A girl with wet hair and bare arms put her hands on Walter's shoulders and hopped along to the music on the grass. She wasn't a great dancer, so he felt okay jumping, too. *You'll take away the very heart of me.* They kissed. It was easier than he'd thought.

"Where are you staying?" she whispered, as if this were urgent information. She knew how to do this.

In his room, he put *Let It Be* on the turntable and set down the needle while "Play That Funky Music, White Boy" pounded up through the floor. He offered her tea. His mom had told them: you always offer a beverage. He gave her his mug and sat in the butterfly chair. She moved her head to "I Me Mine" and told him she was a swimmer. If he just waited, he thought, something would happen.

When the needle bumped at the disc, he turned off the light. Things were winding down outside. Then he lay next to her, and it finally began, what he'd imagined a thousand times, with Carrie. He tried to pull the reins, but couldn't; it happened quickly, and he found himself laughing out loud. So this was sex. But the girl was a random person; he didn't even know her name. The music hadn't started, the soundtrack that was supposed to run under his life.

All night he wondered if he would still be able to meet Melinda downstairs as usual. He wanted their morning doughnut. At dawn, the girl blinked her eyes open and dressed. "We do lake laps in the morning." She smiled at him and left. He thought of his mom. You lived every day with someone and then you left, and even if they were failing, you lost your virginity; your lives weren't interdependent anymore, though you'd once been everything to each other.

The frat house had a balcony the guys let him hang bike frames from. He sanded while they sat above him smoking cigars.

"Lookee there." He heard one whistle.

"But you know, you don't want a cute woman," another said. "A cute woman will expect you to take her out to nice places. She'll ask for this and that and the other thing. What you really want is an *ug*ly woman. An ugly woman will suck your dick." They laughed in the twilight. "She'll be so grateful she'll do anything."

For no reason at all he thought of his mom. Had someone mocked her? That could break a person. But his mom wasn't ugly.

The swimmer, whose name was Cathy, came over most nights now.

Rory stumbled downstairs using a hand to steady himself. Walter could tell from the way he stepped, dance-like and unstable, that he was buzzed. "Hey, a lot of the guys, we've been talking about these bikes and we think white's a little sissy."

Walter counted up orders in his head. He had enough without them. He'd use the white paint.

Cathy asked to talk. This meant either she was dumping him or wanted to go steady, Melinda said. But it was something else.

"I've been faking." She took up breath quickly. "Please don't be mad."

Walter draped an arm around her and patted her back vaguely. The film archive was playing *Tokyo Story*. Leaves outside waved and beckoned, but he did what he was supposed to. Her hands rested on his head, guiding him as obliquely as a Ouija. He recognized the smell his brother carried as a kid from sucking two fingers. Finally, she made a noise, pulled her knees up, and curled into a C. He looked out the window. Someone downstairs put on the Stones. He wished he felt in love with her. But how did he even know what other people meant when they said that?

Carrie wrote to him. The joke writers were all old, in their forties. This had been her mom's idea. Her mom was big on finding things re*lat*ed to what they cared about—for her brother, who dreamed of becoming a stand-up comedian, an internship with an entertainment law firm. Carrie should be glad to be writing at all, according to her mom, even for a game show. They gave her stacks of magazines for inspiration. She wrote gag lines that made her literally gag. The only thing she liked about the job was the eggplant parmigiana lunch from the Source, and now her mom said the Source was run by a cult. *It's nice to be back in LA, though,* she wrote. *Bonfires on the beach at night.*

Walter had never been to the beach at night. Once when he was twelve, he'd taken the bus over the hill to the beach with two other boys and they'd seen graffiti on the pilings: VALLEY GO HOME.

Guess that's us, one of them said, giggling nervously.

15.

Lina ironed her best blouse, then blow-dried her hair. She didn't really know how.

"Do I look better?" she asked Donnie.

"You look different," he said. "I don't know about better."

The sky turned deeper blue. It was five o'clock, then six. She instructed Donnie to answer the phone, then went to the alley. It took a while rummaging through the neighbor's old newspapers to find an ad. The concert started at seven thirty. If the scooper didn't call soon, they wouldn't make it. A slow hour passed. Finally, she took off her good blouse, hung it up again, and put on a sweatshirt to ride her bike to the ice-cream shop.

Weirdly, he was there, too, sitting in a back booth, flanked by two guys with strange smiles. The tall manager observed, curiously.

"Called your number," the scooper mumbled. "Said it was disconnected."

She stood there, feeling heat on her face. Their phone had been disconnected? She tried to remember the last time it had rung.

"Spent a lot for those tickets," a guy next to him in the booth said.

"Maybe our phone's broken," she said, stupidly. They stopped talking to her then.

She ordered an ice cream, conspicuously paid, and rode home. She left her bike on the ground, ran in, and picked up the phone. Dead. In the chalky kitchen light, she ripped through a pile of bills on the counter and found one stamped URGENT. Another, from Pacific Gas and Electric, said FINAL NOTICE. The next morning, Lina rode her bike to an office and handed a yellow check to a woman behind a grille. They had to pay forty dollars extra to turn the service back on. That didn't seem fair.

"No, it don't, do it?" the woman said. "But I got to charge you."

The woman's name was Linda. Every month, Lina returned to her.

Walter sent four twenty-dollar bills folded inside lined note-book paper. Lina gave one to Donnie. The scooper never asked her out again. She mostly understood.

16.

Ken invited Walter to Modesto for the Fourth of July. Bring Cathy, he said. Walter counted up the money he would lose by not working and took the weekend off. There was something pathetic about being a single man budgeting for your own pleasure, but he didn't invite Cathy. Whatever they had seemed untranslatable into public. Rory drove and brought along a laugher named Sally. Walter sat with Melinda in the back. At the end of the long road trip, Ken stood wearing an apron under a sycamore. A stereo, connected by an extension cord, was playing classical guitar music. Ken's parents had gone to a wedding in Sacramento, but before leaving, his mother had rolled manicotti for them.

It felt adult to sit at a table outside with wineglasses and cloth napkins, facing rows of walnut trees. They were two couples and Walter. Ken carried out a hot casserole dish in mittened hands.

"Did you always live here?" Sally asked.

"We moved when I was nine. My parents wanted to live in the country. They imagined us riding horses to school. But I never liked horses and my brother's allergic." Sally found this hilarious. "A neighbor told my dad he could pay the property tax with walnuts. So we planted five hundred saplings by ourselves in a week. My dad's lucky. Horse-riding turns out to be the most expensive thing a kid can do, and by the time our trees matured, more Chinese were becoming middle-class, and people wanted nuts." Ken lit a candle on the table as the branches knit together, making the dark.

Each of them talked about their parents. Melinda's parents met in college, which was where they made all their friends. Since her father died, these friends were making sure her mom had something to do on the weekends.

They talked with unusual politeness, napkins on their laps. Ken said he was afraid that after college nothing would be the same. "Friendships change for most people."

"My parents don't even have friends," Sally said.

Ken didn't think his parents had had friends either, until recently. The whole time he and his brother were growing up, it was only work and family. And walnuts. Sally laughed.

"They travel with two couples now, both Asian, all doctors. They take cooking classes. She learned this in Tuscany."

Such good food and no parents present!

"My folks didn't go to college," Rory said, "but they have friends. My dad played varsity and he still knows the guys from the team. My mom went to secretarial school after graduation, but her friends are all from the West High cheerleading squad. They don't have careers like they want for me." Six players from the Berkeley team injured themselves last year and the coach sent them home. Rory was beginning to understand, he said, that football might not matter so much when he got older. "It was just my way in." Rory had to finish an incomplete. The lady poet was helping him. In the distance a train rumbled, trailing a moan.

Walter kept quiet. He didn't want to talk about his parents.

"For most people," Ken said, "college is probably the last period in their lives they spend time like this with friends."

"Let's vow that that won't happen to us," Melinda said.

The next day, Walter took a walk after lunch to give the couples privacy. It was hot and still, the trees motionless and buzzing. A tractor rolled in the distance. Rory's athletic talent was turning out to be worth less than he'd thought. Walter, too, had had glory whispered into his ear at home. He'd once believed he was exceptional. Watching Melinda work out chemistry reactions, he'd learned that he was only average. Architecture was easy for him, though, the way equations were for Melinda. Maybe he could plan cities. But he needed to make money. When he came to Berkeley, he'd felt lucky. His mom had always been proud of her degree; they'd carried the framed diploma from apartment to apartment. She'd considered herself equal to his classmates' moms, even when the feeling wasn't mutual. She'd probably feel superior to Rory's mother. Walter's lack of means, she thought, was due to a personal misfortune: the Afghans. Rory had a football scholarship for tuition, but his dad paid for the dorm. What would he think of Walter applying for financial aid? (Walter had turned in the papers with a note saying his mother couldn't find her 1099. He'd applied for the scholarship, too.) Rory's dad might not like his tax dollars paying for another father's negligence.

They sat on a hill watching fireworks, the girls inside the half circles of their boyfriends' arms. Maybe he should have brought Cathy. He imagined her under the clustered walnuts still growing inside their green padded skins. Cathy was so easy to please. His mom loved him, but that was a small mark among a thousand frets. He liked being able to make someone happy.

17.

Lina called Walter at the fraternity and cried. He waited until she could talk. "The phone got turned off," she finally said, and then he had to wait again. Evidently, it was back on.

"Do you think she's improving at all?" he asked.

"She said she was going back to work. Then she went to sleep."

He would have to stick it out in chemistry. Jan Tudor made jokes about unemployed architects. If he got into medical school, he'd have a career. His kids could be architects, he thought.

After Lina hung up, he sat in the big fraternity room, unable to move.

He received a postcard from Carrie with only one line.

Don't you love the smell of the Valley summer nights?

She could write almost nothing and it was a poem. He'd never told her that he'd once lived in the Valley, and that his mom had plotted to get them out of there. He believed that Carrie would understand everything that had happened to him. She was like a fairy tale. If he were with her, he thought, his whole life would be different.

Cathy told him she loved being in water, where everything you heard bent and hushed. She knew, though, that no one would ever pay her to swim.

"You could teach swimming," he said.

Her eyebrows pressed together. Her mother was an accountant. A swim team friend was studying nutrition. Her roommate from Beirut was majoring in feminism. Cathy planned to major in physical education or maybe nutrition, but when he asked her what would she be then, she looked cornered. "Or maybe something else," she said. Her mind seemed a small, guarded animal.

One morning, they drove her mom's old Pontiac to a lake covered with a thick layer of fog. She slipped neatly into the water, a letter L tipping, hardly disrupting the surface. She could talk while swimming. He was gasping, the moon and the rising sun both in the sky.

All day his body felt loose in a way he hoped would last.

They went to a showing of *The Apu Trilogy*. Walter's boss grabbed his tickets before they were torn and paid Walter back, out of his own wallet. Walter loved being known here. They sat in the full, expectant room as the lights dimmed. Then they were in a small town in India.

When they came out, it was late and lights were on along Durant Avenue. If he could go to films and then come up into a lighted world, Walter would be happy. Movies—middle-class entertainment, his boss called them—were attainable pleasures. He'd begun to collect those. One of his white bikes sped by in the dark.

They ducked into a stand-up hot dog place, next to a real restaurant. He took a napkin from the dispenser and drew. In the used bookstore, he'd studied sketches of middle-aged people in a book called *The Joy of Sex*. They hadn't had a vaginal yet. They were getting close, he thought. The angle was critical. If he were higher, friction would increase. She blushed and crumpled the napkin.

On the street, a guy from the dorm—a shoulder-rubber—opened the restaurant door for two girls, one holding a small white dog on a leash. The other was Carrie, in a sleeveless dress and tippy shoes. The shoulder-rubber had his arm on her back. It was eleven o'clock and they were going into dinner!

"I'm just here for one night," she said, as Walter made introductions.

Later, Walter jerked out of bed, hearing rain. A dozen bike

frames hung from the balcony. He and Cathy hauled them inside. The surfaces were pocked, traces of raindrops trenching the finish. He'd have to sand them down again. They peeled off damp clothes and slipped back into bed. Her head fitted in a spot below his shoulder. He looked down at the part in her hair and wondered if he should feel more.

"Was I your first person?" she asked.

He admitted it. Another gust of rain pattered the windows.

She always scooted to the edge of the bed to put in her diaphragm, a rubbery circle that flipped like a tiny boomerang. These times together were so private they felt like experiences he had with his own body, corners of his mouth felt by his tongue.

Wind howled in the chimneys. It was almost enough. His sketches worked. And she looked so happy afterwards. Years later, he would still remember the expression.

I could be this person's luck, he thought, and then, like the second beat of a footstep, but I don't love her.

When he held his summer bike sale, Cathy brought the whole swim team with their boyfriends. He sold out again. Success, it seemed, was only a matter of paying attention. $920. More than the last sale. But next to what he still owed and the bills piling up on the bungalow's kitchen counter, it was barely a nick.

18.

All summer, the bungalow seemed to loosen and settle. Mornings stayed quiet. Donnie lay in his bed reading comic books. He liked doing things that amounted to nothing. Lina's shifts at the ice-cream store started late in the afternoon. Most days, she rode her bike to the clay room, open for summer school, before work.

One morning in August, Donnie and Lina heard a noise in the kitchen. The boarder was never up this early. The sky was clear outside, not yet infused with the splash of midmorning brightness. They knew from her footsteps it was their mother. They both ran and gathered around her at the stove, where she was lighting the burner.

"I thought I'd go in today," she said.

They stayed near, helping her with breakfast in a way they never had before and found excuses to go in and out of her room while she dressed. She fretted about her makeup and her hair, sagging at intervals until their encouragement buoyed her and she left through the side door.

"Do you think she can drive okay?" Lina asked.

Julie had been taking the car around the block every week to keep it alive. Their mother drove off, slower than they remembered.

"Her job won't be there anymore." Lina tried to call Julie, but there was no answer.

Their mother came home in the middle of the afternoon and took off the outer layers first, the jewelry, the heels, then the clothes. She spent a long time washing off makeup. Then she put her nightgown back on and went to bed. She seemed content; when Donnie asked, she said it was good to see everyone, but she was tired from the drive. She slept through dinner.

Donnie sat at the counter and, between customers, Lina made him a shake. He was hungry, and not for ice cream. They served sandwiches here, too, but Lina told him that when the tuna grew mold, they opened another three-pound can and mixed it in, to dilute the clumps. Only the ice cream was clean. She wore clogs. Everyone who worked there did. They needed the lift off the sticky floor.

"I could call Walter," she said.

"But what can he do?"

Lina locked the front door of the shop and mopped, while Donnie cleaned the glass cases. Then they called Walter from the pay phone, using quarters from the tip jar when the recording broke in to say they had to deposit more coins. Walter called back. When they told him their mother had driven out in her car, he was silent. Lina floated the idea of going to their dad to ask for money. "Well, that's a last resort," Walter said.

"Ask our dad," Donnie said. "That sounds more normal than it is." They'd not seen him for almost a decade.

"I think of him as our *biological* father. No savior. I could look for a real job," Walter said. "Quit school for now."

They knew he shouldn't do that but couldn't think of alternatives.

"Could you get a good job?" Lina asked.

"I don't know," he said.

Their mother would have to leave them; Lina felt this as a catch in her throat. The idea burned: *our father.* Like the prayer. He might help them, even if he never had so far. He'd summoned his children to Las Vegas to attend his third wedding; Donnie was not yet four, their mother thought too young to fly without her. But in the end, she put them on the plane in their best clothes. In the hotel banquet room, there had been two sides for the wedding and they were the only people on his, two boys and a girl, scrubbed that morning at home, not neatened since. Lina had felt amazed when their father leaned down to kiss the gnome he called Lucille. The bride had worn a camera around her neck. But as far as Lina knew, her father and Lucille were still married. Their longevity seemed a verdict against her mother. They'd received drugstore cards from *Lucille and AA* some birthdays, but their mother had rarely been able to reach him. She would dial and a recording would click on saying that the number had been disconnected and that there was no new number. Eventually, they'd hear from him again, often from overseas. He and Lucille traveled to Macau, to Rio, to Singapore.

Lina had yearned to go along on these exotic trips. "You have school," her mother said. "That's more important. They have the money. We have the education." When her mother said "they," Lina understood she meant Lucille. Lina's father had studied in London. A classmate's mother was rumored to be a Chinese spy. Lina thought her father could be a revolutionary. She'd known that Afghanistan was still ruled by a king.

She asked Donnie to find their father's address on the school's mainframe computer.

Donnie hadn't gone to the computer room all summer. He thought of Evan eating his sandwich from home and laughing at jokes in his book. He rummaged in Lina's desk drawer while she was at work and found an old Christmas card with a stick-on return address label under Lucille's name, printed by the Red Cross. Donnie copied that down and gave it to Lina. He didn't care about their father.

But Lina did. She wondered if it was because she looked like him—she touched her eyebrows. Or because she was the opposite-sex child. Walter and Donnie never said one thing against their mother. The bus to Reno, she learned, took a little over eight hours.

19.

The air rang with hammers in the residential neighborhood. An old house had been undressed, down to a skeleton of browned two-by-fours. Three guys perched on parts of the structure. Walter went to see what they were doing.

"Configuring stairs," a young woman said, bending over a makeshift table. "It's a narrow footprint."

Walter caught a glimpse of the drawings.

He noticed a carpenter, who had to be fifty, wearing painter pants with a book in the back pocket. *Ulysses*, by the same author who'd gotten the tall comp lit major out of Bakersfield.

Walter imagined a curved staircase. The assignment for his design class was to sketch *your ideal family home*. He was drawing a house not for the family he might someday have, but for his mom, brother, and sister. By the time he could afford to build anything, even Donnie would probably be on his own. Walter had heard Arizona was cheap. He wanted somewhere his mom could walk into town when she got older, to meet a friend, take a class.

He and Ken moved into a Northside Craftsman co-op full of divinity school students, who'd years ago claimed the bigger rooms. They were given a small attic double with eaved ceilings and had to work only six hours a week. Walter had lucked out again.

Walter ran up the steps of Sproul Hall two at a time and then waited five hours on a plain wooden bench to see the director of financial aid. He had a 448-page book by Jane Jacobs. After an hour a woman, who looked no older than him but wore nylon stockings under a triangular skirt, went into the director's office. Walter took a break and sketched the window, with its deep stone ledge. Another imaginary staircase. The young woman came out of the director's office, carrying a stack of folders. Walter liked the geometric figures architects drew next to buildings for scale. He added the woman with the triangular skirt to his staircase. Then the director emerged.

"I'm going to lunch," the man said to him.

By the time he returned, Walter had missed two classes and finished Part II of Jane Jacobs. The director seemed surprised to find him still there. "Give me five minutes," he said. "Vicky, will you pull this young man's file?"

Eventually the director, whose nameplate said Mr. Josiah Matthews, called him into a large office with windows on two walls. Walter sat before a long wooden desk.

"I looked at your utopia," the director said. Walter stiffened; from what he'd just read in Jacobs, he understood his proposal was seriously stupid. "I don't know much about city planning, but your Berkeley is the kind of place I'd like to live in." He asked about Walter's parents' professions. Walter told him that he didn't know his father and that his mom was a nurse but that now she was sick.

"I'm sorry to hear that. Is she getting treatment?"

"I don't really know," Walter said.

The director looked at him, not saying anything. Then he seemed to make a decision. "How have you been paying so far?"

Walter unfolded the paper from his wallet on which he'd kept track of what he owed. The next minutes felt leisurely—Mr. Matthews was on the phone, pencil in hand, and asked Walter various questions—his social security number, his mailing address, his middle name—and in less than an hour he arranged for Walter's balance to be converted to a low-interest student loan. He told Walter that as of October 1 he'd be on scholarship, full tuition, with a living stipend and work-study hours. As he stood, he asked Walter if he planned to pursue a degree in architecture.

"Oh, no. I love architecture," Walter said. "But I'm pre-med."

"I'm surprised. Well, whatever you do you have a talent. Take classes in anything that tugs at you. That's what college is for."

Walter shook his hand too long, thanking him.

He could have made it to the end of his last class, but instead he wandered along the creek. The sun felt intermittently warm, shafts of light pierced through branches, leaves waved in show-offy motion. What had just happened, he understood, would reach into his future. He should be happy. Instead, he felt still. Able to feel the day flitting around him. He hadn't told anyone about his disaster, so now he couldn't think whom to tell of his luck.

He found Susan and Carrie leaving the sorority to walk to a dance class. The *Berkeley Poetry Review* needed a designer, Carrie mentioned.

One by one, Walter delivered bikes to people on his wait list. He kept one for himself and brought a Raleigh to Cathy in the apartment she shared with her roommate and the Labrador retriever her roommate brought from Beirut.

When the students in his class presented their "dream houses for your family," most of them, like Walter, had drawn homes for their parents. His high school pals would have drawn houses for themselves, their future families. Their parents already had homes.

He had a paycheck from the Princeton Shop and another from the archive. He loved the deposit numbers the teller stamped in his book.

I could save myself rich, he thought. If he didn't have to send money home.

20.

Donnie sat with his mother in the kitchen. Birds peeped intermittently outside. She didn't look the way she used to. It was as if her prettiness were a mask she'd lost.

"What do you want now, Mom?" Donnie asked. "Do you want to go to the doctor?"

She nodded her head as if she had been waiting for the question. "My mother is expecting me home," she whispered. "I'm late."

Years ago, she had taken them to her mother's funeral. She'd told them then how her mother had been unkind to her. But now she sounded like an obedient daughter.

Lina called Walter with a convoluted plan. Another episode of her endless romance and disappointment with her father. *Her father* was how Walter thought of him. Walter never wanted to see the guy again. But Lina intended to take a bus to Reno. The boarder was attending a conference on intuition refinement in San Francisco and could give Donnie a lift there and then drive both of them home.

"Wait. You wanna take a bus to Reno and then another bus here? How do you know he'll even be home? And anyway, wouldn't it be better for Donnie to stay with Mom?"

"Julie will camp out here. She's circled all the old movies playing on TV. They'll have fun."

Walter knew he had few rights. He wasn't there. "Pretty nice of Julie," he said.

As Walter and Donnie strolled through the campus, two white Berkeley bikes whirred past. Walter felt proud. This was the first time his family had visited. Donnie gazed at the campus buildings with reverence. Walter had to take tickets for a screening of a film called *American Graffiti*. He and Donnie slipped into the back row. They loved the movie. Walter couldn't stop watching Cindy Williams; her legs stayed straight when she jumped and she was always jumping. Donnie fell asleep that night in Walter's bed. The next morning, Walter worked at the Princeton Shop. Mr. Barsani said that the kid could be a model and gave Donnie a tie.

At five, they waited for Lina at the designated coffee shop and ordered cappuccinos. A sandwich to split, an hour later. Donnie looked at everyone who passed on the sidewalk. Lina had said four thirty, but there was no way for her to reach them if something went wrong.

They sat outside and it was becoming cold. When Walter finally saw his sister walking up University Avenue, hair disheveled, eyes wet, returning from one of her life's odysseys, he wondered for a second if there was something wrong with his own lack of feeling for his father. No. He'd far rather talk to Ken's dad.

Before they said anything, she unfolded a check and laid it on the table. Three hundred dollars, made out to Lina Aziz, their father's signature written with a flourish.

The asshole thought he was signing the fucking Declaration of Independence.

The end, Walter decided, again.

Lina told them he was handsome still, mostly bald. Walter touched his own hair. At a stoplight, they'd pulled up next to a convertible, and he'd begun speaking Dari. The other man spoke Pashto. They both switched to French. Lina sounded proud. But what good was French? Three hundred dollars was an amount their mom had once sent to Greenpeace.

Lina told them about their mother typing up his PhD dissertation. "'We were a great team then,' he'd said with his accent."

Walter repeated this, rolling his *r*, with the generic foreign accent of the movies. He'd picked up that much from his job.

"He told me, 'There is someone in my life, Lina. We have fallen in love. Her name is Christine.'"

"But what about his wife?" Donnie asked.

"'So now you know my secret' was the last thing he said."

They sat outside under heat lamps and a fine rain, as the streetlights went on. Lina ate a grilled cheese sandwich. Oddly, this was a happy time. A guy on stilts hobbled by. Donnie looked continually amazed. "But I won't get in here," he said. "I'm not smart like you guys."

That might actually be true, Walter thought. Donnie had been in remedial classes. "What you're liking isn't specifically Berkeley," Walter finally said. "It's college. And you'll get that, too."

Donnie and Lina both wanted Walter to stay here in school.

And they wanted to hold on to the bungalow. They wanted to keep what they had.

From his attic window Walter showed them the Bay Bridge, strung with lights. The city skyline, across the water, looked more drawn than built. Donnie fell asleep on the bed as Walter read Carrie's poem:

> She squats
> shaking a plant,
> holding roots
> in her palm.
>
> A pine,
> six inches,
> sways in rain.
>
> He wakes
> brushing drops
> from oily skin.
> He rolls up his bag
> to move on.
>
> A surveyor kneels
> measuring the dimensions
> of next year's gymnasium.

Walter was blown away again by Carrie's talent. Lina looked down. She wanted all this for herself, too, but now she couldn't be sure she'd get it. She probably remembered saying Berkeley wasn't good enough. She had straight As in all her honors-track classes. California public school administrators were unabashed about segregating their students according to what they deemed their abilities. In a hundred years, Walter thought, people will consider this primitive and cruel.

Lina slept and Walter kept watch at the window. When the

boarder's VW Bug pulled onto the street below, he nudged them awake, trooped them down the creaky stairs, and piled them into the car, then stood watching the taillights melt into the dark.

21.

By the time Lina woke, the boarder was speeding past fields where thousands of pipes sprayed fans of water into the air. They turned off the freeway at eight thirty, an hour she would normally be in homeroom. But here, shopgirls not much older than Lina stood with take-out coffees. A guy in front of a restaurant hosed the concrete. So this was going on every day, too. She would forge her mother's signature, saying they'd had doctors' appointments. The truth, as usual, was impossible to explain.

When they pulled up in front of the bungalow, Donnie bolted out before the boarder completely stopped the car. The curtains in the front bay window had never been closed before. Julie was asleep on the couch, her arms folded, her mouth open.

Donnie skidded to their mother's room. "She's gone," he shouted.

But where could she be? Donnie was running through the small house, opening doors as the boarder thunked her suitcase over the threshold.

Lina grabbed Julie's shoulder, shaking her awake. "Where's Mom?"

Julie sat up, rubbing her eyes. "Come, let's sit at the table." She was not wearing stockings, and her legs looked indecently white. The boarder walked in and opened the refrigerator. Julie said, "I'd like to talk to the kids alone."

The boarder hopped up on the countertop. "You guys don't mind, do you? If something's going on, I should be in on it."

Lina made a gesture. Boarder, no boarder—she didn't care.

Donnie looked straight at Julie. "Where is she?"

Lina knew now she shouldn't have gone. This was her fault, her stupid fucking pitiful hope for her dad. She hated him; he had cost them everything.

"While you were gone, your mom started to get frightened of I don't know what. I heated up fudge for sundaes, I made jokes. . . . Then yesterday morning, I couldn't get her up. When I finally had her standing, she could hardly walk, so I called Learhoff. We had to take her to the hospital in an ambulance."

So here we go, Lina thought. The long terror had finally begun. They had to hold on. Eventually it would be over. Or did it just seem it would because the other terrors she'd known, man-made roller-coasters, had been built to scare and stop? Maybe real terror had no end.

Donnie sobbed. Lina hadn't seen him heave since he was a baby. He looked ugly. The boarder hopped down from the counter. Lina had forgotten she was there. "So what does that mean for me?"

For her?

"We don't know how long this'll be," Julie said. "We're hoping not long. And, kids, I thought while your mom's in the hospital, you'd move in with me."

Move in. With her. With Julie. Donnie had his head in his crossed arms on the table.

The kitchen was incredibly still. "Our stuff's all here," Lina said. "And we've got school."

"Where do you live?" Donnie asked from inside his arms.

"I'm in Beverlywood."

"I can't be babysitting," the boarder said. "I have work. Auditions."

What work? The boarder was trying to be an actress. From what Lina could tell, she didn't do anything.

"We don't need *baby*sitting," Donnie said.

"Well, you kinda do, no offense. I can't be responsible for two kids. What if something happened?" She added, apropos of nothing, "My dad's a lawyer."

I'm sure he is, Lina thought. With exaggerated patience, she asked, "Has anything ever happened?"

"I've found keys in the lock. Or the back door open. Today's the sixteenth. I always pay her on the first of the month."

"Just pay the same as always," Julie said. "I'm not familiar with her financial doings. I don't know the landlord."

"I do," Lina said under her breath. "You won't even know we're here."

"No offense," the boarder said, "but it's just too much responsibility."

"I can sleep on the couch," Julie said. "We'll take it one day at a time."

Book 2

A Moral Treatment

22.

Walter never fully understood how it happened, but from the first phone call with Julie after his mom went into the hospital, he never again felt he should be where he was. What he couldn't figure out was where he should be. Home, he thought, but then Julie told him not to come, not yet. There had to be jobs he could apply for, but when he reached this point in his thinking, he pressed his hands to his temples. The sweetness of the night his sister and brother slept in his attic room had dissolved. For three hundred fucking dollars they'd left her alone. Because Lina couldn't admit the truth about their dad.

What he'd pieced together was that his mom had been with Julie, who'd tried to make a party out of things they used to like. But his mom had asked for her kids. Julie offered a movie on TV. She had food ready. His mom told her to leave, get out of her house. Julie retreated to the living room after Diane slammed the bedroom door and shoved a dresser against it.

Julie thought of her cats, she said. If Diane didn't want her, she would just as soon go home. "But I'd promised the kids I'd stay." She had no way to reach them.

Julie had awoken in the living room at dawn. She hadn't thought to close the drapes the night before. She pottered in the kitchen, letting Diane sleep. At nine o'clock she knocked. By then she was worried. She pushed at the door until the dresser moved and when she saw his mom, she panicked. Diane looked more out of it than someone asleep. Julie knew the difference. She tried to wake her with a wet towel, but Diane slumped like a rag doll.

Julie didn't know what to do, so she dialed Learhoff. Was that what people did in emergencies? Call their bosses? Walter wondered. Ambulances cost over a thousand dollars—Julie didn't know how much Diane's insurance would cover. Learhoff didn't pick up; her call went to the service. She dragged Diane to the kitchen; she got her sitting up at the table and managed to brew coffee. She held the cup to her lips and Diane let the coffee dribble out. Julie knew then that she must have taken something. Diane in her right mind would spit, not dribble.

Julie took apart the sheets. She found an empty canister. Barbiturates.

Then she called the ambulance, price be damned. You're careful all your life for the once you have to spend.

"I'm not going to say anything about the pills to your sister and brother," she said. "So don't you either, maybe." Julie followed the ambulance in her own car to UCLA Neuropsychiatric. They asked Julie whether she was next of kin. On all the papers where it asked for a signature she signed, and in the box for relationship, she wrote *Friend*. While they were pumping his mom's stomach, Julie called Learhoff again.

At nearly midnight he finally arrived. A young woman doctor was in the room asking if Diane had had any unusual trauma.

Julie let Learhoff talk. Nursing, he said, was demanding work. Patients relied on Diane. They asked for her in particular. Julie was surprised he knew that. Patients did ask for Diane, but he was never there to hear.

The young doctor recommended a hospital commitment. She believed in something called moral treatment, which was already a century old. The idea started with doctors in France. Then Quakers in the English countryside opened a retreat, using rest, conversation, and manual labor for their cures. A period of slowed-down life to take apart the patient's system of habits and to learn new ones. She asked about Diane's insurance. A nurse checked her chart. Learhoff didn't say anything about the insurance running out; Julie took this as a good sign that he'd keep her on the books. Learhoff wasn't known for generosity.

The young doctor said Diane couldn't stay at UCLA for more than seventy-two hours. There was a new law Governor Reagan signed: Lanterman-Petris. His mom was on something called a 5150—involuntary. She could maybe get a 5250, saying she was a danger to herself, but the best thing would be to go in as a vol— voluntary. To the state hospital in Norwalk.

"Do you really think a big state hospital is the best?" Julie asked.

Did she have family members who could take care of her? Julie told the young doctor that the family members were seventeen and thirteen years old. What about me? Walter thought. Didn't Julie think he could take care of his mom?

The young doctor knew the superintendent at the state hospital. Learhoff had bent down and kissed Diane's forehead. Walter didn't like hearing that. He couldn't say why.

Julie stayed until five in the morning and then went home to feed the cats. She drove to the bungalow to get Walter's number. Walter smiled thinking of that patch of wall with the numbers written on it. But that morning, Diane woke up in the hospital and she didn't like it one bit. They told Julie she hit a nurse. "I don't believe it. And if she did, the nurse wasn't hurt. I've been hit by agitated patients. Bitten, too." By the time Julie got there, they had his mom in a geri-chair and they'd given her Haldol. A terrible drug, Julie said. She called Learhoff to say they had to get her out. He agreed, saying there was nowhere worse than an urban acute care unit. Diane wasn't in any state to talk to about where she was going. And now the nice young lady doctor was nowhere to be found. Julie stayed all day waiting for his mom's spasms to wear off. By around dinner, Diane was calm, but in a flat, bad mood, as if she'd seen the ugly workings at the back of everything.

"Do you know me, Diane? It's me, Julie."

"I know who you are," she'd said.

"Listen, let's talk about what's best. To get you back to being yourself."

"Oh, I'm myself all right."

"The doctor here thinks you should go to a place called Orchard Springs, in Norwalk. It's on a big piece of land like a park."

"I bet they want me out of here."

"Well, we all want you out of here. Don't you want that, too?"

"Where are the kids?" she asked, after a while.

"Walter is at college, Donnie and Lina are on the way."

"Lina wants to get her hands on my skirt. Or maybe you've already given it to her."

They went around and around. They had been friends for such a long time that Julie knew Diane wasn't herself, but she was a little herself, and there's only so long you can take meanness when it's pointed at you. She finally went to the bungalow to wait for the kids. The poor cats had had nothing to eat since dawn.

"I meant to call you then, but after all that emotion I just fell asleep." She'd pulled the drapes shut this time. She woke up when the kids clomped in. She thought maybe they could talk to their mom, but Julie didn't want them to see her in the psych ward, not in that chair. Norwalk was the countryside, at least. The hospital had to release her tomorrow and they needed to know to where.

"I don't want to tell the kids about the pills," Julie said again. "But, with them not knowing, they'll want her home." That's why she was calling him. "You're the only one she'll really listen to."

"Julie, what do I know? You're *there*." Still, he was glad she thought he was the one his mom would trust. "Where do you think she should be?"

"I think she has to go in somewhere. She hasn't gotten better."

He told Julie he'd hitch down. He'd be there in ten, twelve hours.

But that wasn't soon enough. Julie said he had to talk to her on the phone. Now. She'd drive over to the hospital and hold the receiver up to his mom's ear.

Okay. He would try. And he'd come down tomorrow.

But she didn't want him then, either.

"Let's just get her in and settled. They won't let her have visitors right away."

It wasn't really a conversation.

"It's me," he said. He heard a thump on her end and knew she recognized him. Then she began crying. She was ashamed, he could tell. "It's going to be okay," he said.

"Really?" she asked in a small voice.

"Yes, but now, you should tell them you'll go to that place. You need rest to get better."

"Even with Lina and Donnie?"

"Julie's there. They'll be fine." It was bittersweet that she didn't worry about him.

She would be transferred the next day. Julie sounded relieved. But Walter didn't know where that left him. He thought he needed to get home.

Julie promised to call in a day or two.

Cathy asked again and again what was wrong. He told her his mom had had a breakdown. That she was in the hospital now. He had never before seen a person's mouth drop open, as if from a busted hinge. Clichés are true, he thought. They come from life.

"Was she normal before?"

"Normal for me."

"That's hard to believe."

He didn't know how to explain. "Then don't." He couldn't deal with her now, thinking about his mom and sister and brother in LA.

He became vague about his schedule. She left two messages at the co-op, then showed up at the archive.

He wrote her a breakup letter in a hurry: *You're a great person,* and slid it under her apartment door, late at night. Her roommate's Labrador barked and he ran down the cement steps, three at once, his heart knocking.

He told his bosses he'd need time off, but when? He was waiting to be called home. Maybe they would fire him. But as soon as Julie told him, he would hitch down. He didn't know how long he'd be gone. People missed classes for no reason, joked about sleeping in. College teachers didn't even take roll.

He told Ken the least he could. "My mom's in the hospital. I have to get home."

"Rory and Cub can fill in your jobs. I'll go with you." No one had ever offered anything like this, but what would he do with Ken there? Melinda sometimes talked about her father's long illness. Mental problems were different, though. They smudged the sufferer. People didn't offer food or flowers. They lowered their voices, as if discretion was a kindness.

At first, Julie told him, his mother fought. Even after she'd agreed, she went back and forth. She wouldn't sign the paper to be a voluntary admit. Finally, she did.

23.

Lina lingered in her mother's bedroom. They'd rented the bungalow furnished and painted the rooms where she and her brothers lived. They'd never gotten to this one. The flocked wallpaper would have had to be scraped off. But they could have at least moved out the owner's twin bed frames and ancient drapes. Julie had opened a window, so the room was cold. Her mother's bureau had been moved back to where it had always been, with a cloth on the top and her hairbrush. What was her mother doing in Norwalk without her hairbrush? Lina took it in her backpack to bring. They couldn't visit for two weeks. Julie now thumped into the bungalow late at night. They saw her mornings on the front couch, with her clothes on, under a thin blanket. They understood that they were allowed to stay in the bungalow because of her.

They went to school on not enough sleep. Twice, Lina was called on and didn't know the answer. She liked the ice-cream store better now. Scooping spherical balls was absorbing—she forgot about her life for minutes at a time.

On a Wednesday morning, day 11, Julie said, "Let's play hooky and just go." Julie wasn't a hooky sort of person, but she drove, her hands light on the steering wheel, her fingernails surprisingly pink. Lina had never before noticed Julie's hands. "I thought Norwalk was more in the country," Julie said. "But I suppose California doesn't have much country left." She kept up a running patter.

Lina tightened her arm over her backpack and felt the bristles of her mother's hairbrush poke through. They were passing the generic development that gave LA a bad name: stucco buildings in no particular order. *Back east,* Lina thought, then felt guilty.

"The place isn't all I'd hoped," Julie was saying, "but it won't be for long."

"What exactly does she have?" Lina asked.

"I haven't heard a diagnosis. Everyone says she needs a rest."

A rest. That didn't sound bad. But hadn't she already been resting?

Behind a high chain-link fence, they saw trees. They rode in under an arch made of greened copper letters spelling the hospital's name: Orchard Springs.

"We'll see her and then after, we can try to find the downtown and get something to eat."

Norwalk's downtown! Did Julie think they were *sightseeing*? But in eleven days Lina had learned to quell her sarcasm. Julie cared about their mother. Who else did?

A girl on a bike flew in front of them, making Julie slam on the brakes. The girl pedaled standing, red hair bouncing on her back. Lina remembered a picture of her mother young, leaning on handlebars. This girl had the same coloring Lina's mother had always hated on herself.

"Most of the people here have bigger problems than your mom," Julie said. "But your mom knows, hospitals have the acute and the chronic, and at first, your eye goes to the worst."

Julie got out of the car, saying, "Wait here a minute," leaving her bag on the seat next to Lina. Their mother would never have chosen a purse this drab—Julie must have bought it on sale, a color no customers wanted, like the hide of a mouse. Poking out was a yellow legal pad.

1. *Lawyer—temporary guardianship?*
2. *Call my nurses' retirement fund. Need to wait till 65 or can I withdraw?*
3. *Diane's landlord*

Lina didn't know how much nurses' retirement money was, but it had to be more than three hundred dollars.

When Julie returned, they stepped outside and the sun lay on their arms like thin weights. In the distance, orange trees weighted with fruit stood behind a white house, under a high, pale blue sky. Julie told them they were going to the library and they followed her across the grounds. The library turned out to be a high-ceilinged brick building that had once been the hospital's kitchen. There were two tables of smudged, used-looking novels and a dozen standing shelves holding journals. No librarian sat behind the metal desk.

They waited a long time and then she was there, their mother, walking slowly up the ramp. They ran to her like younger children; Donnie gasped, even Lina felt a choke—"Mommy" escaping from her throat. Their mother seemed already different; the clearest thing wrong was what she had on: they'd put her in someone else's mismatched T-shirt and pants, brown and blue, with a faded pink sweater too small for her.

After their initial clinging, they stood in the empty, echoing room, trying to think of what to say. They'd never had to make conversation with their mother. Julie asked if she had gotten some sleep. "Mm-hmm," she said, as if she weren't convinced. That was the only word she'd said so far.

It took them a moment to register another person, a woman with stiff curls wearing lipstick, who nudged them all outside onto a path. They passed a young man, with his arms outstretched, walking as if on a ledge. He made a buzzing sound. The building she took them to was old, with a gabled roof. Lina noticed that what looked good in the distance was not quite right here up close. The lipsticked woman, whose name was Shirley, showed them around the ward where their mother lived. She opened the door to a sitting room, where the only furnishings were scattered wicker chairs and a television. A thick-bodied woman stood doing an elaborate hand game with the wall. They followed Shirley through a dormitory, each bed with an arched white metal frame, to their mother's small alcove. The shabby stuffed elephant from her bed at home was on the pillow. Julie must have brought it. Lina wondered why her mother had her own room. That seemed like a good thing.

In the small dining room, a smell of long-cooked food came in waves. A woman wearing a hairnet scooped mashed vegetables onto a plate next to gray chops, the bones showing bloodstains. Lina's stomach twisted. In the high school cafeteria, she limited herself to black coffee. She stood up to get a cup here.

Donnie ate with his head close to his plate. He shrugged, as if this was where they belonged, here at this institutional table. "Better than it looks," Julie said. Was Lina the only one who wanted to scream? Their mother held her silverware delicately, the way she always had, pushing a limb of broccoli under some mashed potato. Shirley reached over to cut her meat. Her curls looked shellacked. Lina would never be able to explain this day to her friends at school. She had a revelation: if this was going to be her life, it really didn't matter what she scored on the SAT.

Women shuffled in line, all wearing the same white cotton booties that her mother had on. Many moved stiffly. One woman had symmetrical features and a pretty hairline, but then all of a sudden she winced, making a horrible face. Lina watched her, expecting it to happen again. After an interval, it did.

Their mother didn't say anything besides "Mm-hmm." She seemed to be aiming her gaze at them particularly. Shirley showed them a sheet of paper with colored blocks. Her schedule. "She told me she likes flowers. When she's settled, we'll take her to the garden. Someone will have to sign permission. Do you know who has power of attorney?" The three of them looked at each other.

Lina just then noticed a mural on the long wall—a line of women moving forward, with angular faces. She asked Shirley who'd painted it. The figures had a grim consistency.

"A former patient. We had a good art teacher here for a while."

Their mother walked slowly to the sitting room, with Shirley's hand on her back. Donnie and Lina pushed next to her. They wanted her to remember they were here.

"It's the Elavil," Shirley said.

So that was why. A drug had slowed her and made her vacant-seeming, with a scratchy fear in her eyes.

"See the head, the way it goes down. She's tired now. Time for her nap."

They followed Shirley through the empty dormitory, a TV down the hall emitting the hollow sounds of a laugh track. Their mother nodded on her bed. She ran her hand through Donnie's hair. She didn't want to return with them, as Lina had feared. It was startling how quickly they'd waned for her. Their mother was still beautiful, in a way not obvious; it opened to you.

Leaving, they passed a young nurse lining up paper cups of medicine.

"Excuse me. Are you giving my mother anything besides Elavil?" Lina asked.

The young nurse was dressed in a white uniform. "Lithium, it looks like. But it's mostly Elavil."

"She seems kind of out of it."

"Really? It's a good drug. It usually helps. But I'll make a note for the doctor."

The woman was still standing, playing her hand game against the wall.

"I'm glad it's all women," Donnie said, kicking gravel.

"That Shirley grew up in Norwalk," Julie said. "Her mother was a nurse here, too. The head doctor lives on the grounds. I'll show you the house when we drive out."

As they rode in the cola-colored Chevrolet (did Julie seek out shades of mud?), she asked, "Hey, Lina, do you have your license yet?"

Their mother hadn't let Lina practice. "We need *me* to work," she'd said, and Lina had never asked again. "We had only the one car," Lina said now.

"This wouldn't be the worst place to teach you," Julie said. Then, "Oh my gosh, I haven't taken Diane's car out for a week. I hope it'll start." *Car* would become another item on her list.

Julie asked about the landlord. Once, a long time ago, Lina told her, when her mother needed an extension on the rent, she'd driven to the landlord's house and sent Lina in. She thought they'd hesitate before evicting a polite high school girl.

"That's Diane, all right." Julie laughed.

Mrs. Haley had opened the door wearing a white floor-length quilted housecoat with an ostrich-feather neckline.

"You know who they are, right?" Lina asked. She explained, Jack Haley had been the Tin Man in *The Wizard of Oz*. The day Lina went inside their house, he was slumped in an old blue bathrobe at the kitchen counter. Mrs. Haley offered Lina a glass of orange juice. Lina said yes, please, and Mrs. Haley took a carton of Minute Maid from the refrigerator. Lina's mother always bought fresh-squeezed. Mrs. Haley asked her how she was doing in school.

Lina said good. "School's easy."

"Well, that's wonderful. Just wonderful," Mrs. Haley said.

Finally, Lina blurted, "My mom's hoping we can pay late."

"Oh, sure. Tell her the end of the month is fine."

The whole time, a rerun of *Gunsmoke* was playing on a portable TV.

Tonight, in the car, Julie asked, "Do you think she's up to date now with the rent?"

Lina and Donnie looked at each other. "No," Donnie said, and they all three laughed.

At home, they searched for financial records. Every drawer they opened was stuffed with stationery. Ferns pressed into handmade paper. Pretty, unmarked envelopes. They found a savings account in an accordion file, but it was depleted; they could see the stamped withdrawals. Lina found the statements from her mother's nurses' retirement fund. "Here's some money!"

But Julie said they couldn't touch that without a penalty. "She's still young. We'd best leave that be. Diane may need that someday."

Lina felt slapped; Julie had seen her thinking of herself. But she also felt relieved to hear the word *someday* in the same sentence with her mother.

In the leather checkbook, Lina and Julie found that the last rent check had been entered five months ago.

"We'd better pay," Julie said. "We don't want the landlord sniffing around."

"Are you sure?" Lina asked. The back rent would empty her mother's account.

Julie said she'd put in another thousand. She looked serious, filling out the deposit slip. Julie drove them in their mother's car up to the landlord's ranch house.

When Mrs. Haley opened the door, she lifted a hand to wave at the car and asked, as she had the last time, "Does your ma want to come in?" In the dark, she couldn't tell the difference between Lina's mother and Julie.

This time, Lina handed her a check. Mrs. Haley pulled the paper tight between her hands. She didn't look particularly happy. "Can she manage? We don't need it all today."

"It's okay," Lina said.

"Well, good. She must be doing well, then."

This time, Mrs. Haley didn't offer Lina juice or ask how school was. Running back to the car, Lina remembered something her mother had once told her that she'd never believed: people *liked* to help you.

24.

Walter drew 3-D letters on the back of a spiral notebook during class.

LA.
MOM IN HOSPITAL

He was copying signs he'd seen hitchhikers hold on the side of the road. VIETNAM VET, one had Magic Markered. Most named destinations. FRESNO. TIJUANA. ANYWHERE BUT HERE. He remembered the guy from Bakersfield and hoped his mother had recovered from her operation.

But Julie still told him to wait. Every time he hung up, after hearing the equivocation in her voice, he sat still, furious and relieved. The feelings didn't cancel each other out but left him exhausted. Did she think he'd be in the way? His mom had gone into the hospital at the end of October. Now Julie was talking about him coming home at Christmas. He should stay there at school and do his studies. *That's what she would want* was her refrain.

Walter only talked to people who already knew. Ken, who'd told Melinda. Susan suspected something, he thought. Probably Carrie had heard, too; he trusted she'd understand. His other friendships went dry. Cathy blamed his mom for their breakup and he avoided her. He spent hours in the co-op's garage working on bikes. He spun the wheels just to listen to them whirr.

He studied the way he always had, but facts fell through him. The TA handed back his chemistry midterm with a D.

Walter carried the graded test up to the sorority. He still hadn't told Susan or Carrie about his mom. His own failure felt easier to explain. For the first time, he was more eager to find Susan than Carrie, and there she was, reading with her legs up on the porch railing. She didn't say the usual things. Cub had said, *You can still pass.* Walter kind of wished she'd say that, too. But she asked, "Do you really *want* to be a doctor?"

"It's not a question of do I want medicine, it's more whether medicine wants me."

Susan left her book and pencil and jumped down from the porch. As they walked, she talked about doctors. She had the habit of saying things to keep your dignity intact. "All day, they're touching bodies that aren't always clean. Everything's a matter of life and death."

"At least doctors make a difference."

"Lots of people make a difference. Teachers. Architects. Social workers. Florists. My parents would say real estate agents. Doctors keep people alive, but for what? There's being alive and there's meaning. My mom's best friend married a surgeon. He missed all his kids' birthday parties. The human body isn't the same for him, after seeing illness all day long. She says he doesn't touch her." Did she mean sex? "What kind of doctor do you want to be?"

"Maybe psychiatrist," Walter said.

"How's the summer girl?" Susan had never once used Cathy's name.

"We broke up."

"You feel okay about that?"

"What was it your roommate said, love is the business of the stupid?"

"*An occupation of the idle.* But, seriously. You don't miss her?"

"Not now. My mom's in the hospital."

She didn't look away, so she must have known. "What's going on with that?"

He told her what he'd heard from Julie.

"Do you feel like the doctor's good?"

"I *think* so. It's something called moral treatment. Like a rest." He'd been reading; those ideas Julie told him about started the asylum movement, here in the States. A schoolteacher named Dorothea Dix met the English Quakers. Susan kept asking questions. Lina had told him their mom seemed out of it; Julie had asked the doctor to cut back her dosages. Susan was so curious. Walter's mind, at a certain point, turned off, like an overheated appliance.

They circled back, and up on the sorority porch Carrie stood, a triangled scarf on her head, its back corners fluttering. A scarf! Pure ornament, Jan Tudor would say. He liked watching Carrie from a distance. He didn't have the energy now for more. A convertible honked. The driver looked straight ahead and she ran down. She jumped with unbent legs like the girl in the movie and hopped in.

Melinda brought home a cat with a metal electrode sticking out of its head. Graduate students had botched its surgery. The ragged edges of its furred skin had healed roughly, like a browned bite out of a peach. When Melinda set it down on the floor of the attic, it wobbled, walking unevenly underneath Ken's bed.

Susan handed Walter a box of stationery in class. To write to his mom every week, she said. She pulled a coil of stamps out of her pocket, pretty stamps, with pictures of trees.

"I could just use notebook paper." The stationery was nice. "I mean, I don't know how much a letter will mean to her right now."

"At least you'll be doing something. You should probably make a schedule for calling the doctor, too."

Maybe she was right. He had no idea. Nothing like this had happened to him before.

Mr. Matthews, the director of financial aid, turned up in the Princeton Shop.

"Did you know you have a future architect working for you?" he asked Mr. Barsani.

He bought the first suit Walter showed him. Walter held the tomato pincushion as the older Mr. Barsani, working on his knees, adjusted the trousers. He hardly ever spoke, hunched over a black globular sewing machine in the back room.

Dear Mom, Walter wrote, then stalled. *It's foggy today.* He balled up the expensive sheet of paper. It was foggy every day in Berkeley.

> *Berkeley's the same. Foggy. Like when you drove me up.*
> *I hope you're getting better.*
> *I love you.*
> *Walter*

"Pretty basic," he told Susan.

"You'll get the hang of it. Have you called the doctor?"

He hadn't. Passing a pet store, Walter bought a toy mouse stuffed with catnip. When he set it under Ken's bed, he could see the cat's eyes gleam from its defended corner. It lived among the coils inside the box spring and came out only at night for food and water.

Walter dreaded his conversations with Julie. You couldn't end a call without cutting her off. Normal pauses never occurred. He made himself dial. She answered on the second ring. Julie was never not home.

She had been getting to know Norwalk, she said, so the kids could have some time alone with their mom. Julie, who had no children, had a reverence for family, Walter noticed. One street in Norwalk was lined with antiques stores. "Your mother liked antiques," she reminded Walter.

Likes, he thought but didn't say.

She told him about seeing incarnations of remembered furnishings from her Michigan childhood, now placed in a white-walled store, with extravagant price tags. Where were those lamps from the living room on either side of the couch they used to call "the davenport"? Who knew they'd become antiques?

They should have held on to them, she'd written to her brother in Michigan. Walter was beginning to understand that Julie considered the true part of her life incomprehensible to her brother. His mom had felt that way about her family in the Central Valley. They wanted to hear about the Rose Bowl parade, Julie said, and whether she'd seen any celebrities. Once she'd seen Anjelica Huston in Gelson's, weighing a peach. For years, she'd reported her glimpses of Hollywood stars in her letters home.

His mom herself probably seemed a celebrity in those letters.

Doodling on his binder's inside cover, Walter pictured Julie walking through antiques stores intimidated, never buying a thing. He wished he could buy her some small treasure. She told him she'd discovered an ice-cream store in Norwalk that made weekly flavors and brought two pints back to the hospital.

"Your mother always loved ice cream," Julie said.

Loves, Walter thought.

The years of their friendship, Julie went on, going out for dessert was the pretext for their conversations. Our excuse, she said. Julie missed those talks. She now realized they'd been the most important of her life.

She'd once heard a young nurse complain about her fiancé: *He's dying to get off the phone with me, always interrupting me to conclude, when we should be starting an endless conversation.* At the time, Julie felt sorry for that young husband-to-be. *An endless conversation* seemed a tall order, but now that she'd had her own—what had it been? Eight years? Nine! You were in fourth grade!—she was beginning to understand what it meant for something like that to end.

Walter rubbed his neck. He had never once thought about his mom's friendship with Julie.

At the beginning, Julie said, she didn't propose an outing too often, knowing Diane was busy with the kids. Eventually, though, they talked every day. During a dull afternoon Julie looked forward to the evening when she could call Diane and tell about her day, its net of insults and specks of pleasure. She bought a long cord so she could pull the phone around her kitchen, feeding the cats while they talked. She still sometimes felt that pleasurable feeling arise while she was driving home from work, Julie said, before she remembered—she couldn't call Diane now. "Say, I've been meaning to ask you," Diane had once begun a conversation, "why *don't* you like Goldie Hawn?" They'd decided together to throw over their family allegiances and vote McGovern. They'd each saved for silver plate and selected the same pattern, Autumn Rose, though Diane bought hers on layaway. Julie thought now that really she could've helped her friend. Maybe never again would someone care what she thought of Goldie Hawn. She laughed.

That was probably true. Later, Walter realized he should have said: *I care.*

When she returned to the ward, she said, after a few hours in Norwalk, Lucille Ball was jumping around on the TV, the kids patted a spot for her next to them on the slumping couch, and they all ate ice cream. Lina had professional opinions on the flavors. Her favorite was cactus. At five, they shuffled into the dining room with the mural Lina stared at from different angles. The ward no longer seemed so terrible. There was a bread pudding Donnie liked. Driving back, Julie let Lina get behind the wheel. There were only a few cars on the road. Lina was cautious; she didn't want to take her foot off the brake. Last week, when she finally did press her sneaker on the gas pedal, the car jerked forward, shaking them up.

"Do you think Mom's getting better?" Walter asked.

"It's hard to tell," Julie said. "I think so."

The person Walter told next, after Susan, was Em Ball, the librarian.

"Moral treatment," she repeated. "I like the sound of that."

Mrs. Ball took care with her outfits, the way his mom had, but his mom had dressed to look pretty. With Mrs. Ball it must have been for another reason; she was married and had a full head of white curls, a style she called a "permanent," although, he later learned, it wasn't.

———

Walter delivered Mr. Matthews's suit to a *My Three Sons* house. This was 1973 Berkeley, where people walked barefoot caped in serapes, yet a woman opened the door in a pleated white tennis skirt. The style of an epoch didn't, apparently, reach everyone. She offered Walter a glass of water.

That night, he checked under Ken's bed, but the toy mouse remained where he'd left it. The cat, evidently, had no desire to play.

25.

Walter began to ask his mom questions in his letters. *Was there anything I could have done to make you happier?*

He asked Lina if she could get her to talk to him on the phone and she said, "It's not like that, Walter."

"Well, tell me what it is like, then."

"It's just . . . it's just really different than it was up in Berkeley."

"What can I do? Tell me and I'll do it."

"There's nothing you can do," she said. "Just live your life."

Mrs. Ball gave him an old book. *On the Construction, Organization and General Arrangements of Hospitals for the Insane with Some Remarks on Insanity and Its Treatment* was embossed, gold on brown, peeling leather. "I learned, believe it or not, that almost all the um, asylums in America," she said, "were built according to one blueprint, made by this Quaker psychiatrist. He was superintendent of what they called the Pennsylvania Hospital for the Insane. He used an English model but made his hospitals bigger. And these Kirkbrides—that was his name—were grand, with high ceilings and sweeping staircases. He landscaped views outside the windows." She showed him pictures: A gracious living room. A full hospital orchestra.

The chapters were pretty specific: *Economy of Curing Insanity; Drainage; Size of Rooms and Height of Ceilings; Dust Flues and Soiled Clothes Hoppers; Washing, Drying, Ironing and Baking; Different*

Classes of Hospitals for the Insane; Remarks on the Number Employed and Their Compensation; Separation of the Sexes; Should the Curables and the Incurables Be Separated?

"Wait, was this guy a doctor or an architect?" Walter asked.

"Well, the book has plans and elevations, but he was a psychiatrist, I gather. This was the age of institutions. We had orphanages. Homes for unwed mothers. Places for incorrigible girls. Of course prisons. Penitentiaries, we used to call them. Reformatories."

None of the design classes Walter had taken at Berkeley talked about asylums or orphanages or prisons. But they all had to be built. Maybe if they were designed better, they would work the way their founders hoped.

A world opened.

When Walter understood that his letters to his mother wouldn't ever be answered, he stopped asking questions. But without them, the letters seemed too much about himself. Still, he wrote every Sunday. Susan had been right; at least he was doing something.

One night when he came back to the co-op, Cathy was sitting on the steps, her hair in front of her face. "I thought you were falling in love with me," she said.

He looked up at the pediment. When people talked about falling in love, they probably meant a hundred different things and one he hadn't experienced. She wasn't crazy to hope. At moments, last summer, he'd wondered if he might be falling in love, but now he couldn't touch any live feeling. They sat side by side. Her features were distorted from crying. He waited until the agitation worked itself out of her. Finally, she stood, tied the belt of her coat. "I'm sorry about your mom," she said, and left.

She'd probably always believe he'd stopped falling in love with her because of his mom. Maybe it was kinder to let her think that.

He walked with Susan on the streets below the Claremont Hotel.

"Maybe I should move back home? It's not like I'm doing so great here."

"What's going on with that?" she asked.

"Chemistry? I'm still hanging on. I study with Cub."

"I meant your mom. Do you think she's getting better?"

"Not yet." He was annoyed that Susan didn't care about chemistry. He still had a life. Or maybe he didn't. No one else was on the wide, quiet street. Did the rich never step outside their houses?

"Have you been calling her doctor?"

"I can only talk to a few people. And they aren't the ones I should call."

"How about your mom?"

"It takes a long time for a nurse to get her to the phone. And then, she just says 'Mm-hmm.' I think I tire her out."

"But you're writing to her."

He wrote on other days, too, now, not just Sundays. The box of Crane was almost empty. "I'm not sure she even reads my letters. I ask if she got mail and she says 'Mm-hmm.' It's kind of freeing. They're like these long open letters to God." *I'm sitting in the church we passed when you brought me here. It's completely empty. I have work in an hour. Do you ever pray? I know you went to Catholic school.*

"When you talk to your sister, does she say to come home?"

"They all say, Stay. But maybe it would be good to be together."

"School will always be here." He wasn't expecting Susan to say that.

"They're busy, though. Julie's working. I might be in the way."

"Maybe that's why you want to be a doctor. To help your mom."

Susan always made him out to be more noble than he was. He told her about Kirkbride, who thought mentally ill people could still appreciate books and music; how he'd budgeted for a library and a concert hall.

"That's not how I think of those places. Does your sister say it's nice?"

"They were pretty upset at first. But this guy Kirkbride said half his patients recovered."

"That's really something, when you consider they didn't have the medicine we do."

Susan invited him to a party that the sorority was giving, with the theme Come Dressed as a Bird.

"Oh, thanks, but, you know—I have a smaller world now."

Every week, Walter counted out bills, debating the second twenty before folding it with the other in notebook paper. They were trying to keep the bungalow. Walter picked up a new job doing layout for the *Berkeley Poetry Review*. After printing costs, he'd get what was left over.

On a clear evening in November, Ken and Melinda left the co-op in matching penguin suits. Walter swept the rooms and fed the cat. Then he sat at his desk and dialed the hospital. He heard the scrabbling that meant the cat was finally eating. "Dr. Moss here." Walter hadn't expected the doctor to answer. He introduced himself and explained that he was calling about his mom, Diane Aziz. He hoped the doctor would remember her. He heard papers shuffle.

"Your mother is settling in," the doctor finally said. "I gave her headphones to listen to music, but she doesn't like them."

"My sister said she seemed kind of doped up."

"We're still adjusting the medication. She hears voices. They taunt her, put her down. It's difficult to quiet those without making her what your sister calls 'doped up.' The drugs are big hammers we're using on a needle. One day she's alert and anxious, and the next, on the same dose, she droops. It's not perfect science." That seemed to be all he had to say.

Walter didn't want to hang up. "I read about a guy named Kirkbride."

"He was one of the founders of psychiatry in America," the doctor said. "Asylum design was his legacy. He believed the hospital building itself helped the healing."

"That's what architects think! About all buildings! Was there a generation after him that concentrated on institutions?"

"He's the only one I know of. Architects don't generally understand mental illness and doctors don't have the talent to tinker with buildings. He made it all up from scratch."

"People got cured, his book said. More than half."

"They still do. Some do," the doctor said. "Maybe not half."

The doctor gave Walter his private phone number. Walter wrote it on his wrist.

———

On the way to Wurster Hall, Walter saw Cathy again; she ducked, pulling her books closer to her chest. He found Jan Tudor packing. She was teaching only one class in winter. She was an adjunct, she said, paid half what the regular professors got. Who all happened to be male.

Like Julia Morgan, Walter thought, whom you don't like.

Jan Tudor was wearing a T-shirt with the sleeves rolled up. "Let's see what you've got," she said, reaching for his sketchbook. She leaned over it, pitched on her hands. Her arms had small muscles. He imagined having sex with her.

Under the drawing of his favorite house, he'd written, *Why is this corrupt?*

She scribbled with a red pencil. *New materials make architecture better. Think of the arch, the flying buttress. Reinforced concrete.*

Beyond utilitarian needs, he'd lettered beneath a dog on a porch. She flipped the page to Carlos's table. *Beautiful tools.*

He hadn't told her about his scholarship; she'd disapprove of his utopia. The director of financial aid lived in a traditional house.

"I just want to be respected by a few architects I respect," she said. "But they have their little club."

He remembered what Em Ball had said about pillows and chintz. "I respect you," he said. "But why don't you like Julia Morgan?"

"I don't know. She's corny."

26.

With an aerosol can of shaving cream, Lina tried to stencil a plausible Santa onto the ice-cream shop's glass door. Outside, people rushed by with bags of store-wrapped presents. Lina felt a shy longing; then, with the fury of the once duped, told herself that people were controlled by the military-industrial complex's advertising, to spend money on things they wouldn't love or use. She swerved to dodge a memory of the gift-wrapping station at Sears Roebuck, Fucking Christmas, and set her thoughts instead on the new flavors: pumpkin, and eggnog with dark chocolate chips.

Could you even go to college if your mother was crazy?

She'd signed up to work every day the week after Christmas, when nobody would come in. She could write her applications then in the back booth. That was the trick, to do something for herself while being paid. A long time ago, she, Lauren, and Jess had written away for brochures that showed students milling in front of ivy-covered buildings. It was harder to picture that future now.

Julie drove Lina and Donnie to Norwalk every Sunday. The light had gained a winter clarity. If their mother was getting better, her improvement was as gradual as the growth of a plant. Some weeks she was distant or desperately sleepy. Or she seemed to find them a bother. Last Sunday, she'd looked at Donnie's face a full three minutes, lifted her hand to his cheek, and made an effort toward a smile.

Their routine at the hospital was familiar. At lunch, Lina drank only coffee, studying the odd mural, and then she did her mother's laundry. They watched TV. Julie's warning their first day there had been prophetic: Lina saw more freaks then than she ever did again.

Every Sunday, she looked for the redheaded girl. It was a game she played with herself. For years, when she was in elementary school, every time Lina went to the library, she'd reached for the O–P volume of the *World Book* to see the red-haired girl. Then, a decade later, the picture had come to life; a girl with freckled skin had ridden by on a bike. Lina imagined calming her down, tucking a strand of wild hair behind her ear. She wondered if this was how guys felt, tender toward someone weaker. But she hadn't seen the girl again. Teenagers had their own ward. Perhaps the girl had been discharged and was home again, in her life.

Every Sunday, on the way back, Julie pushed Lina to drive farther. Lina was ready to take her driver's test, Julie said. But Lina didn't want to; the more things that happened, the harder it would be to resume where they'd stopped, and when her mother returned, she and Donnie would no longer be the same.

Lina was hauling her bike in through the kitchen door (the fender scraping the tire; once before, Walter had fixed that) when she heard voices in the living room, one unfamiliar. She found Donnie talking to a woman she definitely didn't know.

"Who are you?" Lina asked the woman.

"This is Joanie," Donnie said.

The woman stood and offered a hand. She had dark, heavy hair pulled back in a ponytail. She was dressed like a school art teacher. "We were talking about basketball," she said.

The afternoon bent stranger. Since when did anyone here talk about basketball? Lina stared at Donnie, who didn't play basketball. He spent hours in a windowless computer room.

"Do *you* have a particular interest?" the woman asked Lina.

"Getting through this freaking year." Lina had edited herself; why? Her mother hated it when she swore, but she hadn't edited herself with her mother.

Donnie smiled at the stranger. Why was he like this?

"Do you have any close relatives?" the woman asked. She was taking notes!

"No," Donnie said.

Julie banged in through the kitchen carrying paper bags of McDonald's, the smell of warm oil sailing out.

"Family friend?"

"Julie," Donnie said. Julie's face bloomed.

There was a momentary pause and they heard the woman's pen.

"Can I eat?" Donnie asked.

After the woman left, Julie shook her head. "You know you could move to my place."

She pulled a pencil from her mouse-colored sack and drew the layout on a napkin. Lina could have the sewing room, and Donnie would get a pullout in the pantry. They began to discuss storage—but it seemed too horrible and they decided to wait.

Julie had put in a request to bring their mother home overnight for Christmas.

Later, Lina sat, folded up, on the floor of her mother's closet, the hems of dresses brushing her cheek. She had been here like this once before. She had come home late, and her mother had beat her with an open fury. Donnie had woken up and seen Lina, crouched in a corner, her arms over her face, but Walter had slept through it.

_____

One afternoon the week before Christmas vacation, Donnie sat writing code in the computer room and took out the slice of cold pizza he'd brought from home, the cheese congealed back to its original lace. Evan opened a lunch box full of small, wrapped packages and sighed.

"What's the matter?"

"My mom's food. An ancient problem. She cooks health food because she thinks I'm fat." The word "fat" had a sad little ping.

Evan *was* soft looking. His narrow shoulders made his belly seem wider. Donnie examined the lunch box. An open-faced sandwich, turkey, with strings of vegetable on top.

"You're not going to eat it?"

"I don't detect much edible. Maybe the apple." He opened a small container. "Ugh. Asian pear. They taste like perfume."

Donnie and Lina bought what they wanted at the store, trying not to spend too much, but Evan's lunches reminded him of what their mother used to fix. From then on, every lunch, Donnie and Evan met in the computer room and traded food, each pleased with the exchange.

Lina gave Julie three out of every four paychecks from the ice-cream store—Julie told her to deposit at least one into her own savings account—and at the end of the month, they paid bills. Julie calculated how much she needed to deposit; she frowned, adding the string of numbers. Walter sent two twenty-dollar bills every week. Most nights, Lina ate ice cream for dinner. That saved money. Still, she knew she should have insisted on giving Julie all four checks.

Julie told her the doctor said it would be best if they had Christmas at the hospital.

27.

Walter stood by the highway, weeds slender as thread around his boots. He wasn't scared of hitching anymore. Enough had already happened.

The minute he stepped through the back door, after midnight, the bungalow felt infected. Floorboards tented up. His chemistry grade card, curled at the edges, remained on the refrigerator. Everyone was asleep. Light from the boarder's lava lamp leaked from under her door. All there was to eat was ice cream. He finished a pint of eggnog chip.

He slipped into the room he used to share with Donnie and lay on his old bed, hearing his brother breathe. Why hadn't they let him come before? Lina said it had been their worst Thanksgiving. The hospital turkey was orange. He'd never thought that holidays were any big deal. Well, what do you know, it turned out they were.

He got up, tore down his grade card, and threw it out.

The next morning, Lina and Donnie looked like themselves, only less good versions.

Norwalk, when he opened Julie's car door, felt hotter than any place should be in December. Everyone in Berkeley hated LA, as if it were the bottom of the state, where everything had gone wrong. Strip malls. Freeways. Benighted parents. Smog. For the first time, Walter saw Northern California's collective point.

The grounds of the hospital looked enormous and shabby, like a neglected park, probably a hundred acres without any apparent plan. What had happened to Kirkbride? Buildings of wildly different styles had been thrown up on the vast lawns—which up close proved to be crabgrass—their only commonality being poor construction values. Trees grew randomly. He followed his sister and brother past a clutch of women, smoking.

His mom, when he finally saw her, actually looked mentally ill. But her posture lifted as she recognized him. She patted the chair beside her. "This is mine," she said to the woman next to her.

"The one she's proud of." Lina picked up a laundry hamper with angular bitterness.

"She's doped up," Walter whispered, but he knew it wasn't just that. He felt guilty knowing, but also pleased. "Let's take a walk," he said, pulling his mom up.

"She comes along." His mom nodded toward the woman next to her.

"Come on. You can take a walk with your son."

"She's on thirty-minute check," said the woman, who introduced herself as Shirley and turned out to be a nurse, smiling but definite.

"So we'll go for thirty minutes." Had they examined her for something like a brain tumor? He planned to ask what happened. He needed to get her alone. Donnie and Lina didn't know about the pills.

"Julie told me." It came out sounding like he was mad. He hadn't wanted to sound mad.

"What?" She tripped over a root. She wasn't wearing regular shoes, he saw now; she had something gauzy and cotton on her feet.

"The pills."

"Oh, that. I was feeling down."

"You have to think why."

"It's only sometimes."

When did she get like this? The place wasn't what he'd expected. Where were the vistas? The orchestra pavilion? Inside the fenced perimeter, a factory spewed gray smoke. They passed a coffee stand that sold muffins wrapped in too many layers of cellophane. At one point, his mom jerked and ducked, as if dodging an attack. But there was nothing. Not even a bee.

They stood under an enormous copper beech. Walter would have liked Ken to see it. Maybe a hundred years ago it had grown from one blown seed. His mom's hand was sharp on his arm. He loved her and that love exhausted him.

"I'm trying to hold on to my mind," she said.

"I know, Mom. You have to keep trying."

He was relieved when Shirley ran over to say it was thirty minutes. "They like to get back to the ward," she said.

They. She's not a *they*, he thought.

Back in the big room (*the parlor,* Shirley called it) where chairs faced every which way, his mom rested a hand on her belly, which was bigger than it had been.

"It's the medicine," Shirley said. "Bloating."

"I'm like a Biafran."

Walter laughed, glad his mom could still make a joke. Lina

returned with a hamper of neatly folded clothes. Back in real life, their mom had screamed at her to pick up things from her floor. Here, she held up a tiny garment. Her mother's good blouse had been shrunk in the hospital laundry to a doll's size. Next week, Lina said, she'd bring iron-on name labels.

Julie summoned Walter for what she called the grand tour. They walked in the hot, stinging air as she pointed out buildings, which he couldn't have cared less about, the sexes segregated, Julie said, except for the open ward, where his mother could eventually be transferred.

Eventually. How long was Julie thinking she'd be here?

"That one's for older women. Menopause Manor, they call it." Julie walked briskly. "The kids shouldn't really be by themselves. If Child Protective Services knew, they'd have social workers all over us. One already came. I think that boarder must have called." She'd told Donnie and Lina that they could move into her place but they didn't want to, at least not yet.

"Would *you* ever consider moving in there?"

"Me?" She had a lease, she said, and two cats!

Were cats not allowed? The four years Walter lived in the bungalow, he'd never seen the landlords. But Julie had a life—cats, an apartment, friends, even a book club (Em Ball was a member of two)—and she was electing to keep its small pleasures. Later he winced, remembering his presumption.

"This is the beauty shop," Julie said, and inside what looked like a garden shed stood two old pedestal sinks. "They open Thursday mornings. Your mom and I had our hair done. They don't get hot water."

A young man Walter's age, wearing a vest like someone a generation older, passed, taking small steps, with his arms out to the sides, as if for balance. He made a buzzing sound.

"Trent," Julie said.

The smokestack expelled steam. What was a factory doing here?

Julie pointed. "There's the doctor's office."

Walter wanted to meet Dr. Moss. A secretary sat eating a sandwich at her desk. She waved him in; he was surprised how easy it was.

The doctor had close-cropped hair. Glasses. A narrow face. Maybe Jewish. Walter said he wanted to ask about his mom.

"Your mother is . . ." They made small talk while the secretary squatted at a file cabinet, her heels lifting out of her shoes, then delivered a folder.

"Diane Aziz. Yes. You and I spoke on the phone. I have a lot to learn about her yet. The voices seem less insistent. We have conversations about trees. There are hundreds of different species here. She's the only patient who's taken an interest. Your sister and brother come every week. That helps. And you're at Berkeley? How do you like it? You have friends?"

"A few."

"Good, that's important. A girlfriend?" He looked pained, asking.

"No."

"Your father's foreign, isn't he?"

"He's Afghan but he lives here now. I don't know where." Then Walter asked, "What exactly does my mom have?"

The doctor started writing something on a piece of paper.

Walter stood to examine a framed black-and-white photograph of a brick building that looked like a castle. A name in silver cursive said: *Greystone.*

"That's one of your Kirkbrides," the doctor said, standing up and handing Walter the paper, folded over.

"I thought it was an orphanage." Walter's mom had been left in an orphanage when her own mother went into the hospital. She had driven them once to see it. They sat parked in front of the old brick building, which was empty by then. Her memories of the orphanage sounded fond. A young nun snuck a record player into the dormitory and taught them the Watusi. Every year at Christmas, his mom sent that nun, now in an old nuns' home, a card with a check. She was enraged that the Church allowed priests to own houses and boats and left the nuns impoverished.

Outside the window, a redheaded girl streaked by on a bike.

"A lot of Kirkbrides are empty now, too," the doctor said. "When the state opened this hospital, they had a parcel twice the size of what we have now. They kept their own cows and chickens, and planted kitchen gardens and orchards. The patients worked—either in the laundry or outside. The place was almost self-sufficient."

"Like a commune," Walter said.

"But we can't do that anymore. There was a case. Alabama cut their cigarette tax, which paid for mental health. So they had an overcrowded hospital, five thousand people, three doctors, and ended up with a lawsuit. The newspaper compared the conditions to Auschwitz. And what came out of it is that now you can't have uncompensated patient labor." They stood before the photograph. "Greystone is where I grew up," the doctor said. "My parents were psychiatrists. Family business."

"I'm not sure if I want to be a doctor or an architect. Maybe I'll design hospitals."

"You could be the Kirkbride for our time. You'll see as you visit your mom. It's not so bad. We have movie nights. We hold dances in the spring and fall."

Em Ball had located a biography of Dr. Kirkbride. After his first wife died, he married a former patient. Walter wondered if Dr. Moss was married.

"I read that Kirkbride ended up marrying a patient," Walter said.

"An ex-patient, I think she was. They say his life exemplified the Wild West of early psychiatry—he was shot by one patient, sued by another, and married a third."

Walter's mom was a pretty woman. Maybe she and the doctor would fall in love. That would be a good end to her story.

Walking to the parking lot, Julie pointed out a large Victorian house. "Dr. Moss lives there. The other doctors have cottages." In the distance, they saw laundry lines hung with sheets.

"Shirley told us patients used to clean the doctors' houses," Lina said, "but they outlawed that."

Maybe the Alabama law wasn't so bad. Walter was relieved that his mom was spared the indignity of being a maid. That idea bothered him almost as much as her being insane. Did men fall in love with women who scrubbed their floors?

Julie let Lina drive. She steered smoothly down a long road, then turned onto the two-lane highway.

"You're surpassing me," Walter said to his sister. He reached for the paper in his pocket. "The doctor gave me a diagnosis: *DSM 296.33, major depressive disorder.*" Eventually, these terms would become blankets to throw over obscure painful shapes. Now, they felt like stabs. Walter didn't say the final word: *Recurrent.*

At home, the boarder offered to read Walter's tarot, but he refused. Lina volunteered. The boarder began, but then her face stalled. She shuffled again.

"You see bad things?" Lina asked.

"I'm perceiving disturbance."

"Does that mean we'll lose the house?"

The boarder seemed to grow an inch. "But I signed a two-year lease."

"I'm sure it's fine, then," Lina said.

28.

Julie talked over Frank Sinatra crooning Christmas carols on the car radio. Her gift had been delivered in Michigan. A popcorn popper. Last year, Lina remembered, had been a washer-dryer and the year before a TV. She wondered if the Michigan brother blamed them.

When they rode in under the arch, the Arts and Crafts letters spelling *Orchard Springs* were draped with pine.

Their mother was dressed horribly in a pink sweater with gold buttons, but her hair smelled clean and she was excited, saying, "Come on. It's starting." Her face, upon seeing her sons, rounded with joy. Her mother loved her, too, Lina knew, but with complication. Did she see her own illness inside Lina?

———

The auditorium was full, the hanging lamps lit over three flocked trees on the stage. A choir huddled behind a Black woman with an enormous echoing voice, who stood forward and began "O Little Town of Bethlehem," her arms out to the sides, earrings catching glints of light, singing as if she believed something. A man with a tambourine shuffled.

Lina's mother rocked, singing along, off-key. She used to be the one who started the fun. She'd always been puzzled that Lina wasn't like that. I would have been, Mommy, Lina thought. I didn't know how.

A Santa Claus walked down the aisle, a belt slipping to his hips. Lina's mother looked expectant, like a child. At the microphone, someone introduced the California secretary of state. He wore a shirt and tie under a pullover and talked about how important what they were doing here was. He had presents for the kids, he said. Donnie was still a kid but he wouldn't count. The gifts would go to the kids who lived here. Lina looked around for the redheaded girl. She hoped that she'd gone home.

"You see Dr. Moss?" Walter asked.

Lina didn't. He probably took his family to Mexico, or skiing, like Jess's and Lauren's families.

The chorus sang. The mentally ill didn't have bad voices.

Her mother's foot tapped. Nurses in white angel costumes passed out cookies. Lina bit into a star. Her mother licked the sugar off her fingers. She'd always loved Christmas. Lina took three more cookies, wrapping them in a napkin.

A rabbi spoke, then a priest with a guitar sang a prayer. Lina's mother was holding her hand and kept squeezing. The world narrowed. Lina squeezed back.

By the time they filed out, their mother said she wanted to go to bed.

"Oh, Diane, what about the dinner?" Julie said. "You don't want to miss that!"

Shirley said, "You did so much work on those centerpieces."

"Next time," she said, her eyes flickering down. "Next time I'll go."

Under an ill-shaped tree, one of the nurses had convened a group to carol the bedridden patients. The carolers stood studying mimeographed sheet music. The nurse blew a pitchpipe.

"She would love this normally," Julie said. "Remember, Diane, when we caroled at Northridge. The LVN who couldn't sing leading the pack!"

"She used pieces of trees on the tables," Shirley said. "You'll see."

Julie wanted to take a peek. Get a bite before the long drive back. "You can go to bed right after, Diane."

Lina's mother stuck out her tongue at her.

Julie looked down, shamed.

"It's the medicine," Shirley said. "When it says sleep, she turns off."

Lina walked her mother back to the ward, hearing carols in the distance and her mother's own small voice humming along. She'd been moved out of her alcove into the general dormitory. Progress, Julie said. Lina helped her mother take off her blouse and pull the nightgown over her head, her arms up like a child's. Her mother's body had changed, her stomach was looser. Her mother was the only patient here now in the long room full of beds. A nurse sat knitting in the corner.

"Well, that was the best Christmas ever," her mother said, as she said every year.

She wanted Lina to crawl onto the small bed with her and Lina did, her face on her mother's back. Once her mother was asleep (she snored now; Shirley said that was the medication, too), Lina got up and began the long, slow trek. The night was cold, the stars white, and Lina dreaded the cafeteria.

She was used to the other patients by now, but their visiting families alarmed her. She stood at the door. It was almost beautiful inside, the room with seemingly haphazard piles of cedar on every table, candles burning on wooden spools, the uplifting smell of pinesap. The same kitchen ladies as always tonight wore pins shaped as wreaths and importantly served prime rib under orange lights. They made sure everyone got a thick slice and a ladle of juice, proud to be serving this good meal. Just then, Lina decided to become vegetarian. She felt clean, with her plate of mashed potatoes and Brussels sprouts, which the ladies heaped as if to compensate for the bewildering lack of beef.

"It's a good cut," Shirley said, noticing Lina's plate and reminding her that the staff chipped in for top-quality meat for the holiday supper. In her peripheral vision, Lina saw the doctor, who was not skiing after all, but sitting with the redheaded girl and the politician. It took a minute for Lina to make sense of these three together. Oh. So the redheaded girl was not a patient. A revision. She was the doctor's daughter. Lina had thought she could help the girl. Now, it turned out, she was the one beneath.

Still, Lina went to meet her at the dessert table. The redheaded girl looked her over, asked, "So what's your deal?"

"My mom is a patient," Lina said. Her heart sped. At school, she went to the clay room to avoid the social jockeying in the cafeteria.

The girl's red hair went to her waist. "Are you into something? Like me, I'm into art."

Lina considered saying that she hung out in the clay room, but it would have seemed she was copying, even though it was true. "I work at an ice-cream store," she said.

None of the girls at Pali wore lipstick, only eye makeup, in a vague allegiance to the sixties, which they'd just missed. But this girl, whose name turned out to be Isabel, had dark red lips. Her clothes didn't look like clothes people at Pali wore, either, not the flared cords from Rudnick's or Theodore, if they could afford it. Isabel had on old Levi's and a black crepe top that could have been her grandmother's. Lina craved that top. "Are you in college?" she asked.

"Michigan," Isabel said.

Now that the girl was a real person, Lina was not sure what she felt about her.

29.

Dr. Moss introduced Walter to the secretary of state. "This young man attends your alma mater. You went to Cal, didn't you?"

"After seminary. I loved Berkeley, but I was an older student. Less carefree."

"He's studying to become a doctor and an architect, isn't that right?" Dr. Moss said.

"I've been reading Kirkbride."

"That's the psychiatrist who designed the hospital most American asylums are modeled after."

"Do you know about Geel?" the secretary of state asked.

"I lived there the summer I was ten," Dr. Moss said, turning to Walter. "Geel is a Belgian town where, for over a century, mentally ill people have boarded with local families."

People came over to shake the doctor's hand. Walter wished his mom hadn't gone to bed. He hoped Dr. Moss hadn't seen her in that sweater.

Walter asked the politician if he had a family member here.

"No, no. Dr. Moss and I are old friends and I like to visit on holidays. That's not to say there's no mental illness in my family. We just manage it in-house."

"Walter, you got me thinking about Kirkbride," the doctor said, sitting down. "The end of his life was tough. The next generation thought he was a dreamer. They trampled his career. Every generation thinks they can do better and the young always win—for a while. Then, too, as soon as there were state hospitals, people drove out their elderly and left them. With facilities understaffed, moral treatment didn't work as well."

"So people blamed him?" Walter asked.

"A few patients published exposés, one in Charles Dickens's magazine. Neurologists started treating people with electricity. Kirkbride wanted to keep the chronic and the curable together. The curable lent a little glamour, a little aspiration. We still mix paying and Medicaid, but we lost most of the curable to outpatient therapy. And then the state wanted the asylums to be only for those they deemed the deserving poor. By then Kirkbride was in his seventies, still living in his hospital. He died there. People left hickory nuts on his grave."

"Nuts?" The politician laughed.

"Where's your mother?" Dr. Moss asked. "I see Julie."

"She fell asleep."

He frowned. "Maybe we do need to reduce her dosage."

Walter thought of the strange pink sweater and his sister's sorrow about the shrunken blouse, her frantic efforts to make their mom look the way she used to. Walter had considered all that attention to appearance a vanity. But now he saw its utilitarian value. If the doctor fell in love with his mom, he'd give her special attention. Maybe she'd recover.

"Should I be here, do you think?" he asked. "I could take time off from school and go back later."

"You can't be waiting," Dr. Moss said.

Walter felt relieved, as he did every time someone told him to stay in school, but also unnecessary.

Dr. Moss would have been handsome, Lina decided, if he weren't so old. He resembled the picture of Kafka that Mrs. Anjani stapled to the back of "A Hunger Artist." Even when the doctor smiled, he looked pained.

"Merry Christmas," Lina said. "I wanted to ask you, is my mother going to get better?"

"I believe she will. Your mother has something. A spark."

This was a large gift. Lina looked away, to hide her happiness.

Lina drove all the way back in the dark. She had to keep a heightened concentration to manage the field of haloed lights. Isabel had given her a sip of liquor.

On Walter's last day in Los Angeles, Julie asked him to walk around the block. She said that Dr. Moss hadn't ventured an end date, but that it sounded to her more like a year than a month. That was the feeling he'd gotten, too. "So a year," Walter said. That wasn't forever.

"We'll have to let go of the bungalow," Julie said. "The kids can move in with me."

So Lina would have her last months at home in Julie's apartment. What had been an emergency would now become just life. Still, their mother would get well. The doctor had said that to Lina. Walter felt that assurance like a coin in his pocket. "Should I talk to them about moving?"

"Not yet," Julie said. "We still have time."

A generous sentence. *We have time.*

Walter imagined the doctor and his mom in a restaurant, his mom herself again, her hair bouncing up at the ends. She would be grateful to the doctor for curing her; she would smile and listen because he was a man, she would laugh along. He would be careful, a little paternal, she would be the fun. But if they got married, would she have to move into that Victorian house on the grounds? Would Donnie live the rest of his childhood in a state hospital? Walter rubbed his temple. That wasn't the ending he wanted.

Walter brought the peeling leather-bound Kirkbride book to Jan Tudor. "This guy designed an alternate city for ill people. A little smaller, a little safer, but with some of the same pleasures and recreation. Everybody lived in one structure, the doctors, too." He showed her the plan: a building shaped like a bird, the sickest people at the wingtips. "What if I want to be an architect who builds institutions? Asylums and orphanages. Even prisons. Are there classes for those?"

"Maybe at Ball State. Not in architecture school. We don't even talk about money in studio. You're supposed to be making art."

"Can't art be useful?"

"Art is useful. Just by being art."

"Corbusier built a housing project," Walter said. "Where is Ball State, anyway?"

"Indiana."

30.

Lina locked up the store and took her bowl of Tahitian vanilla to the back booth. A dishwasher brought her one teabag of Earl Grey every time they worked together. She'd saved today's to make another concoction not for sale: three scoops of vanilla with hot tea poured over. The brown tannin crashed against the billow of cream.

Lina took out the folder of applications she'd sent away for when she was a different person. What she'd feared then had by now already happened, and the prospect of convincing people around a conference table that she should be chosen seemed hopeless and absurd.

Describe someone you greatly admire, living or dead.

Lina didn't admire. She envied. She envied the distinctions Lauren parsed; she envied Jess's mind. She envied both their houses. Envy didn't require time or peace. But admiration?

What questions would you ask him or her if you could spend an evening together?

She didn't admire her mother—almost the opposite—but she was the only person, living or dead, who contained the answers Lina needed.

Were we happy once?

Was it me who ruined it all?

But an evening of questioning her mother was inconceivable. The answers might be locked inside her forever.

Her mother had always cried. She cried easily. Lina had heard that phrase about other women, but this was different. Lina's mother sobbed, she railed, she fisted her hands at the ends of straight arms, and then, for as long as Lina could remember, she went to her room alone to let air out of herself. She stayed that way—flattening—for an hour or a day, before rising again, shy, ashamed, repentant, moving in the kitchen to make herself a morning egg.

The sadness was always there, an underground cascade. For a long time, Lina and her brothers could pull her back, to remember other parts of herself. Now their powers had dwindled. Maybe it had been only Walter. But Dr. Moss had said she would get better. . . .

Sounds Lina had been ignoring for a while under the music were identifying themselves as knocks on her out-of-date stenciled Santa. Two people, an adult couple, wanted in. The woman, wearing a fur coat and glittering earrings, squatted to a kneeling position and held her hands together, mock-praying. The man opened his wallet.

Lina walked toward the door. She could give them free cones and magic their night. But it was late, the money was counted, in its bag for the chute. She still had to do applications. *If I had a box just for wishes and dreams that had never come true.*

Sorry, we're closed, she mouthed through the glass.

They made one more attempt at sad clown faces, the young woman standing on tiptoe, then they left, bumping together on the sidewalk, arms around each other, not even angry. They were too happy to be mad. Would she ever be like that? She watched them straggle down the street, then unbolted the door and called, "Register's closed. I'll give you cones on the house." They asked for one scoop of chocolate to share.

The guy left a fifty-dollar tip.

She slipped it in the deep pocket of her overalls.

Whom could she say she admired?

Lauren had written about Eleanor Roosevelt. Jess had picked some scientist, a man, not Madame Curie. Why does it have to be a woman just because *I'm* a woman, she said, an opinion she would change her mind about two decades later. Lina ran through her teachers. Clumps of Mrs. Anjani's hair had fallen out, but she was alert as an owl, in wire-rimmed glasses. She'd loved a poem Lina wrote at the beginning of last year but by the end told her she hadn't lived up to her potential.

Finally, Lina wrote about Mr. Riddle. "Dean of Art," he called himself. He ran the clay room. The only Black teacher in the school, he wore overalls and yellow work boots. He cared that they all kept the room in good order. He made mumbled references to his time in Vietnam and to his own work, which Lina had never seen. "I used to paint horses and shit. Watts Riots changed that," he said.

Years later, she realized that he had been stoned. Teaching high school was his day job. He probably hated it.

But Lina did admire him. Overalls had become her uniform, too. Her hair carried the smell of slip. But she wasn't going to say *that.* You couldn't write about hair in a college essay.

One of the schools Lauren said was good, *not Harvard, but still good,* asked you to imagine interviewing the person.

> *One New Year's Eve in Nam, all the guys in my platoon got wasted. I woke up next morning facedown in a ditch with my mouth full of dust and all the Vietnamese people were sweeping the dirt in front of their huts. They cleaned on New Year's Day. That's how they celebrated. I want this room clean.*
> I'd been washing a bucket. I asked him if it was clean enough.
> *Can I eat out of it?*
> Not the outside, I said.
> *That's okay. I don't eat from the outside.*

Lina was making up answers from things Mr. Riddle had said while people cut clay with wire, to see that all the air bubbles had been kneaded out.

> *Went to college on the GI Bill. I didn't party. I was back from a war. Didn't need all that.*

There was a fee for every school, just to apply. She'd checked the box for financial aid. The pouch of money for the bank and the stack of envelopes for the post office jostled in the basket of her bike. She knew how this would end: she would stay home.

She wanted to go to one of the faraway castles in the brochures, but her hopes had lowered. She went to the bank, dropped the pouch down the chute, then rode to the post office. She stood by the mailboxes. She could dare the world, send in applications to only three schools back east, rip up the others, and leave it to fate.

It was dark. No one was watching. When they were children, she and Donnie had entered sweepstakes. Chances dropped into the mail. Once she'd sent away her three entries, she tossed the others into a trash can and sped home.

31.

The first weeks their mother was gone, Julie had slept over. They were relieved when she began to leave after they were in their beds. She called, "Are you in for the night?" They called back, "Yes, thank you," but they would wander to the kitchen later. The boarder wasn't home most of the time; she'd caught them only once without Julie.

The boarder was usually asleep Sunday mornings when they drove to the hospital, but today she was in the kitchen, a towel turbaned over her hair, when Julie arrived with a bag of bagels, car keys dangling from her hand. "Hey guys," the boarder said. She was poking a knife into the toaster, as they'd always been told not to do. "Listen, I'll be moving out today." She must have thought that was enough, because she stopped. When the three of them stared at her, she stammered, addressing Julie. "It's too much for me. I need to settle. And you people have a lot to deal with, without worrying about obligations to me. But I did"—she shot furtive looks, one brush over Lina and Donnie—"I gave Diane first and last months' rent and a deposit. I'd appreciate if I could get the deposit back. Here." She bent over the counter and wrote on a scrap. "My new address. I wish I were leaving for a lead on a hit series and I could just forget about it." She stood, her foot on the other knee. "I know you're having trouble. Just whenever you can." This was the height of her generosity; they could sense her stretching to reach it. As they were leaving, she asked, "You think Diane'll be okay?"

"We sure hope so," Julie said.

I'll never see her again, Lina thought. It was strange not to feel more. This wasn't the first time Lina had knocked against this wall of not feeling. She *could* care about people, even a boarder, she thought, only a different one.

"Are we going to give her deposit back?" Donnie asked, and

Julie said, "I can think of a thing or two ahead of that on my to-do list." Their drive started jollier than usual. To get deposits back, Julie explained, you had to give notice. Thirty or sixty days. But whether or not they refunded her deposit (they did, though not until the summer), her departure would mean no more help with the rent.

"What's going to become of us?" Lina asked.

"You'll go to college," Donnie said.

"I doubt it," Lina said.

"Of course you will," Julie said, sitting straighter. "Best years of your life, people say."

Evan's parents hired a tutor, a UCLA math graduate student, to pick him up from school. Middle school math *was* slow, but Evan wasn't as interested in math as his parents liked to believe, and his mother also instructed Dino, the tutor, to make Evan more physically fit, in which he had no interest at all. She was fine with Dino schlepping Donnie along. She hoped he'd be a good influence. Dino dragged the boys fishing at Malibu Creek Canyon, where he caught two crayfish himself and threatened to make a fire to grill them over. He coaxed them to the LaBrea Tar Pits, but after the old empty halls, they said no more museums. They continued to refuse the tennis club and the park, which Evan contended was too green.

"Can't we just stay here?" Donnie countered, in the computer room.

"You guys know how to play chess?" Dino asked. Friday, he said, he had to go to Chinatown.

They wanted to go along. They were bored with everything else.

Dino drove the long Wilshire Corridor to Chinatown, where neither of them had ever been before. They followed Dino into a steaming, droopy park.

"Now you guys stay close and watch," Dino said. "Don't say anything."

Old men, most of them Chinese, sat paired at square tables playing something that looked like chess but wasn't. The board was different. Dino sat at the first table for about twenty minutes, then stood up and moved to a different one. He played nine games. The old men (they were all men) gave him cash and spoke to each other in what Donnie and Evan assumed was Mandarin. Dino drove them home in a lighter mood. The boys said they wanted to learn.

From then on, they played every day. In Chinese chess there was no queen, and during the game the pieces changed value. It was a realistic game, Dino said, more than Western chess. Both boys had good memories. Donnie visualized the board and tried to go twenty or thirty moves deep into a game. "It's like counting," he told Evan. "If you interrupt, it throws me off."

Dino always beat them. But the games grew longer. The board was divided by a river. In Chinese chess there were elephants in addition to horses. Donnie sometimes woke up with a move in his head.

People thought game strategy was about intelligence, but it wasn't that, Dino said, it was a capacity for fine work, dropping into a zone where you do one small thing with intensity.

In Chinatown, when Dino lost he fell into a dark, silent mood. He played for the money, the boys understood by now.

"We can practice more," Donnie said. "That's probably what helps, right?"

"Sometimes I play ten hours a day," Dino said. "It's like an addiction."

"Can't you ask my mom for more money?" Evan suggested.

"She's unhappy with me already. She wants you guys on a tennis court. I think she expects you to lose weight," he said.

"That was mean," Evan said, and Donnie agreed.

When it started to rain, Donnie and Evan directed Dino to the ice-cream store. Dino had a credit card from Evan's parents, but Lina wouldn't let him pay for their sundaes. Because it was still pouring, Donnie let Dino drive him home. His sister was hush-hush about their address, as if it would be a crime if anyone found out, but it didn't seem to Donnie such a big deal. Dino asked if Donnie's sister had a boyfriend. No, Donnie said, and looked at Evan. The bungalow was still and empty. There was no boarder, only the swept room and the water bed she'd left behind.

Donnie said they could play inside. They set up boards on the landlord's dining-room table. From then on, they played in the bungalow after school, and Evan and Donnie looked at each other whenever Dino mentioned going for ice cream.

They left hours before Julie arrived. They never went to Evan's house, which had wall-to-wall white carpet and his mother.

In the bungalow now, no one was watching. They didn't have to worry that the boarder would call social services. Strangely, though, at night, Donnie and Lina stayed in their rooms. Julie arrived earlier and didn't go home until late.

Julie called Donnie and Lina to the kitchen table. They had to give sixty days' notice to the landlords, she said. "I told myself that if Diane wasn't back by the summer . . ." They would move in with her in June. "At least when we're all under one roof, I can make sure there's a decent dinner on the table every night."

"Where you live, it's just far from the ice-cream store," Lina said.

"Honestly, you were ready for your driver's test months ago. The thing I've been worried about is your allergies. But I've got the name of a doctor and we'll get you shots. If worse comes to worst, a nurse I know will board the cats."

Donnie was looking at Lina; she was not allergic to cats. Once she'd been sick and Julie got the impression that it was an allergy to her cats and Lina had never corrected her.

Lina's mother had once said the happiest part of her day was returning home. She'd had a particular gait; she stinted forward, Lina remembered, carrying a stack of manila folders. Lina bolted up in the morning, thinking she'd slept in. She pined for regular days, which used to include heat, bees, a messy room, songs, a crush. Now she would never have them again.

College letters arrived April 15. Lina arranged not to work (finding a sub was easy; kids who scooped ice cream weren't in great suspense about college admission) and arrived home in the still-hot middle of the day, when no one else was there. Three envelopes slanted in the mailbox.

The first, which she ripped open standing, was a no. She sat. Her chest lost its pattern of breathing. Her fingers tore open the paper ahead of her. Another no. The last one said she was on a wait list. She remembered the envelopes she'd thrown into the trash. Her grades had been high, they'd not dropped, and her scores were better than Lauren's. Her recommendations, maybe? Mrs. Anjani had asked her once if anything was wrong and she'd not answered. Still, Mrs. Anjani liked her. Jess would stand out in any pool of applicants. Lauren had gone to nationals in debate. Still, still, Lina had believed that the world *recognized* her and some magic would trump any fumbled evidence of her value.

She'd hoped to move far away. She hugged her knees. Now that she couldn't go, she desperately longed for college, any college. Maybe she really wasn't as smart as Walter. His friends had talked about national economies while her friends talked about boys. She should have applied to UC. Everyone did. Sending in only three chances had seemed a way to dare the universe to give her what she wanted. The universe had called her bluff.

She ate by rote. Donnie had no idea. Julie breezed in the back door at seven, and Lina's chest clenched when she said, "It's April fifteenth." But then Julie made a joke about taxes: "Who knows the difference between a taxidermist and a tax collector?" This must be what it was like to be in prison, Lina thought, when you'd secretly believed you were a princess.

"What about Berkeley?" Lauren asked, her voice shrill. "You had to get in there."

"I didn't apply."

"You didn't apply? Lina!"

Mrs. Anjani stood at the blackboard wearing a full, thick wig. "So where are you going?" she asked the class. People shouted out their colleges, looking at the slanted desktops. UC San Diego! Colorado! Mills! Santa Cruz! Lauren mumbled New Jersey.

"How about you?" Mrs. Anjani asked, standing in front of Lina.

"Nowhere," Lina said.

"Yeah, right," the teacher said, and the class laughed. They loved her nimble sarcasm. Mrs. Anjani was ancient but fluent in their demotic.

"It's true," Lauren whispered, with an ominous tone.

Mrs. Anjani's face turned all business. She told Lina to stay after class.

"What is your grade point average?" Mrs. Anjani asked. "How could UC not take you?"

"I didn't apply. I'm on the wait list for Barnard."

"Barnard is a fine school, but the wait list is a wait list. Why didn't you apply to UCLA? I graduated UCLA." Mrs. Anjani talked about a library where she'd done her homework that had record players with headphones and Persian rugs.

Lina shrugged. "I'll just stay here and work."

"That's a terrible idea. Tonight I'll write to a woman I know who took her degree at Barnard. I have another friend who is a lecturer at UCLA. Come to my house on Saturday. I see the doctor at one thirty. Be there at four." She wrote down her address.

Scrubs grew up against the dirty stucco of the small house. Lauren drove here once a month to file the teacher's insurance claims. She'd told Lina that there was no evidence of any Mr. Anjani.

Mrs. Anjani opened her door wearing a caftan, her head bald, a kitten in her hands.

"I would make tea but I'm not feeling well today. This is for you." She held out the animal. A plastic tub by the door contained a bag of litter and cans of cat food. "I've made mistakes in my life, but my only real regret is waiting until my fifties to adopt a pet."

The small, warm thing clutched at Lina and rooted under the bib of her overalls, its claws sinking through her T-shirt into skin. "Oh, I can't. I'm moving in with a family friend who already has cats."

"Your guidance counselor thinks you should write a letter. I'm drafting one for you to sign. I'll mail it; I'm not taking any chances. Absolute madness for a California student not to apply to UCLA. The best bargain in the world. I called my friend who lectures in history. There's not a thing she can do. Not a thing. Not even if you were her own daughter."

Lina pulled the kitten off herself.

Mrs. Anjani folded her arms. "Try. I'll take him back. See how you feel in a week."

What would she do with a cat? Lina spent all her free periods in the art room now. She liked the feeling of centering clay as the spinning metal sawed down her fingernails. All day, she smelled slip in her hair.

32.

"That's not bothering you, with your allergies?" Lina had brought along the kitten, with the litter box on the back-seat floor, and Julie—the cat lover—was not charmed. From the rearview mirror, she detected the creature hanging by its claws from the upholstery and told Donnie to keep a hold of it. But when Lina set it on the polished floor of the ward, their mother danced toward the tiny animal, a flicker of her old self. She made small noises as the kitten rubbed against her bootie. The ward was unusually quiet until, from down the hall, there came a piercing scream.

"She likes the cat," Shirley said, passing with her arm under the elbow of a young woman Lina didn't recognize who stared at the floor.

Their mother wanted to take the kitten outside. She stayed alert for an hour, without swatting the air or grinding her teeth. She held the kitten, petting him with her thumb as she walked through rows of bolted herbs. The kitten squirmed out of her hands under the leaves, and Donnie and Lina stumbled to recapture it. Lina slid the litter box underneath her mother's white metal bed, in the long dormitory. The blinds here were cordless and couldn't be lifted or lowered, so gauzy stripes fell over the blankets and on the floor. Lina dumped the clothes from her mother's hamper and sat down to sort the white from the colored. Name labels she'd ironed on had curled up at the edges; some had fallen off. Another of her mother's sweaters had shrunk. She made a separate pile of clothes she didn't recognize.

The laundry room smelled of bleach. She pushed the garments that weren't her mother's into a separate bin. In an hour, she would fold her mother's clothes on the long metal table. She liked this. Her mind went smooth.

When Lina emerged with a pillowcase of clean clothes, she saw the redheaded girl, Isabel, on a bike by the industrial kitchen, an aroma of bread in the air. Lina found her presence jarring, as if someone she'd made up during lazy hours alone had swelled to life. Lina remembered that she needed a white dress for graduation. The school had sent out a letter. "Where do you buy your clothes?" she asked.

"I'll take you there," Isabel said.

"Oh, I can't leave," Lina said.

"It's not outside." Her voice had a laugh in it. "Hop on. Hold my waist."

From a moving bike, the hospital grounds seemed hillier. Isabel stopped in front of a round building with boarded windows and left the bike on its side. Lina held on to her clean laundry. The dim, round room was filled with desks stacked on top of each other and a tower of chairs. They climbed a rickety staircase, the banister replaced by rope, to an attic. There, the floor was strewn with suitcases, open like clamshells, their contents spilling. Lina hugged the laundry. Everything looked dusty. Trunks held name tags with addresses. *Mrs. Fern Goodale, 28 Flintwood Avenue, Northridge. Miss Mabel Eason of The Arroyo, Jack Hammer, the Miracle Mile.* "Whose stuff is this?" Lina asked.

"Old patients."

"Please don't take anything of my mom's. She doesn't have much."

"I would never touch a belonging of someone here."

The ink on the tags looked old, sepia. "Why didn't these people take their things with them when they left?"

"Some of them lived out their lives here. There used to be a cemetery. They dug it up when they sold the farm."

"But people don't die here now."

"Only in Geri. You worry about your mom, huh? Has she always had problems?"

"No. I mean, normal problems. Like everyone has."

"My mom died seven years ago. But I have my dad." Isabel tossed a fur shawl to Lina with a head and paws on each end. Next, she held up a pink party dress.

"This is all just yours?"

"It's like a vintage store. Mostly I take tops." She opened a small cardboard suitcase, pulled off her T-shirt—she was wearing a pink lace bra—and put on one that said *Marquette Makers* in a swirly font.

Lina felt the familiar downheartedness of shopping. That mimeographed paper said girls were to wear white dresses, no more than two inches above the knee. Before, Lina would have made fun of this pomp. But now that she wasn't going to college, she thought she'd better wear a dress to graduation. If she told Julie she needed a dress, Julie would buy her one, but Julie paid for too much already.

Isabel pulled the pink dress over her head and looked at herself in the cracked mirror, canting one leg. In every picture of Lina's mother, she'd assumed that very same pose. She'd believed it slimmed her calves. "You're not that into clothes, huh?" Isabel asked. Isabel's panties made Lina's underwear look like a grandmother's.

"I guess not." Once, Lina's mom had come home with a pantsuit for Lina, a Theodore knockoff. Lina had stuffed it in the back of her drawer. It mattered to her not to try.

"You could be beautiful," Isabel said.

Lina and her mother had argued about clothes: her mother thought a beautiful woman was most beautiful in a beautiful dress. Lina thought in jeans.

"I have to wear a white dress for graduation," she said.

"We could look in my mom's closet. My dad saved her clothes for me."

"When they dug up the cemetery, where did they put the people?"

"Some families moved their own relatives. A rabbi in LA took the Jewish bones. The rest are here. I'll show you."

Lina rode on the back of Isabel's bike again, feeling her hips move up and down, the laundry between them. They stopped at a small patch of land, backed by cypress. A patient had made copper plates with names of the dead and the dates they were born and died. It was a minimal cemetery, the very least that ought to be done for a life. The guy who made the plates was buried here, too.

Lina sat inside Dr. Moss's house. A man arrived, clomping through the swinging doors of the old-fashioned kitchen and, nodding incessantly, put two loaves of bread on the table.

"Thank you, Artie," Isabel called after him. Then: "He never talks."

She cut slices, dropping them into an ancient toaster. From the rounded refrigerator, she dug out celery, a cucumber, a carrot, and something Lina learned was dill. After avoiding it at the ice-cream shop, it had never occurred to Lina that tuna fish could taste good.

"You grew up here?" she asked.

"Until they sent me to school in Ojai. The other doctors' kids were my friends. We never had babysitters. We ran everywhere. It was all fenced in. Patients wandered around the grounds. One guy used to walk reading a book."

She went upstairs and returned with an off-white Indian gauze caftan. "Her wedding dress. They were hippies." From holding it up, though, they could tell it was too long for Lina.

Maybe I won't go to graduation, she thought. A girl in the clay room, who made neat coil pots, had already lined up a job in a department store.

Lina had been away too long. She ran, tripping, into Ward 301, hugging the laundry, and found her mother sitting with Donnie watching TV. The kitten licked water from a bowl. She held the fresh clothes up to her mother, but her mother closed her eyes. Maybe it didn't matter if her mother wore other people's clothes. Maybe Lina's efforts were useless. But her mother would care, if she were herself. Was this important, though, if the self was no longer here, or if it swam inside somewhere loose, unattached, beyond reach? Still, this morning she'd danced toward the kitten, singing *Di-di-dit-di-di-da*. If that melody was still inside, more must be. Maybe all was recoverable yet.

Julie returned and they sat in the parlor that was nothing like a real living room. Lina asked about Julie's Michigan brother. Talking to Julie took work. Still, if Lina had told her she needed a dress for graduation, Julie would have bought her one.

When it was time to go, Lina bent down to collect the litter box and just then noticed Shirley's shoes. Oxfords. "Are the booties only for patients? I thought they were to keep the ward quiet."

"No shoelaces," Shirley said. "The cotton does polish the floors."

There was another woman now in the alcove.

"Don't let me forget to have you sign permission for your mother to work in the garden," Shirley said, "so Sacramento knows we're not making a slave of her."

Lina lifted the cat from her mother's lap.

"Why don't you leave him?" Shirley said. "We won't tell anybody."

Lina hoped Mrs. Anjani wouldn't be mad that she'd given away her gift.

"Where you been?" Mr. Riddle asked Lina. "Haven't seen you for a season."

Later, she would think of this year as time not lost but spent, outside the normal course, days given to something she couldn't name. She'd felt alive, though.

"Nowhere," she answered.

Mr. Riddle told the room at large that he was getting the hair waxed off his back. "For the ladies," he said.

Lina folded her mother's dresses, which she knew by heart. They were finally packing. From the small box on the dresser she lifted out the familiar jewelry, tried on the gold bracelet. Three rings rested on her palm, making bars of light. Should she bring them to Norwalk, even if they could get stolen there? Maybe her mother would take pleasure in the colors. But her mother didn't care about beauty now. Better guard them for later, when she became herself again.

Once, long ago, her mother sat at the dining-room table, with piles of lined paper. "I'm writing a book about my life," she'd said. "You'll see."

Lina had felt afraid that inside the book she would be a bad daughter who backtalked. Now she looked through the bureau for written pages, the beginning of a story. She rampaged through drawers, first carefully, then becoming wanton, and found endless unused stationery, blank pages—with whom had her mother hoped to correspond? Her mother would never write a book now. Lina's meanness would be forgotten.

She found handwritten lists of prices for curtains, slipcovers, chairs. Bills stamped PAID. So much that Lina had taken for granted her mother had struggled over and finally managed to bring home. And where would it all go? Julie was arranging for storage.

Julie's apartment was small; they could bring clothes, books, and their mother's jewelry. For even this Lina knew they should be grateful.

But it was tiring having to be grateful all the time.

Lina finally told Walter about college. He thought of her as the type who always raised her hand. It would never occur to him that she could do something this stupid.

"What about the wait list?"

"Total long shot. I can apply again next year. I don't think I will, though."

She told him about packing up the bungalow—his stuff, too.

"I trust you," Walter said. "Anything you think I'll want, maybe put in a box."

Lina stretched the phone cord from the kitchen to the hall and surveyed the boxes, labeled *Goodwill, Storage,* and *Apartment.* He was in Berkeley with that fairy-tale bridge over the water. It did not seem right.

"What doesn't, Lina?" he said, and that did it, the hint of deliberate patience in his voice as if she were being histrionic.

They screamed until she banged the phone into its cradle and leaned against the wall, stunned.

Walter arrived the next day with Susan.

"Put me to work," he said, looking rumpled from the drive. It was like Walter to have a helper. They took what he intended to keep to Susan's car. He could store it in her family's backhouse, where Susan's nanny once lived.

33.

Everything Walter dreaded had begun. For a long time, his family had been stuck. Now they were moving. He found Julie with his sister and brother, all of them dirty, among towers of boxes and goods from their previously private life strewn on the floor. Susan turned out to be talented at this. While Walter stared at old books, she emptied the refrigerator. In an hour, she volunteered to get sandwiches and took orders. Then she brought back more sandwiches, but also pickles, Greek salad, drinks, cheesecake, and extra cookies. A warm clutter. They unwrapped the food on the landlord's heavy table. While they ate, Susan told them about the sorority party she'd missed to drive Walter down. She and Carrie had bought domino masks at the swap meet. People had to wear them and dress as a character from a book. Susan chided him for not having his license. Everyone was displeased with Walter. "Nothing's stopping you," Susan said. "You can borrow my car. Did you even get your permit?" He had not. When they finished eating, she suggested that they call it a night. Julie agreed; she wanted to get home to feed her cats.

Susan offered to take the three of them to her parents' house. She held within her the sense of a floor. Even misery only went so low. You still got to eat and rest, even when packing up the bungalow you'd dearly hoped to keep. Donnie and Lina wanted to sleep here one last night, so Walter stayed, too, on the boarder's water bed, which sloshed when he moved. The place didn't feel theirs anymore. It was as they'd found it: an old house with ugly furniture.

He woke to the sound of his sister and brother talking. They'd always talked between themselves, and when he came near, they stopped. They cleaned the garage, throwing out their mother's treasures. Hand-painted dishes. German stuffed animals. They were probably worth something, but Walter had no idea how to sell them.

A truck arrived to take the furniture to a storage facility. Donnie scoured the bathroom. Lina started sweeping at the front of the house, gathering fluff, bits of paper, and dirt. She swept her pile to the back door, caught it in the dustpan and carried it out to the alley, then stood under the peach tree, laden with unripe fruit. They wouldn't be here to eat the peaches this year.

Julie's apartment was small. Donnie's room had been a closet, his bed separated by a curtain from the washer-dryer. Lina burrowed in her room. Walter tried to talk to her about college, but she was snippy. She had an interview to be a salesclerk, she said. This was the sister for whom Berkeley hadn't been good enough.

"It's been our worst year," he said. "We lost our parent."

"We have two, technically." She never gave up.

"He's useless. You wanna talk about college at all?"

She did not.

He called Dr. Moss, who said that his mom was working in the garden. Another patient, the owner of a Japanese plant nursery, was teaching a small group, the doctor included, to train bonsai. He'd spoken to Walter's mom about the Midsummer Revel. "She told me she'd come and dance."

Walter jammed his hands in his pockets and went to the car, where Susan was waiting with two cups of coffee.

They had finals in a week. Walter and Cub had worked out regular study sessions with Melinda, and his average was up to 90.1. He slammed the car door and they took off. A feeling stayed with him all the way back up to school, a tenderness in the upper gut, as if he'd had the wind knocked out of him.

Three weeks later, Walter returned for Lina's graduation.

"Why are you here?" she asked. In a way, she was right. He

wouldn't have been standing on that tiered lawn if her life weren't a disaster. "Is this what it's come to? We're celebrating me getting a high school diploma?" But her flip dismissal—only a *high school* diploma—rested on assumptions about a future instilled by their mom, who'd once lived in an orphanage. No one had expected their mom to attend college.

A few teachers looked at Lina sadly. Mrs. Anjani stumped over with a cane. "We'll be in touch," she said.

After the ceremony, Lina drove Walter to the place. She had her license now. Amazing to be in the car with Lina driving. The air was hot, with a low wind. Their mom wasn't in the parlor of 301, though, or in the dormitory or the garden. They finally found her in a room off another building filled with flowers in buckets, the kitten at her ankles. She stared at stems on a metal-topped table with a concentration bordering on terror. She didn't turn when they burst in.

"Lina graduated today," Walter said.

"Mm-hmm," she said, still looking down.

It was so hot. Norwalk was unbearable in summer.

"She got her diploma. You have two graduates now."

"Mm-hmm." Her eyes fixed on the geometry of stems.

They finally found Shirley in 301. "Oh, when she does her flowers," she said, "she can't think of anything else." She led them to another small building, where a woman plinked at a typewriter, and showed them the arrangement their mother had made. The blossoms were papery, petals already falling, mixed in with woody branches. Walter wasn't sure it was pretty. He noticed blown dandelions. Had she forgotten that those were weeds?

Her life in the hospital seemed settled now. She'd gained weight and her hair and nails had grown.

Walking to the parking lot, Lina said, "Julie rails about the stigma. She says, *If your parent had cancer . . .* but, you know, sometimes I think this really *is* different. Cancer takes over cells but this, it infects love. She turns away from love." She started to cry. Walter looked at her young fingers on the steering wheel. He felt idiotic being unable to drive.

"I'd hoped," she said, gulping. "I wanted to . . ."

She needed him to understand that once, her dream had been attainable. He had to believe that, now when she had nothing. She looked over at him, almost shy.

Walter agreed that UC *wasn't* the Ivy League, okay, but college was still college. The real disparity was not between this college or that college, it was between learning and working. "Like your job. You scoop ice cream, talk to customers, sweep the floor, right?"

"And replace the cans. Count the cash. Deposit it at the bank."

"And not one of those skills has anything to do with your development. Or figuring out what you're naturally good at."

"I may not be naturally good at anything. I have an application in at the May Company," she said. "That's a real job. My arms are already uneven from scooping." This prompted another gale of tears.

Julie had looked into community college. Lina could transfer to UC in two years. "And UC is really good!" Walter felt sorry for Lina; she wasn't even beautiful anymore, her hair in a tight ponytail, her face puffy.

34.

While Walter stood laying out pages of the *Berkeley Poetry Review* on a Ping-Pong table, the editors, lounging on couches, spoke derisively about every submitted poem and decided to set up a display of old issues. Someone said there were boxes of them in the attic. They located the trapdoor but couldn't find a ladder. The next day, Walter asked Carlos, who lent him one from Buildings and Grounds. He climbed up and pulled on the overhead bulb from its chain. A whole room was up there. Not tall enough to stand in except at the center. One at a time, he carried down the boxes of back issues. The cottage had everything a person would need: a bathroom, stove, and refrigerator. Someone must clean the place, he thought, though it wasn't especially clean. But the attic lightbulb worked; it stood to reason that the Pelican Building, named for a defunct humor magazine, received at least sporadic maintenance.

———

"Is it the cat? Does the noise bother you?" Ken asked. Some nights, the cat scratched the bottom of his mattress. Walter hadn't thought Ken would care about him moving out.

"I like the cat. Moving won't change anything." But as Walter said that, he knew that their friendship had changed. Walter had loved their dorm room, with Ken a solid weight on the other side. They were the same amount of neat, the same amount of social. The soft huffing sounds of Ken's horn had soothed Walter. They'd never fought. Here in the co-op, the nights Melinda stayed over, they closed the door and Walter heard them laughing in the dark.

But Walter didn't like seeing the person he might have been if his mom were well.

He stacked his boxes on a borrowed dolly, pulling the thing downhill with Ken walking alongside, steadying the turntable on top. Ken declared the hidden attic a treehouse. Downstairs, he opened the oven. "We can throw dinner parties," he said.

"You can't tell anybody," Walter said. "Seriously."

After finals, the student editors adjourned for summer trips to Europe and internships at the *LA Times*. Walter had the cottage to himself. He and Carlos painted the attic walls, beamed ceilings, and floor planks with Buildings and Grounds standard white. Walter bought a sterilized mattress and box spring from the Salvation Army and had them halfway home before he realized they'd never fit through the trapdoor. He had to buy a futon that rolled up.

He loved the emptier Berkeley. A sorority sister in the 1950s had planted berry bushes, and now more grew than the young women could eat. Carrie and Susan, both staying this summer, thought they could find a waffle iron at the swap meet. Walter went along. Susan insisted they get there at six, when the dealers were unwrapping their wares.

She lifted a rusted two-piece cast-iron contraption that looked like a clamshell from a box on the ground. "Use it right over the burner," the seller said. They bought it for a dollar. Then Carrie spotted an electric waffle maker for two dollars. They bought that, too. The prices amazed Walter. Here was an alternate world where he could afford things. He found an hourglass coffeemaker, which Susan bargained down to three-fifty. She'd grown up flea marketing. Her parents had organized vacations around their perennial search for old things. She remembered a hideous town in the Luberon where she and her brothers goofed around while they talked to dealers. Some of those people visited Los Angeles, recognizing the cabinet or table they'd shipped halfway around the world. Susan's dad had started out as an architect.

"Why didn't you tell me that?"

"Well, he didn't have the best experience. He couldn't get a job; that's why he went into real estate. It's probably different now."

Not different enough. You needed another degree past your BA, and even then, newly credentialed architects weren't getting hired in California. "You might as well be a poet," Walter said. He'd continue pre-med classes, quarter after quarter, and keep up with design, too. Drawing his useless utopias.

"I'm thinking of library school," Carrie said.

It was relaxing to stroll through the aisles, with resurrected junk on both sides of them. Walter found a French library ladder that unfolded from a pole but the man wanted seventy-five dollars. "Probably worth it," Susan whispered.

"Not to me." He could knot heavy-gauge rope from the hardware store.

Back at the sorority house, girls in pajamas blinked in the kitchen as the waffles came out, purple with berries. "Real maple syrup," Susan said, pouring from a bottle.

Walter had never known there was such a thing as fake syrup.

Walter read on the futon under a salvaged lamp. He'd bought an army blanket his second time at the swap meet, when he'd run into Jan Tudor, with a large German shepherd, negotiating for an Eva Zeisel teapot. Painted, his attic looked like industrial space in Berlin she'd shown on slides.

So now he and his brother and sister had all moved while their mom remained in Norwalk. Maybe getting to know the doctor in their bonsai class. He hoped she was wearing decent clothes. He still sent money home, but there was no longer a clear cause. They'd already lost the bungalow. Lina and Donnie lived with Julie and he tried to help her out. He should have felt relieved, he supposed. But Lina no longer thanked him on their Sunday calls. She wanted to become a shopgirl now. Not long ago, she'd been certain to go to college. This kind of slip probably happened all the time.

"You can't never again go to a party," Susan said.

"For now, I can not go, can't I?"

"You have to have your life, too. You want her to have hers, even there. Didn't you tell me she was going to a dance?"

"My mom actually likes parties," he said.

He'd have to ask Dr. Moss if she'd gone to the dance. If she danced.

35.

Julie left every morning before it was light, in her white uniform. She'd asked Lina and Donnie if she could give Diane's colored uniforms to a young LVN, who didn't earn much. Lina hated being asked, as if her mother's chance to recover was being prematurely snatched away. She'd felt this when she'd passed her driving test and the lady behind the DMV counter asked whether she'd agree to be an organ donor. If she were lying on the road, they might grab her organs when she could still have been saved. With Lauren watching, though, Lina checked the box yes. It would be years before she realized that most morality worked this way. We do the right thing so others think well of us and, eventually, we feel grateful that we did. "I'll pay for new uniforms when she comes back," Donnie said. He was working on an arborist's crew this summer, cutting down a historic live oak infested with termites. That morning, he'd awakened thinking two points diagonal. No jump. The elephants, in Chinese chess, couldn't cross the river. The king was never allowed to leave the palace.

Julie carried the uniforms out, draped over her meaty arm.

As the morning drifted toward noon, Donnie felt a pollen-soft breeze and remembered they lived with Julie. Tonight she was making lasagna again because he liked it.

Lina worked double shifts at the ice-cream store, where the manager kept threatening to quit. The owners disappointed him daily. They'd promised more cans and a new freezer, but—he shook his head—no follow-through. "You care too much," Lina told him. He couldn't get it through his head that this was a stupid job.

A girl from the clay room had turned in Lina's application to the May Company. An anomaly at Pali, she hadn't even applied to college. Her father thought his daughters were pretty enough to get married and have babies.

Lina's mother had smuggled her into Pali to lift her out of exactly that mentality.

Lauren and Jess dropped by the store, but their solicitousness felt like pity and embarrassed her. She gave them free cones and was relieved when they left.

A manager called Lina for an interview to be a stock girl, and the girl from the clay room offered to come see her closet, to help her decide what to wear.

"You're looking at my closet," Lina said. "I have these jeans, overalls, and T-shirts."

The girl, Kim, offered to lend her a dress. Lina owned only one dress: the white one she'd worn to graduation. Lauren had said her mother bought two and that it was too late to return either. Lina hadn't believed her, but accepted it anyway. She wore it now to meet the manager. Kim said she'd have to spend her first month's salary on a wardrobe.

But it turned out that Lina could wear jeans in the stockroom. She was hired to make price tags with a machine, to affix them onto garments with a small gun that shot out plastic stems. It was mind-numbing work, only occasionally broken by the noise and color of salesgirls, not allowed to eat on the floor, bursting in for breaks. They looked costumed and of a higher rank than Nancy, Lina's supervisor, who sat most of the day, tightly packed into her gabardine slacks, checking inventory and complaining. Occasionally, she sent Lina onto the floor to count sweaters to mark against the stock list. Enormous chandeliers shed flecks of light.

When Lina tried to give Julie her first paycheck, Julie refused, saying, "You save that."

"But what about all you paid into Mom's account? Shouldn't we pay that back?"

"No need."

Lina began to wear makeup to work. Kim told her what to buy. The manager, a pert woman named Sue who wore jewel-colored clothes, always a tight top and matching voluminous pants, asked Lina if she would like a piece of advice. No one had ever asked Lina this before. They'd just given it.

"Sure," Lina said.

Sue led her to the mirror in the grimy bathroom. "When you do your top eyelashes with mascara, do the bottom ones, too."

Was that all? Lina had thought the advice would be about life. Sue brushed the hair off Lina's face. "Do you ever blow-dry?" She held Lina's hair back, twisted it, and walked her out that way, asking the others, "What do you think?"

"Definitely," the salesgirls said.

"She's got a perfectly proportioned face," Sue said.

The salesgirls' murmurs made this feel intrinsic, while other people's advantages (Lauren's house, her father) felt like accidents of fate, which could just as easily have fallen to Lina.

A very thin salesgirl, on high platforms, said, "Looks like you blow-dried."

Lina had. Quite a production.

"Do you want a tip? Bend over like this. Dry the back first. That's how you build volume. Then you have to decide about your ends. My boyfriend likes mine straight, so I iron. But if you get a round brush, you can flip it up or under. Depends."

"Well, how is it now?" Lina asked. "Up or under?" She thought she'd prefer the opposite.

"Kind of neither. That's the problem."

The thin salesgirl was named Marci, and Nancy said she lived with the drummer of the band Geronimo. There were no windows in the stockroom, only a loading dock, where trucks idled, beeping, as uniformed men carried in boxes.

Lina wanted to work on the floor. For that she had to up her look. Becoming a saleswoman would be like getting cast.

Julie hauled out the heavy, bulbous sewing machine from the closet. She could sew. She had a number of invisible talents that you wouldn't discover unless you lived with her. Lina had often imagined her mother's life changing on a dime; by luck, she would meet a man who would fall in love with her and move them into a mansion. Or hire her to run a modern clinic. Julie was overweight, with thinning hair. Lina tried to imagine something wonderful happening to her, but it was harder to picture the details. As they knelt on the carpet piecing out a Vogue skirt pattern, the phone rang. Mrs. Anjani, wanting to schedule an SAT practice session for Lina's applications next year. They'd met once already in the old typing room. Mrs. Anjani stood at the dusty podium drilling her. Since Lina had started at the May Company, though, she cared less about college. She promised to read the SAT prep manual just to get Mrs. Anjani off the phone.

Julie pinned pieces of brown-yellow tissue to the fabric. They hadn't had to shop for material. Julie had a trove, full bolts of cloth that impressed Marci when Lina brought in swatches to work.

Julie had been collecting lush fabrics for years, buying on sale and saving them. What life had she imagined? Caring about Julie was painful; Lina feared that the world would be unfair to her. Together, they picked a matte, dark green silk. "But don't you want it?" Lina asked. "Can we make a skirt for you, too?"

"Let's do yours first. I don't have to be anywhere I need new clothes for."

The owner limped into the stockroom and thumped a wall of boxes. "These should be on the floor!" he yelled. "People are buying pre-fall!" He wore thick cardigans and loafers too feminine for his pale, sockless feet. Nancy pushed her layered flyaway hair off her face and assumed a proper tone, with a hint of scold. "Allen, this is Lina, my new assistant. We'll get the stock on the floor today."

He looked Lina up and down, then turned to Nancy. "All of it?"

"Yes, Allen. All of it." She smiled at him. She stood then, and took a scissors to one of the boxes, tilting back on her spike heel. He swatted her butt, then left.

After he was out the door, she mimicked him, dragging her leg. A few days later, Lina heard yelling when she punched in. She and Nancy ventured out of the stockroom to see Allen limping fast to the elevator and Ceci, the Frenchwoman who did the windows, sticking out her tongue at him. She could get away with this. Her windows were known for their flair; he needed her. Ceci was the most elegant woman in the store. Nancy called Lina back in. She mimicked Allen's limp. Sue, sitting at the stockroom table with coffee, raised her eyebrows, and Lina understood: Nancy and Allen were lovers.

Marci walked in stiffly, as if on stilts, looking even thinner than usual. Her boyfriend hadn't come home last night, she said, opening her lunch box. Inside, she had a thermos of soup and a wrapped sandwich. Her face was bare and the structure of her bones apparent, a skull evident beneath the hair. She smiled a way that exposed more teeth. "If he doesn't come home tonight, that's it. Everyone I've lived with always wants to come back because I make a good dinner, a protein, a vegetable, and a starch. I don't do that for them, that's the way I eat. But once it's over, for me it's over."

Sue had a sly smile and announced: a television writer, a regular customer in menswear, spotted Lina kneeling by a sock drawer and asked Sue for her number. "Should I release it?"

"How old is he?" Nancy asked.

Middle thirties, Sue thought. "But young-looking, not too tall. Maybe five eight."

"Rich?" Marci asked.

"How would I know that? He buys a suit whenever he has to go to a wedding. Two already this summer." This caused excitement. Salesgirls stopped in to the stockroom and picked up Lina's hair, forming it into putative buns and uptops. He was a prince, they decided. And she, their creation. Lina didn't mind being dandled over.

Saturday, Sue rushed in. "Look. He's over there."

Lina couldn't tell if he was cute or not. His hair looked pressed down like a cap.

"Oh, go out with him once," Marci said. "He'll take you for a good meal."

Lina went home every night to Julie's apartment, which always stopped her the moment she walked in because it had a different smell. Not a bad smell, just different from the bungalow.

"Do you play tennis?" Sue asked. "Maybe he can teach you."

The salesgirls discussed what Lina would wear. Marci had white tennis shorts Lina could borrow. Sue advised a crisp white T-shirt, white socks and sneakers. But when the man left a message on Julie's machine, Lina didn't call him back. She couldn't say exactly why. She liked the idea of tennis.

When Donnie complained that Dino kept trying to teach him and Evan tennis, Lina told him he should learn. It would be another thing he'd know how to do in his life.

"Why don't you if you're so eager? He'd be happy to teach you."

Dino picked up Lina early on a Saturday morning. He had a racket for her and they were the first people at the park courts. He showed her the grip, putting his hands over hers. He dragged a machine to the other side of the court and then jogged back and stood immediately behind, his arms around hers, and they pivoted and swung the racket, hitting together. It felt good to be enclosed and then, when her arms caught the rhythm and could time the swing to meet the ball, a thrill ran up her shoulder. By the end of an hour, he pushed the machine into a corner and he tapped balls over the net to her. A good hit made a sound she felt in her chest.

He told her about Evan's mother grilling him and his mentor in the math department and chess downtown, but then abruptly stopped, saying, "Enough about me." He asked when she'd started working at the store. Why had she quit the ice-cream place? Did she miss it? What did she want to do with her life?

Lina felt like an ant under a spotlight. She didn't *know* what she wanted to do with her life. She mentioned Walter at Berkeley, as if to prove that, normally, people in her family went to college.

At Nate 'n Al's, he urged her to order both the scrambled eggs and the blintzes. He watched her eat as if she were a young animal. He paid for their meal in cash, extracting from his pocket a wad of one-dollar bills held with a rubber band.

Kim hurried into the stockroom to say that Mrs. Anjani was waiting for Lina near Costume Jewelry. The teacher seemed incongruous, blinking in the bright pavilion, wearing a floor-length muumuu. She looked Lina up and down with an expression curious and severe. Lina was wearing mascara, eye pencil, and lipstick. But Mrs. Anjani only said that she'd received a letter from her old friend, the Barnard alumna, who had taken up Lina's cause. Lina had been moved to the top of the wait list. All it would take now, Mrs. Anjani said, was for one girl to get knocked up or sick or to decide she was afraid of the big, bad city. Lina felt grateful for this glimpse of an alternate future, but also conscious of Sue watching her from across the floor.

"Thank you," she said. "I better get back."

Mrs. Anjani progressed toward the revolving door, a dark, slow-moving figure. Had she seen that Lina was ashamed of her?

Book 3

*A Building
Somewhere in California*

36.

Nights in the Pelican Building could turn against Walter if the book he was reading didn't enclose him. Once, during a storm, he missed his mom. The university phone wouldn't put through long distance, so he pulled on a windbreaker and sprinted to the student union, then stood, wet through, in a smoky booth for forty minutes (ten dollars in change) until the nurse said she wouldn't come to talk.

For $175, Walter purchased a device called a blue box from guys who sold them out of a car trunk. The box mimicked tones Bell used that allowed him to make long-distance calls. Bell billed companies somewhere and Walter tried to believe that those charges were the equivalent of pennies. "Less than the multinationals owe the people," the guy he bought it from had said.

He checked in with Dr. Moss every week. They were more than halfway through his mother's year of recovery.

"She's starting to laugh again," the doctor said.

One Sunday morning, Walter woke with a racing pulse and heard banging. He'd knotted his rope and could slide down like a fireman, but if this was Buildings and Grounds, he'd better lie low. After he heard footsteps leaving, he found a waffle maker outside his door.

How did they know he lived here! Furious, he confronted Carrie and Susan. They cascaded into laughter. They'd gotten it out of Melinda.

"It isn't funny."

Melinda and Ken arrived unexpectedly that night, with full bags. Melinda lifted a frying pan from her backpack. He'd move soon, she said, when the editors returned, so they decided to have a dinner party.

Walter wasn't so sure he'd move. "Why here? The co-op kitchen is bigger."

"We thought of that or the Delta house, but . . ." Ken shrugged. "Other people."

"Nice to have privacy," Melinda said, "for a change."

Ken held open a bag of tomatoes to smell. In a mason jar, he'd mixed rosemary and roses. Susan burst in with a large straw bag.

"This feels so adult," Melinda said. "Like we really live here, not just because we're students."

Ken washed carrots under the faucet.

"What are we eating?" Walter asked.

"Pasta." Ken took a tomato from Melinda and showed her how to slice it. Ken's hair was long, his flannel shirtsleeves rolled up. He had muscles now and knew how to cook.

Carrie dashed in, wearing a button-down shirt with no bra, handing him a bottle of wine.

Susan took a cloth out of her bag. "Just a sheet," she said, shaking it over the Ping-Pong table. She dug out candles from that bag, too.

"Are you declaring a bio major?" Melinda asked.

"Architecture," Walter said.

"That's always been your love," Ken said.

Walter didn't want to be highfalutin. For him, for Ken, too, and Rory and Cub, a pulse urged them to think: How will you support a family? "I'm not dropping biochem. So don't assume you're the last one standing," he told Melinda. He asked Susan and Carrie how they liked Berkeley summers.

"I had no choice," Carrie said. "My mom sold our house, but this one"—she aimed a thumb at Susan—"could be home in her parents' mansion."

"Not a mansion," Susan said.

"But isn't the architect famous?"

"Cliff May. My parents sell real estate, so we moved nine times by high school. They're moving again." Her father, a realtor all these years, had finally designed a house for them. "He says he loves residential architecture." She looked at Walter. "I know that's not what you want to do."

In class, he'd seen exotic-wood dressing rooms, master baths perched like tree houses. She was right; he didn't want to build rich people better houses. "But I want to *live* in a nice house."

"Most people do," Carrie said. "I do."

"Where'd you put your stereo?" Ken asked. Walter pointed upstairs.

"There are different kinds of residential architecture," Susan said. "Like Eichler's ranch houses. Even public housing."

"I don't see why architecture—even for rich people—can't be meaningful," Carrie said. "Most art before the twentieth century *was* for rich people. Even . . . can't a pretty dress be art?"

"Seems more like a product," Walter said.

"Why? Does it really matter if someone buys something to wear or to put on a wall?"

"A painting lasts longer," Melinda said.

"A house lasts longer than that," Susan said. "Think of ruins. There're a lot more foundations of dwellings than there are cave paintings."

"Still not forever," Walter said. "But a building can serve a purpose."

"A pretty house or a beautiful dress can give a hurl of joy!" Carrie said. "Somebody feels lucky. Happy."

Walter thought about Carrie the way he thought about art-for-art's-sake buildings. Her beauty altered his breath and seemed to elevate him, but he couldn't figure out how he could contribute. "I'd like to build a hospital that's useful for a time. After that, fine, the wrecking ball."

"Sometimes I think you're allergic to fun," Carrie said.

That stung. He was having fun right now! He wasn't wild enough for her. When she was slipping into restaurants in scant clothes, he walked around Berkeley in the dark. Carefree, the politician had called college students. Walter had cares, but he'd also had days at Ken's house; he'd gone swimming in a pond at dawn with a girl he almost loved. His first day in the dorm, the glimpse of gold under the cloth draped over Ken's French horn. He wouldn't have swapped his own youth.

"I want more summer," Ken said. "Let's put on something." They climbed upstairs to go through Walter's albums. They put on *Catch a Fire*, *Abbey Road* waiting to drop when the B side finished.

That night, late, Walter wrote *Call Lina* on his list. Julie said his sister liked being a shopgirl.

The season for the sweetest berries ended (mulberries, from a tree on the wide front lawn), but small, harder blackberries still grew in the sorority yard. Susan continued waffle Sundays. There, on the terrace, overlooking the lawn where a circle of young women played Duck Duck Goose, Walter bit down on a seed and a line of shock ran up to his ear.

Susan drove him to the student health services, where he stood holding the side of his face. The resident told him he had to have his wisdom teeth out and wrote down the number of an oral surgeon. The cost for the procedure was $180. A receptionist asked, "Do you qualify for public assistance? He takes it." She even told him where to apply.

Walter qualified for food stamps, too. He made an appointment for the extraction.

The oral surgeon anesthetized him with nitrous oxide and told him afterwards that he'd clawed the air. Cotton wads jammed his mouth; the surgeon gave him a prescription for Tylenol with codeine.

"You look like a chipmunk," Susan said. His face had doubled.

They had to wait in the pharmacy. A television mounted on a wall showed the president, flanked by a red-and-white-striped flag on one side and a blue one on the other, reading from a sheaf of papers. Walter's cheeks throbbed. He's really doing it, someone said, behind the counter. "America needs a full-time president," the even voice came from the TV. "A full-time Congress." If the president weren't resigning, would the pharmacist work faster? Walter also wondered whether, if he'd been a paying patient, the surgeon would have given him pills to tide him over before this roar of pain.

A night nurse coaxed his mom to the phone. To his surprise, her voice belled out. A long *Hi*.

"You sound good. Are you getting better, do you think?"

"Well, ye-es," she said, as if being tested.

"Do you think you'll be able to go home soon?"

"Not right away. I've started to do flowers, you know."

"I saw your flowers, remember? When I was there for Lina's graduation."

"Mm-hmm."

Once Walter's face returned to normal, he tried to buy groceries with the food stamps. The checkout girl looked at him. He would turn twenty-one this year; a grown man, on food stamps. He thought of Carrie and felt ashamed.

"Here," he said, handing the booklet of stamps back to her with cash. "I don't need these. Could you give them to someone who does?"

Someone braver. Someone more desperate. Maybe those were the same thing.

37.

Ceci, the French window dresser, passed out invitations to her house in Malibu. "Come swim," she said. "BB will bar-b-que."

"That's her husband," Nancy explained. "BB and CC. He's some kind of businessman." Most of the husbands were businessmen. That was what you were supposed to want, Lina gathered, not a drummer. They all still liked the idea of the TV writer, who hadn't come back to the store.

Lina hoped to be like Ceci when she was in her thirties. Ceci was so consistently elegant it seemed effortless, like a bird's coloring. But the party was on a Sunday. Julie said to just skip a week of the hospital. Donnie promised to wash their mom's clothes, and Lina drove Kim to Malibu in her mother's old car. The only other guest they knew was Nancy, who, a beer in hand, had on the same clothes she wore to work every day. Everyone was older than Kim and Lina. Coming was a mistake. Lina wished she were at the hospital with her mother. Here, outside, Ceci didn't pout the way she did in the store. With BB, who stood at the grill, she was deferential.

"Aren't you going to swim?" she asked the girls.

Nancy refused to take off her clothes. Lina felt reluctant, too, but she followed Kim on the path to the ocean and waded in. She'd learned to swim years ago at the YWCA, but that water had been flat, restricted to lanes. The sand under her feet felt unstable and she had to pay attention and jump when the big waves came. Kim was an even, pretty swimmer in the hectic water. She'll make a good mother, Lina thought. Just then, a big wave pushed over both their heads. Lina gulped and flailed, and it was exhilarating to bob up again. The temperature of the water seemed the same inside of her and out. They each stood in the shallow waves, their hands to the side, rowing, the water knocking their legs out from under them, so they had to balance again on the ridged sand. Her own thighs were tight, her belly shallow, like a hammock slung between bones. She looked over at Kim as they trudged out. The sun felt good as the salt dried on Lina's skin. She'd wanted one life, but she could glimpse another here, far away, soft and forgotten and gentle. She felt Californian, looking at the small heads dotting the ocean, and was happy.

When they high-stepped out, BB was serving hot dogs on paper plates. Sue arrived, trailing miniature children. For the first time, Lina noticed a gap between Sue's front teeth. That was something, Lina instinctively knew, Sue would have wanted to have fixed. Ceci's house was narrow and white, her needlepointed pillows the only color.

Lina and Kim sat on either side of Nancy and asked her questions about the store. How long since she'd started? (Can you believe five years?) Had Allen always been the owner? (His uncle founded it.) Ceci limped over, impersonating him. "I am telling you. For*get* him." Ceci took Lina's leg onto her lap and wove a bracelet onto her ankle, then held up the foot. "Look at you, you're small but the perfect shape." She turned to Nancy. "Will you be mad if I steal her mornings? I need an assistant for the new season windows."

"As long as you give her back for inventory." Nancy looked at Lina. "She's been dying to get onto the floor."

Lina felt pleased, also guilty and disloyal.

Ceci scooped strawberry ice cream into cones. They ate outside, their skin eased by the sun and salt and breeze, the frozen strawberries rough on their tongues. Just then, Marci arrived in a T-shirt that didn't reach the top of her jeans. A man with a ratty ponytail followed, his hand on the skin of her back. The drummer.

On the way home, Kim told Lina she'd met a man at the store. She named a famous actor, in his fifties. Her father worried that he'd pressure her for sex before marriage. So far, he'd been respectful. But last week, when they were kissing, lying down in front of the fire, she wanted more, too. "What about your guy?" she asked.

"Dino? We just play tennis."

Lina went to Norwalk all the other Sundays that summer, leaving earlier because the old car's air conditioner gave out only thin ribbons of cool. She, Donnie, and Julie stayed for lunch, not dinner, now and left her mother stroking the cat. Before, they'd tucked her into bed.

Lina saw Isabel there one more time. She'd worked on a gubernatorial campaign in the Central Valley and then gone on a bike trip with her cousins in British Columbia. She came home a few days before returning to college. Her dad looked old, she told Lina. She found him staring at tiny wires, trying to train a bonsai.

Lina's mother was in that class, too. Lina had met the teacher's daughters. They brought their father full meals in stackable boxes and told Lina they blamed the government for his breakdown. A lot of people here blamed the government, but their father had been in an internment camp when he was a child. His mother had died there.

Isabel took Lina to see her artwork, in the art therapy building. She did portrait photography. Lina recognized Shirley and the cook from 301 and Artie, the guy who delivered the bread. Isabel's grandparents, who'd both been psychiatrists, too. They'd run a famous asylum, a nicer one than here, where Woody Guthrie was a patient and Bob Dylan visited him once.

"Did you go to the asylum for Thanksgiving?" Lina asked.

"We stayed in their apartment. Their asylum had different rooms for different classes of people, like on an ocean liner. Some rooms had big marble bathrooms. Woody Guthrie probably had one of those."

"My mom used to work in hospitals, and those rooms were identical."

Isabel never seemed interested in Lina's mother, though. The only thing she ever asked about was the department store. She wanted to know if Lina would get discounts.

"Are you going to be a psychiatrist, too?" Lina asked.

"No. I want to live in a city. Maybe do something in design. Fashion. You're going to apply to college for next year, right?" Lina thought about Mrs. Anjani's friend, the Barnard alumna.

When Lina returned with fresh laundry to the ward, she found her mother strewn across her bed, snoring extravagantly, the kitten by her feet.

Every time the phone rang in Julie's apartment, Lina froze wherever she was, imagining something magical; but it was never Mrs. Anjani. Apparently none of the accepted young women got pregnant or sick or afraid of the city. Jess and Lauren flew east for freshman orientation. It was painful to see them leave without her, but after, LA seemed easier with everyone finally gone.

The salesgirls stuttered on their heels into the stockroom at lunchtime and collapsed around the table. "What happened to blow-drying?" Marci asked.

Lina looked to Nancy for help. "Sue said she liked my hair back."

"But there are ponytails and ponytails." Marci demonstrated bending down to gather the hair concentrically. All her techniques involved bending over.

Almost every day, one of the salesgirls had a suggestion for Lina's appearance. She was a project. Only Ceci frowned. "Don't go overboard." The morning Lina wore her new silk skirt, Sue lifted the hem and complimented Julie's even stitches, but Marci said, "You need a platform with that."

Sue pushed a rack of suits into the stockroom to be marked down. "Try one," she said. Lina wouldn't. If she put one on, she would want it. But Sue stood waiting, holding the jacket open for her.

Dino slouched by the loading dock to meet her after she punched out. Lina had brought her tennis shoes in a grocery-store bag. After an hour of rallying, he said, "I won some money playing street chess downtown. Wanna get some food?"

As they stood eating messy tacos over napkins, he showed her a course catalogue for Santa Monica College, some of the classes circled. "You said you like art stuff."

Visual Talent Exploration: Excavate your unconscious and use creativity to make a living. The teacher's name was Feather Brown. Lina read the description aloud, as a joke, then decided to try the class. Maybe she could learn something for store windows.

The course was on Tuesday nights. She didn't tell anybody. The people in the class were all adults but different than the adults she knew. Every one of them, the first night, said he or she wanted their life to change. The teacher began the class with a five-minute meditation. They closed their eyes and concentrated on their breath or ambient sounds in the room, observing where their minds went, only to fasten them back on the peg of regular breathing.

Lina's mornings with Ceci started at dawn, when the Mustang's horn tooted in front of Julie's apartment. Lina ran out, passing the already-set table. Julie laid out a whole breakfast each morning: grapefruits cut around the sections, toast, and eggs. Lina missed most days. Ceci drove fast on the empty streets to the flower mart downtown, where they strolled through aisles of watery blossoms. They filled Ceci's trunk. One day, Ceci was running late and, at the flower mart building's entrance, said, "You go that way, I'll go here. Meet back in twenty."

"What should I get?" Lina asked.

"Surprise me."

Lina chose branches of eucalyptus with the buttons attached, twigs with acorns, and stalks of milkweed pods. Ceci looked perplexed. Then she grinned her small-toothed grin. "You have a good eye, *ma étudiante.*"

They walked through the May Company's top floor before opening time, picking clothes to display. When Ceci was half done with a window, a pile of jackets heaped on a chair, she sometimes picked up her needlepoint and stood stitching as she looked at her display. By now, Lina knew that she painted the patterns on the netting herself. She liked rich colors, deep blues, purple, magenta, dark orange.

Lina and Dino played tennis Saturday mornings. Lina enjoyed the feeling of improvement. His hands over her grip, he showed her how to tilt the racket for spin. She noticed stalks with shiny dark pods to the side of the courts. "Could I cut some of those, you think?"

Dino extracted his Swiss Army knife.

Lina began to collect things for windows in the corner of her room, by the sewing machine. She had a paper wasps' nest, pussy willows, dry beach grass, cocoons, a fallen bird's nest, and two tree stumps from Donnie's summer job.

Dino's apartment was smaller than Julie's but emptier. One wall had floor-to-ceiling casement windows that opened to wild rosemary on a hill. It was a calm place. Dino lay on his side, on the floor.

Did Feather Brown give homework? he asked. (Yes, this week they had to seek out paradox, odd combinations of things created and found.) Was she close to any of her high school friends? (She was, kind of. She'd received two letters from Lauren that she still hadn't answered. It was hard to write what she was doing.) Was there a book she loved? He asked too many questions! She was a slow reader. Julie always had a book. What about college? he asked finally, hitting a sore spot. You going to apply again?

Lina looked around the room, considering the corners.

"How much rent do you have to pay here?" she finally asked.

Dino explained it was student housing. He could never afford a place like this if UCLA didn't own the building. But even the subsidized rent sounded like a lot.

Ceci squatted in the store window, with birch branches Dino and Lina had scavenged and two garbage bags full of red and brown dry leaves they'd collected from UCLA's sculpture garden. Lina carried an armful of furs down from a refrigerated room in Couture. Shearling jackets, a fox cape, rabbit fur hats, and a mink coat in a cloth bag. Fun fur, Sue called it. Allen wanted a window of winter clothes. Outside, people walked by in flip-flops. By noon, the temperature in the Los Angeles Basin would rise to the eighties. Caltech climatologists would record October as the hottest month of 1974. No one was going to buy fur. "Even fun fur," Ceci said. Ceci wanted the branches to drape from the ceiling, so Lina was standing at the top of a ladder with the industrial stapler when Sue came in to say there was someone on the floor to see her.

Lina's head bumped the chandelier. She backed down the ladder, her heart tapping her spine. If it was Mrs. Anjani to offer her a place, she'd have to leave all this.

But it was only Isabel, wearing clothes from those ancient suitcases. They were all wrong; Lina saw that now.

They talked in unfinished phrases, observed by Sue, who raised an eyebrow, prompting Lina to return to the vitrine, where *A pile of fur!* was written in red cursive on the window glass and birds' nests were scattered on the floor, waiting to be placed in birch branches, now upended to look like trees.

On the first floor, Kim sprayed Lina with a different perfume every day. Today, Lina stopped. What is this? she asked. L'Air du Temps, Kim said. Lina stood still a moment. It was as if she'd stepped back in time, to the bungalow. Her mother.

———

One night in November, Nancy found Lina near closing time to say that two men were asking for her at the loading dock. The security guard sounded suspicious, so Nancy went along.

"We own the ice-cream store. We got a call this afternoon from one of the girls. The door was locked when she came to work. So we drove up from the Valley and found this." He handed her a note. *No new flavors, no cans, no support. Maybe Hawaii will be better. . . .*

So he'd finally gotten out. Good for him. Lina hoped Hawaii would be better.

"We're wondering if you'd take over."

"What exactly are you offering her?" Nancy asked.

Even before she heard the terms, Lina knew she wouldn't go back to the smell of old ice cream in her hair.

"Do you want to have sex with me?" she asked Dino.

"Have you ever had sex?"

"Fifth Amendment," she said.

"You're not ready yet. Turn over. Let me rub your back."

He was good at that. "How do you know I'm not ready?"

"You're not in love with me, I don't think."

"Is that a prerequisite?"

"Your first time should be . . . I guess sweet, at least." Now he was chopping, which she didn't like.

"Down," she said. From there, he knew where to press.

Lina was helping Ceci arrange a handbag display. The hem of her pants swished on the floor. Sue had advised this length. She liked all skirts and trousers to brush the floor. By now, Lina owned a pair of platforms.

Ceci pointed out the paper wasp hive Lina had foraged for the display and Allen paid her a quick compliment, head down, then limped away. Lina felt a thrill run up her nerves; *I can succeed here.*

Ceci was tying a scarf on the strap of a bag when Lina glimpsed Mrs. Anjani outside the ornate front doors, a hand on her dark sunglasses. A flutter of hope rose up and up in her chest. But it was November. Wasn't it already too late?

"There's a slot," Mrs. Anjani said. Her friend had received the call. A girl scheduled to return from Taiwan after midterm break had not shown up.

They could hear as early as next week.

The floor, still and calm, looked like a painting, salesgirls neatening their stations, Ceci with her hands on her hips, surveying. Lina would have to leave. Ceci had put her up for a raise. Sue was holding a jacket for her until the after-Christmas sale.

She would miss it all. When she walked in the door of the apartment, Donnie had his head down in his arms while Julie was going on about his homework.

Julie couldn't make him study. Lina did, late at night, at the kitchen table, where they ate ice cream with their books open. But who would coax him when she was at Barnard?

The week passed and then the next. Mrs. Anjani said if she didn't hear by the end of the third week, she would call.

Julie's phone rang at six in the morning. Mrs. Anjani had just gotten off with New York. She was furious, she said, and so was her friend, the alumna. The girl from Taiwan had withdrawn all right, but another girl beneath Lina had leapfrogged over and taken the spot. Her grandfather had given money for an arts center. He'd apparently written another check, just last week.

Okay, Lina thought. She would buy that fucking jacket.

"So. I'll come over on Sunday with the Santa Monica College course catalogue."

Lina blushed. Mrs. Anjani didn't know she was already attending.

Her life felt random now. She'd gotten off the track, and now she was lost. Lina asked the salesgirls how much they paid for rent. None of them had gone to college, either. Probably most people in the world went from one thing to the next. From an ice-cream store to a stockroom, eventually to another job. School hadn't worked out; maybe she'd save for an apartment. For herself and Donnie. But then, a thought nagged: What about Julie?

She filled her pockets with scraps of paper covered with numbers.

38.

Tuition at Berkeley in 1974 was $212.50 a quarter, a price that did not then seem remarkable. Walter was by now accustomed to the waiver that had once made him feel lucky. Professors passed out enrollment cards larger than their hands. Walter filed his in the basement of Sproul Hall, below the steps where Mario Savio, founder of the Free Speech Movement, had a decade earlier warned against being processed by the university machine.

The *Berkeley Poetry Review* editors resumed their Wednesday-night meetings, leaving ashes in cups and a hole in the arm of the sofa. The only one who knew that Walter lived in the attic was Carrie. She sometimes looked at him with pity.

Em Ball told Walter that a model of the campus would be delivered to her conference room. Wealthy alumni would be paraded in to see where the university could erect new buildings with their names on them. Names on existing halls could be sandblasted off and re-carved, for the right amount of money.

"Rich pigs," Walter said, quoting Patty Hearst. For her release, the SLA was demanding seventy dollars' worth of groceries for every person on welfare in California. As someone who'd recently received food stamps, Walter thought there had to be a less humiliating way to help.

"Development needs someone to serve tea and cookies," Mrs. Ball said. "I told them we should hire a design student."

"I'd rather make the model," Walter said.

"May I say you'll do tea? Different presidents want different things. This one wants to build."

Walter thought she was talking about Gerald Ford, but she meant the university president. Walter wouldn't mind meeting rich people. Maybe one of them could teach him how to make a million dollars. *He* could be rich and not a pig. He'd never get rich from architecture, that was for sure.

When the model arrived, Walter and Mrs. Ball recognized the Campanile and Sproul Hall, but otherwise it didn't look like

Berkeley. The colors of buildings were off. Pillars and steps were missing. There were only two kinds of trees, triangular and those with foliage the shape of a child-drawn cloud.

Field Studies had made drawings of Berkeley's trees, Ken told Walter. They'd catalogued over two hundred species, twenty-two varieties of pine and twenty-one of oak. The next day, Em Ball showed Walter a catalogue of small wooden trees you could custom order, made by a father and son in Alabama, for toy train collectors.

Walter spent the weekend trooping through campus holding a color chart up to buildings. He repainted the model and glued in three tiers of stairs to Sproul. Nights, he still took tickets at the film archive. In a group streaming out of *The Umbrellas of Cherbourg,* he spotted Cathy and her Phoenician roommate with the dog. Cathy looked away, as if she were afraid of him now.

For the first potential donor meeting Em Ball wore what Walter recognized as her best suit, a dark wool with large buttons. Walter knew her outfits by now; she never wore the same one twice in a week. How did she keep track? The custom-ordered trees from Alabama arrived, but the colors were off. "Let's stick them on anyway," Em said. "We can paint later."

Walter yanked at one of the triangular trees. It wouldn't loosen. Em left and returned with a serrated knife. They managed to pry off two. This became hilarious.

You got to know people a different way working with them.

The young woman from Development, Sarah Voss, had a head shaped like a melon. Except for being on that sloping curve, her features were pretty. A rich man, who wore cowboy boots, unrolled a large aerial photograph of a property on top of their model, which he treated as an encumbrance. What you're seeing, he told them, was the largest privately owned lake in California. Privately owned by him. He wanted forestry professors to survey his soil. He needed depth charts and microbial analysis. "They can bring along their students," he said.

However outlandish the man's proposal, Sarah Voss nodded, Walter noticed, as if in agreement, and then tried to redirect the conversation. This didn't seem to be working. After a half hour, the man rolled up his picture, slapped his hands on the table, and said, "Call me when you round up my soil scientists!"

Walter threw out the untouched tea and returned the uneaten cookies to their box, then ran outside, where design students lounged on concrete furniture. One girl's Fiat was collecting parking tickets on University Avenue. She planned to do interiors. Most of the girls did. A large picture of the politician he'd met at his mom's hospital, who was now running for governor, was fixed above a table. Walter bought a button for a buck. Two years in, he understood what Jan Tudor had said about Ball State. The only institutions discussed in design classes were museums or universities. At Berkeley, Yale, or SCI-Arc, beauty didn't need to be useful. At least not useful for the unfortunate.

A short banker and his tall wife, who parted her hair in the middle, had the idea of building a meditation grove. Their daughter had been interested in Buddhism, the woman said. Walter noticed the past tense. "Outside. A place kids could sit still," the man said. "Wouldn't be expensive."

Sarah Voss's eyebrows told Walter that she didn't want to go in that direction, but she said that a meditation grove was a wonderful notion. Ideally, it could be in the courtyard of a new building. Of course, she went on, that would be up to the building's sponsor.

Em Ball told Walter afterwards that the couple's daughter was a divinity student who'd jumped out of the Campanile three years ago. Their other daughter attended a small Catholic college, and the two institutions were vying for their wealth.

Everyone was trying to pry money out of somebody else's hand, and the person holding on made it his life's business to clutch.

"I don't know why you're paying me," he told Em Ball. "No one will donate a building. They don't even look at the model!"

"You work on the poetry magazine, don't you?"

"I do layout."

"That building was a gift. A contentious one." Later she slapped a file on his table. "For your amusement. I have to run to the beauty parlor. Lock up when you leave."

The next day, the curls of her permanent were more tightly coiled. "Your permanent looks more permanent," he said.

Walter read the file during a Truffaut film. *A building for the undergraduate humor magazine ("The Pelican") is at the bottom of everyone's priority list,* a dean had written in 1954. *But President Sproul believes that in order to secure a large unrestricted bequest in Anthony's will, he must be humored.*

A pun, Walter registered. Then *President Sproul.* So the president got his name on a building. Earle Anthony became rich selling Packards. He was the first businessman to introduce neon signs in the States, on his Packard showrooms. He invented what we now call a filling station. But the money he gave Berkeley was strictly stipulated to pay for a cottage to house the humor magazine with a statue of a pelican in front of it. There it was again. The one with money and others trying to pry open his fingers. Noting that Anthony had only one son, they'd decided to indulge his whim. Earle Anthony had been a founder of the *Pelican* magazine when he was an undergraduate in 1903. Then, the word *pelican* was slang for an ugly female, Walter read, which was how the founding editors of the magazine characterized the then-new Berkeley coeds. Seventy years later, the *Pelican* magazine was defunct and its building housed the *Berkeley Poetry Review,* a poetry journal with a female editor.

"Anthony had insisted Maybeck be the architect," Em Ball said. "Maybeck designed his Packard showroom and also a medieval Renaissance castle in Los Feliz, where he lived."

"A medieval Renaissance castle?"

"Architects have never had an easy time making a living."

"I'm losing my respect for Maybeck."

"He was too old anyway. He no longer even had an office. A faculty architect drew the plans. For the dedication, Anthony wanted dance girls and a flock of pelicans. Bob Sproul sent a dean to Palm Springs to talk him down to one live pelican."

Two young guys told Sarah Voss to start a programming school and called the dean of engineering "an imbecile." A portly man who'd bought a seersucker suit from the Princeton Shop stopped by on his way to the Bohemian Grove, carrying *Time* magazine, with Walter's politician on the cover. Walter started his own private ranking of the millionaires. It felt like shopping for fathers. He hadn't found one yet that he much liked.

Carrie sometimes lingered in the Pelican Building after meetings. Once she wore a sweater that showed her pronounced collarbone and Walter thought of her the next dozen nights. He still hoped they'd eventually marry, but that seemed less possible than before. She and Susan invited him to a sorority party. But normal social conversation felt off to him, slow. He liked to be at jobs where he was being paid. By November, the other editors figured out that he lived in the attic and they treated the cottage with more care, the way they would somebody else's parents' house.

He still got up before dawn. He liked those hours alone. Every Monday, he made coffee and left a message for his mom's doctor. Today, Dr. Moss answered himself.

His mom did go to the summer dance, he said. And she danced. "She didn't stay long, if I remember. She can't make the winterfest because she's level one. She's still attending bonsai class. It's down to the two of us and the teacher."

"What is level one?" Walter asked.

"If you earn four fouls in a twenty-four-hour period, you're put on level one."

"How did she get a foul?"

"You get a foul for abusing staff or another patient. Hitting, biting, spitting. I think your mother hit a nurse. She got agitated."

"My mom hit Shirley?"

"Not Shirley. There's one nurse she doesn't like. But I talked to Diane. I told her she could come to the party after this one. I asked her to save me a dance."

"You dance?"

"Our parties are the only time I dance. I'm not sure what happened with Diane. She has the nurses she likes and some she doesn't."

"Does she have friends?"

"There's one woman she pals around with. Now that I think of it, I don't see her talking to Julie as much anymore. We show movies in James Hall, but your mother doesn't go. She's a bit of a loner."

For no reason, Walter told the doctor that he'd had his wisdom teeth out.

"Ouch." The doctor urged Walter to see his friends. "Don't be afraid of a party."

Walter remembered the costume party Susan and Carrie had attended, dressed as wrens. He thought he could live without that. "But you don't go yourself, except in the hospital, you said." Outside the Pelican Building window, the creek poured over rocks.

"You're young. I chose my world a long time ago. You're still finding yours."

His world. Some design students stayed late at night in Wurster, drawing and arguing about city plans. Walter hoped his mom was the doctor's favorite patient. He wished she hadn't hit a nurse. What getting well would mean, now, was hard to know. She could still get better. She would have to find a new place to live and start everything over. He pressed his hands to his temples. Sometimes he couldn't find the happy ending, even in his own imagination.

The day the politician who'd worn a pilled sweater at Christmas won the election to become California's governor, Walter got back his biochem midterm with a C. He didn't go home for Thanksgiving. Instead, he studied all day, and in the evening, took tickets for *It's a Wonderful Life*. Em Ball came with her husband.

He'd stopped living like other people. He burrowed like Ken and Melinda's cat, which never came out in daylight. He walked around the empty campus at night. He hadn't lost respect for the university; his reverence only increased with his disappointment in himself. He called his sister and brother from the Pelican phone. Lina sounded like a regular shopgirl, thinking about her next pair of shoes. "That's normal for her age," Julie said. Walter couldn't get Lina to talk about college applications for next year, and they were due right after Christmas.

"I could care less," she said.

39.

The next millionaire wore what Walter had learned to recognize as a bad suit. Walter asked where he was from, just to say something.

"Marin woods." He looked at Walter. "Where are you from?"

"Who, me?" Walter's fingers opened on his chest. "I'm just a work-study student. From LA."

"I don't know what I'm doing here," the man said. "I'm not going to donate a building. The kid who walked me over said it wouldn't help my daughter get in, no matter what I gave. State school, he said. Regulations. My daughter's not sophisticated like some kids. She's grown up with animals in nature. I think a lot about her and my wife, after I'm gone."

"Do you have just one child?"

"Just the one. I married late. She's a junior in high school. And she's been through a lot—her mom suffers from depression."

Em Ball walked in and Walter got up to get the tea and coffee. When he returned, the man was touching a tiny building on the model. He was Walter's favorite millionaire so far. The afternoon opened in the panoramic window: gray clouds over the hills with patches of blue and gold showing through.

When the man left, Walter followed him to the elevator and asked, "How did you make your money?"

There was a pause. Nobody, Walter supposed, likes you to mention their wealth.

"Well," the man finally said. "That's a long story."

"Maybe I shouldn't have asked."

"No, no. I was a little taken aback. Heck, I suppose I wanted something from them, too. Hoping to give my daughter a leg up."

"It's just, can you think of a way I could make a million dollars?" Walter asked.

Now the man laughed. He pulled a wallet from his trouser pocket and extracted a card. "Come to my office. I'll take you to breakfast."

As the elevator doors started to close, Walter jumped in.

"You must be good at school. To have gotten in here."

"I'm okay. I make money selling bikes."

"Tell you what. For success in business . . . you don't have to be a genius."

A valve opened inside Walter. He held on to those seven words.

But between the December afternoon he took Lawrence Wimmer's card and the morning he climbed the steps to his office building a few weeks later, the world changed.

Walter had to go to LA for a crisis with his mom, just when she was supposed to be nearly well. The doctor had never given them an exact date for her recovery, but Julie and Walter both thought it would take a year, from around last Christmas. Walter had been counting down the months. The night he got the call from Julie (a problem, your ma, you better come), Walter jumped on a bus. He didn't tell his friends. His family never held still. His mom had been improving, he'd thought; he'd been worried about Lina. He had his own problems, too. The roof of the Pelican Building had a leak. Carlos could submit a work order, but if a crew came to repair it, they'd discover his nest. So he and Carlos patched the broken shingles one by one and tested them with a hose until there were no drips. But one day, Carlos said, a leak would spring, and that would be Walter's eviction notice. "May-be we patch it good enough to get you the diploma," he said. To Carlos, a diploma was valuable. Walter wasn't so sure anymore; *We don't need no piece of paper from . . .* might pertain to universities as well as city halls. Walter knew two architecture graduates who still worked at the film archive.

Against the Greyhound window, he felt the hum of wheels on his cheek. Anthony, the Pelican donor, seemed to have had fun making money. He'd owned the Packard franchise, and his best friends owned Buick, Cadillac, and Ford. They'd called themselves the Good Roads Movement and bought a full-page newspaper ad urging San Francisco to build a bridge. What would be the equivalent now of cars at the beginning of the century? Bikes were probably the opposite. Walter had two more buses to Julie's apartment. Her cats, he recalled, stalked everywhere, even on the table.

This time, though, she penned the cats in the kitchen and made up the living-room couch for him. All night long, light slanted in from a streetlamp.

In the morning, Lina looked older. Better than the last time he saw her, but too much makeup and ridiculous shoes. She didn't look like a student anymore. Donnie was quiet, shuffling. "You coming along?" Walter asked, but Julie said he couldn't miss school before finals. Walter had finals soon, too. And college mattered more than eighth grade. Why didn't she ever worry about him?

They drove with the windows open.

His mother had been settled nicely, Julie said. God, it's over a year now. She was doing her flowers. Then, starting this past summer, she was always with that lady from Pasadena. "I could never get her alone. They had little jokes between themselves. Once I thought they were making fun of me and I said to myself, Well, crud, here I drive all the way down. So I asked what they were laughing about. Your mom whispered, 'Ward secrets.' And then I thought maybe it was good that she made a friend. I liked her having someone to sit with at meals when I wasn't there. They could go to that little beauty shop open Tuesdays. I made sure she had cash. I didn't see this coming."

Julie stopped talking. Then a startling thing happened: she began to cry. Walter wasn't used to being alone with Julie. He searched the car for Kleenex. She lifted a balled napkin to her eye.

"Your mom kept saying that woman from Pasadena was the first lady, that the president didn't want her in Washington because it was too dangerous now, things were going on the public couldn't know. The Pasadena woman nodded along. She probably told Diane in the first place. But then the Pasadena woman got transferred to a facility nearer to a nephew. Your mom said the president had sent for her to join him in the White House. She told that to other women on the ward, too, because when they watched the news and the president came on with Betty Ford, one said, 'Where's your friend, Diane?' Taunting her. Your mom said the Betty Ford on TV was really an actress. And there was that one attendant she never liked. I'm sure it wasn't as bad as the attendant said. She said your mom hit her and then bit her. Hit her and bit her, my foot. That attendant's a whiner. She has the arm bandaged up so you can't see. Her wound is probably a mosquito bite."

She was in a different building now, in an unfamiliar part of the property. The hospital was on a large parcel of land among old trees, but the place today felt ill-built and untended. Even the grass looked poisonous.

"She was fine before," Walter said. "I don't understand."

"I know it," Julie said.

They made their way to the ramshackle building, where Julie asked for Walter's mom by her full name. A nurse, preoccupied, pointed them down a hall of polished linoleum. They found her on a cot covered by a sheet, her wrists and calves in worn leather restraints, her ankles swollen, bare feet sticking out. The skin under her eyes appeared bruised. She wouldn't look at Walter.

"Mom," he said. "What happened?" He touched her shoulder.

Nothing. A small flinch under the skin. She exhaled audibly then as if disappointed but not surprised, and shook her head, as if everything was too futile to explain.

"You can tell me. I'm on your side, you know," Walter said after a while.

She shook her head again, stubborn, as if to mean nothing they could do would get it out of her. She kept her eyes on two points on the wall.

"It's Walter, your Walter," Julie said, in her overly enunciated whisper that sounded like scolding. "He took the bus down from college to see you." The new way Julie talked to his mom made Walter inordinately sad.

It went on like this, his mom refusing to look at them, until a nurse ducked in and wrote something on a clipboard. Walter asked when the restraints would be taken off. The nurse looked up from her chart with complete dryness, as if he'd asked what time it was. "The doctor should have been here already. He's late. He'll come in the next few hours."

The next few hours. He's late and he'll be here in the NEXT FEW HOURS!

Walter didn't know until the end that he'd been shouting.

The nurse shrugged. "Welcome to hospital time."

His mom fell asleep.

Julie stood up, rubbing her pants legs. "I'm antsy. Maybe I'll walk over to 301 and bring something for her to wear tomorrow and her elephant."

Walter stayed where he was. Surprisingly, this was easy, like settling deep in a hole. It was plain that he needed to sit here and wait. Eventually, the doctor would come. Walter wanted to see him, though he felt furious that he was late.

He heard noises, distant and close. Even with her like this, drugged, he liked being next to his mom asleep, hearing her breathe. He took a small book from his backpack. For once, he was exactly where he should be. The book he'd grabbed when he'd left for the bus station was about Corbusier's chapel in Ronchamp. A picture showed the building in the rain. Water ran off the slanted roof, a sheer fall.

Walter stayed in the chair between the bed and the wall while the light changed on the ceiling of the small room, as noises clanged and then subsided in the dormitory behind him. Nurses poked their heads in and left; they were together, her sleeping and him sitting, and in that period, Walter made peace with everything that had happened to her and would happen still and he understood that she did not blame him for being unable to stop her fall, but appreciated that he was here and wanted forgiveness. He could not say why he knew this—she had moved only once, and her eyes hadn't focused—but the knowledge sifted into him over the hours. She'd been here a year and two months. At first there'd been the scare of other people and the medication. Then she'd seemed to settle into a primitive safety. She did her flowers. She ate eagerly. She was heavier than she'd been and careless of herself. And she seemed less interested in them, her children. Walter accepted this, too. Maybe she was, as the doctor once said, still in the beginning of her illness. Walter no longer blamed Dr. Moss. He was just a man, guessing, too. Hoping for the best as they were. Perhaps the illness had a life even he couldn't see. This was the end of a belief Walter hadn't even known he possessed; that someone was watching, someone knew, someone powerful was on his side. He'd grown up without religion. When Ken had asked him once if he believed in God, he'd said he'd didn't know. He didn't think so. But he had trusted something to bend the arc of time in his favor. He no longer had that feeling.

Julie returned with a small, foreign-looking man who had a thick mustache. "This is Dr. Baqri." With a tool, he unlocked the restraints. Last, he unbuckled the thick belt around her waist. Her eyelashes blinked. "We'll have you out of here lickety-split, Diane."

"It's about time," she answered.

She still didn't look at Walter, but he felt warmth fall on his left shoulder.

"You'll be back in 301 soon," he said. "I promise."

Walter's lips felt big inside. How had it come to this—that the best hope was a return to what had once seemed unbearable?

"I didn't want Donnie or even Lina here to see," Julie said.

Walter couldn't answer. He nodded. For the rest of his life, he understood that experiencing this day of his mom's humiliation changed him.

40.

The superintendent was not in his office. Walter and Julie waited. Walter was disconsolate. For months, he'd been fantasizing about Dr. Moss and his mom falling in love, and now, this. She'd been in the hospital more than a year. She was supposed to be getting out.

Today, he was missing the week eight lecture and study session for biochem.

Still waiting, Walter found a pay phone and fed the machine quarters. A secretary in Sausalito asked what his call was concerning.

"Oh, well, I asked Mr. Wimmer how to get rich and he offered to buy me breakfast."

The secretary laughed. "That sounds like him. Can you come in on the nineteenth?"

"Yes," Walter said, not considering how. But he needed a tether to some future.

Finally, two days later, the doctor swung open the door. A middle-aged couple filed out. Dr. Moss was wearing slippers.

He sighed. "I'm sorry I wasn't here. I went to visit my daughter and ended up in the Ann Arbor emergency room. Food poisoning. A bad shrimp. I understand they restrained her. That shouldn't have happened. The charge nurse was on her third shift. I spoke with her. She'd been working thirty-one hours. The night person hadn't shown up."

"She won't even look at us," Walter said. "She wasn't like that before."

The doctor pushed his glasses up his nose. They slipped down again as he read something in a folder. He looked older now. "They took the restraints off, but we'll keep her in the closed ward another week. It's protocol. I don't like to go over the unit supervisors. For her safety, too. If she's agitated, she could hurt herself."

"That's the building where we've been seeing her?" Julie asked.

"It's a good ward. Becca Vronsky is head nurse. One of our best. The only difference is Diane can't go in and out by herself."

"Can she still do her flowers?" Julie sat forward in her chair.

"After a few days. I can see that someone takes her over to the gardens."

"And the bonsai class?"

"That's Friday. I'll walk her there myself."

"When we talked last January," Walter said, looking at Julie, "we thought she might be coming out around Christmas this year."

"It's a setback, but she'll regain her equilibrium."

"Where I work, in convalescent hospitals, a lot of doctors say that people like Diane do better in a smaller setting," Julie said. "Someplace in the community."

"That's the prevailing thinking. In universities, at least. So I've been reading," the doctor said. Everywhere in the room were towers of stacked books. Maybe you should read a little less and go supervise your wards, Walter thought.

"What would she do in the community?" Walter said. "She can't work yet."

"They try to set up group homes like households," Dr. Moss said. "But they hire unskilled caregivers because they're cheaper. She's better off here. Let's get her stabilized, back to 301, and then see."

"I have to move more of her things over if she's going to stay there another week," Julie said. At the door she asked, "You don't think that attendant was exaggerating?"

Dr. Moss said he'd seen marks on her shoulder.

"Does this disqualify her for the dance?"

"The next one isn't for a while. We'll see what we can do."

The doctor smiled, sadly it seemed, his fingertips touching.

"Do you ever worry that you'll end up like Kirkbride, marrying a patient?"

"That couldn't happen now. We believe in transference. Once a patient always a patient."

Walter felt deflated. This romance of his mom's had seemed more likely than any of his own.

"I have a friend who teaches at Pomona," the doctor said. "All the beautiful young men fall for him. He waits until they graduate. But by then, he says, they've always lost interest."

"For a long time, I hoped you would get together with my mom." Walter could say this now because it seemed too late.

"When my wife was alive, she picked out the prettiest young women to clean the house and the running joke was I never even noticed." The doctor looked down at his papers. "Romance is not what your mother needs. And I think she knows that."

"She wanted a husband. Our dad didn't work out, but she revered that kind of life. Marriage. Family."

"Sometimes you outgrow even a cherished dream."

"I thought the only way to get over a dream was to achieve it."

"It's another thing you learn getting old. You can have a desperate longing and one day realize you never obtained it, but now . . . you don't need it anymore."

"You don't think my mom still wants love?"

"She has love. At our age, our children are more important than romance. She needs peace and a sense of purpose. And she has those here."

"Peace seems like a poor trade for love."

"At your age I'm sure it does. It would be."

"Don't you think dreams are important?"

"They are important, absolutely. But not as endings. I care less whether a person 'gets' her dream than whether or not she has one. Dreams are billboards, promising something ahead. By the way, I asked your sister, the last time I saw her, if she'd send a picture of herself at her job."

"And she didn't do it?" Walter asked, suddenly furious.

As soon as Walter walked out of the office, he returned to the pay phone and left Lina an angry message on Julie's machine.

Donnie was in trouble at school, Julie told him, driving back. "He made fun of somebody. That guidance counseling lady. She's a big gal, did you ever meet her? Donnie drew a picture of her sidling up to the principal—you know, he's tiny, and she's batting a huge eyelash. He drew it seven feet high on an outside wall. Because he's so darn talented everyone recognized who was who. And Mrs. Graver, that's the lady, was so embarrassed, mortified really, at the picture of her, her size, which nobody spoke of, certainly not in her hearing, so she'd maybe imagined that it wasn't so bad and that other people didn't notice. I'm that way," Julie said, simply. "And now there she is in a mural—huge—for all to see, next to the basketball hoops, a laughingstock. She stopped going to work. No one knows if she'll return. He feels awful. He likes her. Why he did it, I'll never know. But he never imagined it would get blown up into something like this."

"Has he apologized?"

"He's written her two notes. She hasn't answered."

"Maybe it's time to think about Hollywood High. Be a lot closer."

"He'd be the only white boy there," Julie said. "He's saving for a motorcycle to ride to Pali."

"He's not even fourteen. He can't drive."

"There's something called a hardship license. He's done research."

"Let him be the only white kid at Hollywood High. He'll learn something."

"I'm thinking about safety."

"Be safer than a motorcycle."

"He promised to wear a helmet."

"I hate thinking of that lady," Walter said.

"Kids do stupid things. It shouldn't ruin his life. But the way the school is carrying on, you'd think . . ." She shook her head.

So his little brother would ride a motorcycle.

The old-fashioned downtown of Pacific Palisades hadn't changed. Two women hovered over a sewing machine in a store window. The fire department building had a FOR RENT sign. Walter could see these old buildings joined, a playground in the center. But how could he ever get the money?

He walked to Pali, waited until it let out, found his brother, and they strolled to the diner where Susan and Carrie used to meet their friends. He told Donnie their mom would be in the place longer. He'd planned what to say when Donnie asked, How long? But Donnie didn't ask. Walter knew he should talk about the trouble at school, but he didn't know how. He told his brother he could always call him. "You know that, right?"

Donnie nodded.

Then Walter took a long bus ride into Beverly Hills. He felt like a bum walking on the glossed floor of the May Company, the air frantic with perfume molecules.

Someone went to find his sister, but she'd already left.

As the Greyhound passed downtown LA, Walter noticed an empty department store that had been turned into a garage. The plate-glass windows showed the top halves of cars.

When the Pelican roof gave out, he told himself, he'd return.

41.

The year Walter had been counting down was over. There was no new end date. His mom wasn't going to marry the doctor. The doctor had told him so.

In Mr. Wimmer's office, he found himself standing before a framed picture.

"My first penny building," Mr. Wimmer said.

Walter wanted to ask what a penny building was, but said, "I'm here on my own. Nothing to do with the university."

"Good. Then you're not going to ask me for a research wing."

"I want to learn how to make money," Walter said. He wasn't as bad off as he'd been. He had the scholarship now and three jobs. But you never let yourself get sent back to Go.

Mr. Wimmer clasped his hands. Whatever Walter said seemed to give this man mirth. "You're how old?" Walter was twenty. Mr. Wimmer talked about his own youth. "You could start out at a commercial brokerage firm like I did. Learn the fundamentals of real estate without risking your own money."

A real estate agent? Whoa. Walter wasn't in college to become a real estate agent.

"But I got out fast. In real estate, the incentives are all wrong. They motivate you to sell the most expensive property whether or not it's the right move for your client. I didn't like who I was becoming."

"Do all brokers want to become developers, then?"

"Most hope to but few do. They spend their salary on life-style. To buy something and improve it"—Mr. Wimmer shook his head—"takes discipline. Delayed gratification." Mr. Wimmer cupped his hands as a scale. "Agent or owner."

Or doctor, Walter thought. The bus ride to Sausalito had taken two hours. He had to study for the biochem final. Mr. Wimmer was now talking about why shopping centers started after World War Two. "Air conditioning! That's what made malls possible." He paused. "What do you need all this money for?"

"Home in LA," Walter said, "there's a fire station I'd like to buy. I love old buildings." Walter sensed the man's interest in him; he felt like a pet.

Mr. Wimmer leaned over his desk. "Listen, I'm not so smart like you kids at Cal. But I learned early. When I had one client, I made it my business to make that client happy. I know a Chicago company that's looking to put stores in California. They need sites. That'll take scouting. Do you have a car?"

"I can get one." Walter still didn't have a license.

"They want commercial space, not for damaged goods or overruns, but a lower price point. Outlets. They want to try the Central Valley."

"Would they pay a finder's fee?"

"They would lease it."

"From who?"

"From you. That's the opportunity."

"But I can't buy a building. I don't have the dough."

"Let's not get ahead of ourselves. It's a long shot, you understand. I'll put in a call to my friend. What are you doing for Christmas, son? Are you going home?"

Walter hadn't figured out Christmas yet. Christmas could wait, he thought, until after he found a building.

"Go home," Mr. Wimmer said. "No business will get done this month."

"What do you do?" Walter asked.

"My wife is a Christmas person. She had a painful childhood— the mother drank—so she knocks herself out for our daughter. But she pushes herself. I'm always relieved it's January."

"What's a penny building?" Walter asked from the door.

"You don't know the J.C. Penney Company?"

Back in Berkeley, Walter biked to the co-op and told Ken, "I have to find an empty building in the middle of California. You've got to help me."

Walter finished biochem with a C. If his MCATs were high enough, he could still maybe get in. Cub had the statistics.

"You never loved it," Susan said. "It's always been your safety."

"Some safety."

"Worst-case scenario, you could go abroad. My cousin got his MD in Costa Rica and he has a huge practice."

"It's just, do I always want to feel behind?"

She shrugged. "Being a doctor isn't the same thing as junior-year biochem."

Now he had to find that building. Even if it took him a year. And it did.

For Christmas he went home for a few days. Lina was working on department store windows, as he supposed she would for the rest of her life.

The fat lady returned to the counseling office right after the holidays. She'd joined Weight Watchers and had lost fifteen pounds. No more mention was made of Hollywood High. "But I think he's smoking," Julie said. "He says no. I'm not sure I believe him." Also, Donnie was making different friends. Julie didn't hear much about Evan anymore. She wasn't always so sure where he was, either.

Julie was taking a cooking class. She and their mom, she said, always meant to take a cooking class together.

42.

Lina's days assumed a familiar rhythm. Nancy and Ceci competed over her, Nancy relenting when Ceci asked, then pouting. Allen complimented another of Lina's displays. The saleswomen liked Dino. Even Julie did.

Still. Her life felt uncharted. Marci drove her to see an apartment on a quiet, tree-lined street in Hollywood.

The girl who showed her the room was on the phone. She apologized, whispering, "An audition." The room had a honey-colored wood floor. Two windows; each faced the blank side of a stucco wall, interrupted by a glossy cluster of bougainvillea. Lina had almost enough money saved, but there was still Julie. And though she'd told Walter she wasn't trying again, on Saturday she sat in Dino's apartment staring at the empty college application forms she'd had sent to his address.

———

At the staff Secret Santa, Lina received an easel from Ceci. To sketch fashion, she said.

This year, Lina was giving her own gifts: for Donnie, a nice button-down shirt, still short-sleeved so it looked like him. For Julie, she and Ceci were making a dress with one of Julie's fabrics, a soft olive wool, on Ceci's old French sewing machine. Lina had drawn the dress in her class, and Ceci revised the placket and added pockets. They made a pattern. It took them three days to piece and assemble it. For her mother, Sue let Lina buy a German nightgown at half off. She picked out a hat for Mrs. Anjani. She'd forgotten Walter. At closing time on Christmas Eve, Sue gave her a good deal on a wallet.

Dino picked her up at seven on Christmas morning to play tennis before she drove to Norwalk. He pelted her with questions from across the net about the hospital Christmas.

"Why don't we ever talk about you?" she asked.

"I'm so bored with myself."

He gave her a tennis racket. She didn't have a present for him.

Everyone in the store compared Christmas presents. No one was impressed by Lina's racket. The movie star had given Kim a diamond bracelet. But when she tried to put it on, he lifted it from the box and fastened it on her ankle. She rolled down her sock to show them. In the bathroom, Kim offered Lina the lingerie she'd gotten from the Secret Santa. The actor liked her in her regular cotton underpants. She couldn't keep it in her house, either; her father would have a cow.

Lina looked around at the white industrial staff bathroom. It needed something.

Sue promoted Lina to assistant stylist. Lina would finally earn a decent paycheck now when she had no real use for money, except to buy more clothes. She had nearly a thousand dollars in her checking account, but it didn't feel as important as what she'd managed to save from the ice-cream store when they'd needed every dollar.

She wished she'd insisted that Julie take all her paychecks then. Julie wouldn't accept her contributions anymore and the bungalow was gone, rented to other people.

She no longer minded time in the stockroom. Nancy was relaxing. And since Christmas, Lina owned a suit. Sue had let her buy it with a 70 percent markdown.

Lina hauled a birch stump into the corner of the staff bathroom and placed rolls of toilet paper on top.

She was sorting ribbons with Kim to stock the gift stations with spring colors and put away the holiday wrapping for next year.

Sue had promoted Kim to the top floor. Dating a movie star made her a celebrity. But sometimes an hour would go by in Better Dresses without any customers, Kim said. And some of the women wanted an older salesperson. "To understand my lumps," one said.

Then Sue called Lina's name and she looked up to find Mrs. Anjani's face hanging over the counter. Lina knew; she gasped before she even heard the words. A girl from Texas had become homesick. By her second week back, she couldn't get out of bed. Her parents were flying in today. Mrs. Anjani's friend had stayed on top of everything. "I sent her flowers. They're going to put you in the Texas girl's room. We still have to sort out the money. But you're going. They want you there next week."

Lina knew her relief should have been complete, but this was so fast. She and Kim had both registered for a course in buyer training. As Mrs. Anjani rode up the escalator with Lina to the office, she looked down at the first floor with its tiny movements like the internal workings of a clock. Lina led Mrs. Anjani around tables of fine china to the office, at the back of Housewares. "They've given away all the aid for this year," Mrs. Anjani said. "We'll start on paperwork for next. There's a deadline for Pell Grants. I called Julie. We'll pool resources."

Mrs. Anjani waited while Lina reluctantly told Sue and Allen, who shook his head. "We can't give her a reference now, can we?" he asked Sue.

"That's okay," Lina whispered.

"Does Nancy know?" He limped toward the elevator.

Sue's smile turned upside down. "You would have made a good buyer."

"What day do I have to leave?" Lina asked Mrs. Anjani.

"You go to New York Sunday. You leave here today. Now."

"Let me at least stay to finish the ribbons."

"Do what you have to do," Sue said.

There was a commotion downstairs. Marci had taken home a dress to wear to a music industry gala, then brought it back and processed the return. Allen had let her go. Just like that. Marci blamed Nancy for ratting on her and Nancy was crying.

They gathered—Ceci, Sue, Nancy, and Kim—and handed Lina a huge box with a bow. They'd chipped in to give her a winter coat. Camel hair. Kim and Nancy gave Lina a hug in the stockroom. Ceci, on a ladder hanging silk cherry millinery blossoms from a chandelier, blew a kiss.

Lina still had the card Mr. Moses had given her the night she, Lauren, and Jess went to jail.

On the twenty-ninth floor, the law firm's reception room felt importantly quiet. Mr. Moses's office was bigger than Julie's living room. On the wall was a small framed picture of him arguing *Jarndyce v. California* before the Supreme Court.

"I'm glad you'll be joining the fellowship of scholars," he said, lifting a stapler, then crunching a small stack of paper. "The University of California is as good as any other. Better, in fact," he went on, "because the students are there because they're smart and *they work harder.*" Why was he telling her this?

"I'm going to Barnard," she said.

"Oh. Well, Barnard is a decent school, too. But I'll say to you what I say to Lauren: kids at Hunter and at UC are nipping at your heels. They work harder because they're *not* at Barnard."

Mrs. Anjani had written out the numbers for tuition and the larger sum for the dormitory and meal plan. He studied the index card. Lina explained that she would be eligible for financial aid next year.

"You'll need a job," he said. "But you're used to working. Unlike my daughter. I'll cover part of the tuition. I'd rather be writing a check to University of California Regents."

"I guess it would be cheaper."

"Not only that. I prefer to pay real costs. Do you think the professors teach better because they're at Barnard? Or that *they* get a penny more from Princeton than from Berkeley? Margaret!" When the secretary gave Lina the check for $7,500, she was disappointed; in her daydream on the Wilshire bus, Mr. Moses paid for all of it.

Thank you, Mr. Moses, wherever you are, Lina mouthed years later, a well-worn, silent prayer. By then he was dead. As was Mrs. Anjani, who sent Lina her own library, boxed up, during Lina's second winter in New York.

43.

The phone rang in the Pelican Building at ten o'clock one January night. Had to be something bad, Walter thought, the doctor or Julie. But it was Lina. Breathless, crying.

"I need all the money you can give me."

She was going! He felt it like a basketball just caught. "I'll give you all I have." He left only one hundred dollars in his account.

44.

Dino promised to keep an eye on Donnie even if Evan's mom fired him. He told Lina that Donnie was turning out to be cool. Kind, Dino said, but also oblivious, which equaled confidence to the high school population. Lina decided, on the spur of the moment, to have sex with Dino. She wouldn't go to college a virgin, then. She wanted to say goodbye. This time he went along with her, but it didn't quite work. It seemed the parts didn't fit. If she was technically no longer a virgin, that was all. They lay in bed, but the night felt unfinished. Dino still wanted to celebrate Barnard.

"Let's go for dessert," he said. "I'm in the mood for a soufflé."

It was raining when they stepped outside, and he drove them up the wide, palm-lined streets of Beverly Hills.

"Where're we going?" she asked.

The Beverly Hills Hotel. Evan had talked him into going there once after he'd won in Chinatown. Dino turned off of Sunset onto a winding driveway. On top of the hill, one valet took his keys, another opened her door. A large sign said PARKING $10. He guided her through the lobby to a dim room where a saxophonist played soulful music. She should have been more dressed up. She wished her mother and Julie could see this place.

"What kind of soufflés do you have?" he asked the waitress.

They both wanted chocolate. He ordered two. That must have cost a fortune.

"Do you know this song? 'In a Sentimental Mood.' Coltrane has a version with Duke Ellington's band." He pulled her up into a slow dance. She shuffled her feet. "Here, follow me—do you know the box step?"

Another thing he taught her.

Lina woke abruptly, early and scattered, never lighting on one thing, and then slumped back to sleep, waking again only after Julie and Donnie left, having missed one of her last breakfasts. She panicked: so much to do, she could hardly summon her attention. She remembered her mother but couldn't bear to; her mind darkened and a pain started in the center of her head, as if her brain had cleft and air was shrilling between the lobes. Maybe this was what people called a headache.

It was going to be awful to say goodbye. What would her mother understand? She'd been proud when Walter went off to college. Lina would call from New York. Donnie could dial from the booth in 301 and give her the receiver. Lina had to convince her that she'd be back, in the summer.

What if her mother thought she'd died?

She drove to Norwalk and found a cardboard sign on the door of the sitting room, which had been transformed into a make-believe beauty parlor—*Spa Day!* in pink cursive. The wicker chairs, which normally faced every which way, had been put into order. A long table was set against a wall with a mirror leaning on it. Two patients sat getting their hair done. Several more wore rollers. Most of the women were watching a rerun of *I Love Lucy*, the volume turned high. An aide Lina didn't know was giving her mother a pedicure, and her mother's mood was lively. A laugh track roared predictably every few minutes. It was nearly impossible to get her attention. On one end of the long table were open containers of makeup. The woman who played hand games against the wall was using her fingers to draw blue spots on her cheeks.

Lina waited. She had time. The hours between her two lives hung like weight in a hammock.

A pile of clothes made a haystack in the corner, probably from Isabel's trunks. A small, tight-muscled woman crouched near it, pulling garments out by their sleeves and whipping the floor with them.

Shirley dropped the needle on the record player and a waltz began, a melody Lina recognized from a childhood music box. Some of the women stood to dance. They wore ruffled dresses over their clothes and hospital booties; several had clownish circles on their cheeks.

The dire importance of looks, a given all of Lina's life, seemed a spoof here. Even Lauren and Jess, the intellectuals, would admit that appearance determined everything. Today, though, not only patients but nurses, too, were dressing up for fun, all meaning rinsed away. Being pretty no longer mattered here.

Isabel had once told Lina that her dad hated these beauty days. He said they made his patients look more insane. The nurses planned them anyway behind his back.

Two women fought over a blouse from the pile, their hair wild with ribbons.

Someone was shrieking hysterically in a mask.

From the threshold, Lina squinted to see an enchantment. The rickety music-box waltz repeated. She could almost catch the tail end of an old feeling. Once upon a time she believed the four of them possessed majesty.

Shirley wheeled in a cart with thermoses of hot water and tea sandwiches. "Oops, someone had an accident," she said.

A small lump of feces in the corner. The woman next to Lina

drooled. The one who played games with the wall was doing it again, stamping blue handprints. Her own mother made a sucking motion with her mouth. Tardive dyskinesia, a side effect of the Elavil, Lina had been told. She knelt, took her mother's hand.

"Mom," she said. "Remember, Walter went to college. Now it's my time."

Her mother was not paying attention. Her hands had changed. There was dirt under the nails and her cuticles were ragged. Lina remembered her oval nails, the neat cuticle—once her pride.

"Look," Lina said. She picked up scissors, pulled her hair down, and cut off a foot-long hank. Here, she said, giving the tail of hair to her mother.

"I'll keep it for you," her mother said.

A woman in a crushed red velvet coat squatted by the door, making lewd gestures.

Lina kissed the top of her mother's hair—it had a taste—and left.

In the car, she closed her eyes. A rounding staircase, clean wooden floors. A vase of tulips on a still table. Her future. But could her mother be there, too?

Julie insisted on paying for a beautician to at least even out Lina's hair.

Walter sent $2,300. Julie took out an equity loan on the Michigan cabin.

The last brutality was Donnie. The worst part was his acceptance. "Other people go. Walter's there. I'm kinda looking forward to some time alone. Being less watched."

He was trying to make it easy for her. Julie and Donnie were better people. Virtue was a luxury Lina couldn't afford yet.

She was ruthless and she did it.

She left.

Lights from the vast ground of Los Angeles hung in the oblong window, but then the jet pulled free and Lina stared out at pure black.

Mrs. Anjani had told her her roommate was from London. Lina had the dormitory address in the pocket of her backpack. Julie had given her money for a taxi "just this once." A lot of money.

Long before the ice-cream parlor or the May Company, Lina had been hired at Sears as a holiday wrapper. Her first job. She'd stood in a line of women at a counter facing spools of paper on dowels. A salesperson would bring down packages, each with its torn pickup slip, and Lina would wrap the item in the chosen paper. She learned to fold paper on the sides of a box as symmetrically as an envelope. After three days, she could make a neat, perfect package. She could do that still.

At the registers in Clothing or Kitchenware or Farm Equipment or Fine Dining, there was a sign that announced the wait time for gift wrapping. Often, people left and returned to the loading bay, where, in a room like a tollbooth, someone matched the ripped tags, taped them whole again, and gave the person their holiday package.

Her second week there, Lina's mother took a weekend job in sales. "What are you doing here?" Lina said. Her mother treated her as if they hardly knew each other. She would bring a box to Lina, Lina would wrap it, tape the ripped half tag on top, and send it to pickup, where Donnie would later hand in the other half and carry the package home on his bike. Lina no longer remembered how her mother had explained the plan. She did remember being scared.

It worked as silent choreography. They stole a blender, a toaster oven, and a space heater. Those things Lina could almost abide. Her mother had earned little. But there was more: garden tools for a garden they never planted, clothes they didn't need. This thinking started a painful whirlpool in a spot Lina later identified as her liver.

The stewardess asked if she wanted a beverage. Lina said no, thank you.

The seasonal jobs had finished on Christmas Eve. Whatever happened to those appliances? Lina hadn't seen any of them for years. Had they made a difference? Maybe they'd helped her mother, as she'd scanned the bungalow, take pleasure in her life.

Last year, after the social worker came and quizzed them about their interests, Lina had woken up startled every day. Or had that begun even before, when the three of them committed a crime? It was over now. Julie, of all people, had saved them. Lina had liked the rhythm of days working in the department store. But when she'd told Mrs. Anjani that they'd said she was good at decorating windows, she'd hissed, "You want a career in design? There's a long line of girls in good colleges. You've got to get in that line. Even if you can't see it, the line is there."

Lina jolted awake when the jet bounced in a bumpy landing.

She looked out the window at dry, cold land.

Those afternoons at Sears, they could have been caught. The three of them.

But she had pulled free.

Book 4

The Bouquets

45.

Lina was finally East. For years, her family's humiliating lack of money had made her anxious. She'd kept the secret of their address. And her mother. She'd loved her, tried to protect her, and again and again come up against her mother's disappointment in her. She always knew that someday she'd get away. Here she was. But without those agitations, she felt meager. Unformed. Qualities in herself she'd trusted no longer seemed to work. In Los Angeles, she'd never doubted that she was smart, and that confidence had given her a freewheeling bravado. The class had fallen silent when she'd said Mrs. Dalloway was a rich, silly wife.

Here, though, Lina was subdued. She'd carefully packed her suit from the store and the camel hair coat, but no one dressed like that here. She reverted to her jeans from high school. The beautiful coat revealed itself to be merely ornamental in the cold, brittle air. She wore it with a sweatshirt underneath.

She and her roommate never quarreled, but the girl belonged to a social world into which there was never any question of bringing Lina. Lina made other friends in the dorm. They all hated their mothers. They all complained about the food. Lina listened. Anyone watching would have assumed she shared these opinions, but she liked the cafeteria meals. She discounted what they said about their mothers, too. She didn't doubt that those women were irritating, bewildered, and critical of their daughters, who after all had better chances than they'd had. She would have loved to be able to hate her mother the way they did, with a breeziness carried by a fundamental trust in a home with a set table and dinner cooking.

Walter called sometimes and told her about his building. She wasn't really listening.

"So everything's okay with you there?" he always asked at the end.

He told her to send a picture of herself on campus to pin over their mom's bed. She said she would.

"I mean, do it," he said. He'd asked her before, she just remembered. Why hadn't she sent a picture? Still, Walter had never con*tend*ed with their mother the way she had. He hadn't been there for the worst of it. And their mother had always been different with him. Lina desperately wanted not to be*come* her. Walter never for a second even considered that he could.

Mrs. Anjani told Lina to take a foreign language. Dino suggested Chinese. "There'll be over a billion Chinese people by the year 2000." But her mother had studied French. The phrases she dropped into ordinary conversation, *je ne sais quoi* and *fait dans la vie*, seemed what she most enjoyed from her education. Lina enrolled.

The May Company suit went to the back of her closet.

Her new friends in the dorm talked about sex. All of them had had it. Kim believed she'd given her whole self to the actor, but these girls were nimbly able to have sex and come out unnicked.

A tall Deerfield girl discovered that she loved econ. "It comes naturally to me," she said. So far nothing came naturally to Lina, though she was studying more than she ever had. She didn't like one class above the others. No teacher showed a particular interest in her, either. She had a job interview at the college store. After six minutes, the manager hired her. Maybe this is what comes naturally to me, she thought.

A handmade sign in the student center said *CLAY ROOM*, with an arrow pointing to the basement. She recognized the mineral aroma, like the bottom of a well. Electric wheels sat in rows, and only one woman was throwing a pot. Lina asked her if you had to pay. "Student?" the woman asked, then said all she had to do was sign in with Troy. "He's loading the kiln."

In a moment, a guy her age emerged, tall, Black, with long hair in tiny braids. He copied down the number of her student ID.

"Can I fire, too, and glaze?" Lina asked.

"Got you set up now. Just sign in every time. If I'm not here, leave the clipboard on that nail."

She reached into the barrel of clay, redder than what she was used to and mixed with damp, discarded pots fallen in on themselves. She wedged a cool lump, slicing it with wire to check for air bubbles. She hadn't felt clay for a long time. After she graduated, she'd never returned to Mr. Riddle's room; she would have been ashamed not to be in college, and, working at the store, she'd become careful with her clothes. When the clay was smooth, she sat at a wheel and pulled the ball under her hands; she'd always loved the feeling of centering. The first few pots wobbled. It took her a while to find the rhythm of pulling wet clay up between her knuckle and fingers. The guy, Troy, was watching. When she looked at him, he glanced away. She threw eleven pots and kept one, lifting it off the wheel with a wire.

"You're no beginner," he said, sliding her board onto the firing rack.

"High school."

He was a student at Columbia, an art major. She hadn't seen a lot of Black kids at Barnard. Running up the steps, she felt good. The wheel had bitten down her nails, her hair held the mess and smell of slip. So four days a week, for six hours she sold Barnard regalia: mugs, sweatshirts, blankets, notebooks, and umbrellas—then ran down to the clay room.

She wrote Julie and asked her to send her old overalls.

Troy told her she should take a sculpture class. There was a great one, over across Broadway, he said, but she'd be the only girl.

In the library, for her great books class, she read Descartes' a priori proof of God. She looked up the word *ontological*. The dictionary declared it an adjective "relating to the branch of metaphysics dealing with the nature of being." Then she looked up *metaphysics*, which turned out to be "the branch of philosophy that deals with the first principles of things, including abstract concepts such as being, knowing, substance, cause, identity, time, and space." She set down the heavy dictionary. From what she could tell, Descartes was proving that God existed because he'd thought of him and nothing that he thought was so wonderful could not not exist. But how was that proof?

It seemed like her mother's logic.

Around her, the only sound in the stately library was the rustle of pages. After all the trouble Mrs. Anjani and her alumna friend had taken to make up for her stupid, proud mistake and all the money she'd borrowed (she hated to think of what it took to transport her here to this carrel), Lina was turning out to be only an average student. In the department store, Ceci had trusted her instincts and Sue had recommended her to be a buyer. Maybe that was where she belonged. After another hour (two more readings of Descartes' proof), she packed up her books and left. Outside, the leaves were lacy with light, breeze, and shadow. Spring. She was very far from home.

Lina had been counting down the weeks to go back to LA, but Mrs. Anjani decided she should stay at Barnard over the summer to make up the semester she'd missed. She felt an acute longing for home, but she complied. Financial aid had come through for next year, but there was still a shortfall and Mrs. Anjani was helping Julie pay her expenses. Mrs. Anjani figured out that if Lina took twenty-four credits a semester and stayed two summers, she could even graduate early.

"Will you explain to my mom?" Lina asked Julie.

Troy turned out to be staying, too. "See, I got in as an *underprivileged* student," he said. They were making him take remedial classes all summer. "Reading and shit."

She asked him about the Columbia art department. "Come on along," he said.

She didn't have to be anywhere for another hour, so they walked across the street and under the Columbia gate. She followed him into a cool hall. Through an open door, Lina glimpsed a phenomenally large nude woman luxuriating on a plinth, the bottoms of her bare pink feet dirty and a dozen young men sketching her.

A girl passed wearing peacock-green tights and Doc Martens. People in the art building looked less normal than in the rest of the school.

Lina bought a peach for dinner at the corner Korean market and ate it on the stone steps of the art building. She bit into the tight skin and, inside, fine chains of crimson beaded through the orange. Juice sprayed her hands. She'd check out a class.

That first summer, she wore overalls with tank tops, and her hair carried the stony, cool smell of clay. She added a drawing class. The teacher arranged still lifes and roamed the room with an eraser. He erased the part of your drawing he wanted you to do over. Look again, he said. Look better.

When Lina asked Julie if she'd told her mother why she wasn't there, Julie quickly told her yes, yes, she was fine. She understood. Lina doubted that.

"Still liking school?" Walter asked. Now it seemed she liked it more than he did. When she asked him about graduating, he changed the subject. He'd finally gotten his license, he said, and was driving to the Central Valley every day. Julie and Donnie sounded good, he told her, maybe better than ever.

Now that I'm gone, Lina thought. "What about Mom?" Lina called the ward, but her mother was so quiet on the phone. Lina could hardly get anything out of her.

"Me neither. I've stopped expecting much."

She didn't tell Walter that she was taking two art classes in fall. It seemed a wise thing to keep from a person who was helping pay for her education so that she would eventually have a means of support.

Most of her Barnard friends were gone for the summer. Jess had a job in a microbiology lab; Lauren was in Mississippi, interning for some southern center for injustice. Or justice, it must have been.

In the art department lounge, there was a pot of bitter coffee and people stood around talking about Arshile Gorky. More than one loved Picasso, most revered Pollock. Troy stomped in and fanned out pictures of graffiti he'd photographed downtown. The rumor was that a kid did it, a Black kid, still in high school. The department was mostly guys, but there were a few Barnard girls taking classes.

A girl in a slip dress and combat boots painted standing beside a large dog asleep on the cement floor. Her canvas was abstract and layered, thick with paint but still pretty. Lina's eye kept going to one spot of orange. While she worked, the girl whistled a raspy melody. Another girl wore white blouses every day and, even drawing with charcoal, her cuffs stayed white.

She also knew how to use a drill, Lina found out the first week of fall classes. In Introduction to Sculpture, when the teacher asked everyone to say what they wanted to build and what tools they'd need, the girl in a white blouse said she planned to build a dollhouse. Lina wished she'd thought of that.

The sculpture class was all men, besides the girl and Lina. Barnard girls take painting but they don't sign up for sculpture, the teacher said. It wasn't only the students. The sculptors they talked about and loved—Calder, Brancusi, Arp, Judd, Noguchi—were not only men, they were men who'd all known each other. Calder, it turned out, had a degree in mechanical engineering and had worked as a forester and on a boat. Thinking about his accomplishments made Lina tired.

Her Barnard French class was all women and one gay guy. The thing about French was it made you realize how little grammar you knew, even in your own language.

46.

Walter bought an eleven-year-old pumpkin-colored Karmann Ghia for six hundred dollars from Rory's dad's car lot and Susan invited herself along on one of his expeditions. "We'll see the world," she said, and put her feet up on the dashboard. She had nice feet. She slid in a cassette. Dance music.

"I brought the Stevie Wonder and Keith Jarrett," she said. "For those too brilliant for fun."

"If I'm driving, maybe no music yet."

"Are we visiting random towns?" She said she was moving to Sacramento for a summer internship in the new governor's office.

"I met that guy once at the place for my mom. He was secretary of state then."

"Good that he was there. Maybe he'll do something for mental health."

"Yeah, but look at Kennedy. I loved Kennedy. And he was the one who started all the trouble."

"Why? What did he do?"

"He passed the law that emptied out the institutions. Kennedy had a retarded sister. She could read *Winnie-the-Pooh* but not much else."

"You know that's not a good word to use."

"I didn't mean it like that." He wanted to explain, but once someone thought you were a jerk it was hard to prove why you weren't. "She fell down curtsying when she met the queen of England and they gave her a lobotomy. She was in a hospital the rest of her life. So Kennedy hated institutions. And shut them down. It was the last bill he signed."

"How's your mom?" she asked, after a silence.

He shrugged. "Pretty much the same."

They saw six buildings that Saturday: a canning factory, a barn, three warehouses, and an abandoned school. None met the criteria the man in Chicago had given Walter over the phone. Visibility. Access. Plenty of parking. Walter was planning to take only two classes in fall. Once he found the building, he could catch up. The worst that would happen? He'd graduate late. His sister was in college finally. His brother and Julie were quiet. No one needed him.

Carrie was camp-counseling in Yosemite. He liked thinking of her there, her brown stick-legs in shorts. Ken trucked back and forth to Blodgett for soil science research in the mixed conifer forest. Melinda worked in a sleep lab. He saw *Jaws* with Melinda and Ken, and when the theater rocked with screaming, Walter walked out to go home to bed. He left at six every morning. He'd become a nimble driver. At the end of the summer, when school started, he still hadn't found a site that excited Chicago. Once classes began, he stopped talking about his fugitive trips, because his friends looked at him with things they weren't saying. He hoped Mr. Wimmer hadn't lost faith in him. At dusk, when he took the Ashley exit and drove uphill, it seemed amazing to see Berkeley still intact, cool and waiting.

On October 23, Walter found an old high school, the name "Central" inscribed over the door. Gutted, the brick walls painted, it could be beautiful, he told Mr. Wimmer from a pay phone in Clovis. Central was the seventy-third site he'd seen, the ninth he'd submitted to Chicago, with Polaroids and specs. And six drawings: his.

47.

On parents' weekend, Lina took a bus to Princeton to see Lauren, who'd written that she was in love with one guy and best friends with another. The best friend came along to meet Lina at the station. As they walked to campus, he and Lauren argued about the idea of government, something that had never interested Lina but now did, as they disputed who should be paid more: janitors, surgeons, or artists. They ran into people Lauren and the best friend knew; Lina was introduced; those friends joined; they ate; she lost track of time and she was never once, not for even a moment those thirty hours, alone. Getting ready for a party while still debating whether people who loved what they did for a living ought to be paid less because they received nonmaterial compensation, Lina asked, "Do I look all right?" and Lauren said, "Of course."

Lauren seemed surprised by this new insecurity. In high school, Lina had always known she was beautiful, behind her shield of hair. Here people didn't see it. "Really? You look the same to me. And you're much more open to ideas now. In high school you were so unimpressed with everything. Remember how you hated Virginia Woolf?"

"You mean I can think better, even if I'm no longer good-looking."

At the party, while Lauren stood in a cluster of young women furtively glimpsing the guy she was in love with, Lina talked to the best friend. He told her that he and Lauren had the same values. For both of them, friendship was the most important thing. They were both trying to figure out what to do with their lives. They wanted to be useful. That mattered. "We can't all be artists!" he said. Lina flushed. She'd told Lauren her secret ambition, in private. The best friend said he wanted to marry Lauren but understood that he would have to wait. He kept glancing at the man Lauren was in love with.

On the bus back to Barnard, Lina already missed Lauren, for whom friendship really was the most important thing. You might be small and anonymous in the world, she'd decided, but you could be deeply known by your friends. The bus hurtled into Port Authority. Still, Lina had to do more. She owed the world. She sometimes wondered what her mother's life would have been if she'd had only Walter. Just by being alive, Lina had harmed her. She needed to justify being luckier than her mother.

At the bottom of everything was always her mother.

Back at Barnard, parents were everywhere. Her roommate stood with two white-haired people in a whispered colloquy, which resulted in an invitation to join them for dinner. But Lina had to work at the store. By closing time she'd sold out the BARNARD MOM mugs, and only seven BARNARD DADS were left on the shelves.

Lina hadn't known that de Kooning's wife, Elaine, was a painter herself. She'd read that Lee Krasner, Pollock's wife, was an artist, too, but she hadn't heard that she practically worked as his gallerist. Krasner was still alive now and painting, even with arthritis. The girl who wore white blouses worked for her twice a week. A small group stood on the sidewalk outside the Hungarian Pastry Shop. Vistas were opening. The girl who painted in a slip dress (with a plaid coat thrown over it now in the first snow) held the leash of her straining dog. She and the woman with white blouses were characters in Lina's life, not friends exactly, but they mattered. The girl with the dog was a better artist than Lina. The one in white blouses caused a different agitation. Looking at her dollhouse, Lina felt she could have made it, if only she'd thought of it first.

There was a bookstore across from the Columbia gate that Lina used as a library. She walked over that afternoon—the sky seemed to be wringing its light out early, in the winter dusk—to look for a book about Elaine de Kooning. She couldn't find one. She did see a picture of her in a book about her husband. Elaine was beautiful. Lina stood for an hour, leafing through the book. When she heard a name she didn't know in class—and nearly every day there was at least one—she would look for that name in the art section here. One cold Sunday, she'd sat in a corner and read a whole book. No one seemed to mind. The people who worked here barely noticed her, except for one kid who was always shelving and said, hey.

48.

Susan told Walter she didn't have a date for the Winter Ball. "So you wanna come?" Carrie would be there; would it be strange to show up with Susan? He'd never been either's date. But the truth was obvious: Carrie wouldn't care. So Walter asked Mr. Barsani if he could borrow a suit. Mr. Barsani said, "Sure. Fits you. You're lucky. Most people have to at least hem. Just make sure no one spills on it."

At eight in the morning on a December Wednesday, Walter was eating cereal remembering that yesterday Susan had asked if he had a tuxedo, when the phone rang. He didn't have a tuxedo. Mr. Barsani kept tuxedos in a special closet, only one in each size. Susan had said a suit would be fine, but now he wished he'd said no to the whole thing. Who could be calling so early? It had to be something bad.

The man at headquarters in Chicago said they were giving him the go-ahead and asked for a fax number. Walter jumped. The Wurster library had one of the new machines; he sprinted over and explained the papers in a rush to Em Ball.

A work-study student walked in while the new beige machine was clacking and asked, "What's coming in?"

"Oh, that's Walter's future," Mrs. Ball said.

The window of the Karmann Ghia didn't go all the way up, so Walter fastened a seat belt over the papers as he drove to Sausalito. Mr. Wimmer put on his glasses and read while talking on the phone, then hung up and called, "Cheryl! We're going to Chicago."

They sat next to each other on the plane, the plastic gray trays open as Mr. Wimmer reread the paperwork in the small circle of light. When they landed, it was snowing.

Walter had stayed in a hotel only once before, a Motel 6 at the edge of town, for the funeral of his grandmother long ago. This bed on the twenty-ninth floor was deeply luxurious, but Walter couldn't sleep. In the morning, he put on the tie Mr. Barsani had given him for Christmas. In a glass tower, they were shown to a conference room with views of the city seamed by fast, evenly falling snow. A long table was set with folders, mechanical pencils, and pens where the knife and spoon would usually be. Uniformed women offered coffee, tea, and rolls from a basket. They were both pretty, like stewardesses.

The man Walter had talked to on the phone introduced the legal team.

"You don't have a lawyer?" he asked Mr. Wimmer.

"I have a lawyer but I didn't bring her. I also have a daughter I didn't bring."

Was this non sequitur a joke? People didn't laugh. Mr. Wimmer took out pictures of Violet, though, and then other men reached for their wallets and the table became cluttered with white-bordered pictures of kids, toothless girls with pigtails, freckled boys, ugly babies, each evidently cherished.

They finally opened their folders. The headquarters team gave speeches. Mr. Wimmer occasionally scribbled a note. He asked a few questions and each time nodded, accepting their answers. Plates with menus were placed before them by the silent, smiling women. They ate lunch right there, on china with cloth napkins.

Until late afternoon, the terms discussed had to do with dates of occupancy, square footage, breach of contract, and penalties. Mr. Wimmer asked for a two-and-a-half-year window for renovation. They demanded occupancy by June 1977. That seemed a long time from now. Mr. Wimmer stayed quiet. There was a round clock on the far wall. Finally, Mr. Wimmer said, "Well, if you need that, we'll have to get it to you. I'd feel a lot better, though, if we could stretch it to September and split the difference." Walter wondered if Mr. Wimmer wasn't a pushover.

One of the women now pulled down a screen, flicked off the lights, and projected a slide—Walter recognized one of his Polaroids! He looked to Mr. Wimmer. The next slide showed an overlay of the site with proposed parking lots, arrows to indicate streams of entrance and egress, and a truck bay station for deliveries. They talked for an hour about arteries. But where were his drawings?

Then they projected a slide simulating an all-new building on the site. A sound escaped from Walter. He looked again to Mr. Wimmer. A new building! The beauty of Central was its symmetry and lines. He'd scouted for months to find it. They spoke of "templates" and "the company brand" as the sky outside darkened and someone turned on the lights.

Walter was relieved when they called it a night; he needed to get alone with Mr. Wimmer. But as the women brought the men their coats, someone named a steakhouse.

"You've got your slaughterhouses here, all right," Mr. Wimmer said.

The executives took them to a low-ceilinged restaurant where a saxophone played loudly enough that you didn't have to talk but if you wanted to hear, you had to lean in to understand. "They're famous for aged beef," the man next to him said twice. Everyone ordered martinis. Walter sipped his, which at first tasted like medicine and then became smooth. The saxophone seemed to be pleading, as if the musician understood him. The steaks were enormous, served with baked potatoes and shredded green beans amandine. By the time the waiter took away their plates, the music had stopped. Walter was the only one who ordered dessert. His sundae arrived in a frosted silver-pedestaled bowl with a ceramic pitcher of hot fudge and small ramekins of blanched almonds and whipped cream.

They all watched him eat.

Finally, Walter was alone with Mr. Wimmer in a taxi. Suddenly shy, he asked what he thought.

"Just fine," Mr. Wimmer said, rapping the file on his lap.

"But those square boxes are a formula. And Central has a beauty worth preserving. The architects in Wurster love it! This is supposed to be something new, not just another store. We have to fight for the building's integrity."

"The thing I want to fight over is the lease term," Mr. Wimmer said. "They're at five years. I want to punch that out to ten. Even fifteen."

"Sure. I'm fine with that. But we have to keep Central. At least the edifice. This is my chance to make something."

"What you came asking me was how to make money. You wanted to earn a million bucks, if I remember." Mr. Wimmer took out a pencil and drew numbers on the back of his folder. "A change from five to eight years could end up being worth nine hundred thousand. You want to gussy up pretty buildings, that's a whole different business. One I'm not in. They have their ideas. Most of those details, I'm inclined to give them. I'd rather get any lease with Sears Roebuck than no lease. Remember, we don't own anything yet. This could be your first building. They're not hiring you for your architecture degree."

"I don't have one yet."

"Don't tell them that, either."

On the plane home, a stewardess brought them each a warm chocolate chip cookie. Mr. Wimmer mentioned that negotiating a commercial lease generally took three to four months. The sixty-one-page contract stipulated square footage of the building and the parking lot, entrance and egress, and a thousand other details regarding plumbing, loading facilities, and electrical grids, but it didn't explicitly say new construction. Mr. Wimmer knocked on the folder. "We'll take this letter of intent to the bank and we'll have a mortgage for 110 percent of the purchase price. We've already doubled the value. It's a no-brainer for the loan officer."

Snow fizzed outside the small oblong window. Carrie didn't love him, Walter remembered, and she was the first woman he'd loved. But he had this.

49.

A sound wove in and out of Walter's dream. Eventually it became the telephone. Someone wanted something. He slid down the knotted rope.

"Are you coming?" Susan's voice, but smaller.

The Winter Ball. Walter and Mr. Wimmer had landed in the afternoon. Walter had taken BART, then walked to campus and went straight to bed. He'd forgotten all about the dance. "Be right there," he said.

She was sitting alone in a cream-colored velvet gown, her arms long and bare, like a portrait, her hands on her lap, fiddling with pearls. Understanding sifted into him: he was very late. He hadn't picked up the suit from the Princeton Shop. She must be furious. She'd always been there, first an annoying girl who raised her hand in class, then a friend so constant that being with her was like being alone. But tonight, she didn't look like herself.

"Should we still go?" he asked.

"They'll have finished eating. People will be dancing." She *was* mad.

"I'm a pretty bad dancer."

The dress was tight, the small mound of her stomach newly revealed and sexual. They decided not to drive to the Oakland ballroom. Instead, they stayed sitting in two wing chairs, like parents waiting for teenagers to come home. He told her what had happened in Chicago, remembering Mr. Wimmer taking out the picture of his daughter. He explained the letter of intent. She stood up to get a paper and pen and smoothed her dress over her hips before sitting again. He wrote the numbers, subtracted taxes, federal, municipal, and state, as Mr. Wimmer had explained to him, estimating electricity and power. It still left a huge profit. "That can't be right. I guess the big question is renovation versus new construction, which turns out to be cheaper. I'm the only one who cares if it's beautiful. And every added dollar of renovation comes out of what I earn."

Susan wanted him to talk to her father. Or a lawyer. Both. She said that twice, then admitted she was starving. They decided to go for hamburgers.

The night marked another beginning. A hundred times, he'd thought about lifting the hair from Carrie's neck and bending down to kiss her, but now, with Susan, he imagined more carnal movements. He wanted to cup the small mound of her belly from behind and pull her against him. He felt his body in his pants and followed her upstairs.

She emerged from her closet in tailored slacks, loafers, and a ribbed sweater, still with her formal earrings on. She asked him to open the tiny clasp of her pearl necklace. Her neck smelled like fresh green peas. He'd always thought she was uptight. Sure of herself. Too something. But tonight corners were melting.

They both knew that this was a date. They walked up the hill to the Claremont Hotel.

Walter understood that he was someone who could always take on more. The addition of a new job calmed him. Still, Susan argued, this was different. "You really have to call my dad," she said. "They're in real estate. It's what they *do*."

He'd always known Susan liked him. He could say anything to her. But he'd drawn a line around himself. That had made it easy to be close. She'd climbed up the rope ladder and seen his Pelican loft with the bed unmade. She'd probably seen Carrie's poem, framed. He'd gotten nowhere with love and now he was twenty.

They ate cheeseburgers in the hotel dining room, sipping from goblets of red wine. Over a dessert they split, she fought with him about his design, her spoon aggressive in the sundae dish, digging around the bottom corners. He wanted to show her; he had close-ups of the building, but not here, back in the Pelican. So he drew the layout on a napkin.

"That doesn't look like a store. It looks like a high school."

"So people can shop in a place with history. Everyone remembers high school."

"Not necessarily fondly. I think if it's important to you that this works, do it their way."

"Their way is a shoebox. They have dozens of them already."

"I kind of like the one in Santa Monica."

She kept up with this long after Ken would have said, *Do what you want*. Even if what Walter wanted wasn't best for him. Walter felt an inkling of what this could be: someone who fought to tell you the truth you didn't want to hear, because she had a stake in your future. He picked up the check. She didn't lift her purse. It was a date, all right.

The walk back to the sorority was downhill, but cold. "The problem with walking," Susan said, "is walking back." At the door she said, "I'm scared."

Under the streetlight, diffused in fog, her earrings glowed. *Friendship* was the word that came to mind, not *love*, but friendship with a halo. He could imagine dinners like this, her leaning in to listen and then giving advice, her voice sharp, for his benefit. Almost involuntarily, he moved toward her face, a buzzing feeling; he tried to aim for the side of her mouth, not straight on, but her lips caught his. Kissing Susan could change everything.

"You got them to sign a lease for a building you don't own?" Susan's father sounded surprised.

"I guess we own it now," Walter said. Just saying that—that he was an owner—started a wave of dizziness close to nausea. The bank had approved the loan, 110 percent, as Mr. Wimmer predicted. Lina had called the morning Walter skipped class to BART over to the city to sign papers. "How's school?" he'd asked her, and only half listened to her answer as he stretched the cord to the mirror above the sink and tied his tie, the way he'd learned from tying other people's at the Princeton Shop. It was different on your own neck.

Now, sitting in the room Susan shared with Carrie, he scanned the small print of the sixty-one-page contract. "It doesn't *say* we own it. It says we promise to deliver the building September 1, 1977." Mr. Wimmer hadn't claimed anything untrue. What would he have done if the men in Chicago had asked when they'd bought the building? For almost an hour, Walter talked to Susan's father, whose dark, fast-moving legs he remembered from the day they left for college, and who now delivered the death sentence for his dream. "You won't get earthquake insurance, not for a California brick building constructed before World War Two."

"The wrecking ball," he said when Susan returned. "I did twenty-seven drawings to scale. That beautiful building. If only it weren't brick."

"Kill your darlings."

They hadn't had sex yet or even made out lying down so that the points of their bodies touched, but that would probably come. Thinking of this gave their conversations gentle electricity, like the tickle of a feather.

Mr. Wimmer had arranged the loan through his banker. He owned 15 percent of the project. He'd given Walter two names for general contractors in the counties closest to the site, but despite regular invitations, he still hadn't seen Central. "It's your building," he said. Before winter quarter midterms, Walter would have to hire his GC, file for permits, and draw mechanicals. Em Ball hired Rory for tea and cookies. The lady poet gave him a reference. Quitting the film archive turned out to be so easy it was insulting. Before Walter had finished explaining, his boss started filling in his blocks on the schedule. All along he'd been that replaceable.

The Princeton Shop would probably have to go. "You're not in college to become a suit salesman," Em Ball said.

But it was only Saturdays and Walter still coveted that promised suit. "For a graduation I probably won't have."

There was no way he could graduate in June.

Walter called Mr. Wimmer to ask him again to come to see Central. He offered to pick him up in Marin. Mr. Wimmer was leaving, though, to appear as Santa Claus at the Sausalito shopping center he'd built. He did this every year. Walter had forgotten his wife's obsession with Christmas.

50.

Outside the airplane window, snow continued to bullet down. The pilot announced another delay. All the months Lina hadn't seen her mother weighed on her, as people rustled in their seats. By the time the plane taxied on the runway (a wing's red lights blinking), it was three hours late.

Julie was waiting at LAX. Dinner was ready at home, she said, they'd head down to Norwalk tomorrow, but Lina had to see her mother tonight. She asked to borrow the car. Julie insisted on driving. She'd pack up dinner, she said.

"What about Donnie?"

"I'll leave his on the table. He knows." She left a large portion in a glass casserole.

When they arrived at the hospital, Julie knew where to park. She lagged behind as Lina ran to the parlor, where her mother sat with a blanket covering her lap.

Lina fell on her. For a long minute, it felt good to cry. But when she opened her eyes, her mother looked fearful. She had raised her arm, as if to protect herself.

"It's me, Mom," Lina said. Had she forgotten?

"Oh, hi," her mother said, playing along.

Lina took in more now. She didn't recognize one article of clothing her mother had on, and in these other garments—which must have belonged originally to other patients—her body looked different, too. Her cheeks were fuller, burying the bones of her face.

Julie stepped closer, carrying the bags of food. "Here's Lina, her plane was late. Come, Diane, we brought dinner." Julie knew where to find plates in the dim kitchen. The three of them sat at a long table and ate an Indian chicken dish, delicately spiced.

Julie said she made larger portions now and brought some of whatever turned out to Diane. "She enjoys it," she said. "Her sense of taste is, if anything, more."

During the Christmas show and dinner, Lina's mother ignored her.

"She's mad," Julie said. "You were gone. She can be like a child."

Her mother wanted Donnie to walk her back to 301 to bed.

Christmas morning, they drove down again with presents for their mom and the cat. Julie brought food that they ate at a picnic table outside. Her mother seemed to accept Lina now the way she accepted Julie, as an acquaintance to whom she had to be polite. She remembered Walter.

He shook his head. "You got to stop waiting for her to come back the way she was," he said. "We've got to move on."

Before they left, Lina stopped by her mother's bed. There were pictures taped on the bare wall: Walter at graduation, her mom as a girl on a bike, she and Julie in their pointed white caps the day they graduated as nurses.

Walter, Lina, and Donnie went to see *One Flew Over the Cuckoo's Nest*.

"It isn't like that," Donnie said, coming out of the theater.

"Those people weren't real," Lina said. "They were *com*ically crazy."

"Like to see the Norwalk guys on a basketball court," Donnie said. "And that nurse."

Walter asked Lina, "So everything's still okay at school?" If all went right, according to the lease he kept in an accordion file, he could pay for her last year of tuition.

"I love it," she said.

She didn't seem to remember him convincing her to go. He told her he'd be able to help; she could maybe stay four years instead of taking so many credits to graduate in three. But she might not even need him. She'd received a Pell Grant. She said she didn't mind a five-course load. He told her again to send a picture of herself in front of a Barnard building for their mom's bed.

Maybe her mother didn't remember her, Lina all of a sudden thought, because she'd never sent a picture. She hadn't sent a picture because she wasn't beautiful anymore and she didn't want her mother to be disappointed. Her mother had always loved having a beautiful girl.

51.

When a wrecking ball swung at the brick edifice of Central, Walter felt it in his chest.

Piles of trash littered the ground, possibly things that should be salvaged, but where could he sell them? He was supposed to be memorizing Shakespeare. Jackhammers blared. Heat rained onto his arms. A huge crane lifted debris, dropping a screen of dirt. Walter made a list for the GC, whose clipboard rested on the shelf of his belly.

"Don't you have some test you got to study for?" the GC said.

"I have to pass this quarter," Walter said. "I've already taken the money."

On a legal pad, Walter numbered eighty-seven tasks. He'd hired two graduate design students at minimum wage to draw the electrical grid. He needed them, to remember his other life.

The crew talked about pussy. White guys, Black guys, Hispanic guys, two Asians, bragged in the relentless sun about getting ass. And all were getting it, apparently.

Susan and Carrie had already memorized their lines. Walter was still reading from the book. But he had a massive loan from the Bank of California. That felt more pressing than *Much Ado About Nothing*. To file for a leave of absence, he needed to tell Mr. Matthews.

"You'll still graduate," Susan had said last night, on the sorority porch. "Only later."

"Someday," Carrie had said, yawning. She'd slept on a sidewalk in front of a San Francisco district court to watch the Patty Hearst trial. She had a reporter's card from *The Daily Californian*, but she still didn't make it in.

Walter pocketed a tape measure, grabbing a hard hat from the pegboard on the trailer wall, where a *Playboy* pinup calendar had appeared this morning. He wanted to measure the yards between the perimeter and the future footprint. When he finished his calculations, he found the GC on a bulldozer. Shouting above the noise, he said that the nine-inch red linoleum tiles heaped in the dumpster should be salvaged. "Full of asbestos," the GC yelled, ramming the machine into loud reverse. By the time Walter took the Ashley exit and drove uphill toward Berkeley, he admitted that architecture had nothing to do with this project. He'd found a beautiful building in the middle of California and was demolishing it to build an ugly one.

In class, he'd been the one to say, "What about the client? Some of us hope to make a living at this."

"We know *you'll* succeed, Walter," a girl behind him once said.

He'd liked being the straight man in Berkeley, but maybe only there.

52.

All the time that Lina was working in the Barnard store, throwing pots in the clay room, sitting in classes, doodling, listening to her dorm friends complain about their mothers, Donnie was growing up in Julie's apartment. Lina called Walter to talk about whether this was even okay. "I mean, when we moved there, the idea was a year maybe. This summer it'll be two."

"She might like having someone there with her, besides cats."

"I'm sure the cats never gave her as much trouble."

"Donnie's a good kid. It's not healthy for people to live alone."

"You don't think we should ask Julie about it?"

"We don't have any alternatives to offer."

Lina remembered the kitchen next to Donnie's room, Julie's tense grip on the handle of a pan. Julie had become a real cook. Those lessons. Indian cooking. Thai.

"How's art?" Walter asked before they hung up.

Lina had finally told them about her major, over the holiday. They'd merely nodded, which was also infuriating. It hadn't mattered, she decided, because she was female. They thought she'd get married. That would be her career.

Only Mrs. Anjani was disappointed. "Oh well, you can always teach," she said. "It isn't the worst life. You'll have your summers."

At least Walter made a choice, she thought. He'd taken those pre-med classes. She remembered his fucking A-plus on the bunga-low refrigerator. He could have become a doctor, but he de*cided* on architecture or building or whatever it was he was doing instead of graduating on time. Lina thought what she was trying for (even the name "art" seemed pretentious) was, though she'd never say it, noble. She hadn't even picked it, exactly—this was all she could do, even a little, and it happened to be the hardest thing in the world. She doubted that she could succeed.

The college store manager caught Lina drawing when she was supposed to be refolding sweatshirts and fired her. But then, the same day, Troy gave her his morning hours in the clay room. Unlike Lina, Troy had taken to education. He'd come to Colum-bia knowing he wanted to be an artist but then fell for the core curriculum.

"The fucking great books."

"Do you swear even in your thoughts?" he asked.

Her mouth had driven her mother crazy, she told him.

"Of course. She's a mother. See, around Judy, I stopped calling her mama when I was eleven, I keep it to myself that I love the god-damn *Odyssey*." At dawn, Troy still subwayed downtown, looking for new graffiti by the artist called SAMO, which he said stood for Same Old. Lina thought he didn't sleep enough or that she slept too much. He was dating a straight-up Kenyan nursing student.

By now, she and Troy talked most days, she went to the Hun-garian Pastry Shop with other art students, and even attended the occasional party, but she was still in preparation for life, while her mother was still in recovery.

53.

Walter waited for Ken in the trapped light of the co-op's entry. In the summer, Walter thought, the two of them could drive to Clovis together and life would feel the way it used to when Ken was the person he saw the most. They couldn't plant for another year, the irrigation and hardscape had to be drawn.

They walked for an hour, stopping in the eucalyptus grove so Walter could unroll his plans on a stump. "I can't wait to show you the place."

"What are they going to sell in this future emporium?"

Walter hadn't considered what people would be *buying* inside his building; they'd be shopping, obviously, but for what? The Outlet, they'd named it. In design class, Jan Tudor had talked about the imperative of use. "Whatever they sell," he said, "business'll probably be good because there's not much else to do in Clovis. I saw a sign for a rodeo . . ."

"Maybe we can build them something to do," Ken said.

Jan had shown slides of apartment blocks designed to echo medieval town squares. He and Ken sketched a playground with a fifty-yard sandbox. "At the edges I'd like something fruiting," Walter said. "To screen parking. Citrus, maybe. How much do trees cost?"

"My dad always says it's better to put a one-dollar plant into a hundred-dollar hole."

"How is your dad?" Walter asked.

"Melinda applying to med school hasn't helped. They think she'll leave me for another doc."

The phone was already ringing when Walter rolled his bike into the Pelican.

Ken's father. "No commercial landscaping until after graduation. I told Ken. I'm telling you the same. Finish up first. Get the degree."

In a week, Walter planned to put in the paperwork for a leave of absence.

"I think that's a mistake. But I'm not your parent. Have you told your father?" He must have known about Walter's mom. Otherwise, he would have said "your father and mother."

"My father's not really in the picture."

"I didn't know that. I'm sorry. Well, I've given you my two cents."

Mr. Matthews was no better. All business, he said he had nothing to do with withdrawals or readmittance, there were forms for that. He didn't stand when Walter thanked him. "Glad I could be of use," he said, looking at papers on his desk.

Walter had disappointed the man. Still, he knew he was doing the right thing.

Mr. Barsani shook his head. Then he called his own son, a sophomore at Cornell. "Antonio? Your dad here," Walter heard as he left the store.

Enough of fathers.

Susan knew he was driving to Clovis every day, but no one else did. He hadn't talked much to his sister or brother. Things were not going in order. He'd meant to build his life and then figure out love. He remembered Carrie's hands trembling the paper of her poem, the poem that was now in his possession. He tried to be his best self with Carrie, but always having to be your best self was exhausting. And she didn't feel the same way about him. Susan had picked him and he wasn't sure he could stop it. But why didn't he ever get to pick?

He took his last final in an auditorium. The teacher wrote a question on the blackboard: *How has your reading of Shakespeare's late tragicomedies changed your life?*

Carrie lifted both elbows, pulling her hair into a ponytail. Walter thought for a full fifteen minutes as he heard pens tock on paper around him. Finally, he opened his blue book and began. There was a particular sound in a tiered room of fifty people trying to translate their thoughts into sentences on paper in the spring. After an hour and a half, they stood, one by one, placing their blue books on the front table, and left. The professor stood at the podium, reading a book. Over the quarter, he'd sometimes lectured in a wig and Elizabethan costume; he'd once leaped in brandishing a sword, reciting a soliloquy from memory. Walter glanced at the clock as it jittered ahead. He believed adult love would be like Shakespeare's older heroes and heroines, who reunited after breaking up and joked with each other, understanding their own faults. The room was empty now, except for himself and two others. Walter had already filed the forms to suspend enrollment. This exam had not been as difficult as he'd thought. The other two walked to the front and the professor accepted their blue books. He shook Walter's hand when he thanked him.

There was a feeling of confetti in the air when Walter stepped outside. People stood with radios on the balconies of apartments Walter passed on his way up the hill.

In the co-op attic where he used to live, Walter got down on all fours and looked under the bed. The cat's eyes, from the far corner, gleamed like lit marbles. Melinda was doing the splits on the floor. Ken held a letter. "She got in," he said.

"Remember the English guy who said one out of three?" Walter asked. "You're the one."

There was something so triumphant about the letter that Walter and Ken stood looking at it for longer than it took to read. It seemed amazing. Dr. Melinda.

54.

Walter sat at a tulip table in Susan and Carrie's room reading a clipping Em Ball found.

> *When they opened in 1947, a few blocks east of the Santa*
> *Monica Pier, they had to have police officers for crowd control.*
> *Two thousand people pushed into the store the first ten minutes.*
> *They had a main entrance for pedestrians and also entrances*
> *from the back parking lot. Parking lots were new then. A*
> *decade later, Santa Monica's first civil rights demonstration*
> *was held there in front of Sears. . . .*

A petal fell from a mason jar of roses. Susan's glasses lay on a yellow legal pad. She looked at the grainy news photo of the square, flat building. "I like the lettering," *Sears* in cursive neon.

She knelt by the stereo, flipping through albums. She *owned* Karen Carpenter. Just then, Carrie slammed in, her hair up in a clip. "Oh, hi" was all she said. She grabbed a book from the floor, mumbled "Virginia Woolf," and left, footsteps cascading downstairs.

He'd blown it and ended up with the wrong girl. "She seemed strange."

"She was probably surprised to see you here."

He knew exactly what Susan meant. "Should we say something?"

"Not yet."

Walter pushed his bike into the Pelican a week later and found Carrie sitting in the dark. She wanted him to accompany her on a newspaper assignment, her last-ditch effort to find something she could make a living at that was still writing. She'd already been admitted to library school. Her dad had mailed in the deposit.

"Did you talk to Em Ball?" Walter asked.

"Yeah, she had me over. Thanks for the introduction. I loved her house. But anyway. Tonight." She'd let herself get recruited by some Moonies on purpose. The Moonies hadn't admitted they were Moonies. They never did, but you could tell. "The nude nylons with tie-up shoes." They'd invited her to dinner and she was going undercover. But all of a sudden, she didn't want to be there alone.

The address belonged to an old building on the North Campus. Carrie elbowed Walter; a framed portrait of Reverend Moon in the entry. A woman with long, dun-colored hair led them into a room of low tables that, on inspection, were hollow-core doors on cinder blocks.

A free meal, Walter thought.

The food was unidentifiable: green-brown strands in a bowl of warm, viscous liquid. A skinny guy in overalls next to Walter lifted his to his mouth. When he finished, Walter swapped bowls with him. When the guy finished that, Walter gave him Carrie's. As a wan girl collected bowls, a man with a shaved head called the woman who'd led them in to play the guitar. She stood, head down, strumming, and sang "Blowin' in the Wind." Walter wondered if there would be dessert. Oreos or something. The woman's voice veered and creaked. Pitiful. But when she finally stopped, the clapping continued a long time. No dessert in sight, they snuck out.

On the street, Walter and Carrie talked at once, interrupting each other. They decided that finding a person's secret hope, like that woman's to be a singer, and then praising her for what, in fact, she couldn't do, was a way to hold her captive. If you searched for a real strength, even a pedestrian ability, like knowing how to change a tire or do dishes, and praised someone for that, she might recognize her skill and become independent. The world needed people to change tires and do dishes. A person with a skill could leave you. Whereas the only audience for the concert they'd just heard was this group of Berkeley Moonies.

"Thus, library school," Carrie said.

"It's not the same. You're talented." As they neared the Pelican Building, he asked, "Should I walk you home?"

"Let's have tea."

Stacked boxes of the latest *Poetry Review* towered inside the door. Carrie banged the kettle onto the stove. She asked how he liked his new big job.

He said it was an opportunity, but he missed classes. Their conversation was eerily proper. She was going to grad school in North Carolina. "No one's going to pay me to read novels. This way, at least I'll always be around books."

It was strange to be alone with her. He'd wanted this. For years, he would have done anything to make it happen. They sat on the arms of couches, holding their tea mugs. He told her she shouldn't give up on writing poetry. She said she never would, but poets hardly ever made a living. It was getting late and she was still here. This chance didn't feel like a chance. He almost wished she'd leave. Then she was pulling her shirt over her head, not in a gesture of abandon; the fabric tangled and her shoulders curled in like a child's. She wasn't wearing a bra and her breasts were small and beautiful, the nipples maroon. She looked down, compliant. He felt drawn to lift her chin, uncurl her shoulders, but something held him back. Why now? A campus maintenance truck rattled outside.

Then it came to him: she knew. She'd always had his allegiance. His love, really. She'd had it without a use for it and now she sensed change; she was afraid of losing her reign over him.

"Do you really want this?" he asked. "I don't think you do."

"I don't know," she said.

"You don't. If you don't know, you don't. Come on. I'll walk you home."

She put her shirt back on and they left. For the first two blocks they didn't say anything. Then Carrie asked, "How's your mom?"

"She's okay. Pretty much the same." He realized that though he'd always thought of Carrie as the one who could understand him, it was hard to talk to her about his mom. Susan knew more of the details.

Carrie would always have him anyway, he thought, the way she had him now. Spring smells of dirt and rainwater rose from the ground. Love was a mixed business. As in building, he couldn't afford the refinement he desired. He needed too much. Carrie had been his great romance. He hadn't been hers. With Susan it wasn't romance, exactly. It was home.

He climbed two steps at a time to the room where she sat reading, with a yellow pencil. He could hear an ice-cream truck outside. It was spring break and they were the only ones in the old house. She looked up at him from her book.

There had never been a question.

An awkward twirl, a bump against her dresser, and they were finally on her bed, shoes dropping off the side, one then another.

Okay, it was happening.

She kept her glasses on, unbuttoning her blouse. Was this passion? If the phone had rung, he could have answered. Outside, dense cumulus clouds moved across the blue. He'd thought touching Carrie would have changed him into someone else. He was still himself now, opening Susan's blouse. The afternoon had a feeling of summer.

She stopped everything, stood, walked naked to her dresser, and took out a small box. He missed her on the bed for those minutes. Her legs looked better all in one piece. He'd thought her calves muscular. They made perfect sense now, knees like quivering egg yolks. Her skin had a smell like warm grain. She sat at the edge, frosting the diaphragm with gel. Breeze lifted the curtain. It was a square room, the walls and the floor painted white. The table, where she'd been reading, held a jar of thin-petaled flowers. He burst out laughing after he came.

She laughed then, too, saying, "What? What?"

They lay there, not sleeping, one or the other of them getting up to go to the bathroom down the hall and then returning. There was a tiny sink in one corner of the room. Her white bed reminded him of his mom's in the place. He thought of his mom less frequently now and never for long. At one point, Susan flattened her belly, pulled out the diaphragm, and went to wash it in that sink. A white nightgown hung on a peg. She pulled it on.

When they began again, she retrieved the diaphragm. It sprang onto the floor. She had to wash it once more and start over. He lifted a piece of her hair, looped it around his finger. She was not beautiful, but there were no bad angles. Maybe that *was* beautiful.

Walter put on Duke Ellington. *It don't mean a thing*.

Three times, Susan called restaurants to ask if they could get in and three times they didn't leave the bed. Horns pranced around the ceiling.

Susan scrambled eggs at the enormous sorority stove, twirling from the refrigerator to the counter. She loved to dance. She and Carrie had danced at the same studio as little girls.

"Remember when I was supposed to get a ride up with your family?" Walter asked.

"My mother said something."

"My mom was hypersensitive. Especially about being a mom."

"I won't make excuses for my mother," Susan said. "She's impossible. No one understands that more than I do. My dad spends his life trying to repair the damage."

"Are they happily married?"

"I don't know how he can be, but they are."

Walter smelled like green apples, even in yesterday's clothes, after showering in the airy sorority bathroom. He let Susan sleep and drove to the bakery where they'd gone the first morning of scouting. The bakers gave him a muffin straight from the oven. Blueberry cornmeal. He poured cream from the industrial refrigerator into his coffee, leaving a dollar on the metal table. He allowed himself some luxuries now.

Outside the Clovis city limit, guys lined up for daywork, leaning against a wall, like girls in a beauty pageant. Not all were young. Walter sped up. He hated the idea of his GC pointing: You, You, Not You.

In the trailer, looking at a pinup calendar that showed a girl Walter's age spread in a pose he hoped she'd been paid a lot for, he saw his mom's birthday was last week. He'd forgotten. He'd send something. It wouldn't matter that he was late; he doubted she kept track anymore. Had they celebrated? Julie and Donnie had probably driven down. What could he get her? Susan would know.

The ground underneath the old school was full of rocks. Foundation work had fallen eight days behind schedule and his structural engineer was late. The lighting had to be redrawn before the conduit could be laid in. He bent over the plan. The GC sipped from a green thermos. "You know, the guys say you're a cross-dresser. And a virgin. Think they got you there."

"Please take down this calendar," Walter said.

The grad students trekked the site in hard hats. Walter kept a ledger. He'd checked out a book from the library to learn accounting. But the numbers made him daydream: he'd buy his mom a house. Somewhere quieter than LA. This was his old fantasy, revised. Maybe Donnie would still go along. Walter could buy an undervalued place and fix it up. He'd know how by then. A small town where she could walk, meet a friend. Maybe Julie would move, too. She'd said she was thinking of retiring.

The grad students, holding flooring samples and a color board, came to ask if they could bring a few friends down for a day.

He and Susan had the sorority house to themselves. Walter drove there straight from Clovis every evening. The last night of spring break they baked a chicken and talked about whether or not to tell Carrie. Not, they decided, for now.

The day everyone came back to campus, after work, Walter turned south, for no reason. He didn't feel like going back to the empty Pelican Building. His mom had attended College of the

Sequoias and then transferred to UCLA. She'd loved UCLA and had often driven them through the campus. College of the Sequoias was in a place called Visalia.

His mom had been smart and pretty. He'd seen pictures. College of the Sequoias sounded small, backed by the Sierra Nevada. But he was passing huge agricultural sheds, factories, and strip malls. He had to detour around a bucolic town fenced off for a maximum-security prison under construction. When he finally found the college, the buildings were painted the ubiquitous brownish white of California institutions, including the unfinished prison. He parked. He didn't notice any buildings that looked like dorms. Most were one story, flat. He bought a chicken taco from a cart and asked where the sororities and fraternities were. The kid shrugged, then handed him his taco in yellow paper, darkened in spots from juice. The people he saw didn't look like Berkeley students. They were older, with shorter hair. Can you look poor? He decided yes.

His mom had put herself through college working in a canning factory. She'd also talked about sorority parties. From those contradictory bits of history he'd done what listeners have always done: he'd chosen the romance. Now he saw. College of the Sequoias didn't look like a school that had sororities.

He couldn't have believed, when his mom first went into the place in Norwalk, that she would be there now. He would be graduating with everyone else, he thought, if she was still herself. She would have come to see him walk across the lawn in a cap and gown.

55.

A teacher in the MFA program—"the lady sculptor," Troy called her—was having a show. He and Lina took three subways to the Brooklyn warehouse and walked among huge iron horses. A wall was hung with female heads mounted on plaques. *Trophy Wives* was the series title.

They both admired the work, but on the train back Lina was quiet. Troy kicked her boot until she said what was wrong. "The women everyone likes do work that looks like men's. Big. Monumental. Horses."

"They're broken-down horses. Sad old men slumping on them. Did you see their dicks? They're not heroic. That's her thing. She's the opposite of traditional statuary."

"She's beautiful. That probably helps." Lina knew she sounded pathetic.

"You're plenty pretty," Troy said, and Lina recognized the kindness of this. She'd never been his type. Troy went for tall Black women with big breasts and what he called noble asses.

"That's because I'm Black," he'd once said, when she asked him if he dated white girls.

She hadn't yet found a reliable path to her talent, if she had any, but Lina felt most inspired the closer she came to pain.

"You can be the Arshile Gorky of Barnard," Troy said.

She'd read about Gorky in the bookshop. "Didn't he commit suicide?"

"Not till way later. You can be middle-period Gorky, when he got married and had a kid and became wildly successful."

Gorky was another artist Lina hadn't heard of until this year. She was ashamed of her education. She went to a museum every week and made herself look at one new gallery each time. It would take her fourteen months at the Met, she figured, before she'd have to start over again.

"Why don't you try sculpture again?" Troy asked.

"There's so much construction. Engineering. It's like building a car."

"What about, like, Calder's circus? I bet he made those wire dolls sitting down. You know when he was a student he worked for a police magazine. They sent him out to sketch the Ringling Brothers."

Lina told Troy about her high school teacher, Mr. Riddle, who'd welded together debris he found left after the Watts Riots. He rescued a cash register from a burned-out store. "That store never did open up again," he'd told her. "Korean people. Older."

———

More than halfway through college, Lina's real life had still not yet begun. She was trying to be a painter. But, while she arranged her life around this ambition—was that the right word for it? Maybe the more accurate one would be *wish*—she didn't spend much time painting. She thought about shapes while sitting at the bus stop. And now she stood in her studio waiting, listening to a rake scrape on concrete somewhere outside. She was waiting for some prompting. Not an idea, exactly. More like a hunch.

A group of kids passed below, loud and happy.

56.

Walter was having sex every night. Sometimes twice, once three times. But he didn't feel fully romantic. Or maybe this *was* him fully romantic. He believed, though, that strands of passion ran inside him, still untapped. He remembered Carrie's maroon nipples. Like hearing a scrap of melody. Was that romance?

He and Susan had their first fight. *I don't believe in Valentine's Day* was what he'd said that started it. That Hallmark invented the holiday.

"Hallmark's older than I'd thought, then," she said, "because Chaucer wrote Saint Valentine's Day was when birds find their mates. There's some reference in *Hamlet*, too, I think. And isn't it Mother's Day Hallmark invented? Mother's Day, Valentine's Day, they're not things to believe in or not believe in. They don't have a *theology*. They're opportunities to make someone feel appreciated or to deny them that."

"It's June, Susan," he pointed out.

"I'm not talking about whether or not you'll send me a card next February." She shook her head. "I can't be with a withholder. I won't live with little denials." The way she said that, it sounded like he'd proposed.

She was like a dog trained to sniff out drugs. She'd found the missing strain in his affection. She wanted the Valentine feeling. Probably everyone did. But alone that night in the Pelican, listening to the Beatles, he softened. *That* wasn't there, maybe. But a lot else was. *Fun was the one thing that money can't buy.* They did have fun.

Maybe this was the difference between a great love and a real one.

The next day, after work, he bought daffodils. When he handed them to her and reached for her neck, it felt like proposing. With a slam he realized this had always been the fear. With Susan, there would never be a reason for it to end.

He missed a day of construction for her graduation. The night before, Susan and Carrie gave a dinner party on the sorority porch, with dishes from *The Moosewood Cookbook*. Susan slept in Walter's loft and left before her parents arrived in the morning. She and Carrie would fly to India in a week. Carrie would return for library school. But Susan, usually the most organized of them all, planned to continue traveling, for she didn't know how long. When she was gathering her things from the chair in his attic, he said, "So is this it? I mean, us?"

She asked, "Have you ever read Jane Austen?"

He hadn't gotten around to her yet. She said that Jane Austen had written a book about a brat. At one point, this brat is asking herself whether she's in love with a guy she thinks she's in love with. Because she finds, when he leaves town, she's completely able to be herself. She decides she's "quite enough in love." Susan looked down. "I think you're quite enough in love. Now I have to decide if I need something more. Anyway, you should try reading her."

At graduation, Mr. Matthews told Walter that he hoped to see him walk next year. Carrie stood between her mother and father, holding a bouquet of roses wrapped in green tissue as if she was about to drop them on the ground. Dr. Melinda felt bird-boned in his arms when he hugged her. Everyone was going away, and he was staying. It was hard to explain to people's parents. He'd never convince Ken's dad that the plot of his future would turn on finding Central. He didn't know if he'd come back to school. If he did return, everyone he cared about would be gone.

He stayed in the Pelican Building another nineteen months. Over the Ping-Pong table, where he'd done layouts for the *Berkeley*

Poetry Review, he and Ken redrew the irrigation, moving it two feet farther from the foundation. That first summer, they drove to big commercial nurseries in the Central Valley. Walter wanted roses, but Ken said that they required finicky maintenance.

"You can have roses at your house someday. For here, we need something trample-resistant, like ferns."

Walter didn't find ferns exciting. "Story of my life."

Eventually even Cathy left. He watched her graduate from behind a tree. He still lived in the Pelican, with an almost unimaginable sum of money in a Wells Fargo account.

Then, just after the new year of 1978, the leak sprang.

57.

Lina waited until the kid was at the register. He'd seen her reading in the corner all last year. She wanted him to know she *bought* books, too.

He charged her half the sticker price. She felt a pulse of luck, then made herself alert him to the discrepancy.

"On sale," he said. His name was Etienne Wong. He was half French, half Chinese. He'd grown up in the neighborhood. His mother and dad taught dance. They'd had a studio on Amsterdam.

"Ballet? Modern?"

"Ballroom."

Only a few red and brown leaves were still on the branches outside. Most had fallen.

What was supposed to happen to her? Lina wanted a career, but by the end of her second fall in New York, she still spent more time waiting to paint than painting. The girl in slip dresses stood working whenever Lina passed her half-open door. How did she do that? When Lina asked, the girl, Larkin, said, "I don't think about it."

And other people fell in love, Lina couldn't help noticing. She never had. She didn't count Dino, though she remembered the chaste mornings he'd taught her to play tennis in the dewy park on courts painted like Mondrians.

———

Etienne lived on the ground floor of an old building. He'd made his own sleeping loft. On the walls hung pictures of a female body-builder who turned out to be his sister. He gave Lina the best chair while he cooked. A Morris chair, he explained, and showed her how to adjust the level of the back. He'd found it in an alley and restored it.

He handed her a bowl of pasta with soba noodles, asparagus, peas, and spices. She ate it all. He refilled her tumbler of wine.

She admired the chair. What could they talk about, though?

She unbuttoned his shirt and his skin was smooth, evenly brown. He had no hair at all on his chest. He was beautiful, like Gauguin's women were beautiful, and his face had that wide-boned quality of submission. She liked touching him the way she imagined a man would, touching a woman.

"What are you studying?" he asked, and as she listed her classes, he said, "I was no good at school."

"Do you think you'd ever go back?"

"I'm happy at the bookstore. They promoted me to assistant manager."

They couldn't quite talk.

In her bed, a screen of falling snow against the dull red-brick building out the window, he stopped. "You're not responding to me."

"What do you mean?" she asked.

"From the waist down you're not responding."

Girls on her hall freshman year had talked about the mechanics of sex the way they'd talked about their diets. One had had a vibrator.

She squirmed, ticklish, at the bristle of his chin on her thighs. He asked her, from there, if she masturbated. She hadn't, though her dorm friends had talked about that, too.

"We'll have to teach you."

The orgasm was unmistakable. She sat up, embarrassed that he'd seen her tremble. It felt as if her belly wasn't flat anymore.

She turned her head when he tried to kiss her with that mouth.

"Tell me if it hurts."

It hurt a little, something sharp. But then just a pressure.

So this was the real first time. January 17, 1977. After, she threw a pillow at him. They were both hungry. She made Top Ramen on her hot plate, wearing only a T-shirt and socks. Feet got dirty here from just walking barefoot at home. Lina remembered the model on the plinth and had taken to wearing socks, even to bed.

A week later, she opened her mail to find a copy of *Our Bodies, Ourselves.*

Lina would have liked to fall in love properly, the way people did in the books in her great books class. Maybe the writers had been exaggerating? Still, she thought she wanted that someday. It didn't have to be now. She and Etienne saw each other every two or three weeks, always alone. She never introduced him to a friend. They talked about the books he was reading, by philosophers she had never heard of. Once, she took him to the Met, to the rooms that quieted her, the large, empty galleries of torsos. They walked around the evocative fragments where she could still sense love centuries later, lingering around a hip, or a missing forearm.

In April, three heavy packages arrived. Mrs. Anjani's dishes; they were old, a beautiful green glaze. Lina kept them in her closet, where they'd be safest. Treasures for a future life.

Every time she managed to work, she painted a can of flowers. Flowers drooping. Fresh-cut stems. One blown dandelion in an evanescent silver it had taken her a week to make.

58.

Dino called to ask Donnie why he didn't see Evan anymore. He said it might be good if the boys got together. It would mean a lot to Evan.

Donnie liked Evan fine. He'd just been busy for kind of a long time. People asked him to go to the beach at night. He rode along and sat in front of the big bonfires they built in the sand, sometimes getting up to find a piece of driftwood to throw onto the pyre. This is what high school kids did in Los Angeles during the seventies.

They packed themselves into cars on cold nights and drove to Santa Monica, then trudged through the marine layer toward the loud waves. They lit fires in pits already dug out, lined with ashes and bits of charcoaled wood from older embers. They cooked hot dogs on long sticks and roasted marshmallows with a somber air. Some of them stalked off in pairs, to find a spot far enough away from the circle to feel alone on the sand under a blanket, to talk about their secrets, which mostly had to do with their parents' sadness, and so the shapes their bodies made together couldn't be seen. But Donnie just sat, hugging his knees, and stared into the flames. It felt important to be here at the edge of the world late late at night, uncomfortable, the cold of deep sand seeping up, even through blankets.

A few kids had cars; many more jammed into them. Others hitched rides home. Most stopped at Ships all-night diner for hot single-dish pie à la mode before returning to their sleeping, troubled houses, which seemed more peaceful in the dark.

Before he got off the phone, Donnie asked Dino how he was.

Okay, Dino said. Still the same.

Did you pass that test you were always dreading?

No. I'm taking some time off. Getting some things together. Then I'll go back and take it again. How's your sister? She still liking school?

The day after that call, Donnie went to the computer room, but Evan now played games that he didn't understand. They tried to start a round of Chinese chess, but nothing took. Donnie didn't return to the computer room, but whenever he saw Evan in the halls, he invited him to the beach with people on the coming weekend. And once, November of junior year, Evan went. He sat in his creased khakis next to Donnie on the uncomfortable sand. People offered him food from the long sticks, but other than that they went over and around him the way they would a log or a rock. Evan didn't like any of it, Donnie could tell. Evan shook his head like a bird shaking water out of its feathers. He left at ten, walking to the pay phone to call Dino to pick him up. Donnie closed his eyes, listening to the waves boom.

Dino didn't call Donnie again, and when Donnie saw Evan in the halls that year, he seemed happier. He understood that they couldn't follow each other where they were going. It was a real break, but nothing mean.

That November night on the beach, before Evan left, Donnie asked, "How's your family? Your mom still cooking?"

"It's a little better now that I'm the only one left," he said. "She has no excuse for making stuff I hate. And some of it, I've started to eat." Evan thought he was heading the wrong way, Donnie knew, toward stupidity and even danger.

But there was nothing Donnie could do: this was his one and only life.

59.

Walter surprised Lina, knocking at her door, the fall of her senior year. She felt fluttery in the chest, honored that he'd come. "I had to see you here at least once before you graduate," he said. "Since you don't like sending pictures." Etienne had taken a picture of Lina in front of the art building and she'd overnight mailed it to the hospital. Walter's building had opened; he'd sent *her* a picture of him cutting a ribbon. She took him to the Hungarian Pastry Shop; they bought cookies in the shape of horseshoes and hurried to the clay room, where Lina had to work. She introduced her brother to everyone, even to people she hardly knew. She led him to Larkin's studio, to show him the painting she loved. Lina admired most of Larkin's paintings, but none as much as this one. Lina thought if she ever had money, she'd buy it. She'd never before wanted to own art. "Maybe I'll buy it," Walter said, and a familiar rush of envy welled up in Lina. The painting wasn't even done yet, she said. When they arrived, Larkin's studio was locked.

They talked about Donnie. Walter was moving back to LA pretty soon; he'd found an apartment with a red door. She should move back, too, he said.

One of Lina's teachers was trying to talk her into applying for the MFA program. This same teacher—who happened to be Troy's adviser—was in charge of scholarships. If she got in, she'd stay an extra two years to receive another degree in art.

"What would that degree be worth?"

Troy had asked his adviser the same thing. The adviser took out his checkbook. *Doug Cannon,* it said. *M.F.A.*

"You're pretty sure if you apply, you'll get in?" Walter asked.

Lina wasn't sure. Her work wasn't as good as Larkin's; maybe it wasn't good at all.

"You can't judge yourself like that," Walter said. "This woman Larkin, she may have had a different start."

Lina took him to the bookstore and he bought a book called *Learning from Las Vegas,* which Etienne discounted without Walter even realizing it. She'd been seeing Etienne over a year now, but it wasn't like having a boyfriend. Every three or four weeks, she'd read until closing time in the bookstore and they'd go to one of their apartments. She still hadn't introduced him to anyone.

When Lina and Walter returned to the Barnard studios, Larkin stood working, humming along to what sounded like ancient church music, a cigarette in her hand, the dog asleep at her feet. Lina didn't want her brother to see the painting, propped against the wall, but Larkin showed it to him, saying, "That's the one she likes." Walter glanced at it for a moment but was more taken with the girl in a brown slip dress. He asked her to join them for dinner, but she said she had to paint. Lina opened her own studio. Her brother walked around the walls, standing a minute in front of each painting. He finally said, "She's got nothing on you."

That day, Lina felt as if she had everything. When Walter left the next morning, she went to the Brancusi room in the museum and sat on a bench for an hour, bereft.

Putting her slides together to submit, Lina remembered what her brother said and tried to think of life as an unfair race. She privately hoped she could still win, without handicaps, in the regular race, only later. She was just preparing now. Practicing. Her mother was still healing. It was possible to imagine her own future—in an apartment with old arched windows and white walls, a boyfriend setting croissants on a green plate—but it was becoming harder to picture her mother's. Could she live in that apartment with Lina?

Lina and Troy threw pots past midnight for a Christmas sale.

The night before she flew home, Etienne carried his Morris chair to her apartment. Etienne's sister had won Miss Physique New York, and he was driving her to Ohio for a regional competition. A movement was starting in female bodybuilding to use the same standards as the men's. No more bikinis. The chair was folded; he showed her how to open it and adjust the back. He was giving it to her for Christmas, he said. It was the thing of greatest value that he owned. Should she accept it?

But she wanted it and she did.

At home, Lina drove to Malibu to see Ceci, who'd left the store and started her first clothing line, inspired by surf culture. Sue was wearing braces now along with her kids, Ceci told her. Kim had stopped working. She'd become a customer instead.

Walter took her to see the old aerospace plant he and Ken hoped to make into a mixed-use shopping center. An enormous shed, with concrete floors. In back of his Clovis outlet, Walter said, they'd built a block-long sandbox. They'd hauled in shovels and long black hoses and the place was full of kids now, their moms sitting at the picnic tables drinking coffee.

For this one, they wanted to dig out a pond. But the empty structure, forlorn as a garage, didn't look like a shopping center.

After Christmas at the hospital, Donnie put their mother to bed and they had a late second supper in Julie's apartment, what she called "midnight carbonara" and a saffron cake with cardamom. Walter offered Donnie a room in his new Santa Monica apartment, and Donnie said no, it was okay. Walter asked again and Donnie said, "I'm good. Thanks." Julie glowed, tucking her bare feet up under the couch pillow, pleased that Donnie chose to stay. But why wouldn't he? Julie had become a great cook.

Donnie had a used motorcycle and offered Lina a ride. She rode on the back to see Walter's new apartment, a cottage in a line of connected cottages, with its own fireplace and walled-in garden. Still, Donnie on that thing on a highway seemed to her like a beautiful kid with a needle in his arm.

———

One spring day, passing the trash bins behind the art building, Lina saw the painting she'd loved bent up, in a corner. She gasped and felt a pain in her side hauling it out. The canvas had been slashed, ruined, paint had chipped off. She ran to Larkin's studio, but it was locked.

A few days later, with a group holding to-gos in front of the Hungarian Pastry Shop, Larkin stood with the dog's leash braceleting her wrist, a streak of pink paint in her hair. Lina nudged into the circle where people were talking about Nicaragua. Lina thought Martine was only a little better than she was and that made Lina mad at herself for her laziness. She envied Martine's white blouses, too. Other people, she thought, didn't deserve their reputations. But Larkin had a sheer, deep talent. It was unmistakable.

Lina waited until they were alone. "I saw your painting in the garbage. I always wanted to buy that one someday."

"Wouldn't have sold it." Her dog pulled at its leash. How could someone their age even have an animal?

"Why did you throw it out?" Lina winced at the shrill whine in her voice.

"Couldn't finish."

Two people walked by with their arms around each other's waists, a horizontal S.

"You have a relationship?" Larkin asked.

"No."

"Me neither. And I'm sick of it. Sick of the whole damn thing. I don't think I've ever loved anybody," she said, and patted her dog. "This one's teaching me how."

Lina and Troy both got into the program with scholarships.

Troy said they'd have to get serious now.

"We've been serious," Lina said.

"No more task-irrelevant pursuits."

They stood in the clay room unpacking boxes of glaze. Troy paged through a cookbook. They wondered if their new MFA classmates would be better than they were. Other art majors whose work they admired were veering off, to do different things. Only Martine and another Barnard girl who wore Doc Martens were going to be in the program with them. And one quiet guy they'd always liked who painted arachnids.

Lina didn't want to make a big deal of graduation. Nothing was changing. She'd stay in her university apartment; she'd keep her same job. Her mother couldn't come. But Julie and Walter insisted on flying out, and so she sat and stood and walked through the whole ceremony, all the while thinking of tomorrow, when it would be a regular day. She met Troy's mother, standing in a magenta suit holding a bouquet of long-stemmed roses.

Julie brought a camera. She said she'd send pictures to Mrs. Anjani's nieces. Mrs. Anjani had died in February. Julie was staying only one night in New York because she didn't like leaving Donnie alone.

"Don't you want to see anything? He'll be fine," Lina said without being sure of that at all. She had the sense that Donnie had given cause for worry that Julie wasn't telling her on what she kept calling her "big day." Lina preferred small days. Julie gave her a picture of herself and their mother, wearing white creased nurse's caps, on the day of their UCLA nursing graduation.

60.

Two sculptors had driven an old Chevy truck cross-country. One of them wove on her grandmother's loom. Clumpy, undyed-wool stalactites hung from her studio ceiling, and she'd painted all six walls, including the concrete floor, deep blue. A woman from Southern California cut up old orange-crate labels and pictures of migrant farmworkers to make standing scrap-screen collages. Decorative, Lina thought, even if political. A small woman with a boy's haircut sat by her studio window all day working on layered ten-by-ten oil paintings of clouds. She listened to the radio while she painted with very small brushes that resembled makeup tools. She was trying a technique Rembrandt used to render lace. A tall, dark-haired welder who'd done construction in Montana had somehow landed a CETA job interning for Mark di Suvero his first week east of the Mississippi. He was extremely handsome. That couldn't have hurt, Lina said to console Troy, who'd applied to di Suvero's shop twice and never heard back. Another good-looking guy made big abstract canvases with cratered surfaces by mixing pigments into a tin pot of melted beeswax on a hot plate.

Lina's paintings were still mostly of plants. Weeds and flowers. She wasn't eager to show them to new people. She knew instinctively what the guys would think. She sometimes wondered if Troy really liked what she did. They'd long ago established a mutual respect and continued to confirm, in small ways, their belief that they were more serious than the others. More serious and, though they never said it, better.

Troy's studio was always a mess. He cut out news stories and sometimes single sentences, then glued them onto a base, painted over them, and eventually slashed cuts in the surface to show the layers. He was also making papier-mâché globes, not quite circular (he wrapped the pasted paper around balloons), painted them black, and then did freehand shapes of the continents, some places smaller and others larger than they really were. Lina liked the globes; they were pretty and playful, but she privately wondered whether he wasn't starting too many different things to go deep. His work always suggested a political or moral meaning, though, and hers didn't. But then, even her favorite sculptures—those Roman torsos—weren't particularly moral, either. They were only beautiful.

"Remember Larkin?" she said. "How do you quit art?"

Troy shrugged. "She didn't want the life."

And the life was, if anything, worse. Graduate school proceeded much like undergraduate, except that everyone was now desperate.

A rising star in the ed school was hiring artists to work with public-school fourth graders. Troy got the job. The MFA secretary, an older woman who'd gone through the program herself, promised to find another job for Lina.

"Do you have something to wear for an interview?" she asked.

Lina dug out the skirt Julie had sewn and wore it to meet Harry Beckstein, the owner of the Evergreen Gallery, who hired her after two questions. He needed help, he said, but didn't have much time to train her. She would pick things up. So she took the subway to Chelsea three afternoons a week and sat in the airy, symmetrical room waiting for customers. She wore the skirt with black tights. Another girl worked there mornings and explained how to be when people came in. You busied yourself at the desk as if you were doing paperwork. You had to seem as if you barely noticed them.

The girl who wore Doc Martens walked the halls with the di Suvero welder. Lina wasn't beautiful anymore, she'd decided. She was trying to learn not to mind. She wasn't sure what she thought of romance, anyway. Troy was usually in love and it always ended badly. The women he dated seemed enchanted with him at the beginning, but later became nervous about life with someone who earned nine thousand dollars a year. His current girlfriend brightened up whenever he mentioned his teaching job. She hoped he'd apply to the ed school.

In studio, people criticized the weaver's stalactites. Lina protested. "They remind me of Eva Hesse. Even Rothko. Agnes Martin." The weaver looked at her as if she'd thrown a rope overboard. Everyone else looked down or away.

People called the two weavers "the witches." Lina remembered the hive of discarded clothes at the hospital and thought about what she could do with it. But textile was considered a craft medium; female. She still wanted to be in the major league.

Besides studio, they took technique classes taught by city artists who arrived in taxis.

"I don't like the people they talk about," Lina told Troy. "Why doesn't anyone mention Hopper? I hate Picasso and all that great artist stuff."

"You take Picasso too personally," he said. "Got to admit, guy could paint."

She admitted. She stood before *Boy Leading a Horse* every time she went to MoMA.

Her own paintings felt flat and two-dimensional. When she tried to build up her surface, it looked like mud.

———

The secretary got her hired to teach, after all, a Saturday-morning class on medieval battle armor at the Met. During her afternoons in the gallery, she researched. The original curator of the Arms and Armor Department was a zoology professor at Columbia. He'd first been the curator of fishes at the Natural History Museum. He believed if you displayed a dinosaur with one leg missing, people would think dinosaurs had only three legs, so he hired European craftsmen to make the missing pieces of the armor and shields. To this day, the Met had a smithy and hundreds of tools, still in use. She read for two weeks before even seeing the collection, then went at opening time on a Wednesday. She was surprised by the articulation, the edgeworks of gold. The armor was as fine and intricate as jewelry.

On the street, Lina found a file cabinet and dragged it to her apartment.

She sat on the floor in sweats on a Saturday night with a stack of papers. She was twenty-two years old and trying to be good at the things her mother had failed in. Money, to start with. She had loan statements, financial aid letters, tax forms, and hourly CETA time sheets from the gallery. A W-2 form from the Barnard Student Center, for her summer hours in the clay room. She was filing when she picked up the phone to hear Lauren say she was getting married. She wanted Lina and Jess to be her bridesmaids. "Really? That's great," Lina said, though she didn't envy her friend. Lauren was twenty-two years old, too.

The next morning, leading a clump of middle school boys and retirees through the dim back halls of the Met's armory, Lina had an idea. Maybe she could shape an undulation, in three dimensions, like draped cloth, in a harder material. Could you cast a dress in iron?

She'd crammed for weeks, the names of knights, princes, kings, the dates of battles and tournaments, but the first question she received, from a preteen boy, was "How did they go to the bathroom?"

The codpiece was not removable, the metal molded to the body.

She explained that though we think of armor as military, this one wasn't made for combat; it was a fashionable costume for the entertainment of crowds.

61.

Donnie made it to the Chinatown park by himself. He played a few rounds of xiangqi, but he was stumbling over moves. When he'd been here in this same park, whispering in Dino's ear, they could win. Maybe it had been Evan's presence. Evan hung out now with other nerdy kids who worked in UCLA labs. He had some kind of NSF grant. Neurophysiology. Donnie was still friends with Dino, who no longer played street chess. Dino tried to take both boys to Mount Pinos to see the eclipse of 1979, but Evan couldn't go. Donnie wished he'd come.

When Dino and Donnie arrived, a lot of people were there already, including families with kids and their ninety-year-old grandparents. The sky darkened and a hush came over the crowd. At some point—it was sudden—stars began to pop into bright view. Then shadow bands flew over them, wavy lines of dark. As the moon blocked the sun and the sky went black, the silence was complete: no birds sang, no words were spoken.

Donnie was covered with goose bumps. But it only lasted a minute.

Book 5

Family Week

62.

Dr. Moss called Lina to ask if she was coming west for the holidays. Julie had told him she might not. Was it normal for a hospital superintendent to call a patient's daughter? That's what we get for her being in so long, Lina thought. Customer service.

She looped the phone cord around her wrist. No, she wasn't coming. For two lonely days, she figured, she'd work ten. She didn't tell the doctor this or that she'd run out of money. She said her old friend was getting married here on New Year's Eve and she was a bridesmaid. Her mother didn't need her, Lina told herself. Her brothers would be there. For the first Christmas since Lina's mother went into the hospital, Julie was flying back to Michigan.

"I'll see that we hold her medicine Christmas Eve," the doctor said, in a low, kind voice, "until after you two have a good talk."

As if such a thing were possible. A Christmas five years ago Dr. Moss had promised her mother would recover. Lina held the receiver after he hung up. All of a sudden, sadness flooded her. She'd never not gone home.

On Thanksgiving, she and Troy had cleaned the clay room. Troy was in love again, with another full-figured woman who didn't think that his being an artist was such a good idea. With a below-zero wind-chill factor, Troy wore the gray wool coat that had been his grandfather's when he'd moved north during the Great Migration. They walked out under scarves of color in the sky to the Cuban Chinese place and ordered their usual black beans and rice. Troy splurged on the holiday special. "Have me some s*wine*." By the time they left, the holiday was over everywhere.

But for Christmas, Troy was taking the train home to Baltimore.

Lina had made a series of square canvases, all bouquets, with different backgrounds and varying stages of freshness and decay. But this week she was going to cast a standing metal dress. Hollow inside. A sheath. A friend of a friend was lending her a studio in the corner of a Brooklyn foundry with a setup for pouring molten bronze.

Isaiah Polk, an adjunct with a bigger reputation than any of the full-time teachers since a young Hollywood star began collecting his paintings, was giving critiques.

Lina slipped into the back of the room.

He projected a slide: a suburban house, a sprinkler on. Egg tempera. Lina wondered how the painter had made the beads of water so transparent.

"What's wrong with this?" Polk asked.

People raised their hands, eager to identify their classmate's mistakes.

"Something familiar. That maybe needs blasting out," he said. "Let's have another." Lina had two slides in her pocket she didn't volunteer. Polk flipped through the images, which included Martine's dollhouse, complimenting only one, a piece of plumbing equipment mounted on a wooden rectangle. Lina wondered if it had been cast.

"Flush-valve gasket," the di Suvero assistant mumbled. His hair, from the back, looked as if he'd just gotten out of bed.

"Sounds like it's working out at the gallery," the department secretary said when Lina turned in her CETA work logs.

Lina shrugged. "It's a job."

"You know, sometimes we belittle what comes to us easily. You have a talent for gallery work, but you chase this other thing that may not be as natural."

"You mean . . . art?"

"Don't throw away what you're good at."

Weights shifted inside Lina. Maybe she couldn't do this. The welder who'd mounted the toilet valve was telling Martine about a Christmas party. He really was handsome. He invited Lina, too, writing down his address.

Lina hadn't seen him with Doc Martens recently.

She tried to buy a thick Russian novel from Etienne on Christmas Eve. He rang it up and handed her the book in a bag. He was store manager now. The receipt read: $00.00.

"Fuck," she said to him. "I'm gonna have to find a new store."

He smiled, reached out, and touched her cheek. The time between their meetings had stretched and by now they only saw each other here in the bookstore, as they had at the beginning. But there was something extra.

She bought clementines, bagels, cream cheese, and smoked salmon at the gourmet grocery. As she walked home with the treats, it began to snow.

Flurries fizzed and danced in the airshaft outside her window. Twice, she lifted the phone to call her mother. But it was three hours earlier there. She should have flown home. Finally, she reached the facility. A nurse coaxed her mother to the phone and they had a nearly normal conversation, the first in years.

"Are you doing something now?" her mother asked.

"I'm just in my apartment. Sitting by the window looking at the snow, talking to you." The radiator banged.

"Are you getting ready to go out?"

Her mother had always wanted her to go to parties.

"I was invited someplace, but I may stay in. I bought a bag of groceries."

"Oh, go! Put on a dress and go. You know, Lina, you are a beautiful girl. You've got to let people see you."

Tears crossed Lina's face. She was grateful that her mother still thought she was beautiful. She hadn't been beautiful for a long time. She used to discount her mother's appraisal—she was her mother—but today it was calming, even generative. "I want to work. That's why I'm not there. I'm trying to paint your flowers."

"I know, but one night won't make such a difference."

I know. Lina had told her something important—her work was tied to what her mother did now every day—but she couldn't tell if her mother had registered this.

"Snow," her mother said. "I wish I could see that. Is it white everywhere?"

"It's been swirling. Now it's beginning to stick." Below, on garbage can covers and a low wall, a layer of white had collected. "Are they caroling there?" It was 1978. Lina had been to five hospital Christmases. She knew the rituals. Carolers strolled from the men's geriatric ward to Menopause Manor and from there to the new forensic building, where they sang behind a chain-link fence. Incarcerated patients put their fingers in the metal openings, leaning close to hear.

"I stick to myself. You know," her mother said.

"Donnie and Walter will come."

"Donnie's here. We're playing checkers. He's trying to show me a new game."

She heard her brother in the background. "We have the ward to ourselves. They're showing *It's a Wonderful Life* in James Hall."

After Lina put down the receiver, she sat motionless, sad without the energy of grief. Talking to her mother loosened her. It didn't matter what Isaiah Polk or anyone thought about her slides because art would be made somewhere and it didn't matter whether or not it had her fingerprints on it. She had seen some beauty as the parade passed; there would be more, too, after her time.

The buzzer startled her. For a second, she imagined her brothers here.

Luis, the doorman, said through the intercom that she had a package. She went down the elevator in her socks. A woman in the lobby was objecting to the Christmas tree. "This is not a Christian building," she said. A retired geographer thumped in on a walker. "We're expecting Empire Szechuan," she told Luis.

Lina took the box upstairs to open in the morning, but as soon as she closed her door she tore through the layers of tissue to a padded jacket, no, a coat, a long white coat, light as a T-shirt, made of down. People had been talking about these sleeping-bag coats.

They were warmer than fur, Martine said. Lina put it on. In the mirror, her dark braid fell against the white. She felt augmented. She called Walter and started to leave a message. "Thank you. You didn't have to. I mean I have a coat. Not a warm one but . . ."

He picked up. "I didn't send you anything yet. I've been driving to the Central Valley looking for corners every night. Have you ever heard of Hayward? Neither had I." While she listened, she emptied the May Company box, rustling with tissue, and found a plain index card. *Merry Christmas. From Mom and us* in Donnie's penmanship. But who paid? Lina had received a check from Julie inside a tin of cookies, sent from Michigan. The idea of Donnie with money made her uneasy. How could a high school kid buy a coat?

The past year when the phone rang, Lina's first thought had not been their mother, but Donnie.

Walter asked, as he did on every call, if Lina was dating anybody.

"Not really. How about you?"

"I leave at ten at night to go scout the Central Valley; it's easier to see corners when there's no traffic."

"You're looking for another place?"

"They want two more. It's easy money. But I'm not the best date. What would I say, Wanna come to the rodeo? We'd be the honored guests of the mayor of Clovis. Not a real draw for your urban woman."

"Tonight some guy I hardly know invited me to a party."

"I'd go if I were you," Walter said.

Lina dressed for the party, to honor her mother, trying on most of what she owned.

She walked to the subway in the snow wearing the new white coat. It was light and warm. She'd never really talked to the welder. She wondered what his apartment was like.

Troy was always saying he was looking for his Black queen. Who would be *her* person? Why did love seem so important, especially at Christmas?

Lina panicked when she saw the coat rack in the hall outside the apartment. She didn't want to leave the coat. She unzipped and kept it on.

She didn't recognize anyone besides the welder and, across the room, Martine, who was tonight wearing a white blouse with a lace collar. The welder seemed even more good-looking in his apartment. There was nothing on the beige walls. She noticed two of his pieces on the kitchen countertop among many bottles. Two wooden blocks holding what looked like parts of machines. "Are those cast?" she asked him.

"No, the only cast piece is the one that looks like a boomerang by the window. All the rest are found objects." He drew her attention to a tall totem-shaped pole made of carved wood that looked like a Brancusi. "Bread riser," he said. "From an upstate bakery." A hanging wooden mobile had been inside a primitive 1930s wash machine. "Wanna gimme your coat?"

"That's okay." She was grateful for his attention. She wanted to ask him about pouring metal. They'd never had a class together. Had he noticed her anyway?

He stood next to her and began talking to the group that had gathered. "Yeah, Polk told me I'm going to be the next big thing." He looked modest, even pained, saying this, as if he couldn't help being the next big thing. She was glad now that she hadn't said anything about her work. He had no reason to think she was any good.

Parties were acutely hard. She wanted to talk to Martine, but she never understood how one was supposed to exit a group. Did you need an excuse? She mumbled the words "ladies' room," then found the bathroom (to make the excuse true). In a few minutes, she went to where Martine was, but she didn't know how to fit into that conversation, either. Lina's mother, when she'd been herself, could do these things; she'd smiled, her eyes alight and roving like those of a volleyball player.

Martine had once defended a painting of Lina's when the encaustic guy said her work wasn't *about* anything. "It's just *flowers*," he'd complained.

"And weeds, in an iconic soup can," someone else added.

"It's a moment of peace," Martine had cried out, "on pretty rough ground." The can sat on burned-out crabgrass, littered with cigarette butts. Lina was grateful, though she felt exposed; Martine had noticed her rough ground.

When Martine went to get her coat, Lina got up to leave, too. The welder clipped a single leash on a large pit bull's collar and also a small terrier's and said, "I'll put you two in cabs." It was snowing more seriously now, the broken lines of white slanted and rapid.

Martine put a hand on Lina's arm. "You working?"

Lina nodded.

"Good."

"You?" Lina asked.

"Trying."

"I know."

Martine said she'd walk, so the welder accompanied Lina to the subway. The underground train car was raucous, like a better party. That night, Lina cried looking at her walls. Donnie had never seen her apartment. Her mother never would. There'd been a moment, hearing the buzzer, when she'd thought they were all there, about to come up on the elevator.

She melted wax in a pot on an electric hot plate on the floor of her studio, then dipped panels of felt into it. She wrapped the wax-soaked fabric around balled newspaper to make a form, like papier-mâché. She wanted the shape to be full and voluptuous. It took two days to get the contours right. The sheath was four and a half feet tall but light. She carried it to a corner of the clay room.

Three days after Christmas, she made the ceramic mold. She liked glomping on the clay. She had to wait another two days for it to dry and then she fired it.

It was no longer easy to carry. She wrapped it in packing plastic and then held it across her lap in a taxi to Greenpoint.

She wore gloves and goggles, as she'd been told to, when she poured the metal, but she burned her thumb anyway. The studio smelled like singed wax.

She arrived early the next morning with a hammer to break the plaster casing. It took all day. Her iron dress stood there, as she'd pictured it.

Coughing from the plaster dust, she cleaned the studio, wrote a note to leave with a thank-you bottle of Scotch for the friend of a friend. She needed a dolly to get the sculpture into another taxi to her studio.

One Saturday, a retiree had asked Lina how the Met had transported the armor there. Some suits had been shipped disassembled with elaborate numberings, like a Lego kit.

Others were treated like statues.

Lina tried to keep the retirees laughing. "You could buy a town house for the price of this helmet."

63.

Jess pulled at the neckline of her bridesmaid's costume in front of the mirror. Mrs. Moses had sent them each a lime-green chiffon gown.

"It's just for one night," Lina said.

"But I hate meeting people looking bad."

Lina hadn't thought of that. She'd been worried about whether they had to reimburse Mrs. Moses for the dresses.

At the wedding, it was impossible to ask. Lauren paired bridesmaids with groomsmen. Jess was given a business school student and Lina his skinnier brother, who played guitar and wrote poems.

"A troubadour," Lina said.

He didn't laugh. Lauren told the troubadour that Lina was an artist and Jess was a scientist, as if they were each already what they hoped to become.

Though Lina had known Mrs. Moses for years, this was the first time she'd noticed a deliberate attempt to beautify. Mrs. Moses had a look of settled permanence, a balance undermined, today, by a startling blue powder on her eyelids. People who didn't normally wear makeup shouldn't, Lina thought.

A few people asked Lina if she'd met the art dealer at table eight. She hadn't, but here was the troubadour, bringing her a flute of champagne.

Watching Mrs. Moses arrange the veil around Lauren's face before she walked down the aisle on her father's arm, Lina felt she was glimpsing something important. Mr. Moses had belittled his wife for as long as Lina could remember, but the mother's hope for her daughter's future seemed to have stilled any impulse but joy. Why did *he* get to walk her down the aisle, anyway? But Mrs. Moses had no pride. Instead of being pitiable, this elevated her.

Lina's freshman TA had claimed that troubadours invented romantic love. But was that even a good idea? Lina hadn't experienced it. Lauren was marrying her best friend.

By the end of the evening, both groomsmen had acquired phone numbers.

The lime-green dresses, it turned out, hadn't prevented anything.

The business school brother flew to Berkeley and Lina spent some evenings in New York with the troubadour. On a dull afternoon at the gallery, she wrote a note on drawing paper with orange ink to the art dealer from table eight. *Sorry we didn't meet at the wedding.*

The welder had gotten back together with Doc Martens. Did he think she was a better artist than Lina? He might not have picked her for her art at all. He might have chosen her because he had a thing for toothpick calves.

Lina's note reeled in a date with the art dealer from table eight. Drinks. He told her where. A guy in his twenties who knew hotel bars. She wore the white sleeping-bag coat; she didn't always, though February of 1979 charted record cold. She'd been saving it. He wore corduroy jeans, a shirt and tie, and he ordered a Scotch and soda.

She asked for wine. What could they talk about?

They talked about the same things she'd talked about with the troubadour: college, their jobs, movies, only she was less herself and that subtraction tinted everything. His hair, in the back where it met the collar, curled.

Romantic love, which was not frivolous after all—people lost their minds over it—came down to the high school question of *Does he like me? Does this other person like me* that way? As if *that way* were some anointment. Lina and Donnie believed their mother had fallen off course because of Learhoff, an Encino doctor with a potbelly, a less good person than herself. This probably happened all the time. People gave away their sanity for a person whom everyone else could see was inferior. A too-loud piano player pounded a rendition of "It Had to Be You." Lina was thinking, Oh, no. His forearms were flatter than forearms generally were. Too many feelings started. *This* was what the great books were talking about. A clearing opened. There was a stillness at the center of her petaled feelings, a peace from the focus. The problem was she couldn't speak. And the stakes felt dire: What if he didn't pick her?

A shift took place in her daily life. Her heart beat too fast when the phone rang, leaving a rough tunnel in its wake. She lingered in the clay room to hear Troy laugh, because alone, she no longer felt she was painting, but that she was trying to be the way a young female painter should be. (Larkin, who painted in slip dresses, smoking and whistling. *That* was how a young female painter should be.) This shift was slight but significant.

"D'you know Jackson Pollock baked pie?" Troy asked, loading the kiln. "I'm teaching me to bake."

Six days passed before the art dealer called.

But then he did, and a soundtrack clicked on.

Love was not unlike terror.

They kissed for hours, against buildings, under falling snow. There was nothing rough about the way he kissed, nothing pushy. Sometimes she did a thing back that made him laugh. It was a conversation. His name was Sacha.

He gave her choices. Movie or museum. In an exhibition, he called time out for "a restorative cup of hot chocolate." He was in a book group, reading *To the Lighthouse*. He liked the part when Mrs. Ramsay isn't sure whether Walter Scott's novels were written by Jane Austen or Shakespeare. Lina hadn't read *To the Lighthouse*, but she didn't say.

She wanted to seem better than she was to him.

Every time they met, she gathered some new scrap: today, she learned he loved his father more. Coming home, she stopped at the bookstore and found the Everyman's Library edition of Virginia Woolf's supposed masterpiece, which Etienne rang up for $00.00. He looked at her with an I-know-you expression. They both laughed.

Should she tell Etienne she had a boyfriend now? She wasn't even sure Sacha *was* her boyfriend. He might be, she thought, if she kept still and didn't do anything wrong. She listened acutely for any words suggesting claim. When he finally said they were "going together," she felt a thrill, as if she were now breathing brighter air.

In a basement hamburger place, Sacha asked about her parents. She looked down at the paper placemat and told him her mother was in a state institution. As facts of her mother's illness spilled out, it sounded as if she were exaggerating. Lithium. Elavil. Thorazine. There was no way to translate the truth about her life that sounded sincere.

When she lifted her eyes, she saw his face ratcheted into high alarm. He tried to talk, but his jaw moved without words. "Has she been there long?" he finally managed.

"Six years."

Everything about him was exactly right, even things she normally wouldn't like—his relish for Cokes, for example, or red meat.

"Is she getting better, do you think?"

"I don't know," Lina said. She'd once sent Jess a list of the drugs her mother was on and asked if she could tell her what they did. Jess tried to explain. Lina asked Jess if a normal brain made by itself the compounds that were in the drugs. "The chemical imbalance model, it's just a metaphor," Jess had said. "We develop compounds to treat an illness. Usually cancer. That's where the money is. Say it doesn't work but they notice the trial subjects report feeling a little happier; then they do another trial. So we have these drugs that sometimes work. That's really all we know."

Lina's father was easier to talk about. For most of her life, they hadn't had a working telephone number for him, but now, at sixty, he had the first job Lina had heard of since he'd married Lucille, decades ago. He was the general concessions manager in a casino on the Idaho-Nevada border. She could talk about him the way most people their age talked about their parents, with patient, understanding scorn.

At a subway station, on a gray spring morning, he said, "A good thing about seeing each other once or twice a week is that we make love every time." Lina hadn't known that they saw each other only once or twice a week on purpose. Couldn't they make love more often? She treasured their sex. It always started with kissing, which went on and on. She lost all sense of time. He didn't ask her about orgasms. She slept in the declivity below his shoulder and felt a profound sweetness as she slipped out of consciousness. She started a notebook after their first night, drawing every morning when she got back to her worktable. She drew their bed. His loft, the night it was snowing. Once, at the beginning, he hadn't slept. He'd just watched her. She'd made a sketch of that, too.

Every morning, he put on a shirt and tie. They worked in the same world, but he was on the other side, an arbiter. When she unlocked the door to her dim studio and moved among the unfinished canvases, her attempts felt futile. She was one of thousands trying to be something. She didn't even like saying the word.

Too much depended on how good she was.

She dreaded his judgment of her work but he asked to see, so she cleaned up, the way her mother would have wanted her to, put grocery-store flowers in a water glass.

He stood before the sheath in the corner, then looked at the painting on the easel and picked up canvases leaning against the wall. She told him that they were her mother's arrangements. "From memory." Her heart was beating overly hard.

He seemed a higher authority. If he liked what she was doing, maybe she could relax.

"You don't render the hospital," he said, lifting a canvas from the floor with vague off-white shapes that were the buildings in the background. "But you feel it everywhere."

Decades later, she still feels grateful for his response. Some things, she believes, you can't fake.

Lina flew home for Donnie's graduation and Walter picked her up at the airport.

When he asked, as he always did, if she was dating, she smiled, concealing a mouthful. "I met someone," she admitted.

"I can tell."

Graduation was a ghost town. The same buildings, the same lawns, but no Mrs. Anjani. Julie didn't look like herself. She was wearing the dress Ceci and Lina made for her years ago and she seemed taller—had she lost weight? Or maybe it was just a really good dress. Ceci had insisted Julie come into the store to have it tailored. Ceci pinned it herself. Today, the dress fell a little loose, still elegant. Ceci must have understood, more than Lina had then, how much Julie gave. This morning, Julie had been to the hair-dresser. But that wasn't it either. Maybe Lina had never before seen Julie happy.

Why wasn't their mother here? Couldn't they have driven her up for the day?

"Do you think he's stoned?" Walter whispered as their brother, now taller than both of them, stumbled, crossing the lawn for his diploma, and fell flat on the ground. A wave of applause rose when he got up. He hugged various gowned administrators, tilting the shorter principal, almost tipping him over.

"Remember when we'd be walking and someone would stop and ask Mom if he had representation?" Lina asked.

"I'm glad he's going to college," Walter said. "And a decent one." A small school in an inland town. They both thought that would be good.

Lina told Walter she'd panicked every time the phone rang late at night. He admitted that he, too, felt relieved whenever he called Julie and nothing was wrong.

"She's bringing up retirement more," Lina said. "She owns that cabin in Michigan."

"She told me not till after his first semester. I used to wonder if he'd get in. Worst case, he could live with me. But all those special ed classes and it turned out okay."

"Whenever Julie called to defend him," Lina said, "I got the sinking feeling that whatever she was saying he didn't do, he might have."

Lina wondered what Sacha would make of her life here. There were things she wouldn't tell him yet. She smiled to herself, thinking his name.

After the graduation, Donnie stood with an arm around Julie. He was going to the beach, he said, with friends. Lina looked at his pupils. He didn't seem stoned or drunk.

On the way to the airport, Walter drove her to the construction site of his new shopping center. He didn't like to call it that. It would be a community park, north of the airport, east of the ocean. How do you like the name, Aviation Park? They drove up to what looked like a large empty crater, dotted with bulldozers. The building that had looked like an enormous empty garage before was now a skeleton of wooden two-by-fours.

I wish you could stay and see them build the lake, he said.

At Lina's terminal, they sat in the car.

"Well, it all turned out okay," Walter said, sighing. "We're growing up." Walter was ahead of her, as always, but she was making incremental progress, too—it all rested, Lina thought, on their having left their mother in a state hospital and Donnie in the care of someone who had no obligation to them. Julie had never before raised a child. Once again, they'd gotten away with something.

From the airport pay phone, Lina called Ceci to thank her for her help long ago with Julie's dress. She thought of calling Julie, but that was too big a thank-you to say. Julie would be embarrassed. She wanted to call Sacha but stopped herself. She tried not to call him too much. That may have been the only rule daughters and mothers could agree on in 1979. Not that daughters said so to their mothers. They needed to prove that theirs was a new world in which young men didn't need to be tricked or trained.

Lina attempted to contain her feelings. She pictured a thimble brimming. It took discipline to walk without tipping it. Most of what she felt was longing. She'd swept all her desires into one pile and named it Sacha. It would be decades before she understood that her yearning had little to do with the twenty-five-year-old man.

That first summer with Sacha, they went to see art on Sunday mornings. Sacha always knew a cool bakery, where they could buy coffee and rustic pastries. Lina liked the work by women but also felt competitive with it. Sacha was drawn to some paintings that looked ugly to her. When one of the weavers (the less talented one) found representation, Lina told him that she and Troy had made a vow on New Year's Eve to try to be artists for one more year. "Each year we think it'll be our last."

"We'll find a way to change your life," Sacha said, and the sentence fell into her, a deep charm.

But why did her life need to change? Her socks had holes, true, the elastic of her underwear was spent, but she was painting every day; she read on slow afternoons in the gallery and she'd fallen in love with someone who believed she could be an artist.

She looked up at the old city with hope.

64.

A watercolor of Martine's dollhouse was chosen for a group show in the East Village. Lina admitted she was jealous. Sacha asked if she'd sent in slides to that gallerist. Lina found the rejection note in her file cabinet.

"I don't see why they wouldn't work with you," Sacha said.

A flower opened inside her.

"They rejected Troy, too."

"Troy may not be as talented as you are." Sacha had never seen Troy's work. He was saying, in an offhand way, that he believed in her. It mattered that he worked at a gallery and would know. She felt less like one of thousands.

Even Walter, when they talked, would pause at the end and say, "You really think you can make a living at this?"

"I'm making a living now," she would answer, quietly.

She confessed to Sacha that she was lonely. Besides Troy, she hadn't made many friends in the program.

"That won't be a problem for us," he said.

She trusted him to take her into a thrilling world.

At the end of the summer, they sat at a round table in the sand at a Long Island party with a bald gallerist who had put up a show, which included the welder who'd mounted the flush-valve gasket. The bald man asked Lina what she did. Before she answered, he turned to his date, a flawless blond person, to pass the salt.

"I do nothing," Lina said with white-fingered intensity. "Nothing at all."

The man and his date looked down at their plates. They sat, in the torch-lit dark, as the waves broke and boomed.

Later that night, in a guest bedroom, Sacha suggested, "You could say that you're finishing an MFA program and that you work at the Evergreen Gallery."

She *could* say that, but what she'd said was truer to the spirit of the man's question, which was a perfunctory demand for a display of rank and status. *Impress me* had been his bored dare, fingers flicking ash from his cigarette into a cup. But it was like a joke falling flat. You couldn't explain *why* it should have been funny. Lina didn't answer Sacha. It wasn't that she had no use for rank or status. In fact, her need for legitimacy had ignited the outburst. She felt insufficiently pronounced. Troy would understand why she'd snapped. But Troy was where she was. He didn't know, either, how to make their lives work. Sacha understood the economics of art, and he'd disapproved of her tonight. The exquisite safety she usually felt with her head beneath his shoulder didn't enfold her. Her heart was beating too loud. The crashing of waves came in regular intervals.

"I'm wild about you, you know," he said, but without much push.

The question of whether he liked her *that way* had never been definitively resolved. She believed in *the one* after all. It didn't mean he was the best person, only that he was the one for her. And there was sex. She could still remember every single time. Lina had filled forty-two pages of a notebook with drawings. Tonight, she drew their clothes flung over the four-poster bed. Every night held revelations. They had each cried. She hadn't come yet. She didn't let herself go to that other place; she wanted to be just her with him. She didn't want to miss any of it. She knew this was a high point of her life.

"He's not in love with you," Troy told her as they unloaded the kiln in the clay room in September, "no matter what he says." Troy had been in love four times and claimed he could identify the signs and symbols. But Lina had seen Troy in love. When the Kenyan nurse had entered a room, Troy's eyes had opened too far, as if in astonished pain. He'd crossed his arms, protecting himself from the next atrocity. He'd helped her study for her boards with index cards. And who was *she*? A nursing student with big calves who told him Black Americans were lazy. But to Troy she meant a bold society, dangerous and real. He was miserable but better off when she left, Lina thought.

Troy shrugged. "Learned some anatomy. She has a kid now."

This was their last fall in school. One weaver was moving to North Carolina to take over her grandfather's cherry farm next summer. The department secretary, a person with an abundance of silk scarves and bad news, seemed fond of reminding Lina, the minute she turned in her thesis, the university would evict her. Lina was beginning to understand that New York was a place people came to for a while before moving somewhere with yards.

Troy trekked, even in the October cold, to Lina's apartment, his grandfather's coat buttoned to the top. She baked cornbread in her toaster oven and dripped coffee through a cone. By now, Troy's graffiti artist had been discovered; he was living in a famous dealer's Los Angeles house. "He paints in thousand-dollar suits," Troy said.

Troy got a job at an East Side clay studio, run by a woman in her seventies, where serious potters threw. One had had a solo show. Others sold bowls to Barneys, boutiques in the Hamptons, and private clients. Old women liked Troy, Lina noticed. They found him tutoring gigs. "I'm coaching these kids to make SAT scores that will get them into schools like Columbia, so, after they graduate, *they* can eventually become SAT tutors. Good money but not so good on the meaning-of-life scale."

Walter warned Lina that when she got out of school she'd need health insurance. She asked Harry Beckstein, the owner of Evergreen, and he looked offended.

"I'll have to just not get sick," Lina said.

Troy's new boss said, "If you go to the doctor, just bring me the bill."

This was Donnie's first semester in college. Lina remembered that at odd times.

Sacha had taken a client to a Brooklyn dockyard to see a di Suvero protégé's work and now, three months later, that client was a collector, and the kid and his girlfriend—who turned out to be the welder and Doc Martens—were on the guy's yacht in the Aegean. "I can't believe it," Sacha said, amazed that his actions had effects. The client commissioned three new pieces for a house in Colorado. Sacha seemed to Lina very modest. "I watch the news and follow politics. You're the one with a slash of brilliance," he said. Sacha's boss gave him a bonus check be*fore* Christmas, and when he showed it to her, she grabbed it and ran; he chased her in a spontaneous round of tag in his small apartment, bumping into walls and finally falling down in a corner. They stayed like that, on the ground, their bodies breathing together. Troy thought Sacha didn't love her. But there were moments when he indisputably did.

At the hotel bar, the night Lina met him, he'd said, "I've slept with men before but I don't consider myself gay." They had been talking about a movie. He'd said it nonchalantly, and it had fallen into her like a slender needle.

"What about your bisexual past?" she asked now, out of breath. "Should I be worried?"

"No one can hold a candle to us."

She pressed him for details. Once, a man had looked at him on the subway; they'd both gotten off and walked to an apartment. An afternoon cut out of life. Even after he described it, Lina couldn't imagine what that day had felt like. Or the sex.

"A little dangerous," he said. Did they exchange phone numbers? *No!* He *certainly* didn't want to see that person again.

Lina tried to picture the man. Older, blond. The face a blur. Sometimes when they talked, Lina had a sense of them outside of who they were to each other now, as if they'd stepped into a different room where they were older people.

"What scares me is, since it's harder to be gay still, I think that if you're bisexual, maybe you're more gay."

"You could look at it that way. But you could also say I'm attracted to obstacles. Like a shiksa girlfriend."

"You're wearing that sweater." His last girlfriend. It had been her father's.

"I'll take it off."

"Sometimes I'm afraid I'll never be what she was to you."

"Come here. I just like the sweater."

"But when you talk about her, there's emotion in your voice."

"She left me. That's a whole different thing." He balled the sweater, threw it into a corner. Why *a whole different thing*? Did he mean this time he would be the one to leave?

His college friends were falling into couples. Buying blenders, painting kitchens. Brunch, for heaven's sake, he said. Some of them looked like identical-puppy twins. He and Lina had had dinner with Lauren and Paul; Lina couldn't believe they were their same age and *mar*ried. Sacha rolled on top of her, his eyes closing as he reached his hand down. She numbered the drawings in her book, nearly sixty now. Maybe she was too available. He put himself inside her without kissing.

"I can imagine a situation in which I'd be married now, can't you?" he asked.

"No," she blurted. It just flew out, as it had with the bald dealer who'd asked her what she did. She meant no; she was sure, but she didn't understand why. When she'd doubted the existence of romantic love, she'd been privately hoping for *this*. She'd wanted to fall in love and to be an artist. She was in love, but she wasn't an artist yet, at least according to the IRS. She knew her bank balance exactly. She owed $257.00 every month for her student loan.

Was that a proposal? Had she refused? What did he mean, a

situation? He meant pregnancy, she assumed. The notion made her vertiginous, as if she'd be left behind in a shapeless cotton dress. Of course they were using contraception. It was just now dawning on Lina that the problem of love was more than existential. Not only whether one was loved but why one was loved mattered. She hoped to be loved for what she could do.

And no one could love her for that yet. She was still trying to figure out how to make something beautiful.

When Lina told Troy about the welder and Doc Martens, he got a peculiar smile.

"What?"

"I knew her pretty well once."

"You had a thing with *her*?"

"I don't know about a thing, but something."

"I didn't think you dated white girls."

"I date all kinds of women."

Suddenly, Lina felt bereft; Troy was attracted to white women after all but not her. Then she remembered Sacha saying he could imagine being married. It was a private candy she fingered in her pocket. He wouldn't have brought up the word, would he, if he didn't mean married to *her*? The phrase tumbled in her mind at irrelevant moments, polishing itself.

She called Donnie to ask about college. "It's all right," he said.

Sacha had tickets to an opening at MoMA—this was the glamorous side of his job. Lina was excited but also nervous about fitting in—maybe those two things were the same. She put on and took off clothes for an hour, trying to remember Marci's tricks for adding body to your hair. She finally decided on the old May Company suit jacket over jeans. When she arrived, she scanned the crowd and spotted Sacha, talking to a woman with wild blond hair. Lina's heart beat overly loud. They seemed to be laughing. She bent closer to him. Lina walked across the floor, brittle with fear, her shoes making too much noise on the terrazzo.

Sacha introduced her. Sound echoed in the large room. Lina

felt a knife in her spine, sure there was something between them. "Can we see the work?" she said, maybe too sharply, because they both looked at her. It was a normal thing to ask, though; this was a show, not a cocktail party. Sacha put his hand on her back and they walked to the galleries, leaving the pretty young woman alone in the clattery room.

They stood then, looking at the small mounted boxes. Incredible. It was like being able to see inside someone's mind and finding a joyful playroom.

Lina asked if she could call and invite Troy.

"They gave me only two tickets, but tell you what." Sacha yawned. "When he comes, I'll give him mine. I have to get up early tomorrow."

Lina found a pay phone. By the time Troy arrived, wearing clay-splattered work boots under his grandfather's coat, clusters of people were streaming out the glass doors in beautiful, amusing clothes. Lina hurried Troy upstairs and they stood before each box, reading the cards next to them and the longer paragraphs painted on the wall. "A wholesale fabric salesman," Troy read out. "Never went to Europe. Lived his whole life in Flushing with his mom and disabled brother. Didn't graduate high school. He sold appliances, door to door."

"He had his first show at forty-six," Lina said. "Wow."

She and Troy had talked for years about their work and their careers, or lack of them. They complained about other people in the program. As they stared at the strange boxes, those irritations fell away. They weren't thinking about who was overrated or underrated, better or worse.

"Guy made boxes to send to starlets. Ballerinas," Troy said. "That's probably as close as he came to love. Living with his mom."

They stayed until the lights dimmed and janitors began to sweep the large room where the drinks had been. Neither of them had eaten. But when they came up out of the subway at Ninety-Sixth Street, neither suggested stopping at the Cuban Chinese or V&T. A soft, dense snow was falling, and they each hurried home.

Lina worked most of the night, eating two chocolate bars she'd been saving. At four in the morning, she felt like calling Troy—she wanted him to see a six-by-six canvas of a bunch of violets, held by a rubber band—but didn't. She was ashamed of her old insecurity about whether or not Martine's work was better. After seeing those boxes, none of that mattered. The great belonged to everyone. Somehow this made it easier to work.

The next morning, Troy called; he'd been up at four, too! She walked over to his place to see what he'd done. It was a freezing day. Then he came to her apartment. Then they went to the Cuban Chinese for eggs with rice and beans.

Standing in the bookstore, Lina read about Joseph Cornell. He was born on Christmas Eve, the same year as her mother. He hung out with Duchamp, Rothko, Motherwell, and de Kooning. For years, he didn't sell his work; he couldn't let it go. He once had a thousand boxes in his house, and when he sold a piece, he made another copy to keep. He preferred to give them away. He sent one to Audrey Hepburn.

First, he'd been a salesman, like his father. When he was thirty-seven, he resigned from his job. He kept dossiers on butterflies, clouds, fairies, history, and planets. His little brother played with toy trains. They lived in a rented house on a street called Utopia Parkway.

Later, Lina learned that he'd had a friendship with a young Japanese artist, who'd come to New York after writing a fan letter to Georgia O'Keeffe. O'Keeffe introduced her to Eva Hesse and Warhol. The young artist wrote a letter to Richard Nixon offering to have sex with him if he would end the Vietnam War. She staged a nude "happening" in the sculpture garden of MoMA and had a brief affair with Donald Judd. But then she became friends with Joseph Cornell, who was twenty-six years older, and stayed for days in his Flushing house. They sketched each other. Once, when they were sitting under a quince tree, Cornell's mother poured a bucket of water over them. Cornell, infatuated, made the young artist collages, and gave her some of his work to sell when she was living hand to mouth. They corresponded every day until he died.

After his death, she returned to Japan with a box of his cut-tings, Ping-Pong balls, and dime-store trinkets he'd been saving. She checked herself in to a hospital for the mentally ill, where she still lived now, by choice. She had her first solo show—collages, a tribute to Cornell—two years after committing herself. Lina felt vindicated, for her mother. How different were collages from bouquets?

Lina spent an afternoon at the MoMA Library to find pictures of the collages. There was one picture of the artist nude, overlaid with polka dots. Lina found seven images in all. But she didn't really like the work.

That year, and every year after, Lina went home for Christmas. She drove Julie's car to Norwalk, to be alone with her mother, but they never again returned to the way they'd talked the holiday they were apart. Lina had the iron sheath as a trophy from her one soli-tary Christmas, when she'd had a magical conversation with her mother, looking out the window and trying to describe the snow. Her mother told her things she hoarded for the rest of her life.

Oh, go. One night won't make such a difference. I keep to myself. You know. She remembered her mother saying she was a beautiful girl.

65.

Over eggplant-and-anchovy pizza, Troy and Lina decided to re-up one more year.

"I've painted so many flowers. I don't know if I'm getting any better," Lina said.

"You know what I love? That wire bouquet."

Lina had made a bouquet out of wire, felt, and fabric scraps in a can. She kept it on her worktable. "That was fun. But I can't turn it in. People would think I'm trying to make artificial flowers. You did a whole wall." Troy had directed a mural project on the side of a public middle school. "My brother's on me again about health insurance."

Troy told his seventy-four-year-old boss that a catastrophe

could wipe out his mom. She finally agreed to buy him a policy. But she was getting ready to retire. Somebody had offered her ten thousand dollars for the studio, but she wanted it to go to Troy.

"Ten thousand dollars, that's for the building, too?"

"Just the business. She leases. It's a decent deal. Artists can use it during the day and you could rent it out for kids' birthday parties weekends. But I don't have the ten grand."

"I met Sacha last year. So it wasn't a total bust."

"Well, I should talk." Troy's latest girlfriend had dumped him, after opening his Christmas present. A sweater. She said it wasn't the gift of a man who was ready for commitment. "Probably right," Troy said.

"Sacha brought up marriage once."

"He asked you to marry him?"

"Not exactly. He asked if I could imagine being married now. He said he could."

"Does the guy ever pay for you?" Troy asked. "Like help with the rent?"

No. She had to admit. So 1980 would have to be the year their lives would change.

Troy brokered trades with the guy who painted arachnids so that they would each own a piece of his art. Lina traded a flower painting for a twelve-by-twelve of a bee against a deep cerulean blue.

They subwayed to a small, white-painted room where Martine's watercolor hung in a group show. Lina hadn't invited Sacha; Martine was too pretty. Lina understood that Sacha could never show her paintings; but she couldn't bear it if he signed up Martine.

Still, when she saw Martine's watercolor framed on the wall, Lina gasped. It was beautiful.

Sacha found a new apartment. He hired a painter and was thrilled with the brick walls, newly white. He and Lina felt the uneven smoothness. The walls and floors were so *nice*. Lina admired them but with complication—his old apartment had been better than hers but still a genre she recognized; this one could never be confused with graduate-student housing. In the small extra room, they stood looking out a window that faced the backyard of a church. "You can work here," he said, holding her shoulders. She closed her eyes. She thought he might ask about marriage again, but he didn't.

Lina never felt finished with a painting; she always seemed just on the verge of becoming better. But her thesis was due. She asked Sacha to help pick out what to show.

"What's this?" he asked of her wire bouquet on the table where she kept the turpentine and rags. She couldn't tell if he was asking out of excitement or dismissal; his voice seemed to carry a little of both. He agreed that the most finished paintings were in the series of increasingly chaotic bouquets in old cans, some with the brand labels still on, with weeds and strange pods mixed in, and in the last one twisted old newspaper, bits of garbage. Lina thought of these as arrangements her mother made in the hospital. Troy talked to her about how to contextualize. With a small brush, Lina wrote diagnostic notes (she'd seen patient charts). She could get a pre-scription pad from the medical student Troy was dating. She listed medications and painted a small four-by-four gouache of dentures in a glass (something she'd seen on the ward; her mother still had her teeth, thank God).

While he was in her cluttered room, Lina showed Sacha the two paintings she owned: the bee and Troy's large aerial landscape. If Sacha took on Troy, maybe the two men would get along.

But Sacha was not impressed.

Lina's work hung in the student lounge of Dodge Hall for five days, and a month later, she opened an official letter from Columbia say-ing she would receive her degree by mail in six to eight weeks and would have to move out of Butler Hall at the end of the academic year. Lina showed the letter to Sacha, ostensibly to complain about the lack of pomp and circumstance.

"I guess you could move in with me," he said.

It wasn't much of an invitation. "Okay, maybe," she said.

But Troy figured out a way to petition the housing office for a six-month extension.

By summer, Lina and Sacha rarely went to Chelsea anymore.

Lina had developed an aversion after walking unprepared by a window full of work by the less-talented weaver. The other weaver had moved to North Carolina, where she was making outdoor rooms out of living vines on her family's cherry farm. Sacha had lost interest in galleries that weren't new anymore. They both preferred obscure places farther out in Brooklyn, where they could also shop in junk stores for his new apartment. In a packed, five-story warehouse, Lina collapsed on a plaid sofa. Sacha was carrying a coffee table over his shoulder. He set it down and pulled her up to dance.

She told him about Dino, who had taught her the box step.

"That was the first guy you slept with?"

"Kind of. Not really. But we could talk pretty well. He asked me lots of questions."

Sacha looked at her with keen interest and sadness. "Sounds like a good guy." Sometimes they talked like this, as if they were friends in that other room again.

"I was completely myself with him. With you, it's different; I'm afraid of losing you." She had an impulse to tell Sacha everything, even her fears about him.

He kissed the top of her head.

For no reason, she started to cry. She liked to cry with him.

Then, in September, Lina got a call. It was like being tapped. And it wasn't Sacha who opened the door, offering the glimpse of an empty ballroom, but a middle-aged gallery owner named Sheila Geller who liked Lina's slides.

Everything changed, though in a way nothing had yet. Lina had a gallery. This was an idea more than anything material. But Lina trusted it and signed the paperwork to move out in six months. She had a calm perspectival vision of the future. She would be one of the fortunate.

It was like being picked on the playground. She'd never been first—she wasn't athletic—and it was always excruciating waiting, hoping every time that the name called would be yours. When at last you were summoned, suddenly free, on the good side, it felt inevitable, and you looked away from the others huddling in a smaller group. Troy was in that cluster. And this year when everything began to loosen and move, her mother was still in the place.

Seven years. And she was making her bouquets.

Lina didn't want her brothers or Julie at the opening. She said it was too much travel for just a group show. Only two of her paintings. It seemed wrong for Julie to be at these ceremonies when her mother wasn't. For a second, she irrationally longed for her mother to come; at the same time, she counted on her never seeing these paintings. Those contradictory wishes canceled each other out. Lina had tried to tell her once that her bouquets were models for her own painting, but she didn't think her mother had understood. Would her mother think she'd used her illness for her own gain? And in any case, she couldn't stop Julie from booking a flight.

Lina was trying to figure out how to blow-dry—she'd once known—when Walter knocked on her door, surprising her. He looked up at the corners of her room, as if realizing that to pull his sister up the socioeconomic ladder with him would be more difficult than he'd thought.

"If I were you, I'd try to find another place to live," he said.

"That's not very nice," she said, so quietly it was almost only to herself. The rooms were dark, true; she had no views or real kitchen. But in New York, it mattered that the lobby was clean and that there was a doorman. She'd always been proud of her apartment.

"Reminds me of Donnie's dorm."

From now on, she decided, she'd meet him at the museum.

"I have to move in two months anyway."

Lina was anxious about having to move out. Sacha hadn't asked her again to live with him. For her opening, she brushed on makeup she didn't remember how to apply. Looking at herself in the mirror, she felt downhearted; she'd looked better before. She took it off with a washcloth. She thought of Joseph Cornell, living with his disabled brother and mother. Of Emily Dickinson. Reclusive geniuses. Of course for that you needed to be a genius.

A crowd filled Sheila's tiny gallery. Lina's boss, Harry. Martine with her forty-five-year-old artist boyfriend. The guy from the program who'd painted her bee. Lina had never before seen Troy in a tie. In a corner, Sacha stood with Sheila Geller, the two of them talking like professionals. Lina found it hard to speak to Sheila, whose head stilled like a bird's stiff profile, as she waited for Lina's random words to make sense.

The department secretary entered, unwinding a flowered wool scarf. Strange; she'd seemed to dislike Lina. Lina angled through the crowd, to make her way over, then bumped into Larkin, standing in front of her canvases. She gave Lina a gift. "This book changed my life." By the time Lina reached the secretary, she was pulling on her gloves to leave. Out of the corner of her eye, Lina saw Walter talking to Larkin.

"Congratulations," the secretary said. "I see you've been working."

"Did you like them?" Lina couldn't help herself. She wanted the woman finally to admit she'd been wrong about her.

"I like them, but it doesn't quite come naturally to you, does it?"

"How do you know?" Lina asked.

"Your brushstroke. What you see."

Lina felt punched, airless. She didn't know for how long. As the crowd thinned she found Julie, at Sheila's desk, arranging shipping; she'd bought one of Lina's two paintings. No! Lina had dozens in her apartment. She could *give* Julie one. But Julie had already written the check and insisted she wanted *this* one. Sheila Geller put a small round sticker on the frame.

During the large, chaotic dinner afterwards, Julie asked each of the other artists where they were from while Walter tried to assess Sacha's future earning potential. Troy wasn't there. He'd left, probably thinking of what he'd have to chip in for dinner. Lina could have paid, of course, but that would embarrass him if everyone else was throwing in twenties. It occurred to her that she should have found a way, these past months, to funnel five hundred bucks to Troy, who was juggling bills as they always had, counting the days before his paycheck. He didn't talk about that with her anymore.

Walter insisted on picking up the check anyway.

In the taxi to Sacha's new apartment, she opened her gift: a book called *Enormous Changes at the Last Minute*.

"Big success," Sacha said, pouring himself a glass of grapefruit juice.

Lina told him what the department secretary said. "She doesn't think paint is my medium."

"You're good in three dimensions, too. But the show was a big success."

She'd sold one painting. To Julie.

Something was bothering Lina that she couldn't put into words. She lay on her elbow, facing Sacha. He kissed her forehead, folded his arms, and went to sleep. She sat cross-legged on the bed, sketching him. He was beautiful, even sleeping. His breath made a small whine. She wanted to sleep next to him every night. If she moved in, would she stop drawing their nights? Three sketchbooks already tilted on a shelf.

The morning after the show, Sheila called to say that the other painting had sold and that the buyer wanted Julie's, too; he'd pay more. "It's still here. I could rip up the check. Can't you give another to Julie? You could save her the commission."

Oh, good. Lina could give Julie a painting after all. At Walter's hotel, when she went to say goodbye, she picked up Sacha's favorite book from the bedside table. He'd taken a whole class on it. Walter said a friend he'd once had a thing for gave it to him. A librarian.

"Carrie? When did you see her?"

"Take it. It's a brick. I'm not carrying it on the plane."

When Lina returned to her apartment, her answering machine was full. Sheila with scheduled studio visits. The next day, a man called at the Evergreen, a friend of Sheila's, and offered Lina an adjunct teaching gig, one night a week. Not middle school boys or retirees. Graduate students. Harry looked at her with narrow curiosity, as if frankly surprised that she was amounting to something.

In a week, Lina's studio was almost empty. The collector offered Julie twice what she'd paid for the painting still in Sheila's gallery, but Julie refused to sell.

"I can make you another one," Lina said. "That I'll give you."

But Julie declined. There was just something about this one, she said, that reminded her of Diane.

A glimpse into another vast room. Lina would never understand what her mother meant to Julie.

66.

Lina figured out what had been bothering her: Sacha said nice things about the show, but he didn't seem to love her any more for this small triumph. It didn't matter to him.

"Isn't that what you want?" Troy asked. This was the only time she could remember him defending Sacha.

But it *wasn't* what Lina wanted. She worked for love, to deserve it; she needed that equation to work. If anything, Sacha seemed more aloof. Lina received a letter, inviting her to be in an exhibit of young American artists in Paris. She and Troy had entered many contests; the slide she'd sent was of daffodils, dandelions, and thistles in a can. A foundation would pay for the shipping, insurance, Lina's flight and hotel.

She had never been to Europe.

When she told Sacha, he said, "Good."

"Maybe you can come with me. They'll pay for the hotel."

"I wish."

She told Troy about Paris in a flat voice. Before, in their work lives, they'd always been a we. Unlike being picked on the playground, where you ran to join a team, here, in her success, Lina stood alone.

Sacha hadn't mentioned marriage again. If he did now, Lina thought she'd give a different answer.

After the show, Martine invited Lina to a dinner party. Lina was excited; they'd never socialized together before. Lina buzzed, and from an upstairs window in the cast-iron building, Martine threw down a sock with a key inside. Lina rode up the shaky freight elevator, which opened onto the artist's large loft. "He's been making his grandmother's Bolognese all day." Adults of all ages arrived; a man in his seventies, carrying skis upright, said he'd come cross-country from Westbeth. Someone turned the lights down and the buckets of brushes and years of accumulation blurred, and they saw only the faces of people around the table and the city lights and towers outside. "Candlelight improves bone structure," Martine said. Her forty-five-year-old boyfriend poured glasses of red wine, then walked around the table with a bowl of pasta. Several women in their fifties, all artists, seemed to be partnerless. They looked at Martine with expressions of greed. A wedge of pecorino made its way down the table with a kitchen grater.

Martine's boyfriend bent to tell Lina he'd liked her paintings. Her face warmed. She understood what Martine saw in him. He'd made a life already. He showed at Knoedler. But she wouldn't have traded. She wished Sacha were here. She felt proud of him. Maybe the two couples could go out together. But somehow, despite Lina's hopefulness, she and Martine never did really become friends.

In November, Lina and Sacha bought their first piece of art together, from a Saturday pop-up in a high school gym in Queens. It was white on white, handmade paper textured with stitches done on a sewing machine. The woman who took their money said that the artist was a teacher in Kansas. They split the price.

When Lina called Walter, she learned that he'd bought a house. Dr. Moss said he could pick up their mom to stay overnight when it was ready, he told Lina. A house in the Palisades. Her dream, Walter said. Now she would have it. But no, Lina shook her head, not that he could see. Their mother lived in the hospital. Walter said that Julie had driven her to see Donnie at college. A nice day. They'd sat in a café outside under a huge sycamore.

Lina had called to tell him that she and Sacha bought a painting. But she didn't now. It sounded too small, or just of a different world.

Julie was finally moving to Michigan, Walter said. She was keeping her apartment through December so they could all be there one more Christmas. Pretty soon, he said, everyone could stay at his new house.

———

At a diner, Lina cried on a bright cold Tuesday morning. She'd be kicked out of her apartment at the end of the month. Julie was moving. She couldn't even go home. "You said I could move in with you, but I don't think you really want that," she whimpered.

He ushered them to a booth. "Why do you think that?"

She was blubbering now, aware that she looked terrible. "Once, you said you could see yourself married now, but you never mentioned that again. I guess that means you could see yourself married to someone else." She blew her nose on the rough napkin.

"We can get married," he said. He looked small, slumped in the corner. Lina had wanted this, but she'd pushed him to it. She tried to compose herself. Outside, a breeze lifted trash on the curb. A sheet of ice blew in every time someone opened the door.

"You don't have to say that."

"I know I don't have to."

This didn't seem *enough*. She wanted a declaration, some flourish. But she only said, "You're really okay with me moving my stuff there before I go home for Christmas?"

"Sure."

They'd been together almost two years. Nothing quenched the longing.

"Are we engaged?"

"Yes."

"Should we tell people?"

"Let's wait," he said.

"Maybe just Troy."

"Yeah, sure. Troy," he said.

What would I be doing with diamonds? someone wrote, in one of the books Lina read in college. She didn't need jewelry; she reminded herself, she wanted to be an artist. Still, at a holiday crafts fair, in a booth where the wind taunted the vinyl roof, she picked up a ring from a table and said, "Buy me this." Sacha handed over a twenty, put the ten back in his wallet. She slid it onto her ring finger.

She bought a small rosemary plant for his kitchen windowsill. She moved over her clothes. Of her couch and chairs, he'd said, "They match." She hadn't known that that was a bad thing. He didn't mind the Morris chair from Etienne.

The next morning, he gave her a key. When she stepped outside the building, a man in front of a small shop was carrying out clay pots of geraniums. She tightened her hand around the metal talisman. Better than any ring.

But when she told Troy at Empire Szechuan, he shook his head.

"Be happy for me," she ordered.

She offered him her couch and chairs. He shot her a look.

"It's not the way it sounds." Sacha liked her easels, her table with brushes and cans, she told Troy.

"So he likes some picture of an artist."

They opened their fortunes. *Where there is love there is no question.* Lina slipped the strip of paper into her wallet.

On a gray December day, they carried her couch and chairs over to Troy's tenth-floor studio. Her paints, scraps, nests, and folded drop cloths all fit into one box. She covered her canvases with brown paper and pulled them on a borrowed dolly to Sacha's apartment, while Troy, her easels over his shoulder, carried the box. They were making a second trip with the Morris chair when it began to snow. She let them in with her key. The apartment was quiet and orderly. They moved the easels to the room that overlooked the back of a church. Lina offered Troy coffee, but when she looked in the refrigerator there was no milk.

Troy laced up his boots and left, taking the newspaper to hold over his head.

On the plane home, Lina read Sacha's favorite book. With a pencil, she underlined a passage.

> *There would be nothing trivial about our lives. Everyday things with us would mean the greatest things. It would be like marrying Pascal.*

Lina was twenty-five years old and engaged to the smartest person she knew. He'd been an art major at Bard, so he understood painting; he got her world, but he'd never aspired, himself, to be Pascal. He called himself "average," said, "I'm just the guy who knows how to keep a ledger." He wanted her to be an artist, though, and believed she could be. And unlike the old scholar in the book, he was young and beautiful.

This year, Julie gave Lina the cot off the pantry. The upstairs sewing room was Donnie's now. He slept every day until afternoon.

"Leave him be," Julie said. "It's his vacation."

He'd done three semesters of college and hadn't gotten into trouble. When Lina asked him about classes, though, she couldn't get much out of him. "They're okay." He had acne and an uneven mustache, and his expression was evasive. They'd always been close, but now he didn't seem to like her.

He fell asleep during the Christmas show at the hospital. Lina elbowed him to stop snoring.

Late that night, at Julie's kitchen table, when everyone else was in bed, Lina read more of Sacha's favorite book. She wished he'd call. Once she dialed but hung up before it rang. On Christmas morning, he did call; he sounded excited about a letterpress printer he'd discovered. "We can have our invitations made on it," he said. It took her a minute to understand he meant for their wedding. She dropped into a deep feeling of relief that he'd brought it up. But then she remembered the lime-green dresses Mrs. Moses sent. Did people still expect a bride's family to pay for the wedding? It was 1980. And Sacha knew about her family. Lina wished they could get the wedding over with and just be married.

"Can we do it at city hall?" she asked.

"No," he said, and laughed.

Lina's mother seemed more out of it than last year. They'd been giving her medicine to sleep through the night, Shirley said. She'd been getting up eight, nine times. "The night nurse can't follow her around to see that she doesn't hurt herself. She has a whole ward to watch."

Lina's attention spiked. "You think she'd hurt herself?"

"She tried to go outside at midnight. She could trip in the dark."

Lina stayed over at the hospital. Shirley folded out a cot for her in the linen closet. "I'm breaking the rules, don't tell anyone." Lina thought of Isabel. She hadn't seen her for years. Isabel was probably a working photographer now.

When the night nurse opened the closet door, Lina bolted up. She walked her mother up and down the halls. Her mother's proprioception was off; she bumped into corners. Lina tried to fold her into a chair in the empty parlor. But her mother didn't want to sit. Her arms and legs were stiff. They walked outside on the sparsely lit grounds; cobwebs caught on their faces and in their hair.

Donnie had told her that two weeks ago their mother was pretty much normal—normal for her, that is. He thought the sleep medicine messed with her balance, but to get her off the medicine without medicine seemed impossible, too.

When Lina finally saw Dr. Moss, in his office, after two nights of this, he looked thinner, the lines engraved deeper in his face.

"It's not the medicine," he said.

"Well, what is it, then? Donnie says she was fine two weeks ago."

"I want to say it's life. Illnesses have trajectories we can't always see. I don't think this will last. She's had many long stretches of good days."

Lina delayed her flight. She drove to Norwalk and sat with her mother until she fell asleep. In the morning, she drove back to Julie's apartment and slept in the cot off the pantry to the sounds of Julie in the kitchen. No sleep had ever felt this enclosing; it had the taste of a warm, sweet meal. In her conversations with Sacha, she said that she was staying because her mother was having trouble sleeping. He didn't ask more and she liked hearing about the art world, leagues away. The fifth night Lina stayed in the linen closet, her mother slept through, and, in the morning, sat alert, quiet, aware of Lina's presence.

Lina stayed two more days. Walter took her out to dinner, with Susan, who said, "Remember me? Good to see you again," and then handed her a bag, mumbling, "Engagement present." Lina had told Walter but had made him promise not to tell. Were they going out again, then? Walter shrugged, annoyed with Susan, who was probably hoping the state of engagement was contagious.

Donnie was still sleeping, at two in the afternoon, when Lina left. She looked around Julie's living room for the last time. Her painting, now framed, hung above the mantel.

"You know I met an artist," Walter said, driving her to the airport. "She does fountains. I'm trying to talk her into making one for Aviation Park. I want you to see her stuff."

"Sure," Lina said. But she wasn't thrilled. She'd liked being the only artist in his life.

67.

Julie called from Michigan in February. She'd hired a decorator to refresh the cabin, had a cleaning crew in, and after all that she still wasn't sure she liked it there. It was too quiet, she said. The middle of the woods. She had a nice kitchen but no one to cook for, and it was hard to get ingredients she liked. Lina felt sad, listening, until she understood that Julie was really calling to find out if she'd heard from Donnie. Julie had called him, but the phone just rang. She'd left messages with a roommate, which Donnie never returned.

Lina promised she'd try to reach him.

"How's your painting going?" Julie asked.

"Okay. I don't know. I wish I finished things faster."

"Are you getting out and about?"

"Not really. Sacha's away."

They were admitting to each other that they were lonely.

"Well, let me know if you talk to your brother."

Lina dialed right after they hung up and the phone rang and rang, like Julie said. But halls in dorms were like that. Lina was going to Europe, so she called four or five times over the next few days. No answer. Then she left.

The first afternoon in Paris, Lina closed the door of her hotel room and sat on the high bed, stunned by her luck. For three days, she would live in this tiny, perfect room with a view of French rooftops. Her mother had never seen Europe. She had an eye for color and balance, too. For Lina, the comparison would always be to her mother.

Walter was attending a shopping-center conference in Stockholm and arranged to fly home through Paris. Julie had probably told him she was lonely. They walked through a city park full of children and mothers, ordinary life but in better colors. They looked in store windows. Julie had sent Lina a one-hundred-dollar check to buy a dress in Paris.

Walter pointed to a navy-blue skirt with tiny white polka dots. "You like that?"

"Not really. I haven't shopped for so long I've forgotten how."

After her time in the department store, when she'd worked on herself as a project, she'd returned to the way she'd been before: sometimes she was pretty and other times not, depending on who did the looking. Nothing she could do, she thought, would make much difference.

"It's funny you think that, being an artist. Isn't it all about creating beauty?" Then he told her since he'd started up again with Susan, they saw each other most days.

"I thought she broke it off because you didn't love her enough." Behind them old limestone buildings made a backdrop to early blossoms in the watery March air.

"That was years ago. The thing is we can talk. It's hard to imagine marrying her, but I can't figure out how we could talk the way we do if I married someone else. My wife might not like it."

"I can't imagine you married. You've always been friends."

"That may be more necessary. In the end."

"For you," Lina said.

"Yes. Just for me." Walter smiled, as if he knew her feelings for Sacha were of a different order.

Sitting on a bench by a merry-go-round, they talked about Donnie. "He's gotten through a year and a half of school," Walter said. "His grades may not be anything to brag about."

"Did he make friends?"

"He always has friends. I think there's a fair bit of pot smoking going on."

"Well, that's normal, I suppose." Lina said that, though she'd never liked it much.

"Except when it's not."

"How do you know when it's not?" Walter shrugged. "Any girlfriend?"

"I think the answer would be plural."

Lina thought of Walter settling for Susan. After all these years of being smarter, her brother might turn out to be a businessman, averagely happy. This made her surprisingly sad. She closed her eyes and sat in a room with a curving stairway and a vase of tulips on a round table. A wave of light.

"Hey," Walter was saying, shaking her shoulder. She must have fallen asleep.

The exhibition was in a high-ceilinged room in a pretty residential neighborhood. One of the other American artists was Lina's sophomore-year TA, who'd hit up on her. He'd invited her out to meet artists and then driven her to a creepy empty house in Queens. In the end, nothing happened; Lina asked him questions about his work to flatter him and he drove her home. But the exhibit organizer suggested that she talk about his work. *Une bonne histoire.* The pupil. The teacher.

"You're not doing it, are you?" Walter said.

The former TA wasn't even in France.

Walter stood in front of Lina's painting: a can of flowers, weeds, and thistles. "If I were a museum, I'd buy this." Lina felt grateful that Walter understood that art was important. Most people didn't. Troy's mother didn't.

"Don't talk about that guy's work," Walter said in parting.

That night, when Lina opened the door to her tiny room, with its small, high bed and slanted ceiling, she was afraid that after Walter's hotel it would seem shabby. But she needn't have worried. It was still and would always be a beautiful room.

———

"I don't aspire to happiness," she said back home, at her desk in the gallery. She meant, of course, *mere* happiness.

"What a stupid stupid thing to say," her boss, Harry, exploded.

She and Sacha sat on the bed and called people to tell them they were getting married. Lauren insisted on Amtraking into the city to help. No one had ever insisted upon helping Lina with anything else; not her work, not even when her mother had gone into the hospital. In fairness, Lauren would have come then, too, had she known. Lina had been too proud to tell her. She could have used Lauren then. But what exactly did she need help with now?

"Bridesmaids?" Lauren used her fingers.

Lina didn't want bridesmaids; she couldn't pay for dresses. "Or, I guess you could each just wear a black dress?"

"Do you really want people wearing black to your wedding?"

This was someone who'd sobbed when George McGovern lost. Since when did Lauren care about what color dresses should be?

They decided that the bridesmaids—Lina supposed she had to ask Susan—could wear their own black dresses with some long ivory gloves. There was a glove district in the West Thirties. They spent an hour in a warehouse, selecting.

"And there's your dress," Lauren said. Another finger.

The idea of a dress daunted Lina. Instead, she dragged Lauren to New York's Flower District. While Lauren lingered among tall pails of roses, Lina talked to a vendor whose wares included dried butterflies and bees. "How do you dry a bee?" she asked the woman who didn't speak English. A summoned teenager emerged from the back room, holding a workbook, to say, "Natural death."

No one asked how they would pay for a wedding. Lina had no idea what Sacha earned.

After Lauren finally boarded the train, Lina returned to the apartment. She was toying with a bouquet of twigs, pussy willows, and dried bees, assembling the cluster with wire, when she got the call.

Donnie had stopped attending classes. It had taken three weeks for the report, filed by the resident assistant about his absences, to filter through the channels of student services and finally prompt an assistant dean to dial the number listed for his guardian. Julie had answered on the second ring.

The police found him on the beach, south of the airport, with a cluster of homeless people and a dog. He had a sleeping bag around his shoulders when Walter picked him up at the Venice Station. Julie got on a plane. Walter had called Dr. Moss, whose first question was, How old is he? He told Walter that Donnie would have to volunteer to go into a program. "He's of legal majority. We can't make him stay. And that's for anywhere," Walter explained to Lina. "Because he's nineteen he can just walk out the door. But Julie has influence. And you do. Maybe Mom. I don't."

"What is it, you think?" Lina asked. "Dope?"

"I drove him to the hospital for a blood test and it came back positive for a lot of things, a lot of things that shouldn't be mixed together. You have to come now." Walter had a flight booked for her that took off in four hours.

She dialed Sacha at work, thinking, as the phone rang, what she would tell him. Dope, she would say, the hospital. She wondered what the drugs were that shouldn't be mixed together. But Sacha was at lunch. She tried again from an airport pay phone and left a message saying she was flying to LA for a family emergency. She called Troy. "Where's Donnie now?" he asked. Lina didn't know. With Walter, she supposed. Troy promised to take her armory class on Saturday. She called the Evergreen to tell Harry she couldn't come in tomorrow and didn't know when she'd be back. She'd have to call Sacha when she landed. She felt suddenly as if they weren't a real couple.

But she'd felt that same way about her family sometimes, so it was hard to subtract out how much was just her.

Walter picked her up at LAX and she sank into his low passenger seat as he threaded through on-ramps she didn't recognize to the 405 South. "Where are we going?"

"We put him with Mom."

"But Donnie's not crazy."

"The juvie wing turns out to be mostly drugs. Dr. Moss knew another place in Orange County, but Donnie's student health coverage runs out in June. A few years back, apparently, Julie looked into adopting Donnie to get him on her insurance. She had a lawyer draw up papers, but in the end Mom wouldn't sign it. Would've been better if she had." He sighed. "He might be more likely to stay because of Mom. Dr. Moss says the programs are all pretty much the same, all twelve-step. He says not to be alarmed by the God talk."

Lina appreciated the comfort of Walter's car. He drove in through a different gate of the hospital. The building was newer than Ward 301. They waited in a sparsely furnished room.

"I'm supposed to be in Atascadero today," Walter said.

"The dog," Julie said, rushing in. Donnie had agreed to give the place a try as long as he could bring his dog. "She's been through everything with him, he says." Julie would keep her until Donnie was out of detox. This morning, she'd taken her to a veterinarian to get her vaccinations, and they'd put on a flea collar. Now she'd left her with a groomer. It would take a while; she was matted. Julie was in a hotel near the hospital. It finally registered: Julie had given up the apartment. That was gone.

"You know, you could stay at my house, Julie," Walter said.

"But this way I can check up on Donnie every day and Diane, too," she said. "When he gets out of detox, we'll see. Maybe he can have the dog with him by then."

They were led to a room where fold-out chairs were arranged in a circle. They sat with other families of other addicts. A not-so-old woman stuttered in on a walker. "Diabetes," Julie whispered. The husband was a dockworker and they had good insurance. One tall, thin man turned out to be an uncle, here for his niece, whose father was not in the picture. "Yah, my brother's a real train wreck." Another well-dressed couple had a daughter who had been in and out of rehab eleven times.

"This same place?" Lina asked.

This and others, came the answer. They didn't smile.

Lina was wearing the suit jacket she'd worn to the Joseph Cornell opening. She found a note in a pocket.

cigar box
gigolo father
map of Nevada
Plain ugly land

She crumpled the paper, shot a basket.

The day in the new hospital building was segmented into hour-and-a-half units. They had to introduce themselves over and over. Julie had a hard time explaining herself. When it was her turn, she crossed her arms and said, "Family friend."

"You're way more than that," Walter finally said.

"When do we get to see Donnie?" Lina asked.

"Not today, I don't think," Julie said.

At the lunch break (only lunch? It seemed days they'd been there), Julie pulled waxed-paper-wrapped sandwiches out of her bag. Sourdough rolls with white cheddar and bitter sauteed greens. "I've got a kitchenette there in the hotel," she said.

At a long institutional table, a guy passed out notebooks in which they were supposed to write down every person they could think of whom they resented.

I'm not the fucking addict, Lina thought. She apparently had to do this anyway, all twelve steps of it. Donnie, meanwhile, was somewhere else.

"It's mostly myself I resent," Julie whispered. "Moving to Michigan was a mistake." She'd already left a message for her Beverlywood landlord, to get onto the wait list for her old duplex.

"You shouldn't have to change your whole life," Lina said.

"I didn't like it there anyway." Julie shook her head now all the time.

Lina hated ballpoints. And the list of people she resented was long; it almost equaled the list of people she knew.

Walter doodled. "I can't think of anybody."

Lina covered her list with her arm. Near the top, she'd underlined <u>Walter</u>. "When do we get to see *him*?" Donnie had had real learning issues. But he'd taught himself to code. And Chinese chess. He'd drawn that picture of the guidance counselor on the wall. At college, though, he'd collected eight hundred signatures to get benefits for the cafeteria ladies.

Which side of him would win?

The leader talked about Step Two. What to do if you weren't religious. Think of what you respect most. What you want to be. That can be your higher power. Could Lina's higher power be art? Was that high enough? Or was great art great because it honored a power greater than itself?

Lina meant to see their mother that first day, but by the time they were free to go, she and Walter were so exhausted they sank into his car and opened the windows so the soft air batted their cheeks. When Lina blinked awake, Walter had parked in the driveway of a house. His house. That he owned.

They walked through the quiet entry and Lina ran her hand over the top of a cabinet. Nice wood. There was a sofa. Chairs. She called Sacha from the kitchen phone while Walter stood in front of the open refrigerator. She said, in as few words as possible, what had happened. It was hard to talk with Walter listening. There wasn't much to eat. A leftover burrito, a jar of almonds, and carrot salad in a take-out box. That night, she cried in her bed. A phone waited on the low bedside table, but she didn't call Sacha again. He would be sleeping, and there was too much to tell. She would try him in the morning, when he would be rushing and she could summarize.

This house was so nice. Why couldn't Donnie be here instead of in that institutional ward that felt like a prison?

The next day, they learned about rules. Phone calls were allowed only on Sundays.

No visits the first fourteen days. A visit is a privilege, the man said, that they have to earn. He passed out the schedule. Peer counseling. Mentor meetings. Donnie would have obligations all day long. Group sessions and two twelve-step gatherings. A therapist twice a week. Physical exercise started right after detox. They took them in a van to the gym. They could see a trainer there, but that the family had to pay for. Julie raised her hand. Walter levered her arm down. "My turn."

Week two, they would be given chores. Attend meetings off-site. Everyone got a job in the community after forty-five days. Eventually, the more intellectual ones took classes at the local college. Family week started day 26. The families would watch them receive their one-month chip.

They trekked to their mother in the hot middle of the day. Ward 301 seemed old in comparison. She looked beyond them.

"Donnie is here in the hospital," Lina said, trying not to talk the way people talked to impaired people. "He had a problem with drugs. We have to pray for him," she said, although she didn't pray, really. Their mother fell asleep in her chair. She'd put on weight, the way older people did, tiers of fat stacking on her belly. But she wasn't old. Her legs looked purplish, and she was wearing green cotton ankle socks she would've hated once. No one had been doing her laundry for years. It went in with everyone else's.

They still had time before the afternoon Al-Anon session, so they walked to the superintendent's office. Dr. Moss had become smaller with age. When Lina asked about Isabel, he said she was doing her residency in Oakland. "She's on call eighteen hours a day. Surgery rotation."

So she'd quit art. Lina was shocked. Mr. Riddle and then Isabel were why she'd started. Lina still believed Larkin was a genius. What happened to the work those two women would have made? She wondered where she could see Mr. Riddle's work. Was it for sale in some gallery?

At the end of the day, they finally saw Donnie. His face looked terrible, his beauty marred, maybe forever. He was smoking, right in front of them, as if to flaunt the fact that he had turned into someone else.

Lina started crying. They had been asked to write out what they wanted to say to him, what they were afraid of and what they hoped for.

"I'm terrified that you're going to do something stupid and die," Walter said.

"I'm afraid, I guess I'm afraid, I mean our mother's here, our dad's a gigolo, I'm afraid we're bad, too," Lina said.

"We're not bad," Donnie said, holding on to her hard when they hugged and not letting go. "And she's not bad either."

Lina asked then about school, if he wanted to go back.

"That's the last thing on my mind now," he said.

"Easy, Lina," Walter said, a hand on her shoulder. "I'm a drop-out, too."

School meant too much to her. She knew that.

"I just hope you'll get better so you can have the life that you *deserve*," Julie said.

"That first night I brought him here," Walter said when they got into the car, "I drove home and slept twelve hours. Better than I'd slept in years. Knowing he was locked up safe."

"How's the wedding coming?" Susan asked.

They were sitting in Walter's kitchen. The question startled Lina.

The wedding. Could she even get married with Donnie in there? "Hard to think about now." Lina felt ashamed of her preposterous bouquet. Twigs, cocoons, dead bees. Just then, she remembered the champagne glasses still in the box on the floor of Sacha's closet and thanked Susan. At the other end of the long wooden table was a stack of canvas totes, printed *I've got some real estate here in my bag*.

From the guest bedroom, she talked to Sacha. He asked about her day and she answered in monosyllables. He didn't coax out more. He sighed. "Is there anything I can do to help?" There must be, but what? The casement windows opened with no screens, and a watery smell of dirt floated in.

Lina could have reached out and touched a rose.

Sacha called back after they hung up. Her hopes rose. He had to ask her something. There was too much to tell, but she wanted him to know. He'd scheduled a dinner with his parents the night of her return, he said. Should he cancel? She said no, it was fine. So there would be another meal, in another restaurant. Every meeting they'd had had been in a public place.

68.

The Saturday she returned, they hurried to a midtown Italian restaurant to meet his parents. His mother laughed at her husband's jokes, looking up at him, gold rings on all the fingers of her left hand.

Lina had a feeling she was prone to in certain restaurants (white tablecloths, candles)—*My mother would love this*. And she would never have it. She wouldn't have minded the unevenness between husband and wife, either. Her mother was better suited to her life than she was. Lina wished, for a stray moment, that she could give it to her.

They were complimenting the wine. "Be good for a reception," Sacha's father said.

"But, honey, remember, Lina's from California. She may want the wedding there. And they grow some of the best wine in the world."

Lina looked at Sacha. She was pretty sure a wedding cost more than all the money she had.

As dessert was served—floating island—Sacha's father asked about the surname of their future children. Sacha looked as if he were helpless to stop him.

"I'd like our children to have my family name, too," Lina said, two fingers on the tablecloth, "maybe with a hyphen."

"But your father wasn't even there!" his father burst out, in something akin to laughter that held no merriment.

Both families had had trauma, but theirs was different. It was tragic. Historic. Nazis had hounded Sacha's grandparents out of Europe. Lina respected his family for what Sacha's grandparents had suffered. On her side, she had only the selfish and the mentally ill. Maybe her children could have their name, she liked it anyway. Jacob. These elegant, sophisticated people agreed to take her, but they wanted her pulled free of family, alone.

———

"You have to admit I'm not what they expected."

"Thank God," Sacha said, taking off his tie. "You're not Jewish. You're from California. You propose hyphenation. There's Barnard, though. And my mother likes that you're an artist. I wish you had *more* to poke her with. Seriously, though, do we have to hyphenate? It's so clunky." He asked, "Do you really want to give your father that honor?"

"It's my name, too," Lina said.

Lina's work felt dead after only a week away. She'd left one tube open and the paint had dried. Her canvases felt inconsequential. You will change nothing, they taunted.

She'd felt close to her brothers and Julie; they'd been a family in that depressing place with drab walls and highly polished floors. They'd made their sad confessions and she felt a string of hope. She paged through a catalogue of bright-colored kitchen appliances that had come in the mail. The phone rang and she leaped—thinking, The place? Something about Donnie—but it was only Walter. "They scheduled family week Monday through midday Friday! It doesn't even over*lap* with a weekend. I can't go for five days."

"I think we have to," Lina said. She looked at the room, the shapes of her easels. She had twenty days to fall back under their spell before she'd have to go again.

"You'll be there. And Julie. I'll come as much as I can."

By the time Sacha came home, she was in bed, reading. He clicked on the TV while undressing. When he crawled in, she said she'd have to go back for family week, in May. He nodded, serious and quiet. She didn't tell him her work felt dead. She'd talk to Troy about that tomorrow.

Sacha stood up to get a glass of water. "Is there anything I can do?" That moment, he seemed taller, a dark pine. She fell asleep holding his back. But what had happened to sex? That urgency had ended. Still, she loved the safety; maybe she needed it more.

———

It was spring. Tiny red pointed buds stretched from the tips of branches as she walked along the river, up to see Troy. They met at the Cuban Chinese restaurant. Semipermanent litter rustled in the street.

Troy asked about the place, how the treatment was supposed to work.

"They keep saying we can't control it. We can't cure it. Then what the fuck are we doing there?" It was good to be with Troy. She could sound like herself. "You never did anything like this, did you, no groups? Me either."

"You and me, we never gave ourselves permission to fuck up," Troy said. "I'm kinda surprised your brother did. I'm a little impressed."

"I'm so scared." She took out the schedule of Donnie's days.

The list of NEA grants had come out. Martine was on it and another painter from their program, who'd never said a word. They gossiped. Finally, Troy asked how things were with Sacha. She wished the two men she was closest to would like each other.

"He's going to Florida," she said. "Have you heard of Christo?"

"The guy who wraps things?"

"He's a couple, actually. They use just his name to be taken seriously. Sacha is going to watch them wrap some island. I fly back for family week and here's the weird thing: I'm looking forward to it."

"How's your mom?" Troy asked.

"The same. I'll see more of her in twenty days."

"Hey, I'm learning how to make boeuf en daube."

"Is this all because Jackson Pollock baked a pie once?"

"Bouef en daube, remember? The dinner party in that book you gave me."

Troy had read the book Lina heard about from Sacha that Etienne had given her for nothing. Her three men were invisibly connected.

Lina kept Donnie's schedule taped to her easel. Monday, she called his case manager, who said that despite the wild cocktail they'd discovered that night in the emergency room, Donnie had finished detox and it hadn't been too hard for him.

"So he's clean," Lina said.

"Yes. Now the building starts."

Each week, the case manager reported incremental progress, and Lina felt a sense of pride in that which her work didn't yield.

At the Evergreen, she told Harry about family week. He looked away and asked if she needed a leave of absence. Did he want her to resign? "I think it'll be just the one week," she said.

"Take your time," he answered, not looking at her.

Walter attended family week after all. During breaks, Julie took out the *LA Times* and circled rental listings. Her landlord had given her unit to a family with a baby and, anyway, he'd doubled the rent. "When I went for parents' weekend at the college, he didn't seem so good to me, but he said he was fine. I should never have believed him. The roommates weren't any better. Not a one awake when I knocked at noon. I don't need an upstairs-downstairs. Just two bedrooms. For when he gets out."

The group leader, a tall man with bangs who would have been good-looking if he'd had braces, Lina thought, passed out a list: *Characteristics of Codependent People.* Lina checked eleven of the seventeen traits. (*A tendency to confuse love and pity. An unhealthy dependence on relationships. Do you have difficulty taking compliments or gifts?*) She circled the question: *Have you ever lived with someone who hits or belittles you?*

"You haven't, have you?" Walter asked, looking at her paper.

She was touched by his concern. Their mother had hit her. But she said, "No. Just 'belittles.' Such a perfect word."

They were sent to a workshop on restoring boundaries. A therapist wrote formulas on a green board with blanks to fill in.

When you _____, I feel _____.

Julie bit down on her pencil. She was taking this very seriously. Lina resisted the exercises, dire and terrifying as the situation was. She couldn't help herself.

"When you drive your ma crazy and scare 'er half to death, I feel, I was gonna say mad, mad at my brother, your dad, but what I really feel is helpless," the uncle said.

Everyone murmured. Everyone, that was, except Lina. Julie was one of the louder murmurers.

A few other family members read their sentences aloud. You didn't have to.

Walter had finished quickly. Lina wished she could read his.

The next hour was devoted to consequences. The therapist gave an example: "If you raise your voice with me, I won't share my feelings with you. If you continue, I'll hang up and not speak with you for two days."

But Donnie never raised his voice. He just disappeared.

They were supposed to list their own enabling behaviors. The therapist passed around a cheat sheet. Julie said that she recognized quite a few. Calling to check if he was going to classes. Apologizing for him. Back in high school, explaining his behavior to the administrators when he chalked that picture on the wall. Believing he might be sick when she should've known. She kept shaking her head.

Then they were supposed to write a letter to the addiction.

Dear Heroin,

Dear MDMA,

Dear Vodka,

Lina sat listening to Julie's pencil on the paper. She and Walter looked at each other. It was the end of the day and hard to address a letter to a drug.

Driving home, Walter said that Susan had made rice pudding. "Oh, and turns out this engagement business is contagious."

So the story of her brother had an ending. "Was it Donnie, you think? That tipped you over?"

"Yeah, sure, partly. Made me realize what matters. I don't want to tell him, though. For now, let's just focus on getting him better."

Susan stood in the doorway holding a stemmed dish in each hand. Jess had called and said it was important, she said. But it was already late and they had an eight o'clock session the next morning.

———

She called Jess during the morning break, standing on a strip of dirt littered with cigarette butts. Everyone here smoked. Lina wanted to talk to Donnie's therapist about that.

The troubadour's brother had flown out to look at rings. He pooh-poohed Berkeley jewelry shops and made an appointment to see diamonds in a back room at Tiffany. He told Jess he was proud of her. He understood what an achievement a PhD represented.

Lina was having trouble concentrating.

When she got her first job, Jess went on, he could follow her. "I'm very hireable," he'd said. "But then, later, when we have children, you're going to have to quit." "Quit?" Jess had managed to ask. He'd said, "Being my wife is going to be a full-time job."

"Like first lady." Lina smashed a twisted butt with her heel. It was oddly satisfying. The guy was planning to run the world.

He told Jess she should think it over. So she was thinking. But Lina had to go. The next session was starting. She promised to call soon. After all this agony, Jess would end up marrying him and they'd be rich. It was hard to imagine Jess without science, though. Her little brother, Evan, was studying quantum gravity at Caltech. Lina had always envied Jess's immersion in her work. You did your small piece and it contributed. She'd said that once, and Jess had said, "Sure, but isn't everything like that?"

Art's not, Lina had said. But could it be? She wondered as she hurried to the next session. Two doctors were showing packages of synthetic quaaludes, cocaine, methamphetamine, and heroin. Lina took notes. Cloud Nine. Pearl. Reindeer Dust. Snowball. Woolie. Cielo. White Sugar. She hadn't guessed the language of drugs would be poetic.

A multimillion-dollar industry, the doctors said. Synthetics were sold as incense or tea, labeled "Not for human consumption." Kids melted the drugs with Hershey's bars, froze them, then ate it. Angel dust, Lina wrote down, was an elephant tranquilizer and an embalming fluid. A side effect of something called bath salts was severe strange aggression, the male doctor said. After taking quaaludes, a rock musician raped another member of the band.

Now the doctor wheeled a steel cart to the front of the room to show them containers addicts used to hide their drugs. False pockets. A hairbrush with a handle that unscrewed to reveal a hollow core. What looked like a regular bottle of soda. Two commonly abused categories were pain-relief drugs and relaxants. Diazepams, the female doctor said. And every medicine cabinet has at least one.

But Julie's hadn't. Lina knew that. So how had Donnie started?

They described the myriad ways kids cheated on drug tests. They purchased urine from other kids. "They heat it and keep it in a lined thermos. They wear boxers. Most facilities don't make them pull down their pants."

Lina stepped outside. She had to get air. She stopped at the tea table and filled a flimsy Styrofoam cup with hot water.

When she returned, the doctors were holding up a web belt with what looked like a vibrator attached, with a balloon at the end. The female doctor lifted the apparatus. "They call them squirt guns. Somebody figured out how to drill a hole through a dildo. You can buy them on the black market in any color: white, tan, brown, or black. Some kid told me he was trying to get a patent on it. He wanted to market it as the Weeanator."

They'd planned to take Julie to dinner, but she wanted to give the dog a bath. "Let's go tomorrow or the day after. Maybe by then they'll let us take Donnie."

In the morning, the uncle brought two boxes of doughnuts. They were put into small groups to practice boundary setting.

"No more me stayin' up all night," the diabetic mother said. Her husband, the longshoreman, nodded. "No more four in the mornings."

"No more drug parties in the house. That's my boundary."

But Donnie didn't live with them anymore. What boundaries could they set?

In healthy communication, the goal is to understand, said the leader with bangs and overlapping teeth. (She noticed, behind the bangs, he had thick curly hair.) Most people listen in order to react or respond. True. Often, Lina felt aware of people waiting for her to finish; she tried to hurry up then and tripped.

———

The next day, after lunch, a new doctor from Colorado armed the podium. He looked like a skier—in his early forties, tan, with light blue eyes. The white-coated Robert Redford had once been a patient here, he said. An addict.

So this was the aspiration. Once here as a patient, now back as a doctor flown in from the mountains.

He showed slides of the brain and talked about theories of addiction. Lina drifted off and jerked awake to him saying, "Drugs really do feel different to different people. Some people take one hit and it's all over." This sad, heavy fact dropped into her; there was genetic luck and Donnie had drawn the bad card. He'd had learning problems, too.

The windswept doctor talked about a study in which rats chose dopamine over food. They starved themselves to death for pleasure. Glutamate, he said, preserved memories. Chronic stress caused anhedonia, a state in which a person no longer felt pleasure from the usual sources of happiness.

Lina wrote down the word.

"You want to get a doctor who understands addiction," Robert Redford said, "and doesn't prescribe Ativan to a person in recovery."

He showed a slide with a definition of *addiction*.

A stress-induced (HPA axis), genetically mediated
(polymorphisms, epigenetic mechs) primary, chronic, and
relapsing brain disease of reward (nucleus acumbens),
memory (hippocampus & amygdala), motivation
and related circuitry (OFC, ACC, PFC) that alters
motivational hierarchies such that addictive behaviors
supplant healthy, self-care behaviors.

Lina gave up trying to parse the acronyms. For addiction, Robert Redford said, we should follow the same treatment models as those for chronic illnesses, like post-chemotherapy cancer or lupus or major depression. "I like addicts," he said, quietly.

He let them go when it was still light outside. Julie had obtained permission to take Donnie off grounds, and Walter had heard about a new shopping center, twenty minutes away. Donnie had his dog with him now. She slept at his feet during meetings, Julie said. Donnie seemed himself, but awkward. Someone had given him a haircut. They ate at an open-air restaurant in the newly built wooden mall, and throughout the meal Donnie focused on the dog at his side. After dinner, they wandered in and out of small shops. Donnie looked down, his hands in his pockets. They encouraged him to try on a shirt in a vintage store. Lina had to take the leash out of his hand. They all liked the shirt and fought over who could buy it. But instead he found a collar for the dog. They bought the collar, and Julie snuck back to get the shirt, too. The evening felt like a pleasure trip in a foreign country, one they could finally afford.

Robert Redford was back the next day to talk about "The First Year of Recovery."

Year, Lina heard, first *year.* It had been a month. She'd cast her horizon out three months, even four, to be generous. She was supposed to be married in September.

"Relapse," the Colorado doctor said. "What causes it? Anybody know?"

He wrote the word on the blackboard: what they all feared.

Navy pilots treated for addiction returned to work 96 percent of the time. Outcomes for commercial pilots clocked in at 87 percent. These numbers fell like golden beams slanting into the room. Lina had, by herself, walked to the Palisades Library and looked up the success rates of rehab. She guessed that every single person in this room had. Those statistics were grim; the vast majority of patients became active users again.

"So, we have to ask, what is the *model*?" the windswept doctor said.

Lina liked watching his back move. Taut thighs showed through the light corduroy jeans. He wasn't thin, like Sacha. He was the oldest man Lina had ever found attractive. The chalk squeaked as he wrote on the board.

Medical Detoxification.
Inpatient residential treatment.
Aftercare, 3–5 years.

Three to five years! In five years, Lina would be thirty.

"Now you're thinking, three to five years, what does that mean? Well, it means after residential treatment, a sober-living place. Ritualistic, daily, sometimes even hourly, stress-management activities. Regular testing. Eventually, a return to duty. Service work. Meaningful goals. And finally"—he sighed—"a relapse plan.

"But first, let's look at the things that threaten sobriety.

"Exposure, even brief, to the drug itself. Exposure to cues. Remember, glutamine stores memories. Even now," the doctor said, "I'm twenty-one years sober, but when I landed in Orange County yesterday, there were certain roads I couldn't take. There's a blue door I'll never see again." Regret lingered in his voice, even love. "Cravings aren't all conscious. Picture how you drive home from work without thinking about it. That's where AA comes in . . ."

Trying to imagine Donnie on a three-to-five-year plan felt like deafening noise. The doctor was talking about monkeys now. After a social defeat, a beaten monkey relapses more quickly.

You needed good testing, he said. Twice a week. An experienced tester will notice: Are the pupils blown? Pinned? Sober-living houses varied. Some had a 60, 70 percent rate of going out. Going out meant getting back on drugs.

Would they have to watch him forever? There could be no life for her, then. For a second, Lina imagined him dead, then, guilt flooding her like a liquid—she'd wished her most-loved brother dead—looked at Walter and Julie, relieved they couldn't see inside her.

After lunch, they would work on relapse plans. But not with the blue-eyed doctor. He was flying back to Colorado. "I try to think what it was like for my mother," he was saying to Julie and the uncle of the girl whose father had gone AWOL.

———

The relapse plan turned out to be another letter. Their workshop leader, the tall man with crowded teeth, outlined a formula. The first paragraph read: *I've written this letter to you because I'm cautiously optimistic and hopeful for your recovery, but I'm also realistic in that you could relapse sometime in the future.*

Then they had to write about all the good qualities the loved one had when he was not using. There should be no negatives in this paragraph, the leader said. Only things you've loved about the person in the past, before drugs, and again this month in recovery. The week had done its work; Lina didn't resist. For paragraph three, they were told to use the transition *However* before writing a broad description of the future as you see it if your loved one continues to use. Describe the potential deterioration of his physical, emotional, mental, and spiritual health. Lina looked up at the leader. Tall and lean; he turned out to be handsome after all, in a different way than the Colorado doctor. Envision the loved one's inability to maintain relationships or keep a job, he said. Imagine him dying, prematurely and alone. You can even describe yourself at the gravesite. Use your feelings. When I think of this future, he said, I feel devastated, cheated, and incomplete. He advised starting paragraph four with the transition *But*. This final part should conjure a hopeful future, with relationships, work, a long happy life.

Lina just then realized the difference between the Colorado doctor and this man. It was class. That was all. His teeth had looked to her the way she'd looked to Martine.

69.

They trekked over to see their mother. Diane, Walter called her now. Lina would meet Donnie and his therapist in an hour. Walter and Julie had already had their sessions. In the codependency group, Julie told them as they walked, the leader had encouraged her to write a tough-love statement. The uncle had written to his niece, "If you choose to go out, I'll stop communicating. You will be totally on your own." Julie couldn't write that. "What he said made sense but it depends on how old the person is. I don't think it's the right approach for us."

Their mother wasn't in 301. Shirley told them to check the shed, where she made her arrangements, and they found her there. She had nine or ten dented black buckets filled with branches and weeds—none of the stalks held what would qualify as a flower—and she was concentrating. She didn't want to be disturbed. Walter talked at her ten minutes before giving up.

When Lina found the therapist's office, in a small building on the edge of the grounds, Donnie was standing in a huddle, smoking. The other kids looked hardened. Lina couldn't say exactly how. The therapist was a middle-aged man who clasped his hands between his knees. In the dim room, Lina brought up the crime they'd committed, years ago. Donnie thought their mom had gotten the job innocently and then hatched the idea for stealing from being around so much stuff. "Probably just too tempting."

Her system of theft had involved all three of them. "We could have been arrested," Lina said. She wanted Donnie to acknowledge how reckless their mother had been. There was not much light in the room. The therapist asked about Walter. But Walter hadn't known. "She kept him clean," Lina said.

It was a long, racking exchange. Lina felt she was trying to prove something. She remembered, for a darting second while talking, that she'd never told Sacha about this crime. She never would. She didn't want him to know that her mother had sacrificed them. It was her deepest shame.

"You may never fully agree about the level or tilt of your mother's illness. Lina, you believe she sent you into danger, while, Donnie, you think it was something she fell into herself. Divergent memory is normal. We each have a different experience of our parents."

So she should let Donnie have his adamant, sweet fantasy about his mom. Wasn't that what she was doing with Sacha? Cutting out the parts of her life she didn't want him to see?

While the therapist talked, Donnie took a crushed pack of cigarettes from his pocket, shook one out, and lit up. His long fingers had a finicky delicacy.

Lina interrupted to say, "I want you to quit smoking," and Donnie told her, in a frantic voice, fingers spread, that he was trying so hard and she always wanted more from him, nothing was ever enough, he could never . . .

The therapist sat forward to list the jumbled litany of Donnie's achievements: meetings, working out, reading, helping others, Step Six. She would have to learn. She had stayed up until midnight writing her letter. She gave it to him, at the end. They hugged, standing, and, as they had every time since he'd been here, they held on a long time with palpable intent.

Friday afternoon, the man with bangs and curly hair led the families in a ceremony. He lit a candle. They went around the room and wished each other well. The uncle told the group he owned a boat—he pulled out a packet of photos and passed them in both directions; it was a midsized motorboat—and said that every single person in this room who was sober in one year—you, too, he said to the leader—was invited onto his boat.

The leader smiled a beautiful smile. That moment, Lina wanted to kiss him.

"Reunion on the boat!" the longshoreman's wife toasted, lifting her walker and knocking it on the ground. Then everyone said it, vowing to meet again. Julie and Walter joined. *Next year on the boat.* Someone proposed Baja. Point Reyes. Lina kept quiet. She'd read the statistics. Next year, not all these people would be celebrating. Many would be back in this room or another, with these same folding chairs. She fervently hoped Donnie would beat the odds.

She looked at the leader; he looked back. He seemed to understand. The leader called people up one at a time. Donnie was awarded his token for thirty days.

Walter was driving to Northern California that afternoon and Lina hitched a ride so she could see Jess. She found her in an old building on the Berkeley campus, in a lab where many people seemed to be quietly working.

"I bought food," Jess said. "We can walk to my place." Jess told Lina that since they'd talked Tuesday she'd figured out how many experiments she could run in five years. She'd gone to a gynecologist to ask how long she could put off having kids. If she pushed it to ten years, which the doctor said was risky, eventually she'd still have to quit. If she wanted children. That was what she'd been trying to decide. And she kind of had. She cared about being a scientist more than she cared about being a mom. That turned out not to be a choice, though. *He* wanted them. Thinking of quitting was like imagining an early death. An engagement shouldn't feel like a diagnosis, her mom said. So Jess had taken the red-eye Wednesday. "I had it in my mind that when he saw me, he'd . . . I was shaking. I cried in a restaurant, outside on the sidewalk. He took me back to the airport." This was a lot for Jess to say. She was usually minimal.

Lina was astonished that Jess had said no. Lina didn't know if she could have. They made dinner, talked until midnight, then Lina slept on Jess's couch and woke to the sounds of her friend making coffee. Nothing felt as peaceful as waking in Jess's apartment. Walter came to get her an hour later. Lina had once thought of fixing them up, but they barely noticed each other.

"I'm taking you to see the sculpture I told you about," Walter said, driving over the Bay Bridge. "The mermaid first." Lina looked at him to see if this was a joke. But there were literal cast-iron mermaids, bare-breasted, one nursing a baby that looked like a doll. Cast-iron turtles. Disney kitsch, but Walter loved it. Lina would have bet the artist herself was beautiful. She tried to think of something nice to say. "I like the hair," she said. A group of children pressed close to the splashing fountain.

They got back into the car. "I'm going to show you another." The next fountain was vertical steel, folded to look like paper, surprisingly modern. Lina liked it better. But how could the person who made this have done the first one?

"I want to take you by her house on the way to the airport. We have just enough time. The stuff there; I can't describe it. Fountains are her public work. I don't know much about art—but her work makes you feel something. Like yours does. I tried to commission her for a fountain in Aviation; she said no. I bought one of her pieces anyway. She's Japanese American, from LA. She and her husband have six kids."

So it couldn't be a crush. Lina vowed to be polite. In two hours, she'd be on the plane. The woman's work would be good-intentioned, she thought, overt and virtuous. Lina pictured a pretty Asian woman in Birkenstocks, children crawling at her feet.

Walter parked in front of a small house in Noe Valley. A man with a white beard opened the door. "Albert," Walter said. "This is my sister."

The artist wasn't home. Nothing had prepared Lina for what she saw when the man swung open the living-room door. In a high room with an arched ceiling hung dozens of wire sculptures—light Brancusi shapes shot through with air. A blown dandelion, three feet wide. Lina had to remember to breathe. Her brother, of all people, had stumbled onto beauty.

They stayed in the room until Walter said it was time to go. They thanked Albert, who was reading *The New Republic*.

"Does she have a dealer?" Lina asked in the car.

"Probably. She's had shows. But I don't know how recently. She's been involved in a lot of community projects. She helped start an arts high school here. The piece I bought is like the ones we saw. An older one."

Lina asked for pictures. She wanted Sacha to see.

Lina tried to tell Sacha about the artist. She heard herself; she didn't sound very smart. She admitted she didn't like the mermaids. "But the hanging wire pieces—" She made gestures that were the physical equivalent of stuttering.

"Has she had shows in New York?"

Lina didn't know. Eventually, Walter sent a picture of the piece he'd bought.

"Nice," Sacha said, then put it down. Lina asked Walter how much he'd paid. He wouldn't tell, so it must have been a lot. Lina had envied her brother for many things, but never as much as for this one possession.

She took the picture with her to show Harry when she returned to Evergreen, but when she arrived he wasn't there, and another young woman sat at the desk, wearing a skirt and black tights. She didn't know about Lina. That night, when Harry called to put her back on the schedule, Lina recognized pity in his voice. She would've liked to quit, in a snap of pride, but didn't want to give up the paycheck.

Trish, Donnie's caseworker, said that soon he would get a job. Most kids found work in local coffee shops, but he wanted the hospital, to be near his mother. They usually didn't let patients from the youth wing intermingle with adults, but geriatrics was short-staffed, and Trish was filing for permission.

Did she think Donnie could go back to college in fall? Lina asked.

Trish thought fall sounded too soon. Maybe winter, if the college had sober living. If the testing was sound. With visuals.

"Visuals meaning he pulls down his pants?"

"Yes. He came in—when? March? It usually takes a year all told."

Sacha flung himself on the bed. How long, he asked, did Lina think Donnie would be in the place?

"First they said three months. Now it's already been four." She didn't tell him Trish had said a year.

"You think it's working?

"Yeah. No. Definitely."

"So good." Sacha looked like he had more to say. Lina was relieved. They heard rain outside. A small excitement built; now they would finally talk. He lay on his side, his head propped on an elbow. "Do you want to postpone? Your brother has to be there."

"He'll be out by then, I'm pretty sure." She wasn't, though.

"And he'll be all right, you think, around alcohol?"

Alcohol. She hadn't thought of that. "Would we have to have alcohol?"

"It's a wedding, Lina."

"Walter will be there with him." Was Walter enough? She needed time. To think.

At the Cuban Chinese place, Lina told Troy about the philosophy of the rehab unit, which, come to think of it, ran through the whole hospital. Dr. Moss believed in education as cure. So in August Donnie was starting classes at the local community college. He could eventually become certified as an addiction counselor, Trish said. A nurse in her mother's ward, Shirley, had begun in the hospital at sixteen. Her parents worked there, too. Later, the hospital paid for Shirley's nursing school. That was well and good for Shirley, but Lina didn't like the idea of Donnie becoming an "addiction professional," as Trish called it. As if that were all he could do now.

"Still, probably good to be on a campus," Troy said. "Somebody's apt to be talking about an idea. My cousin, the one that had trouble, he used to say, 'Addicts, we dreamers.'"

Trish had told Lina that Donnie was moving from the lockdown unit to a small cottage with three other young men.

Lina thought of the twelve-step token the good-looking guy had given to Donnie on his thirtieth day of sobriety. Someone probably purchased those tokens by the bag.

Troy laughed. "Could say that about our diplomas or any other damn award."

Lina walked to Sacha's bedroom desk—a mid-century Mogensen they'd found in a Brooklyn warehouse—and he covered a handwritten letter with his sweatered arm, the word *hereditary* crawling out from beneath his cuff.

"My mother," he said.

"What did you tell her?" It came out as an accusation.

"She was going to find out, Lina. Your mother would be at the wedding."

The wedding, Lina thought. Then, *would be*.

They fought until he handed her the letter, a carefully worded note about the heritability of mental illness. His mother hadn't wanted her son to marry into insanity. She was thinking about grandchildren. Lina shouldn't have blamed her. *What if it's in me?* had been Lina's own constant terror. She wanted a better life than the one her mother was living. Was that treachery? Betrayal? At the bottom of the page, Sacha's mother had written *Beauty won't last forever.*

"That's my mother, not me," Sacha said. "You're not marrying my parents."

Lina asked him his true opinion of Walter's sculptor.

"A little domestic, maybe. Craftsy."

Six months ago, he'd brought home an antique papier-mâché bride and groom fashioned to be on top of a cake and had played with them on the table, but his wedding planning had since slowed. Lina had been relieved. But now, she thought, maybe they could get married at city hall, with his parents, her brothers, her mother, and Julie, celebrate with just a cake and champagne. Lina decided to take some initiative. Visiting Troy at the East Side pottery studio, she'd walked past a bakery that made beautiful cakes, displayed on silver stands in the front window. Old men sat reading foreign newspapers. Lina had never before stepped inside.

She waited her turn, then asked about wedding cakes. A baker came from the back and told her that they would make samples. The cakes looked exquisite, lacquered on their pedestals. Fondant orchids spilled over one smooth side. She liked yellow cake with lemon filling. He suggested marzipan and chestnut. Almond. Poppy seed. He would make six kinds.

In a week, she picked up the pink boxes, each tied with string, and tried to pay, but the baker wouldn't accept money. A courtesy, he said, for our customers.

She stepped into the bedroom where Sacha sat at his desk. She stood gazing at his back, his narrow shoulders in the worn brown-green sweater, in front of bookshelves with a small stuffed owl. She didn't want to disturb this tableau. Curls fell onto his collar. Sometimes when she saw him, the world contracted. What she loved about him wasn't the two of them. It was him alone.

They set the cakes on the round kitchen table, each on its own plate. "Like a Wayne Thiebaud," she mumbled. There was just enough space for the table, next to the window. Most of the time they spent together in the apartment was there. They looked down at the small cakes, the dark pressing in from outside. Sacha cut a slice. She ate a bite. It tasted like dust. She tried another. They were terrible. She started laughing. Then he said, "I want to talk." Standing.

They both stilled.

"What?" There was a clear moment, before the terror rushed in.

She'd always known, if he left her, the sting would last. That was the danger of real love, she'd thought. It had the power to destroy you.

70.

For years, Lina had worried that her mother's illness was inside her, biding its time. Now she knew that it was here. There was some relief in this. She didn't have to try so hard. Tears ran down her face as she walked along the river, and she didn't mind people seeing. Her mother had battled sadness for years to stay upright, until Walter was off to college. She'd been more herself around Lina and Donnie. Lina was finally with her. When she couldn't get up one morning to dress, she left a message on the Evergreen's machine, quitting over the phone.

In five weeks, she would fly home. The first time Walter had booked her flight, she'd tried to pay him back, but he'd been awkward, refusing. Now he bought her tickets and they didn't talk about it. He preferred his generosity unacknowledged.

She couldn't tell him yet what had happened. She would have to make adjustments to the blow. When she'd been rejected before, she'd settled into the stockroom and taken a night class. And Mrs. Anjani had been right: most of what was quietly thrilling about school was already there at the community college. Barnard students were younger and better dressed, but no more intellectually daunting. Now, again, she had to start over.

She found a studio twice as expensive as her old university apartment, but it had a kitchen and a view of steeples and water tanks. She brought her canvases, easels, a box, the Morris chair, and a suitcase in two trips. She and Troy carried her sofa there.

She called Jess long-distance on Sunday, when it was cheaper, to learn how to move through the days.

"I just work," Jess said. "I stay late, then walk home and go to sleep without thinking."

But Lina couldn't paint.

Sacha had once picked up a canvas from where it was leaning against a wall and gazed at it. How could he do that and then leave? Could both be true? She remembered him pushing her against a fence in the cold, kissing her before she was fully in love, when she'd still had a choice.

Engagement off, she wrote in a PS to her brothers and Julie. *Can't talk about it yet.*

Lina had too much time. Without her hours at the gallery, afternoons felt long. Her colors looked muddy, her brushstrokes thin. She felt dull. She was supposed to teach in fall, not only her Saturday-morning tour of the armory but a painting class. How could she pretend to tell people how to do what she couldn't? She didn't see friends, except Troy. Two people they knew had shows up. The guy who painted spiders was taking the LSAT. She remembered the restrictions Donnie had accepted.

Tomorrow, she would walk to the university's job board. She would take a regular job, she decided, in a flower shop or a hospital.

Lina made one concession to a future: an expensive every-other-week session with a woman named Dr. Jin. "My DNA is tainted," she told her in a low-ceilinged room, the sound of taxis outside. Sacha's mother hadn't wanted them to marry. *Beauty won't last,* she'd written. Of course, things like this had been said since the beginning of the world and ignored. But not by him.

"Actually, some beauty does last," Dr. Jin said. "Yours will. Because you're dark. You'll have the last laugh. There will be another love."

It had begun raining outside.

When Lina had her heart set on a dress once, her mother told her that there would always be another beautiful dress. Lina didn't doubt that there could be another *kind of* love. Walter's kind. She wasn't sure she wanted that.

She stepped outside, wishing she hadn't told the doctor about crying over a dress. If she'd been a less materialistic child, she thought, she might be a better artist now.

Lina, Walter, and Julie attended a ceremony in a church-basement room where the tall leader gave Donnie a token for six months. Donnie wore a jacket over his cords. A small boombox played Bach's solo cello concertos. Lina reached for Walter's hand.

The next day, they crowded into Trish's small office and she delivered a progress report.

"Better than any teacher conference I remember," Julie said.

Trish detailed the steps of re-integration. Donnie had moved off the hospital grounds into a sober house closer to the college, where he would eventually resume, with a light load. Not this fall, maybe spring. Eight young men lived with a facilitator. There were curfews. Urine testing. When he went back to school, they could set up testing there, once a week. Donnie drove to the hospital to work in the geri unit. He'd also volunteered with Buildings and Grounds to be with their mother in the garden.

"But for how long?" Julie asked.

"How long what?" Trish asked.

"Well, that he'll be living in halfway places. With supervision. And urine testing."

"You want sobriety to become his way of life. It takes a while. But I think by October or November he can move again."

"You say it's all young men in there. What if, going back to college, he meets a girl he'd like to take out?"

"Rehab romance is discouraged. We say nothing for the first year."

They were silent. A year seemed a very long time.

"Think of this as his year of internal reconstruction."

"They keep moving the mark," Walter said when they finally got out.

"The same with Mom."

"I'd like to see him living back at the college," Julie added.

"But we want him to succeed." Lina had never said the word so free of irony.

Donnie shared a room with an emaciated guy from Portland

who operated a vintage record business from underneath his bed. She and Donnie were alike, Lina thought. What little strength there'd been in the bungalow, Walter imbibed. She and Donnie lived with their mother as her illness gained majority, in that cathedral of chaos. Lina hadn't thought they were permanently marked, but maybe only they couldn't see. She and Donnie had inherited the gene.

Driving back from Norwalk, Walter talked to Lina about his wedding. He wanted it to be at Ken's walnut farm. He'd be married long before she was now. Lina had finally finished the book Carrie gave him. Every character she liked ended up with someone disappointing.

That night, Lina took a walk in Walter's new neighborhood, which smelled consoling with intermittent nutmeg lifts of jasmine and long dissolving scarves of woodsmoke. A man ambled down the road with a dog. Every few yards, he bent down to pat it. "Pretty dog," Lina said, passing, and saw the man's pride in his animal.

She'd felt that pride in Sacha once, and, long ago, in her mother.

As if guilty because she had something good.

Donnie was meditating, he wrote. Early morning.

Troy found Lina a gig with a sculptor in her nineties who was a friend of his boss. She worked in a loft that had once been a glove factory. On Lina's first day, she and another assistant hauled a pallet of lumber up from the street.

She'd liked the two guys she worked with fine.

After a week, she had calluses on both hands.

On the day that would have been her wedding, she learned how to weld.

She arrived early and stayed every day until two, when the sculptor took her nap.

After work, Lina stopped to buy a walnut cookie and then walked the sixty blocks to the library, arriving by three, as if it were a job. She set out to learn the history of treatment for mental illness. From what she could tell, humans began studying medicine in Mesopotamia. Most practitioners were priests. Something called the Edwin Smith Papyrus, written in the seventeenth century BCE, was a text on surgery for battle wounds. The first houses of healing were placed near rivers, so evil spirits would be washed away; Greeks and Romans built theirs near springs or the ocean.

Lina read about bimaristans, dated to the lifetime of the Prophet Muhammad, who taught that God would not create a disease without creating a cure. They were mobile, transported by camels. The first was a tent set up by a female caretaker who treated soldiers wounded in the Battle of the Ditch. The earliest permanent bimaristan was in Baghdad, along the Tigris. The founder determined where to build it by hanging pieces of meat several places and picking the one where the meat became least infected.

People could go to the bimaristans for physical or mental illness. They served all people regardless of citizenship, race, religion, age, or gender. Nobody was ever turned away. This discovery pleased her, though she wasn't Muslim and had grown up without her father.

In the morning, Lina helped her boss climb the wide plywood stairs to a seated perch, like a lifeguard's box, where she shouted instructions to her assistants below as they fitted together the pieces, following her sketches. She would redraw what she wanted altered. Lina would run up, retrieve the paper, and they'd begin again. The piece was an enormous staircase that turned in five places and ended in air.

Lina liked talking to the other assistants who knew nothing about Sacha.

Walter called every few weeks. "Are you dating yet?"

"No."

"Well, why not?"

"I suppose Sacha was the one for me."

"Well, then there'll just have to be another one."

"Don't you still love Carrie?" she asked to subdue him.

His voice changed. "I'll always love Carrie. I think you keep loving the people you love, if they're good people. But could I make a life with her? No. I have the one I need."

Sacha had once told her, *We'll find a way to change your life.*

But he hadn't told her he was still deciding. These conundrums occupied her during the months she worked for the sculptor and asked little of herself. Of course Walter would urge her to go out. Walter didn't believe in real love. He was marrying Susan.

The sculptor had never been rich, but she'd managed to buy this factory in the sixties, when she was married, briefly, to a lawyer. Though not much acknowledged herself, she'd been friends with David Smith and Sol LeWitt. Once, finally, there was a retrospective of her work in the Brooklyn Museum, but the *New York Times* art critic reviewed it in one paragraph. Her own favorite artists were Brancusi and Piero della Francesca.

Lina wished the ninety-six-year-old woman was her favorite sculptor; she deserved to be, she worked so hard. But Lina preferred Eva Hesse and Barbara Hepworth. Was she, unconsciously, following the crowd? Lina wanted her taste to be original, for hard work to equal great work, and to love what deserved to be loved.

The woman was still working, but Lina began to discern small problems. One day, the woman's shirt was backwards. Another, her shoes on the wrong feet. Lina began to arrive earlier, let herself in with her key to help the sculptor wash and dress.

Her Saturday-morning armory class at the Met resumed.

"Windows are anathemas," her supervisor said, walking through a gallery where workmen stood on ladders, painting walls. The art had to be set far back from sunbeams. "We want only light we can control."

"Like a casino," Lina said. "Where you can't tell whether it's day or night. Nature is the enemy." These were small facts she'd picked up long ago from her father, probably generic casino lore, but they'd been new to her. And they were new to her supervisor, who laughed for three long minutes and then started over again.

———

One afternoon, Lina turned in to a store. A branch was suspended in the window over a long pillow made from an old kimono sleeve. It smelled like lavender and could fit two close heads. Lina bought it for Walter and Susan, remembering the champagne glasses probably still in the back of Sacha's closet. She felt adult handing over her credit card; it was the first time she'd been this excited about a gift. Usually, she'd felt vaguely deprived.

The sculptor asked Lina what she was eating. Lina offered her a bite. Tabouli with sprouts. The old lady ate more than half. A Filipina housekeeper arrived daily, swept the bedroom and kitchen, and left a meal on a plate, covered with a paper towel. Lina noticed these plates accumulating in the refrigerator. Lina bought her a Macoun apple. An almond-butter sandwich. "California food," she told her.

Thank you, the sculptor said, every time.

On a Saturday in November, walking to class, Lina saw *him*. Sacha. On Madison Avenue at eleven in the morning. He was alone, across the park from his apartment. They said hello and walked by each other on the sidewalk. Her hair wasn't washed.

They would have been married two months.

When Lina called Jess that day, she heard something new in her friend's voice. Jess, she could tell, was getting better. Soon, Lina would be alone in this unexplainable place.

The hospital shall keep all patients until they are completely recovered. All costs are to be borne by the hospital whether the people come from afar or near, whether they are residents or foreigners, low or high, employed or unemployed, blind or sighted, physically or mentally ill, learned or illiterate. Upon discharge the patient is to be given food and money as a compensation for the wages he lost during his stay. This was the policy of the bimaristan of al-Mansur Qalawun. His hospital used music as a form of therapy for mental patients. It remained operational through the fifteenth century and still stood in Cairo.

Another Egyptian bimaristan introduced the safekeeping of

personal items during a patient's convalescence. These Islamic hospitals were the first to treat convicts.

One day in December, Lina let herself into the loft and the sculptor wasn't there. By noon, the three assistants learned that their boss had fallen in the night and crawled to the phone to call an ambulance. She was in Lenox Hill Hospital. They decided to keep working, to get as far as they could. The Filipina housekeeper came and left her plate covered with a paper towel. The next day, they found out that the sculptor had died, her staircase only three-fifths done. They worked again until after midnight to complete the construction prescribed by her last sketch. After that, they had only drawings. But they would make it their mission to finish.

The next morning when they arrived, a lawyer was standing outside the building. She wrote checks against her skirted thighs. They told her that they'd continue to work, without pay, until the piece was finished. Lina surprised herself with her ardor—before, she'd thought of this as only a job—but the lawyer said she couldn't let them. She had instructions from the estate to lock up. They would be in touch with dealers, she said. Realtors. The loft might be worth more than the artwork. She wrote down their phone numbers and said she would pass along their offer. She asked them each for their keys.

Lina never heard from the lawyer. For years, she saw that unfinished staircase in dreams.

"I spent too much time in my life thinking about blouses," Lina said to Troy. "I'd be a better artist if I had a clearer soul . . ."

"And then what?"

"Maybe I'd still be with Sacha."

"You ever think that he's gay?" Troy said. "That would have nothing to do with your soul. You went to California a lot. Maybe one of those times he hooked up with someone."

She left a message asking Sacha to meet for coffee. He suggested an indifferent diner, where they talked awkwardly for forty-five minutes. He kept saying he was sorry. He was walking to the subway when she called, "Wait," and started over. "Are you gay now?"

"I don't think I'm gay." He exhaled. "I have been thinking about men again. But there's nothing to compete with us."

He evidently thought he had to endure this for a set number of minutes and then would be released. This would be their last meeting. Troy had been right. He didn't love her.

Like Walter, Lina believed that the people you loved you would love forever.

"Has something happened?" she asked Jess on the phone. "You sound different."

"Oh, nothing. I guess I'm finally getting over it."

Lina went outside. She walked to the bookstore and bought six self-help books. Etienne wasn't there and she paid. It was just beginning to snow. She couldn't drag Jess into her despair any longer. Consciousness, she supposed, was full of dispositions, slips of paper in a hat. You picked one: fury, joy, boredom, maybe you could drop it, reach in and try another.

Walter called. "I renegotiated the lease of a school a few years ago and they asked me to join their board. They found out their principal is moving to Idaho. They tell me this school is an artistic place." Lina waited for the punch line. "I could get you an interview."

"To run a school? I can't run a school."

"Sure you could. You'd teach art and train up the next generation. It might be a nice life. I'd like that if I were you. Have you met somebody? Is that why you don't want to consider moving?"

"No comment," Lina said.

At the end of their talk, Walter said that Donnie had called to say: *I've made a friend.* An older person, a professor he'd met at a twelve-step meeting. She was in for something else. Not drugs or drinking. Money, Walter thought.

She took the bus home from the library, ate a banana for dinner, took a shower, and then read more. She'd turned the walk-in closet into a sleeping alcove with hooks for clothes. She used liver-colored rubber bands to keep her hair back when she began to draw again. She no longer felt larky premonitions that she could make something fast and get rich and famous. Had she ever believed that? She'd been so immature.

On the telephone, Julie said that Walter got her mother talking about why she—Lina—never wore dresses. They'd had almost a regular conversation.

"I'm on the other side of the country," Lina said. "How does Walter even know what I wear?" She had on her old jeans, a black T-shirt, washed to gray. It was true; she didn't wear dresses. But he didn't know that.

"Well, I thought it was good she was talking. They're taking them on a field trip to the County Art Museum."

Lina hated the thought of her mother in a group of mental patients going to the museum like overgrown children with their hands in loops on a rope.

She had once worried about her mother's looks. It had been years since her mother cared about her own body.

Donnie still had his dog. In the hospital, he'd started running with her. They were up to five miles a day. He still commuted to the hospital to see their mother. Lina wanted to ask him about working up to a full course load. But at family week, he'd promised her he would quit smoking after a year. She wouldn't press him about anything else yet. Donnie told her that Walter was planning his wedding.

For all Lina knew, she would never be married. In fact, she decided that. She remembered details. Cake. Flowers. Dried bees. Days spent on frivolity.

Happiness, she'd thought at the time.

Book 6

The Commons

71.

Donnie's first week in the mixed unit (drugs and crazy), a girl threw a TV set out the window because she thought it was criticizing her. Donnie walked to the window to look. "Probably was," he mumbled. He'd grown up with a mother who came alive when insulted. The guy sleeping across the room, who'd dealt heroin with his now-jailed dad, woke up from the noise and asked, "Are we dead yet?"

"No. You're just sleeping," Donnie told him, and the boy's eyes closed, a thin arm with a tattoo of a serpent hanging down.

Donnie had been terrified when his sister and brother left. Julie stayed, but he didn't see her every day. She seemed to have her own business at the hospital. He ran into her once near the big central kitchen where they baked bread. That was as far into the adult wards as they let him go. The whole first month, he couldn't see his mother. He didn't want her seeing him like this anyway. He wondered if she knew he was here.

There was a girl on the southwest corner of the unit who turned into a horse. She moved on all fours, neighing. Rearing. You had to walk around her.

All day long, they herded him into groups with the other drug people, telling each other the story of how they became bad. It made sense he'd ended up here. He'd been aiming at something for a long time—he just hadn't understood that this place was the target. He liked being on the same grounds with his mother. Even if she didn't know he was here. Some moments, remembering she was less than a mile away, he felt safe. Julie bobbed up, too, surprising him with a sandwich she'd bought at a cheese store. He and Julie had had a lot of laughs in their apartment. It had been a surprise discovering that he could love two people. One day he'd thought of Julie as something inert but useful, like a chair, and the next, they were under a net of love. Once, after the meeting at school, he saw Julie cry. From then on, he tried to stay out of trouble, but that was like walking a balance beam. He had to be always careful.

Eventually, he fell off and followed some kids to the beach. They taught him to surf. Currents ran up from the bottoms of his feet. It felt like he'd been in a whole-body fight, clobbered, then washed up onshore somehow still joined. The rest of the day, his body felt looser. He didn't befriend people one by one, the way he'd once befriended Evan. They made fires at night and, around those circles, a joint traveled hand to hand. Donnie passed it along. But then eventually he fell again. Trouble became his natural habitat. From one toke on the beach to being high all the time took only a heartbeat.

They told him in the unit that that was one of the ways to know. That he was an addict. Most people came from families of addicts, but his had insanity, not addiction. His mother had sipped crème de menthe once in a blue moon from a tiny glass. But he was marked. Lina and Walter had always wondered if he was their full brother. Maybe somewhere in the world he had a junkie dad. Would've explained a lot.

Everyone in high school had found out what happened to his mother. He'd never told, but they knew. Girls wanted to *talk about it*, their voices pitying, hands eager. For the first time, he had the impulse to sock a person. He never touched those girls who wanted to soothe him. He turned remote because he would have liked to hurt them.

Julie had looked into his pupils and he'd fallen back, saying, "Wha—what?" And then cracked up to a joke only he could hear. She couldn't help but trust him.

It was a relief that Julie knew now. She still refused to be mad. But anger had to be rattling in there somewhere.

The unit had incredibly glossy floors. Donnie asked one of the hospital janitors how he kept it up. A block of wood covered with a towel at the end of a pole was all. They let him keep one in his room to polish his end of the hall. He liked the back-and-forth motion. He did the homework here, in a way he hadn't in college, tried to write out the past. Some of it was radioactive, memories that, when he approached, sent out hairline shocks warning *Get down, avoid, divert, detour.* A house in the Palisades Highlands. Xs dotting the coastline, Malibu to Long Beach.

People talked in group. Donnie kept quiet.

Caseworkers shuffled them into a van bound for a gym, off grounds. One guy stood with a clipboard, directing people to the machines or to trainers, for kids who had paying parents. Donnie's name turned up on that list. After the second Thursday, he asked the trainer, a pert, tiny, muscular mother of three, if she could write down a program for him to do by himself. She looked sad, so he said more. "The lady who pays, she's not my mom. And probably has to stretch to do it." He thought of his mother. He was pretty sure she knew he was here.

"Do you ever run? That's how I get my cardio. You're outside, you see things."

He'd hated going around the track in school, but he built the habit every morning and by the third week felt the return loop of reward. His dog, Sylvie, began to trot along.

Running was the first skill he learned in rehab that he could keep.

In group, he finally shared how he'd been happy. On a board out on an empty sea. He remembered the college town on the hill, yellow light pouring out of buildings, old people dressed as if they were young. Donnie saw the homeless with their dogs, shabby men with crescent faces, their dogs happy and bounding. Homeless dogs seemed the happiest dogs in LA.

Everyone around the circle nodded. They knew what he meant.

He saw his mother for the first time and told her he lived here now, within the same chain-link fence. He called it the Humble Place. He told her what he knew she could take. He explained how Sylvie had saved him. They first saw each other on the beach. Donnie was stoned, but he was always stoned then. There was a crusader, with a breastplate and staff, long ringlet hair, bare legs from the knees down, a man's legs with hair. Man on the bottom, girl on top. And a dog, which looked back over its shoulder to Donnie. They trudged on in the fog. Some of the people he followed scared him, but he was wrong about them. They were broken to kindness. When they were far ahead, the dog still looked back. Donnie wanted to steal her, but he couldn't have a dog; he lived in the apartment with Julie and her cats. The dog—she wasn't Sylvie yet—had sores all over her coat. Donnie knew then he had to move. In a lightning-bolt flash, he thought: college. Sylvie before she was Sylvie made him go. Two years after that first visitation, he was low again, enrolled but living on the beach with other people who meant nothing to him, and one day he saw a pack of dogs, near the water. No humans. He'd lost track of distinct days. It was foggy and he'd been stalking alone with a sleeping bag over his shoulders. He'd had one shoe. On the surf, he saw her. He called to the dogs and only she came bounding. "You'll be my luck," he told her.

A week later, police delivered him to Walter. His mother patted Sylvie. Animals went to her instinctively.

While he picked apart wet memories for Step Two, Donnie wondered what the crazies did all day. Did they have groups, too? He asked Horsegirl. She kicked Sylvie with hard heels.

Horsegirl hated Sylvie. She'd bared teeth and bucked at her once before, when Julie brought her in on a leash wearing a bandanna from the groomer.

The night of the youth dance in James Hall, Donnie tried to talk to Horsegirl again. "What do they make you do all day?"

She neighed and two warm words dropped out of the snuffling: "*Stupid stuff.*"

She wasn't going to the dance. Donnie asked if she wanted to see a movie. Caseworkers had hooked up speakers on the unit's roof to hear the movies visible from the drive-in over the fence. They lay on the roof with blankets watching *Ghostbusters* while Sylvie waited on Donnie's cot.

Horsegirl had seen Julie when she picked up Sylvie or brought her back. Donnie had to explain: Julie was not his mother. He told her his mother was here, in the hospital.

"Here, where?" Horsegirl asked. Most of the kids in the unit barely registered that there was a whole hospital here that had nothing to do with them. His mother had come before any of this and they'd gone to live at Julie's. They, he had to explain, were his brother and sister, who lived far away now. Julie had moved, too, to a cabin in the north woods. She'd had a sad goodbye with Donnie's mother. "I really did love two people. I loved her as much as my mom." He was crying then. Donnie hadn't known until he said it to Horsegirl how hard it had been when Julie moved. The apartment wasn't theirs anymore. Other people lived there, cooked their own dinners. He'd gone to college, but she'd always been the same, the same place, the same upbeat questions, and now that life had been folded like a towel and taken away.

She'd invited him to Michigan over the summer. But by then he was here.

They spent a long time preparing for family week. Donnie had never been in the drama department at school, but from noticing his classmates cycle through adrenaline to exhaustion, he thought this was like the annual Shakespeare play, only real, the long rehearsals culminating not in a performance but in face-to-face revelations and apologies, not conversations exactly because they were so practiced, with the people who meant most to you who'd now seen into your box of failures. Your betrayals, your lies, your greed, your cheating—they had seen them and could pick one up to examine.

Julie owed them nothing, but she'd taken them in. She'd laughed with him, told him her daily news, learned to cook what he liked. They'd watched movies together eating Jiffy Pop and almond brittle. But then he'd stopped that and left her to worry while he was out destroying himself.

Not that it felt like that to him at the time.

——

He had a long letter prepared to read, but he couldn't get through it. Julie wanted to take the blame from him and make it all her fault.

He told her not to a thousand times, but she couldn't not be responsible. A switch had been turned on in her once long ago, and it was stuck to that setting now forever.

His brother was a cipher as always. He took Donnie for a walk on the grounds and when they sat down, he zeroed in on Donnie as a man, which he viewed as something completely different than being, well, Lina. "You know how when we were growing up, I was considered, like at least in the family, smart."

"Yeah. You and Lina."

"Well, when I got to college, I found other people way better at school. Even Lina. She likes all that. I'm good at finding things that have fallen apart, like old buildings, and making something out of the pieces. Maybe when you're done with all this, you can come work with me."

Lina kept trying to jump down into the well of the past together. She saw them as twins. And she was this goody-good! He'd never been like that.

In a letter, though, she'd told him things he couldn't forget. She wrote that Mom may never live outside again.

Donnie,

I feel tentatively happy at the end of family week. I'm grateful for the hours I spent with you and for learning how you've been going through your days. Walter said that after he brought you here, he went home and had the best night of sleep he'd had in years. He said he slept twelve hours. This week here I feel as if my life were all in one place again. Norwalk. Who would have thought here? This is the first time the four of us have been together since Walter left for college. It may be the last time; I think I'm finally accepting that Mom may never be able to leave.

The years we lived together in the bungalow, I felt better

than I've felt since and a lot of that was you. I tried to live up to who you thought I was, someone smart and capable and good. I'm not those things without you. Maybe I never was. It was probably all your imagination.

You've always been a cool kid. Popular, like Mom. Now I understand that you had a whole life outside us, a life of danger, maybe with its own kind of beauty also and even love.

But I'm scared of you relapsing. My best art friend said that he admired you. He said that we—he and I and this would apply to Walter too—never gave ourselves permission to fuck up. That requires a kind of privilege, he said. But you didn't have that privilege either. You ran awful risks without a net. That's still true. We don't have the money or the power to pull you out of trouble. If you get arrested, you'll be lost in a web of injustice, maybe forever. In a few years, I could be standing at your grave in my sad outfit and stupid heels, and if that happens, my life will be over, too. You will be taking me with you. And Mom.

If you manage, though, to stay right, you'll have a whole good life ahead of you. You're kind and charismatic and loyal. You'll always find people to love you. I want you to get to have that life that you deserve.

He folded her letter in eighths and kept it in his wallet. He took it out, usually once a day. The folds turned into creases, then began to rip, so eventually it became eight tiny rectangles the size of elementary school photos you cut from the sheet and traded with your friends. He kept those, too. He still had one of Evan.

Lina must have told her friend Jess where he was because Donnie received a package from Evan: a thermos. In the note, Evan offered to visit.

Donnie fingered the thermos. A present! For being here. There was a joke.

It was a very nice thermos. An orangey red.

At this time in his recovery, Donnie couldn't help but keep

track of who called or wrote to him and who didn't. He didn't hear from Dino. Or from any of his college friends.

He wrote to Evan that he would welcome a visit.

One night on the beach, Donnie had seen the Sears building lit like a temple. He and some other people stood on the Santa Monica Pier parking lot, which was made of ancient trees split in half. They were uneven logs, pitted and cracked, loud waves frothing below. He no longer remembered how he'd gotten there. The rectangular Sears building was lit from the ground. He was tripping and could remember the monumental catalogue, years ago. Mid-century children, they'd moved through a series of Valley apartments with wall-to-wall carpets and landlords who harrowed his mother, women with elbows out. His sister lay on her belly, feet up in the air, as she studied the nine-hundred-page Sears catalogue more than her homework or than any Bible. Could she have worn her hair in two braids? Her dark feet in penny loafers? The company was pushing red-and-white calico that season. Shorts, dresses, skirts, pedal pushers—all the same checkered cloth. His sister deliberated because she could get only one. He wanted to buy her another.

For himself, he'd seen a drill with nine bits.

Lina remembered this differently, he'd found out at family week. He flashed on that catalogue again; the children they were, cutting out pictures of his tools and her dress, things they would never even see. The glossy items were "catalogue only."

She did her best, Donnie tried to tell Lina. Donnie never doubted that their mother loved him. She loved Walter, of course, he was first. She struggled to stay her best, can-do self until she saw him off to college. But Lina was her girl and he was her baby; she loved them a closer way. She must have known she wouldn't make it to their finish lines. When Lina left after family week, Donnie mopped the hall, going back and forth. She hadn't even had Julie, not like he did. Their mother walked out on Lina in the middle of her growing up and there was no one else for her.

He could thank LSD for handing him the truth. The night, long ago, in a dirty sleeping bag by the thundering surf, he'd been alone in the dark. The stars sparkled closer. He wasn't afraid to be alone. Then he saw a shape that was really there, not a person, just denser air. The height of his mother. She had tried to kill herself; that was why. The figure stood there, the edge of its density waving a bit in the wind, like a cut piece of cloth. Nobody told him; but the waves and the pressing stars and the figure had given him to understand. She'd wanted to die.

72.

"Are you experiencing cravings?" Trish, his caseworker, asked.

He wasn't, he didn't think. Sawdust in the mouth was a problem. A flat horizon, world without commotion. He'd done drugs to wake himself up.

Trish talked to him about classes at Cerritos College. Small, birdlike, but slope-bellied in pregnancy, she sipped from a fourteen-inch container of iced tea. If he maintained a B average, he could eventually qualify as an addiction counselor. Just what his sister feared; Donnie laughed. He missed the college town on a hill. He thought school would be something anyway. A coffee shop. Used bookstore. Some bustle.

At the end of ninety days, he was allowed to go up to LA for the weekend. Walter would fetch him. He wrote to Evan suggesting that they meet.

He told his group about drawing the counselor and the principal. They took the whole hour on it. He kept waiting for them to turn to the next person. "I can't undo it now," he said, his hands acting without him on his lap.

"That's the thing about damage," someone said.

His roommate, with the snake tattoo, suggested an amend.

"I tried," Donnie said.

"Wonder if there's something else you could do for her. Like if her garage needed painting."

"I'd love to do that."

Some people thought it would be good to try. Others thought, leave her alone. Even giving required a relationship, he was learning. The receiver had to want your gift.

His next meeting with Trish she wanted to figure out a job for him; she had a list of shops that hired kids from the unit.

He hoped to work here on the hospital grounds.

"Because you want to see your mom?"

"Yes. Other things, too. I want to be near her kind of people."

Trish seemed to take that as an acceptable answer.

A calm seeped into him.

Trish put in calls, but the only opening she found was in Geriatrics and the head nurse there would take him but no dog. "We've got more than enough incontinence," she said.

"Sylvie's house-trained," Donnie argued.

"Didn't you say you know a nurse from your mom's unit?"

They called Shirley, who said she needed to meet the dog. Donnie hiked over to the library, and Sylvie folded herself into a perfect triangle at his feet. "She's my luck," he said. Shirley convinced Geriatrics to give them a try.

"New person always takes diaper detail," said the head nurse, whose profile was like the cut side of a key.

Donnie had been handling poop in plastic bags for a year now, with Sylvie. There was a rubberized sheet you flung over the beds. The person either sat down and then spread out, or, for those who were in chairs, Donnie would lift them and set them there. They were fantastically light. Then, as he changed the soiled diaper and cleaned the sagging skin, fixing a disposable on tight, a face would hang at the other end of the bed, looking up at him with shame and gratitude and something else. He folded the soiled paper into a package and brought it to the lidded garbage. "It's not all poetry," he'd once said to a girl who'd asked about his mom and looked at him with pity and romance. But he could do it, with a face looking up at him.

He taught Sylvie to sit near the person's head, and often an arm would reach down to touch her.

"The goal is bowel and bladder," the head nurse told him. They used tricks from preschool teachers to teach them to hold it and use a toilet again.

"Why not just diapers?" Donnie had seen way worse in drug houses. Diapers kept them clean. But the key-faced nurse explained that, out of diapers, families were more inclined to take them back. "Could be the difference between dying here or at home."

Evan wrote that he could drive up to LA. He suggested Saturday lunch. Their arrangements were careful, weeks in advance. Donnie said he'd ask Walter about eating at his new shopping center (maybe an attraction) and told Evan to invite Dino, if he wanted.

I would have loved you to see them build the lake, Walter said, driving him to meet Evan. Huge machines dug the core, a mile alongside the hangar, then a crew lined the cavity with red clay and filled it with two million gallons of water. Walter brought in ducks. He'd show Donnie the catalogues. Machines the height of parking meters dropped feed corn into your hand when you put in a dime. They had to make sure the ducks got the right kind of food. Ken had picked out aquatic plants. Families could feed paper cones of corn to the ducks and buy their own lunches from a dozen different food carts.

In the parking lot, Walter asked if Donnie wanted him to wait somewhere—the restaurant, maybe, where they'd be eating lunch. Walter had booked them a good table. He'd sit by himself in a back booth. But Donnie wanted to go alone. Evan would give him a ride back. He and Evan walked around the oblong lake, which looked natural, with ducks hiding among cattails. Evan said he'd tried to get in touch with Dino, but his phone number had been changed and there was no forwarding number. Evan was living in Pasadena. He'd worked in a lab over the summer, on something called Q switching, which had to do with the spikes of lasers, and he hoped to keep working there, during school. He was thinner and he'd grown a mustache. He talked about a professor he admired who ran nine miles every day and had a tailor make the pockets deeper on all his pants. Almost to the knees. Donnie ran into the restaurant to cancel Walter's reservation; they'd decided on tacos from one of the trucks. At moments, it felt like they were gaining traction;

other times, conversation felt like work. Evan asked Donnie if he planned to return to school this fall.

"Winter maybe," Donnie said.

At Walter's house, Evan stood out of the car to say goodbye. "I'm proud of you," he whispered into Donnie's shoulder. "Wish Dino would do what you're doing."

An accordionist in his sixties played every Wednesday in Geri. He'd been a patient at Orchard Springs when he was young, and drove himself down from Altadena to see his friend Artie, who by now had been here most of his life. After the fifteen-minute recital, the two friends drank together. The head nurse kept their bottle in a locked cabinet. Working in Geri, Donnie began to understand the hospital. Most kids in the unit never did. Their parents checked them in or the court sent them, and they orbited between the unit and town, where they worked in coffee shops and lifted weights at the gym. Some cycled out and back and never knew that the hospital was a world. It had a shoe repair. A barber. What they called the fashion center. A really good bakery that Donnie would miss.

He wrote a letter to the only professor he'd actually talked to at college, saying he hoped to return in a semester or a year. He mentioned that he was taking classes at Cerritos Community. That felt like a lie. The classes weren't much.

He would be moving to sober living. It had taken Trish a while to find one that would allow Sylvie. The house she'd found was in the direction of the college. Donnie would have more freedom, but with that came responsibility. He was strong enough to manage, she said. And she would be here; he could always pop in. "You're going to be dazzled by choices. You'll need your supports. Tell me your dailies."

"I run."

"What else? You'll find a meeting there. Do you meditate or anything? You know I pray."

"I read. I've been reading more."

"You need strong dailies to structure your recovery. Oh, and your house will have its own rules, but one thing we recommend is, and this comes from a lot of experience, the first year, try to avoid romance."

Donnie laughed. "No problem there."

"No cravings for that either?"

His last day in the youth unit, he saw Horsegirl balanced on two feet, looking the way dogs do when they're made to stand. Chagrined. To go from being a beautiful horse to a mental patient pulled up by your parents: talk about a flat world.

Donnie didn't mind the new place. He called it Humble *House*, and he abided by the rules. He ran with Sylvie, five, sometimes six miles a day. He drove his mother's old car to the hospital for work and on Sundays, again, to visit her. She was used to Sundays. Julie, who'd moved to Long Beach, took him out to dinner after. He filed the paperwork to return to college. The professor wrote back after five weeks, when Donnie had given up, and sent him a copy of his fall syllabus. He offered Donnie a place in the class. But fall felt too soon.

January '83 was fine, Donnie wrote.

Returning filled him with dread. "You can't drop out twice," he said to the group he attended in the unit Wednesday nights. "I feel like I'll be falling down the same well." Before, with each failure, came the relief of familiarity. But now he would be trying.

He'd organized workers in the college town. That was the one good thing he'd done. He'd never been a student. He had learning issues. Maybe because of those, he'd avoided homework.

"I have to read everything three times," he said.

"But you were good at organizing," someone said.

"You just collect signatures. Anyone could do it. Convince people to join the union."

"Those are real skills," someone else said.

"Not school skills."

"We're unionized here," Trish said. "It's expensive to pay people a living wage. But you get a better quality of care."

Donnie wondered if he should just stay at Cerritos.

"I get that," said a sixteen-year-old from Santa Monica. "If the other school is too pressurized."

Donnie planned to visit the professor during a fall office hour and bring him a loaf of bread from the hospital bakery.

Over the summer, Donnie tried to teach six geri patients to use the bathroom. The key-faced nurse lent him a stopwatch to give reminders. But getting to the bathroom was a production, and they couldn't go on the hour when they were supposed to. Donnie got to know the signs. Pacing. A twitch in Mrs. Belzer's upper cheek. Artie's eyebrows. He cleared the path from the activity table to the restrooms. Still, it was hard for them. He cleaned up matter-of-factly. The key-faced nurse had given him a tip: he dabbed Mentholatum under his nose each day. Donnie put white enamel urine bowls, discreetly, in several places on the ward.

His mother wore a diaper, too. He didn't know why—she wasn't old—but he didn't ask and he didn't try to train her. They worked next to each other in the garden for an hour after his shift. He pulled weeds and turned the hard soil with a hoe. He bought fertilizer from a nursery and they scattered the pellets, as if they were feeding ducks. They had done that together when he was small. They talked little. One afternoon, his mother said, "See," and lifted his arm to point at a bird. Until then, Donnie hadn't noticed birds, but he became attentive to their differences and eventually found a book in the hospital library. He pointed out birds to her, too. In the dusk, he identified owls calling from a stand of tall redwoods.

Donnie would offer a comment and his mother would nod or make a noise. Their conversations didn't catch, the way Lina needed hers to lock and turn. The hour was more than an hour. Clouds stretched thinner. They washed their hands together in the shed when they finished. He took his mother's hands under the faucet of cold mineral water and scrubbed her fingernails with a brush. He always made her a mug of tea before he left. He set her up with it on a table next to her, in front of the TV.

"Look," she said today, making a commotion, pointing to the screen. It was an ad for detergent. His mother gripped his hand and he suddenly recognized the boarder. She held up a plastic bottle and talked with a bright edge. Her hair had been curled and her face seemed different, too. She looked terrified, Donnie thought. But good for her.

All of Donnie's patients were still there in August. Even Ida Kaufman, the one lady he'd managed to bathroom train. He asked the key-faced nurse if she could call her daughter.

"Wrote to her already," she said. "I'll do it once more the end of September." She patted Sylvie; even she had come around to her.

In October, Trish decided it was time for Donnie to move again. "You'll be starting school soon," she said, her hands resting on the mound of her belly. But there was no such thing as a sober dorm. Walter would drive him to the hill town to help him find a room. Donnie disliked change, though, and the Humble House was between the hospital and the college.

"Can't I just stay there?"

"Sober houses are expensive. All the supervision. You don't need that anymore."

So he and Walter strolled through quiet streets of the college town on a bright day in October. They saw nine rooms in grown-up people's houses, all fine. But Walter insisted they keep looking. Donnie could usually tolerate Walter, but today he saw Lina's point. School, he was beginning to think, might be too much. Walking to the tenth house under a canopy of branches, Walter told Donnie that he had doubts about his wedding. Donnie was seven months sober; he couldn't imagine getting married. But Susan *lived* with Walter. She wore Birkenstocks over pedicured toes; that seemed exactly right for Walter. Berkeley and all. But he was talking about a different woman, who worked in a library.

The eleventh place was a garage that overlooked a garden. Donnie liked the woman renting it, a professor, but young, wearing shorts, and her tanned, muscled legs sparkled with blond flecks of hair.

The geri unit staff celebrated the ninety-first birthday of Ida Kaufman, Donnie's lady, with a cake and still no daughter. Donnie took pictures, they blew out candles, and then he walked her over to the library, where she could talk to her daughter on the telephone. The key-faced nurse had given him the code to dial long-distance.

Donnie roamed over to the metal shelves of periodicals to give her privacy, but he could still hear. *Journal of Mental and Nervous Disease. Crime and Delinquency. Schizophrenia Bulletin. Community Mental Health Monthly. Suicide Prevention. Neuroanatomy.* Donnie came to the library sometimes to sit and think. He'd never been here when the room wasn't empty.

Ida was keeping the conversation going. She asked questions. The answers seemed short. Finally, he heard "I love you. I hope so," and then the phone being put down.

He asked her if she wanted to walk before going back. She said, no, she was tired. "She does her best, she tries," she said, apropos of nothing. "You see, I wasn't a good mother."

Donnie left his boxes on the swept floor of the new place and went out for a long run. Sylvie had stopped running with him in August, in the heat, and she showed no sign of wishing to resume. So after he showered, he took her for a walk. Contentment fell over him in the soft air from being outside after a shower, his body loose, tugged by the light, roving tension of the leash. He'd done what he could and felt released. A squirrel ran in front of them and Sylvie only looked. Donnie had an idea clear as a voice: Why not live on these warm sidewalks, where he could be enough?

Sylvie led him to a church with an open door and, inside, a circle of chairs. A meeting starting. Donnie ducked in, looping the end of the leash again over his wrist. That was where he learned his landlord's name. Caroline.

A guy Donnie's age talked about being addicted to sex. It sounded like bragging. But the guy's own mother had told him to get his head out of his dick.

A pudgy girl said her real addiction was not to alcohol but to love.

His landlord didn't say anything.

He would go back to school, he decided, but not yet.

———

"The elderly and the chronically ill," the key-faced nurse told him. "That's all we'll have here, pretty soon. Incurables. When we had weller people, they spent a season or two and then went back to the world—and that was good for everybody."

Artie tugged at Donnie, asking for an exorcism.

Donnie told his inventories to the ones who seemed right in the head. People, when they're old, will forgive you anything, he discovered, if you sit with them.

His mother was rocking in a chair when he asked, "You going to be okay with me starting back at college? I wouldn't be able to see you every day." She stared at her hands, not answering. "I don't have to go," he said.

"I want you to," she said slowly. "I wish I had gone for a higher degree."

"You have a degree. You're a nurse, Mom."

"I wanted to be a doctor. Like Dr. Moss."

"You may not have become what you wanted, but what you are gave me my life."

For a long time, Donnie didn't talk about his mother in group. She was a box with a lid. Then he finally began. The way he wanted to remember, she was keen-eyed, fun. A very specific person. She didn't like yellow flowers. How can you dislike a flower? someone asked. But he understood; she didn't get to make many things. Not much of her time had ever been her own. Her likes and dislikes defined her. She could turn a small room beautiful. That was true. He promised.

As he was telling these people he barely knew (kids he'd been with in the youth unit were mostly gone) about his mother, he was changing. His life had broken, he'd broken it, it was nearly healed, and now he could feel himself trying to grow. He understood that he would remember this time as the period when his character was formed. This could have happened anywhere, but it happened here, in a run-down never-built-right hospital compound in Norwalk, California. In 1982, the bottom of the world. By the time he met

Caroline, he was twenty, sober, incipiently vaguely Christian, and employed. He saw his mother every day through it all. It could have been anywhere, but it was here that he began his second life.

73.

Donnie had shaved his head. Her little brother! That was the first thing Lina noticed the day of Walter's wedding. He didn't look remotely like himself.

"A mistake, I hear," Donnie said. "It'll grow back. It's teaching me to be patient."

Don't be too patient, Lina thought but didn't say. He had tendencies in that direction. He'd moved out of the halfway place and was living in a garage. This was the first month he was even allowed to kiss a girl, Walter said. Not that he had. But he'd shaved his head and apparently learned to live without his beauty. Why couldn't Lina learn to live without hers?

She'd landed here less than two hours ago, and already she understood that the black dress she'd brought was all wrong.

Neither of them had seen Walter yet. Ken had picked up Lina from the airport and taken her to a ranch house in the middle of an orchard. These neighbors were out of town, he explained, before leaving to pick up someone else. Out the back, Lina and Donnie could see the white tent in a field, huge and whimsical, like something drawn. A bonfire was going in a pit, though it was just midafternoon. The flames looked insubstantial against the sky.

"Why here?"

Donnie shrugged. "Is this the Central Valley? He was always talking about looking for corners."

Donnie had arrived on his motorcycle. "They told me I couldn't bring Sylvie; I guess someone's allergic. So why not ride?"

Lina could think of some reasons why not to ride a motorcycle on an interstate highway, but she didn't list them. She was trying. "Where's Mom?" she asked instead. "Is she with Walter?"

"Julie's bringing her. That's a thing. Julie's invitation came late, because of her new address, and she thought they didn't really want her, so she sent a big-deal gift; she bought them a whole set of forks and spoons. She told me she and Mom did that together. I guess silver was something people were supposed to give you when you got married. But they were two nurses on their own."

"Mom had *been* married."

"Maybe nobody gave her forks and spoons. Anyway, they went out and bought it themselves. They picked the same pattern. Julie made it sound like a happy day."

Lina had never particularly noticed their forks and spoons. Where were they now? She looked around the living room; strange, to be among other people's knickknacks. "Let's go into town," she said. "Maybe I can find something else to wear. Something more western. Like Jessica Lange." Never mind that Jessica Lange was blond and nearly six feet tall. Lina rode on the back of Donnie's bike and then they roamed through small shops. They bought four antique champagne glasses, each a different clear color.

Donnie told her a story then, his shoulder blades moving up and down in the sweater. This was how he'd always been, laughing to himself before he told you the joke. He'd been an addict, maybe would be one forever, according to that caseworker, but he was still himself. Thirteen months sober. "I stopped at a gas station twenty miles south. I'm filling up the tank and somebody at the pay phone is saying, 'There's this guy with a nice enough girlfriend he sort of loved, but he still pined over a librarian. And unbeknownst to his fiancée he made a secret trip to where the librarian lived. I'm on the way to his wedding.' She was talking about *this* wedding.

"There's a dean at the college. Very proper. I turned in my papers to register and he saw my name and asked, 'Do you have a brother?' His goddaughter knew Walter from Berkeley. The dean said she runs a poetry archive. She's engaged to an Israeli scientist. He talked about her as if she were a princess."

There was no punch line, really.

They put on their wedding clothes and walked toward the tent. Donnie looked better than she did in a suit he'd bought in a college-town thrift shop. Lina was getting used to his head. Her shoes were as stupid as the dress; the heels drilled straight down into the dirt. She'd worn stockings, but halfway to the tent she stopped to take them off. She decided never to wear stockings again. Around the bonfire, they sat on bales of hay. It was still early; except for the caterers, they were the first people there. In a few minutes, Walter loped over the lawn in a suit and tie. "Hey. So glad you guys are here." He straddled a bale and rubbed his hands together.

"I hope I'm doing the right thing. You think I am?"

Lina's stomach tensed. What could you say? They stared at the fire, which was boisterous and growing.

"I love Susan," Donnie said. A romp of mischief flitted over his face. "Anyway, dude, what's the alternative now?"

Two girls were lighting torches. Beyond, deep rows of newly leaved trees stood at attention.

"Where are Mom and Julie?" Donnie said. "They landed?"

"She wouldn't get out of the car. Julie called from LAX and we decided: they're gonna stay there. Watch something on TV."

They sat, feeling licks of heat from the transparent flames. So their mother wouldn't be at Walter's wedding.

"Julie bought a dress," Donnie said. "Where you used to work. Your old boss helped her. The one who helped me with your white coat."

"Sue."

"She picked Julie's outfit for the wedding. She picked out something for mom to wear, too."

"I should have called it earlier. I went around and around. It's too much for Mom," Walter said. "At least Julie could have come, then. Anyway, though, it's probably better Julie's with her. And Susan's planning a thing at the hospital. She's hiring a photographer, she'll put on her dress again, and we'll get another cake. Maybe you guys'll come, too."

So she wouldn't be here. After all Lina's agonizing. She felt ridiculous, the cause of her own misery. Walter was probably right, as always. Maybe their mother didn't have to attend.

"I don't know if you guys find this, but . . . I don't like having

Mom around other people who didn't know her before," Walter said. "They ask questions."

Sacha's mother had. "All those years, you didn't notice anything?" Lina had looked across the table to find Sacha to help and saw him waiting for an answer, too. "No, she did a good job," she'd whispered.

"In recovery, people are better, but in high school, yeah. I don't like the questions either."

They shook their heads with unanimity. It was impossible to explain.

Lina and Donnie stayed at the fire when Walter stood to greet guests. "It's pretty wild when you think of it. Marriage is. Forever. Wow. No wonder he's scared." This was Donnie's first wedding.

"But you can see why people want the guarantee. I never considered her not coming to my wedding. I wonder if that would have made a difference. I think the idea of her there freaked Sacha out." Lina would have sketched in her notebook after their wedding. That night would have been one way for her, another for him. "I don't know why he would've gone through with it. I guess he always wanted a kid."

"Guy did you a favor," Donnie said.

"Hey, that coat you bought me. I still have it. Were you already doing drugs then?"

"Yeah. Probably. Sure."

"But you still managed to get me the perfect coat."

"I managed a lot of things stoned. Until I didn't."

Lina knew she should feel grateful. For Donnie, even for Sacha leaving her free. She didn't feel that yet but sensed an opening—an inch more of room inside. This was not the first wedding Lina had attended, but it was the first of *theirs*. It had always been the three of them. Now there were all these other people. Lina and Donnie stood on the edge of a group around a small trellis, without their mother or Julie, as a short rabbi read the marriage service and their brother promised his life to Susan. Beyond them, the orchards buzzed, settling into evening. They both had the feeling they had already had and that they would again only a few more times in their lives: an emptiness that arrived shoulder to shoulder with the certainty of grave importance.

Lina understood that later it would matter that Walter had married Susan, the way it mattered that her mother had been committed to a hospital and that she had gone to college. But right now, there was nothing or, rather, a field that appeared almost still with thousands of minute movements. For these minutes, she ceased to be herself and blurred into the larger landscape. From this rare point of view, it hardly mattered that their mother wasn't here. She was still as much a part of this momentous change.

Julie, too, Donnie seemed to remind her, with a hand on her shoulder.

What had it taken for Julie to brave the escalator up to Better Dresses at the May Company and ask Sue to help her shop? She would have splurged this time, on a dress, maybe with a cover-up. And now she was babysitting their mother in the parlor of 301. But, Lina reminded herself, she would never really know. Julie may have been happier, the two of them alone, missing the party. Her mother, not Julie, was the one who'd loved to dance.

Lina and Donnie found their names at a table, with Ken and his wife, Melinda, Susan's parents, a guy named Cub, and another named Rory, who sat next to Lina.

"Trying to talk your brother into going into business with me," he said.

Walter had seated him next to her, she suspected, because he was rich and single. She looked for her brother in the crowd while seeming to pay attention to what the guy was saying, about a real estate investment trust. Walter's and Susan's chairs remained empty. She scanned the crowd for Carrie, Susan's roommate. She must be here. Rory, next to her, was going on about developing the Central Valley. Maybe he was looking for corners, too.

Across the table, Susan's mom broke into laughter. Lina remembered her—more than a decade ago—humiliating their mother the morning Walter went off to college. Lina had come prepared to hate her. But the sounds lingered . . . *Peals of laughter*, that was the phrase. The woman's head inclined toward Donnie as if she were laughing along to something he'd said. Rory was still talking. If he'd asked her a question, she'd have had to pay attention to answer, but there seemed to be no danger of that.

"The prison population is going up," he was saying. "State's going to be in the business of prison building."

"Why?" Lina asked. But as he began his long and technical explanation, she stopped following and watched the party. She spotted Walter behind her in a circle of men: a handsome Asian man with good gray in his hair, Susan's compact dad, and the man who'd helped him buy his first building. Walter hadn't invited their father. He'd given up on him decades ago. She heard Walter say something about the Falklands. Someone else brought up the breakup of Ma Bell. None of them believed that the price of telephone calls would go down. Lina looked up at the stars.

A nerd in a suit and glasses who nonetheless looked as if parties with eight-piece bands were not unfamiliar to him asked Lina to dance. Susan's younger brother.

Maybe it was better that her mother wasn't here. If she had been, Lina would have felt acutely aware of her every movement, wondering whether she'd eaten, if she was tired, should she lie down? And what would she be doing now, while they danced? Donnie was dancing with Susan's mother to "Billie Jean." Of course, when her mother was still herself, she would have loved it. Dr. Moss had told Walter that she'd gone to a dance. But Lina couldn't picture her here. She tried and just couldn't.

Susan's other brother tapped Lina's shoulder. Then Rory. A dance floor had been set onto the field, luckily, considering Lina's heels.

She and Donnie made a game of seeing who could find Carrie first. When Donnie trekked to the line of porta-potties in the far field and came back with what looked like a drink in his hand, he said he'd heard girls talking about toasts they were going to make. "Did you know Carrie and Susan went to India?" he said. "They studied meditation."

Lina was freaked out about the drink. "What is that?"

"Taste."

Sweet, like a cola.

"A Roy Rogers," Donnie said. They both found that hilarious.

This is life passing, she thought, the leaves of the walnuts heavy on the branches, clouds pulled thin so moonlight shone through the uneven densities.

Donnie could dance (she'd forgotten) without moving much; he made small angular jokes with his hands. He wasn't showy, as most men who could dance were, or straight-backed like Walter. "You're the only one of us who can dance!"

"Nah. Look at Walter. He's Cary Grant."

She asked about Susan's mom. "Really good person," he shouted over the music.

Slices of cake were being passed out, and Susan announced into the microphone that it had been baked by two doctors. Melinda and Cub. "And Ken's mom," Melinda yelled. It was a dark chocolate cake that tasted like cocoa, with soft whipped cream. Donnie hadn't known a wedding cake could be chocolate. He had seconds. Then thirds. Lina remembered the old bride and groom, each figure ending in a tiny stake to set into a cake, that Sacha had picked up at an antiques store. They'd probably once been sold by the bag, as gold bands were somewhere traded in bulk, and the tokens for days and months and years.

Rory made a toast; he was qualified, he said, because he'd taken a creative writing class. At Berkeley, he said, nodding down to Walter and Susan. The third or fourth week, after the teacher had had a chance to read his story, he'd asked her what she thought his chances were. Chances for what? she'd asked. He said, Well, say, of winning the Nobel Prize. People laughed, a soft, murmuring. The teacher told him to lower his sights. How much lower, he'd asked, and she'd said, Let's be sure you can write a great toast for your best friend's wedding. Then he told a story about a food cart, which made two tables of people laugh. Susan stood up to thank her sorority sisters and asked everyone to think of her maid of honor, Carrie, who was in a Jerusalem hospital with her mom, who'd suffered a stroke on vacation. Susan's father lifted a glass and said, choking up, that he considered Walter his third son.

There was a change in the music. "Blackbird," the violin racing up a staircase, the small musician hunched over her instrument.

Susan's father danced with Susan. It settled on Lina as she watched, like a moth landing on her wrist. Happiness.

For no reason, she remembered herself before Sacha. Unbidden, she felt again the way she had loading the ceramics room's kiln with Troy, late, then walking home under a dark sky.

Soon, the grown-ups began to stand, purses tucked under arms, bending to kiss goodbyes. A row of black cars waited on the dirt road. It occurred to Lina that this field with its necessary porta-potties might not have been the bride's family's ideal wedding for their daughter. But they seemed to have loved it all. "We're family now," Susan's father called as he stepped into the back of a car.

Caterers were packing glasses in segmented boxes. Lina returned to the table for her purse.

"Oh, don't go," Walter said. "We're gonna change and sit around the fire."

Ken and his father stood flinging logs onto the flames.

Lina and Donnie made the long trek to the ranch house, changed, and rode back on the motorcycle. "Dirt roads like this are what bikes are for," Donnie said. There were millions of stars.

"You should give it away after you get home. No more highways. You're too old for those risks."

"You know, you're right. I have a dependent. Sylvie can't ride."

The band left and Ken hooked up a turntable and speakers with a long orange extension cord, playing Joni Mitchell. *California*, she shrieked in halting melody.

"Walter made it to the finish," Donnie said. "He's married."

But not in love, Lina thought. He'd wanted that, too, of course. Everyone wants that.

When they returned to the ranch house, it was nearly dawn and there was just enough time to pack. Lina's taxi pulled up with its headlights on.

Donnie held one of the champagne glasses up to the light over the kitchen sink. So pretty. Only twenty dollars for the four. A gift that almost hurt to give. But Donnie didn't drink and she had to get on a plane, so they left them with a note on the counter. *Thank you for your generosity to strangers.*

The New York horizon made a dirty line outside the airplane window. Still, Lina's shoulders dropped in relief.

74.

Donnie got stuck on the steps. He made inventories, but when he tried to offer amends he found no takers. Nobody wanted his apology. His family refused to forgive him; they blamed themselves instead. Julie asked him to absolve *her* for moving to Michigan—"biggest mistake of my life"—and he axiomatically did, twenty times, but that didn't sit well with her either. She said she felt guilty about Diane.

"We all do. And she's our mother. You did way more than any other friend."

"There's friends and there's friends," Julie said. "Your mother was one of the big people of my life."

"You were for her, too, for a long time." Donnie wasn't sure this was true—but friendships were never exactly level. "Not sure any of us is that now."

Friendship was a voluntary activity, his sister said. People who got married promised to stay together no matter how sick the other became, even if the other stopped being herself, which was, Donnie supposed, what had happened to his mother.

"Being married is no guarantee either," Julie said. "From what I've observed. I've known married people who don't honor their vows. But I could've been better. I still call every night. A lot of times she doesn't want to talk to me."

"It's the disease," they both said. They had been saying this for a long time. Years now.

"Will you go back to Michigan?" The professor had hired Donnie to babysit her kids, and he was staying above the garage for the summer.

"Not for good. Maybe a week in spring and fall. When I got there, I realized that I'd lived my whole adult life in California for a reason. And you're all here."

Six weeks after the newlyweds returned from their long honeymoon, Donnie drove up to LA to offer an amend, but he couldn't get Walter alone. He and Susan did everything together. They called each other "my love" with no irony. Walter kept putting his hand on Susan's flat belly and asking Donnie if he thought she looked pregnant. Donnie volunteered to walk Susan's problematic pug, to get out of the house. Sixteen months sober, the din of happy silly married banter slightly sickened him. He wasn't sure why. He walked a long time. Sylvie pulled him to the right, and he saw a low building he'd never noticed before across from the abandoned fire station. Sylvie pointed in a straight diagonal to two crude doors. Stables, it looked like. There hadn't been horses in the Palisades downtown as long as Donnie could remember, but through the windows he saw an old stone trough on a concrete floor. Sylvie sniffed as if she sensed an ancient animal presence nowhere visible in the stark, empty building. The doors were bolted with a thick metal chain. Just then, Donnie noticed a small FOR SALE sign. *I want this,* he registered with a ridiculous urgency, considering he was a student working at a state hospital for minimum wage. Was this a craving? He'd tell Trish. But what would you even do with old stables? He didn't want to live in LA, not now, and if he ever did, he could camp out with Walter and Susan, who ran a sober house of a different kind. They were naturally sober. Sober to the point of wood.

Lina said their mother gazed at Walter with reverence. Donnie wouldn't put it that way. When she peered up at Walter, Donnie saw fear, her attempt to stand her straightest, talk well, and impress. Sometimes Donnie felt that way with Walter, too. He and his mother slumped together in 301 after they cleaned their hands from the garden. They liked watching TV, waiting to see the boarder again. Donnie respected his brother, but he wouldn't have traded lives. He needed slack.

Before he left, he summoned the nerve to mention the stables to Walter, who rubbed his eyebrows. "I always wanted to do something with that fire station. I couldn't afford it then. Tell you what. Let's do it together." Walter took out a pencil and started sketching. The stables and the old fire station could be two corners of a square. They'd have to buy the parcels between, he said. Donnie saw his whim gain volume on the paper. "You babysit that professor's kids, right?" Walter asked. "What do you think families want?"

"Caroline likes a place to read, have coffee," Donnie said, "where she can see her kids a ways away. By themselves but safe."

"Coffee's high profit. And what do you think enchants kids?"

"Other kids. Being away from parents."

"And what about things for a family to do together? If it's not nature."

Donnie remembered the youth unit's roof. "An outdoor movie theater?"

Walter squinted, trying to picture the perimeters, and then he started sketching a drive-in until Donnie reminded him that what he'd drawn as an empty lot was the police station. Susan handed him an eraser. "Thank you, my love," he said.

Donnie had to leave. He thought he'd try to make an amend to Walter-and-Susan, together, though he hadn't done a thing to her.

Donnie's sister was no easier. "We're fine," she interrupted, when he told her he needed to apologize. She wouldn't let him finish.

"It doesn't really matter," she'd said last winter when he wasn't sure he'd go back to college, and he'd known nothing mattered to her more. She and Walter said that to each other about him, he guessed, meaning, in the end, in terms of death, this was true, but in the small races they lived inside, it mattered *cruc*ially. And *it* wasn't only college. It was profession. Status. Books they read touted the nobility of their kind of lives, because the writers of those books had themselves punched in their ten thousand hours and had to believe that that lost time was meaningful, even sacred. All the while other people were making meals and sitting down to eat together. What Lina and Walter finally came to, he assumed, was, Oh well, he's learned how to live some other way. His sister's days sounded as if they were built on adrenaline; she was standing on tiptoes, hoping to be picked by some disapproving deity. Their mother's life had been like that once. Though, come to think of it, on the phone Lina sounded quieter now. Donnie was glad she didn't marry that art dealer. Since last October, Donnie had lived with people who ate dinner together every night.

"I want to be more divorced," the professor was yelling into the phone when Donnie carried in a bag of groceries. "What's the next step *after* divorce?" The telephone slammed; she probably didn't want him to hear that. He hoped she didn't mind him in her house. She put on a record. Two Canadian women country singers.

"Soup for dinner," he said, holding up a bunch of celery.

"I might be late. I've got a department meeting. Was hoping you could stay with the kids."

Donnie and the professor drove to the campus chapel together for their meeting. They stored the box of books in the trunk of her car and set them on the table for new people. Since he'd been given *The Little Red Book* in the youth unit, Donnie kept it in his pocket. It had been written for alcoholics, but this meeting was for any and all addicts. Over Labor Day weekend, the housekeeper at Susan's parents' found empty cocaine vials while cleaning her little brother's car. Walter asked him to help and, on the same call, told Donnie that they were pregnant. That was how he said it. They.

The pudgy girl addicted to love invited Donnie to the beach.

"I can be your friend," he told her, "but not more."

"Are you afraid of intensity?"

"Maybe," he said. "But I don't think so."

She noticed the professor load the books into the box and said, "She's way too old for you."

"I don't care about that."

"Well, she's gonna care," she said.

The pudgy girl was right. The professor did care. But Donnie hoped to wear her down with usefulness. Her kids liked the food he cooked. They already loved Sylvie.

Anyway, there was no hurry. He was still stalled on Step Nine.

———

The professor asked if he missed drugs. He didn't think so. "I miss places they brought me. I don't have as many revelations."

"I wish I'd had even one. I guess you don't get revelations from shopping." She was keeping a journal to discern patterns. "It's like anorexia. You can't completely stop eating or using money. And what is it they say? One hundred percent is easier than ninety-five."

Donnie thought of the pudgy girl whose problem was love. He supposed you couldn't quit that either. Donnie could tell he wouldn't be good at moderation.

The professor talked about irresistible urges. The difference between an expense and the addiction, she said, was just a tingle.

A tingle. That was what Donnie felt about those stables.

She was an assistant professor, an intellectual, with an insufficient divorce, two kids, and an addiction. He found her beautiful. He was in fall when he met her and had no idea in what to major. But he appreciated the tough hot water, voluptuous on his back, in the garage shower after running. In the youth unit, he'd learned to restore order. He'd spent hours going back and forth polishing that floor. He knew that there was such a thing as beautifully clean. Sylvie was always by him. He loved lying in bed with Sylvie.

He didn't want the summer to end.

There was still his mother. Now that fall classes had started again, he drove to the hospital only Tuesdays and Sundays, when he washed her hair. He told her about his courses. A lot flew over his head. Sometimes he brought the books along and did homework, reading little bits aloud. Then he'd read something and say "I have no idea what that means," and they laughed. They could spend an afternoon together not saying much, but when he left he felt nourished as if he'd eaten a light but healthy meal.

Donnie drove up to LA with Sylvie to try apologizing to the newlyweds together. But Walter-and-Susan weren't having his amend. They sat in awkward silence. "You have absolutely nothing to apologize for," Susan finally said. "You're doing a good job with your life." She was grateful, he knew, that he talked to her brother. Donnie suspected his own trouble had tipped Walter over into marrying. Possibly Susan understood that, too.

"Yeah, you're fine by us," Walter said. Then he suggested a walk to their future town square. Walter showed Donnie the wall they'd have to take down between the fire station and an antiques store to make a central restaurant. The sewing machine shop and crafts store could be clothing boutiques. "That kind of thing," he said. "But also service establishments. Post office, shoe repair." The Laundromat would have to stay. "And whatever this place is paying, we'll let them keep the lease," he said, at the chicken shed. "Chicken wings and tacos for the kids. For the parents, the restaurant."

Walter marked the perimeter of a sandbox with his footsteps.

"That'd be one enormous sandbox."

"Size of an Olympic swimming pool. It worked in Clovis."

Walter was already negotiating for the fire station, the stables, and five of the stores. But the old guy who owned the sewing machine franchise was holding out.

Unless they could get them all, Walter didn't want to close on any.

"You're going to buy all these places?" Donnie's head went light. "It was just something we were talking about."

"We'll make it happen. I'll draw up a contract for us, too. A partnership."

"Whoa." Donnie felt dizzy. A bit nauseous. He had to sit down. Nineteen months ago, he'd lived on the beach.

"What? Is it too much to do school and this?"

School was what was too much. Everyone was counting on him to get through. He liked talking about the dreamed-up town square with his brother, but he had to stick to his dailies. Still, he depended on Walter's ability to act. They all did. Walter seemed to be building a kind of permanence for all of them.

"It's just I haven't done anything yet," Donnie said.

Caroline's sponsor told her that clearing out clutter helped tamp down cravings, so she and Donnie held a rummage sale. A guy came in a pickup and paid them three hundred dollars for a truckload of stuff while they were still setting up. He worked the swap meet, he told them. Caroline helped the kids make lemonade to sell while Donnie manned the table, with Sylvie's leash looped on his ankle. At the end of the day, Goodwill hauled off what was left and Donnie started dinner while the professor went running, listening to Plato on her headphones. She stuffed so much into her head.

Donnie mounded couscous on two plates (would be good to have a platter; he remembered that swap meet), poured stew on top, sprinkled chopped tarragon and parsley. He'd potted herbs at the end of the summer. The basil died, but the others were thriving on the windowsill. He marveled at the kids. "When I was your age, I wouldn't touch an herb."

It was a good day. They cleared more than seven hundred dollars. Everyone at dinner agreed: the house looked airier. No one missed what they'd sold.

But a few weeks later, Lily, the eleven-year-old, pointed at her mother in the morning. "You look good, Mommy." Donnie was in the kitchen, sprinkling cornmeal onto the bottom of a cast-iron pan. He looked to the professor, happy for her compliment, and noticed a wobble in her smile. She absently patted her daughter's back and then a horn honked in front: carpool.

"A new blouse," she admitted to Donnie when they were alone. She attributed all her daughter's admiration to that blouse. There was more, too. She'd gone out to the street late the night before to sneak in the bag from the car. She'd overspent.

Donnie reeled. So she was still in that swirl. It was like still using.

He'd thought they were both on the other shore.

She was in debt. She avoided stores, she told him, because once she got fixated on a thing it would circle around and ding with every rotation until the only way to stop the loud cycle was to buy. The two of them sat at the table. She showed him her notebook of expenditures. She used a different-colored pen for the tingles.

He asked why she'd snuck in the bag late at night. Did the kids know she was struggling?

Shame, she told him. "I hope they don't know." She didn't think they did. "There's an isolation to this."

"Do you ever tell anyone before you buy something?"

"My sponsor says I should call her." Her sponsor was an alcoholic. Caroline called her for the big things, a large splurge or a spree, but for the small stuff, like when she went to pick up shampoo for Lily and ended up spending ninety dollars because she loved the feeling of throwing things into the basket like a rich person, she would have felt embarrassed.

"Like a rich person?"

"Feeling careless, I guess. I don't know."

"Call me next time." Donnie wished someone would ask him to be their sponsor.

When Donnie arrived to see his mother, one Sunday in November, he learned that Dr. Moss had had a stroke. He'd been taken by ambulance to Harbor-UCLA Hospital in Torrance. The nurses stood in a huddle. A different doctor had been named interim superintendent. The board of directors would conduct a search for a permanent one.

"They'll decide everything in Sacramento," Shirley said.

"But won't he recover?" Donnie asked. "They may not need someone new."

"I hope so," Shirley said. "But it's not only the stroke. I've been here since I was nineteen. He came to my wedding and paid for my nursing school. A couple times these past months he forgot my name."

Donnie called Walter from the pay phone. There was silence so long after he told him Donnie thought the call had been cut off. "Are you still there?"

"Yeah. I just really love him," Walter said. He wanted to visit him in the hospital. "Once, a long time ago," he said, "I hoped he and Mom would fall in love."

From where Donnie was sitting in the pay phone off the ward kitchen, he could see his mother in one of the helter-skelter chairs. She'd fallen asleep with her mouth open.

"I guess they've aged out of that," Walter said. "But there was something there. They danced together at a dance. He could turn out to be the last man she'll ever dance with."

So the adults had dances, too. Donnie hadn't known. He'd thought those were only for the youth unit. Before he'd met Caroline, he'd thought he should have touched Horsegirl or said something to her before they both left. Now he understood his hesitation; he'd done the right thing.

"Mom'll dance with me and you at Lina's wedding," he said.

Lina had never talked to Donnie about her breakup. The summer before last when he'd been living with nine guys, pulling his pants down for urine tests every night, she'd written a PS in a letter. Ever since, it was a hole in their conversations, until Walter's wedding, when she said a little. He had the sense she was still getting over the guy.

Susan had staged another ceremony in the 301 parlor. They'd brought another wedding cake and posed for a photographer. Dr. Moss was in those pictures, too, next to their mother.

Donnie called Lina next. After a while, she said, "If Dr. Moss isn't going to run the hospital anymore, maybe it's finally time to move Mom."

Life felt fragile. When Donnie had taken Sylvie to a vet to see why she didn't want to run anymore, even now when it was cool again, the vet told him that she was an older dog. That had filled him with sadness. It was only two years ago they'd found each other.

Donnie looked over at his mother again. She was still asleep. Should he take her to visit Dr. Moss in the hospital? They'd been in that bonsai class together.

Lina said they should look at board-and-care places. "When the Dauphin is born."

While Dr. Moss was in the hospital, Donnie's lady in the geri division died. The head nurse left a message with Lily, who wrote down: *Ida Kaufman is dead.* Donnie was shocked. He called to ask, From what? He'd just seen her Tuesday. "She was ninety-two," the head nurse said. Ida's daughter was finally coming. Donnie skipped his philosophy class to meet her. He tried to tell her about her mother, but no matter how much he said he couldn't make her understand how funny she'd been.

This mattered more than school. Donnie had registered for the philosophy class because it was taught by the professor with whom he'd corresponded and because in rehab people had talked about the meaning of life, but he read the assigned papers and could remember almost nothing. The professor had written on his midterm paper, *You don't need to love this.*

"It's hard for me to understand," Donnie confessed during an office hour.

They walked through the campus, under the old trees. "It doesn't really matter," the professor said. "As long as you find something else you like."

When he picked up Lily at another girl's house, Lily showed him her friend's pink room. Lily loved the other girl's canopy bed, but it was day 39 of Caroline's new budget. Donnie looked up the swap meet, and he and Caroline went Sunday morning. "Men hate shopping, don't they usually?" Caroline asked. "Henry James wrote, 'A woman had to buy something every day of her life.'"

"That's not us," Donnie said, and she looked at him as if noticing him for the first time. It was still early. Heat would slam down in another hour even in December. The light, coming back off the mountains, was a tender yellow.

They didn't find anything that could be rigged into a canopy, but Donnie spotted some rolled architectural plans, which turned out to be drawings of mid-century buildings. He found one of a restaurant shaped like a top hat. He bought it and, on a lark, asked the dealer if he could find plans for old buildings in Pacific Palisades. Walking back to the car, they passed faux-bamboo French twin beds, uncanopied, but pretty. Caroline said these would actually be better for sleepovers. The dealer was asking a hundred fifty. Donnie saw Caroline struggling, offered ninety-five cash, and paid himself.

Donnie asked if it would be okay to paint Lily's room pink or if they had to get permission and she said, "Permission! We'd be improving the place!"

Considering how insecure she could be with her department, Donnie was impressed to hear her unafraid of the landlord. He remembered landlords they'd had growing up; one had stormed in, furious, when his mother had put a nail in the wall to hang a picture.

The dealer from the flea market called. He'd found the plan for the stables. Donnie bought the drawings. The building had been renovated twice. Donnie preferred the original open plan. "These'll make the historical preservation board happy," Walter said. Donnie's adviser wanted to discuss his major. What he liked best in college was meeting a friend for a walk. He wished he could major in walks.

Because he'd promised Lina, Donnie asked Shirley about health centers in the community.

"Eight or ten years ago, they had a heyday," she said. "Federally funded places were sprouting up everywhere. But our dear President Reagan substituted block grants, which states can use for anything they want. And states want highways more than they want mental health. So most of the facilities have been dismantled."

They might have already missed the moment to move their mother, he told Walter and Susan, whose pregnancy still didn't show.

"We did the right thing staying," Walter said. "I trust Dr. Moss."

By Christmas, Dr. Moss had moved back into his house. Two nurses from Geri rotated, seeing to his food and medicine.

After the new year, they took him on slow walks over the grounds. The first time Donnie saw him outside, he seemed at odds with himself. The next day, Donnie took his mother over and rang his doorbell. Donnie worried that the doctor's diminished state might upset her, but she linked her arm in his and bore his weight as they walked to the library. She promised to bring him a bouquet. When Donnie took her home to 301, she skipped dinner and went right to bed.

75.

In Walter's house, though the bed was made with crisp linens (better than it had ever been when Walter was single), Lina couldn't sleep. She ventured downstairs to the kitchen, where she found Susan at the table writing. *Dear Betsy, Thank you for taking such good care of our mother, Diane Grant Aziz.* She enclosed a hundred-dollar bill in the envelope and crossed Betsy off her list.

It was after midnight and her list was long. There were nurses, LVNs, aides, and med techs in 301 who took care of their mother. Three shifts a day and a different rotation weekends. This must cost Walter and Susan over a thousand dollars, Lina thought. They believed money could solve problems. Lina trusted its usefulness less than they did but enough to feel so grateful she had to turn her head to keep Susan from seeing her tears.

"You should go to bed. You need sleep," she said, instinctively putting a hand to her own flat, empty belly to indicate the baby. "And anyway, why isn't Walter doing this?"

"Oh, I couldn't sleep," Susan said. "This gives me something to do. Everyone needs a little cash at Christmas."

Down the hall, Lina could see the shape of the tree, in the living room. It must be nice to have someone help you, she was thinking. Their mother had always been their problem alone. Theirs and Julie's.

On the way to the airport, Walter drove her past his town square. Most of the old buildings kept only their outer shells. The concrete floor of the bank Lina knew was being broken with a loud machine.

The only business still operating was the Laundromat.

In February, Walter sent Lina a strange gift: she lifted a stitched velvet jacket out of the box. Fawn-colored heels. Finery. She thought of her early dates with Sacha, the panic of selecting a blouse and the feeling of swooping luck when he picked her, after all.

She supposed she would have to forgo that sense of sudden, giddying elevation.

By now, Lina owned heavy rubber boots and a pair of cross-country skis. The day Walter's box arrived it was snowing.

There are persons who daily examine their condition and give them what is fitting. Opium, music, and massage. Dramatic performances. Prayer. Lina was making a time line: history through the lens of the mentally ill.

She made a model of the Cairo hospital (*large rooms with iron windows*, a twelfth-century visitor wrote), which contained a lecture hall, a library, and a mosque, then photographed the model. When Sheila visited Lina's apartment, she shook her head. "I miss your brushstrokes. You're good with paint. Photography is an already gloomy medium."

When Walter came to town, Lina told him to meet her in the Met's lobby. Her apartment—found in a weekend when she moved out of Sacha's—was twice as expensive as her old Barnard studio that Walter insulted, but no bigger. It had a view of steeples and a water tower, but she didn't trust him to appreciate those charms.

She'd received a small raise for her museum class. The job meant little to her, and because of her indifference, it was easy.

She waited for Walter in the lobby, where the high ceilings and enormous floral arrangements would make him feel better about her position in life. A donor in 1967 had left money to fund fresh flowers in the Great Hall, as she'd called it, into perpetuity. The urns were changed every Tuesday.

"Even the flowers here have trust funds," she said to Walter.

"You're going to be an aunt," he said. "Why don't you come out and work for me?"

"Doing what?" She remembered the printed canvas totes once stacked on his table. *I've got some real estate here in my bag.*

"We've got a couple different things going." He sighed. "But probably not the best use of your talents." He and Donnie had a name now for their town square. The Commons, they were calling it. She thought of her brothers working together. Maybe she *should* go home. It had taken over a year to stop clenching when the phone rang late at night. But she told Walter no. She would try her own life a little longer.

Walter owned a house. Lina had many times been jealous; now

her envy fixed only on the wire sculpture. She'd left behind the paper piece she'd bought with Sacha.

Because Walter had asked to see her work, she carried a large brown folder and, in the museum coffee shop, lifted out one photograph at a time. She could see from his face that he was as unenchanted as Sheila. The department secretary, the person who'd expected least from her, was turning out to be right.

Walter asked, as he always did, about her love life. "Whatever happened to—what's his name, Oliver? Are you still seeing him?"

She'd forgotten; she'd made up a date. "No sparks, really."

"I wonder how many sparks you actually need."

Lina felt more hopeful about Walter's marriage after sitting in the dark Christmas house with Susan. She'd heard a phrase from Donnie, *Forgo the tingle*. He'd told her his friend's problem was not drugs or drinking but money. Which was worse, he said. Because you had to regulate. The friend used the phrase to parse addiction. The difference between a purchase and an addiction was the tingle. Lina's problem wasn't drinking or drugs, or even money. Her problem was wanting things that had no life in them anymore. She wished there were a twelve-step program for that.

The Church founded Saint Mary of Bethlehem Hospital as an almshouse in 1247 and a century later, it became the first institution in England to treat the insane. People were kept in cages, hung from the ceiling and spun until they threw up. Tickets were sold to the public. Ladies sat in ballgowns watching the insane. It was known, by then, as Bedlam.

One night, before she went home from the library, Lina found a room of cookbooks. She wrote down a California chef's salad dressing recipe and made it in a jar. Her dinner tasted like a dish in a restaurant

Sometimes, now, she was happy.

"I'm ashamed I'm not a better artist," she told Dr. Jin.

"Are you equating being a good artist with making money?"

Lina understood that those things were not always the same. Working in a museum offered endless examples of the uncelebrated:

Van Gogh, Gauguin, Vermeer. But the young curators talked about would-be artists in a world-weary tone. They were sure that they knew of everyone even the least bit good.

Lina was working on a clay model of an eighteenth-century Fool's Tower.

"I'm not sure you can be good or bad at art," Dr. Jin said. "It's expression. Deep human expression."

"Money is a thing for me," Lina said. "I have to make a living. But I've chosen one of the only careers in which you can be doing okay and still not have earned ten thousand dollars by the time you're forty."

"You *do* make a living," Dr. Jin reminded Lina.

For years, she and Troy had been re-upping their lives, as if they were leases, for one more year. "I could try to accept that I teach for a living. Be a night and weekend maker." There was no shame in that.

When Lina left the ground-floor office, it was snowing. Taxis moved slowly as in a dream. She skied along the park uptown.

During the long Middle Ages, people believed that moonbeams hitting a person's head while she slept could turn her insane.

The image could be painted on metal. Like the retablos Susan's parents collected.

Lunatics were thrown into the river for the shock of cold.

Lina told Dr. Jin about the day she'd had to go to high school with no college offer.

"You didn't apply to a safety?"

As the therapist loosened those knots in the low-ceilinged room, the sound of jockeying taxis outside muffled by snow, they laughed together at the arrogance. Lina had dared the world to give her precisely what she wanted or nothing at all, then felt like a tragic heroine when she wasn't anointed Queen.

Lina tried Donnie's recipe for muffins, with bran, bananas, molasses, blueberries, and cornmeal. Her apartment was small, but it had a real refrigerator and a stove. Troy walked in as the muffins were coming out of the oven.

Lina told him about medieval olfactory therapy with flowers and about Geel, the Belgian town where, since the thirteenth century, patients boarded with families. "Van Gogh's father considered sending Vincent." Before bed, she read about Tuke, Pinel, and the York Retreat, and Vicenzo Chiarugi, the Italian who removed the chains from his patients. She'd found a used copy of Nellie Bly's *Ten Days in a Mad House* at the Strand. Shirley kept saying: *They die with their rights on.*

Troy's boss was letting him make huge montages in the firing room. And he'd just been given a residency at Yaddo.

She asked him more about his newest piece.

"We'll get to me later. You tell me."

Lina's project would take a long time. She wouldn't invite Sheila to see it for at least a year. By then, Sheila might have forgotten her.

They decided that the story of life was a story of failure. And anyway, that painful binary didn't account for the peaceful hour she'd spent at her sink scooping sweet-scented squash out of its baked skin. Gradually, Lina had come back to the way she'd been before Sacha; life was life, roving, wavelike, with the same quantities of pleasure, discomfort, sorrow, and excitement. Peace at the end of longing. The time with him, she'd thought she was happy. But along with that jolt of victory—*he chose me*—she'd felt a constant anxiety: Would she be able to keep what she treasured?

All that was over. She could be herself now. No one cared.

She flew to California to meet the Dauphin. He was as small as a cat. Lina had never held a baby before. Susan handed him over and she lifted him against her shoulder, Walter leaping up to make sure she cupped his head. "Their necks wobble," he said, suddenly an expert. They'd wrapped the baby in clean-smelling flannel. The bundle against Lina made tiny movements. A circle of wet grew on her shoulder. After a moment, she felt its heartbeat.

They strapped the baby into a buggy and pushed him to a bakery near their house, where they set him in a rush basket on a chair. They described the birth.

"I was pushing and pushing and then this tiny little piece of poop came out."

"Susan was amazing," her brother said.

They looked flushed, as if they'd just finished a race.

"He eats every two or three hours!" Walter exclaimed. After they'd picked at bread and coffee, they ambled home. When they turned in the gate, a smell of lavender and lemon verbena billowed up from the ground. Were roses usually this tall? Blooms came to Lina's waist. Walter and Susan didn't lock their doors.

They lifted the baby carefully out of the buggy. The task seemed to require both of them. It was like traveling with a small molten sun.

76.

A week before Susan's due date, Walter had called at midnight and asked Donnie to drive up. They were going to the hospital. They didn't allow dogs, he said. Donnie had to wake up Caroline to hand Sylvie over. He called Walter back to see if he should try to get Mom, but Walter said no.

"She'll meet her grandson, but not yet. We pretty much want only you."

They didn't want her the next time Donnie asked either, five days after the baby was born. Walter said Susan was just recovering from her own mother's visit.

Julie left Donnie a message, asking if he'd heard anything, wasn't it getting near the due date? She'd been knitting a charcoal gray blanket and booties for a month. Half a tiny charcoal sweater hung from her needles. On Sunday, Donnie's mother wrinkled her nose at it. Julie agreed. "But that's what they want."

Donnie told Walter it really was time for them to come.

"Okay. But not both at once."

Lina had arrived. And she'd already booked visits to board-and-care places. Sylvie could go along for those. Donnie had brought her, against Walter's advice, to the first planning meeting, and the commissioners loved her so much that from then on Walter requested her for all their presentations to the city.

Caroline knocked on his garage door. Lily and Jasper, in pajamas, stood with a box. They'd collected their old favorite toys and baby clothes, which he recognized from pictures, to give to Walter's boy.

"You don't want to keep these?" He looked to Caroline.

She handed him a Hans Christian Andersen book.

"The baby got born at a bad time," he told his adviser, laughing because it was already clear that this small animal was more important than finals. He was a slow reader, and each of the assigned novels was four hundred pages. He had to stop in the middle of the one he'd finally gotten into to start the next one.

And there was still his mother, who had an antipathy toward Susan. During the wedding ceremony they'd staged in the ward with the old doctor and Shirley, she'd made a lifting arm gesture at Susan that meant *Get away*. No one missed it. That was probably why they'd been stalling. But his mother was ill. As Donnie drove her up to meet the baby, she fell asleep. It's the drugs, he thought. Their refrain. Walter and Susan were too sensitive. At the house, he woke her and unbuckled her seat belt. She was hungry. A barefooted young woman stood chopping vegetables in Walter's kitchen.

Donnie fed his mother a banana a piece at a time.

At last they sat her in a large armchair and put the baby in her lap. There it was. A hush. Donnie felt a constriction in his throat. Lina came downstairs to take pictures. After a few minutes, the baby spit up a white cloudy liquid and their mother handed him back to Susan. A good day. Their mother with her grandchild.

Donnie hadn't dared to hope she'd get that.

Two days later, going to look at board-and-care places, Donnie found out from Lina that Walter and Susan were offended. Their mother hadn't said anything about the Dauphin's beauty.

The first facility was in Santa Monica, right across from the ocean. But it was dim inside. The people seemed to be alone in their rooms.

On the drive to the next one, Lina asked about Donnie's classes. They were all right. He always took one English because that's what Caroline taught. But his life was not in school; it was on rides to and from meetings when he and Caroline talked. In the house with her kids. At the hospital with his mother. Lina asked if he still surfed. No, he hardly ever saw the ocean anymore. When he drove up for planning commission meetings, he went straight to city hall.

In the college town, they dropped off Lina's film to be developed and then went home to feed Sylvie before their next appointment. The special food she ate now, for older dogs, had to be refrigerated.

Caroline's house impressed Lina. "It's so pretty!"

She wanted to see Donnie's rooms and climbed up the painted outside stairs.

"It's beautiful," she called down.

"Not really," he said. But he knew what she meant. His rooms had the same feeling of tended order.

The next board-and-care was an apartment complex where aides spoke Spanish over the heads of the sitting patients, who looked sedated. Donnie asked to see the kitchen, which wasn't very clean. But animals were allowed. Their mother could bring her cat.

"That kitchen looked terrible," Lina said outside.

The last place was owned by Beverly Enterprises, which had ties to Reagan, according to Shirley. "They're all for profit," Donnie said. "The hospital is at least state of California. They pay more, because they're union. We don't know how those aides are trained."

"How's the new superintendent?"

"They say he's in Sacramento all the time."

"Walter says you're quitting your job there."

Since Ida Kaufman died, Donnie had cut his hours. "I like being on the inside, though. I could get Mom out to see the baby without any trouble."

"Do you think we should move her?"

"She knows Orchard Springs. I still drive up twice a week."

Lina mentioned saving to buy a building in New York. Friends of hers had bought one in Brooklyn.

"You think you might stay there?" She'd gone for school and lingered; Donnie hadn't considered that she might live there permanently.

They picked up Lina's photos, then stopped at an outdoor café and spread them on the table, Sylvie at their feet.

"You know, Mom's right," Lina said. "He's not beautiful."

"I guess it's normal for babies to be bald, but do they usually have acne?"

They broke out laughing. Walter and Susan couldn't see it.

Donnie made a quick supper: soba noodles, with a fried egg for each person (an over easy for Jasper) and snipped herbs.

"We eat like this every night," Caroline said, opening a bottle of wine and handing Lina a glass. She poured one for herself. "So, how were the places?"

"Not what I was hoping," Lina said.

"Pretty horrible," Donnie said. "I think we're a decade too late."

The adults ate standing. "You know, you could bring her here," Caroline said. "Might be good for her to be around kids."

Here in the kitchen with all the people he was closest to, Caroline had said out loud what Donnie had privately wished. Had she read the longing on his face?

"That's so kind, but she needs round-the-clock help," Lina said. "Did Walter and Susan ever offer?"

"Think about it. I mean it," Caroline called, as they got into the car.

A wild offer. Too big. She was overspending again.

They drove in silence, both tired. "What's the deal with your landlord?" Lina asked.

"She's still pretty hung up on her ex." In almost every meeting, she talked about him. Donnie had been there a year and a half and the guy hadn't visited his kids once.

"Sounds hard," Lina said. "But . . . her or somebody else, you're going to be loved. Of all of us, you're the most apt to be loved."

At the airport, they hugged hard, longer than Donnie did with anybody else.

In May, the guy from the swap meet unearthed more plans: the old Palisades fire station, the bank, and what had once been a haberdashery. For sixteen yellowed tissue drawings, he charged $148.00. After nineteen meetings with the planning board, Walter and Donnie were given tax abatements for ten years, under something called the Mills Act, for the preservation of three historical properties. They came out of the small upstairs city office on a warm September day and walked over to the site with take-out coffees to watch the bulldozers. Donnie thought this would be the end of what he could do to help.

"Just wait till your roastery opens—we'll have way better coffee." The professor cared about coffee and subscribed to bean of the week, from a green roaster Donnie contacted in Berkeley. Walter unrolled the landscape drawings. Ken had flown down already to source the trees. Rows of citrus in boxes were lined up behind the Laundromat.

Donnie said, "Oh-oh. This sandbox is continuous?"

"Yeah, so?"

Picnic tables were drawn around the perimeter of the half acre of sand. "That means if kids get in a fight in the middle, it's a far run, over sand, to break it up." Walter looked from the plans to the parking lot. The plans had been drawn, in dimension, by one of LA's renowned landscape design firms. "Don't know what kind of shoes your Palisades moms wear, to be walking over sand to fetch little Janey and John to go to the car."

Walter called Donnie a week later. "I need you to come up and walk through all the spaces. You have a good instinct for use."

Donnie laughed. In rehab, the word *use* had other meanings.

With each walk-through, Donnie surprised himself by having ideas. They'd keep the Laundromat until the Hamel-Wongs retired. Of course. Walter asked if one of their kids wanted to take over eventually and learned that both were doctors, in the Pacific Northwest. The old fire station with WPA murals would be refitted for a twenty-eight-year-old sober chef, trained at Chez Panisse, whom Donnie met in a meeting. It was a new experience being listened to this way. With reduced rent, they'd subsidize a shoe repair shop, a contract post office, and a barber, who'd once cut Yo-Yo Ma's hair for fifteen dollars. "Keeps it neighborhood," Walter said. This took discipline; they had to resist greed. "We're doing our homework. Where did you find that tattooed historian? Which swap meet?"

The original Palisades commercial district opened in 1948. Katharine Hepburn rode down the hill on her horse to eat a hamburger. Em Ball found bound local newspapers in the Pacific Palisades Historical Society. "See if she can find pictures," Walter said. We can blow them up, even if they're grainy." In the fifties, the chamber of commerce held Brownie troop fund-raisers, fashion shows with afternoon tea, and a pet parade. "A pet parade! We'll do that." They could hire a Santa Claus for Christmas and fill the parking lot with noble firs. "Summer nights, we can make a drive-in, like you said."

"With blankets on the roofs."

"Our insurance company would be all over us. But we'll play classics. And our favorites. Just think, by next year this time, we'll be able to meet here for coffee while Jack is crawling in the sand."

Donnie tried to sneak in the offer of an amend. But Walter wanted to talk about money. He wrote down numbers on a napkin. "You'll have some cash you'll need to figure out what to do with." He began explaining index funds. Donnie tuned out, thinking that money in the bank might make Caroline take him more seriously.

"You finish college in—what, one more year?"

"Maybe a year and a half. Two. Depending."

"When you finish, you'll be able to buy a place. A house."

"If I tried to move them, the professor might bolt."

Walter didn't answer. Donnie understood that Walter thought he should move to LA, to get away from her. At least he knew better than to say it.

———

Donnie drove up to Pali High, where he tried to find Mrs. Graver, but no one in the office had any idea where she lived now. He'd taken too long.

There were still businesses he'd stolen from. He could hit one before heading home. He drove to the Santa Monica supermarket and asked to speak to the manager. He'd come up from the beach once when there were buckets of flowers on risers in the parking lot; usually an attendant stood waiting to wrap the bouquets in paper and take the money, but no one was there that night. Donnie and his friends piled armfuls of the watery stems into the truck and roared off. He tried to explain the basics of this to the current manager, who stored a pencil behind his ear.

"This was when?" the man asked, scratching each elbow with the other hand. He had eczema on the insides of his arms. He was pale, with thinning, pale hair and glasses.

"Five years ago."

"I wasn't here then," the man said.

"I regret what I did and want to repair the damage." Donnie took a roll of bills from his pocket. "I'd like to repay you."

"I can't take your money. I'd have to categorize it as a purchase."

"Can't you categorize it as, say, flowers?"

"Only if you buy flowers."

"Could we maybe say it's a tip?"

"We don't collect tips, sir. We're a supermarket. You'd best just go on ahead with your life and be sure not to do it again."

Donnie noticed the red patches on the insides of the man's elbows; he'd been scratching one and now it was bleeding. Donnie was causing harm. He passed the flower stall. Now, too, buckets of blooms waited without an attendant. He felt a familiar itch of opportunity. That night long ago had started in a joyride of flowers and ended the way too many adventures had: with early morning and the smell of rot.

He sat in his adviser's office at school. He needed to take five more courses to complete his major. He'd chosen history, but that was pretty random.

He just wasn't good at this. Every little hunch that popped into his head for the Commons seemed to Walter like a great idea. Donnie had gotten so he just said what he thought, with no time lag, and Walter acted on all his weird little suggestions.

Nothing he did in school seemed to matter. He got Bs on his papers and people tolerated what he said in class. No one jumped up and down. He looked out the window. In the distance, someone was mowing a lawn.

"You don't have to love this," the professor he'd corresponded with said again.

After Ida died, Donnie had cut down his hours in Geri. When he deposited his first check from Community Commons LLC, he gave notice.

Most Sundays, he and his mother took Dr. Moss for a walk. There were certain trees they checked on. They walked all the way to an enormous bromeliad, near the fence that separated the regular wards from the forensic units, and then turned back.

Shirley told Donnie that his mother asked for Dr. Moss other times, too, and if an aide was free, they'd walk her over. "They talk about plants. You know."

Donnie started to plan a garden for Caroline's yard. Some Sundays, he picked up his mother and brought her there, driving her back in time for dinner with Julie.

Donnie called his sister. "Isn't there anything I could do to make your life easier?"

She was quiet for a while and then said he already had; he'd never guess how many times she'd thought of his kitchen, how orderly it was, when she visited last spring. The neat bamboo rack, counters clear, ripening tomatoes on the sill. Those soba noodles with an egg.

"I could come to New York and clean your kitchen. I'd like to do something bigger."

She sighed. "I wish I saw you more. But that's on me. I live too far."

"You still think you'll stay there?"

"I'm saving to buy a place."

It seemed tragic: they'd once lived together every day, and now they never would again.

77.

Sheila Geller made two more studio visits and left both times with a stern mouth. Lina would have to stop craving her admiration, though it had been her first luck.

Walter continued to serve on the board of the California school and, every few months, called Lina to ask her to reconsider a job there. In early 1984, the school lost its second provisional director.

Lina said no again.

"Okay," Walter said. "But you know sometimes I worry about you."

"Well, don't."

In her early twenties, Lina had hoped to become an artist and to fall in love, not necessarily in that order. But now in the year she would turn twenty-eight, not in the service of either pursuit, she began to look, at first lackadaisically and then regularly, for a home. She and Troy fell in love with a building in Harlem that was almost affordable. They found five people to go in with them. The building had four vacant units, so five of them (two were a couple) could move in right away. The others would have to wait for a tenant to leave or die.

"Maybe before you empty your bank account you should ask your brother who does this kind of thing for a living," Walter said.

"I'm asking you," she said.

Walter arrived in New York on his way back from a shopping-center conference wearing a jacket that didn't look warm enough. They met at the museum and took a taxi up to Harlem.

Lina had saved money. She didn't have enough, she didn't think; she didn't know how much they'd have to put down; she hoped Walter might offer her a loan. But he had been frowning since the West Nineties. When they turned a corner and she saw the building, her pulse quickened. It was a pretty brick prewar on a corner with windows onto Morningside Park. They could fix up the lobby and make a roof garden. By now, she knew older artists; she'd attended improvisational dinners in lofts, cloths flung over worktables, a large steaming bowl in the center. She'd glimpsed a way to live.

But she knew Walter's answer before they'd finished walking through the unoccupied apartments. She opened closets and pointed out views, knocking on walls that were brick under the plaster, until he suggested they go get something to eat. He'd seen enough. They walked down Amsterdam Avenue, but it was the middle of the afternoon and most places were closed. They finally turned in to a tiny restaurant with shelves on the walls filled with jars of jam. They sat at one of the two tables and ordered soup, the only item written on the slate menu. The cook brought out two bowls from the kitchen. Walter said it was the best tomato soup he'd ever tasted. He went on and on, more excited about the soup than the building. His enthusiasm enraged Lina. "You think I shouldn't buy it."

"Nope. Location location location. Plus I don't want you living there. The neighborhood's not safe."

"It's pretty safe and on the way up." He just shook his head. So much for her loan.

"People have been saying that about Harlem for decades."

"Anywhere safer in New York is way too expensive."

"Sometimes you get what you pay for."

"Says someone who can pay." She was arguing longer than she usually argued with Walter, though she already knew he wouldn't lend her money. He would think of this as a matter of principle. She hated his principles.

Donnie and their mother cared more that a person got what she wanted. For a jittery flash-second, she remembered the wrapped packages they'd stolen.

Walter stuck his head into the kitchen and asked the cook about dessert. He ordered two chocolate puddings, the only choice. "How's it going with the new guy?" he asked. He clearly thought love was more important than a place to live. Lina had once thought that, too. She wasn't so sure anymore. She was sure, though, that what she had with the guy she was sort-of seeing wasn't love. She still believed, not only from Hollywood movies but also from *Middlemarch* and Chekhov and even from things Lauren said, in "it"— whatever "it" was. Lauren said with Paul "it" just felt right.

Still, the guy was cute; she could bear to sleep with him.

"I hope you put that a little differently when you're talking to him."

With Sacha, long ago, she'd felt effervescence.

Maybe this was the challenge: to summon romantic feelings for a willing person.

"Hey, I have something to show you." Walter had been carrying a Danish schoolbag. He took out two pairs of miniature shoes: tiny red hiking boots and little sneakers.

"I found these in Italy. You can't buy them in the States. Look."

He extracted a third pair: tiny Mary Janes.

"Who are these for? Is Susan . . ."

"She wants them to be two years apart in school."

"Congratulations." Lina changed the subject. "Are you and Donnie still working together?"

"Yeah, we are. But now he's renovating an old building at the college to be a sober dorm. He still comes up for meetings. He'll make some real dough on the Commons. I suppose once he spends it all, he'll want to work with me again. You've got to see the place. Oh, and did he tell you? Donnie's got his eye on a house he wants to move Mom into."

"A board-and-care?" Lina remembered the ones they saw.

"Susan and I looked a few times, too."

All this kept happening. Finding a place for their mother had been going on for more than a decade, their entire adult lives. No wonder Lina was bad at romance. In her favorite books, you came to a breath-stopping realization that the guy was not bad, or was not, in fact, enamored of someone else, and you trembled there for a moment at the top of the peak, understanding that if he loves you after all, your life will be good. It had felt that way with Sacha. She decided now that she would send a collection of Jane Austen when the new baby was born. The endings of those novels were fast slopes down to happiness. But who could solve the problem of their mother?

The new guy she'd been seeing a few months didn't even know about her. She talked to Troy about her family. He fell into a kind silence whenever her mother came up that made it easy to talk.

"Donnie wants to move Mom in with them."

"Who would be with her all day?"

"Him, he thinks. We'd have to hire somebody, too. He's picturing her with Caroline and him and the kids for meals. I tell him that'd be the end of any hope for romance." He raised an eyebrow. "That wouldn't be the worst thing."

"Has anything happened with them?"

"Not outside his head. You're how old—twenty-seven? Twenty-eight? If I were you, I'd think pretty seriously about making it work with this new guy. D'you ever wonder how Mom has this disease and we got lucky? We just got lucky," he repeated.

"I don't know if I'm lucky. Mom kept it together a long time, too. Maybe it'll happen to me later."

"Oh, no," Walter said. "She always struggled. And you're not like that at all."

This was a large present. He wouldn't loan her money, but this was more. She didn't say anything. She tried to let his confidence in her seep in.

Sitting in the tiny restaurant, saying no to his sister about the apartment she wanted, Walter remembered the day he'd once surprised her at school. She'd jumped up and showed him the whole college; she was totally into school. She was still like that now about her work, though she'd become serious and quiet. During that long-ago visit, he'd told her he wanted to build their mother a house. Maybe Yuma, Arizona, he'd said. Or some Valley town.

"She spent her whole life getting out of a Valley town," Lina had told him.

She'd been right. He should have listened.

He remembered thinking Lina looked different; her hair was unruly, she was wearing jeans that had been too many times through the wash and a T-shirt with dried paint on it. When she'd worked at the department store, she'd been too la-di-da. It seemed hard for her to get it right. She'd been fitted for glasses, at least, which made her look cared for; a regular student. "Any love affairs?" he'd asked. She shook her head, working her hair into a messy bun and sticking a pencil through it. And she used to be this beautiful girl! he'd thought. Compared to the other students, she'd had no ruffle, no flounce. Two lesbians had passed, both wearing black; one tucked in her sweater and wore a slender belt, the other had on baggy clothes. It was as if there was a man lesbian and a woman lesbian. His sister looked like the man lesbian. He'd wanted to tell her to be more like the woman one. Come to think of it, he'd worried about her love life ever since. She looked better now, anyway. He'd once or twice sent her a box of clothes from a good store. She never wore them, that he saw. She still lived in jeans and boots, but either she'd grown into her style or his taste had changed.

Walter bought another chocolate pudding to go. The woman charged him a five-dollar deposit for the jar. He poked his head through the swinging doors to the kitchen, where copper vats rattled on the burners of a huge stove, jam bubbling. He asked the cook if she wanted an investor. She was large, wearing knee socks and clogs. "Write down your number," she said. "I might just take you up on it."

He thought about Lina saying she was like their mom. She was scared that it would happen to her. There was something tentative about his sister; he wasn't like that. His mother must have somehow given him a confidence that she didn't have herself. Still, Lina was an artist. That took courage. He'd made a bargain with life. He'd spend his time gaining the ease they'd once needed. His kids could be artists. He hoped they would be.

He remembered the hanging sculpture he owned. Donnie was supposed to be finding someone to fix it. He knew better than to ask Lina. She'd be furious; the housekeeper had seen a spiderweb and whacked the sculpture with a broom.

He thought of Susan again and how she ran the house.

When Walter had come to see Lina's show, five years ago, he'd taken a secret trip to see Carrie and ask her a question. He told her, without words, I'm ready now. She lived, like a graduate student, in a neighborhood that felt like a vacation. Blooming flowers. Bamboo blinds, music coming out onto the sidewalks. She kept finches in a white painted aviary and rode her bike to the university library. But she'd sent him back to his life.

Sometimes refusal was a gift. His marriage had worked.

His kids would ask him one day about him and Susan. They'd laugh, tell them about their first fight. "Your father didn't believe in Valentine's Day," Susan would say.

"I was an idiot," he'd admit. "But then, later on, I asked your mother on a hot date. Wanna come to the rodeo? We'll be the honored guests of the mayor of Clovis."

Lina wanted this building; he could feel how much.

But someday she'd thank him for saying no.

78.

Donnie had money now, and it surprised him how much he liked spending it. He'd started to pay for more in the house. At first he wasn't sure if Caroline noticed. He'd been living with them two and a half years, and for most of that time he'd been buying the groceries and giving Caroline receipts. She left money every Tuesday night for the farmers market. He stopped leaving receipts in June and let the cash pile up in the empty soup can.

She finally asked about it in August, and he said, "Why don't I just cover that? You've never raised my rent. I can pitch in."

He sensed her struggle. She could use the help; still, she wanted to be fair. "But there's three of us and one of you."

"I eat more," he said.

He was nervous talking about money because her recovery hadn't been as simple as his. She'd had setbacks, more than a few impulsive splurges, mostly clothes that—for a second—she'd believed would change her life.

She resisted, but she finally accepted.

Then one night Jasper's bike was stolen from the porch, where he'd left it on its side. Walter's bike had been stolen once from the bungalow's backyard, and it had never been replaced. Their mother couldn't afford to. Donnie knew that loss had marked his brother. In college, he'd started a whole business with bikes.

Donnie drove Jasper to the town's bike store and let the kid pick.

"Do you have a particular price range?" the salesgirl asked.

"No," Donnie said. He could afford the best bike in the shop. He wished he could give this sense of bounty to Caroline.

Jasper picked an inexpensive bike. Donnie talked him into one with more speeds and safer brakes. Jasper thanked Donnie but he didn't seem amazed, the way Walter would have been. Was Donnie sanding the edges off reality for him? No, he decided, this was reality, too: we do this, if we can, for our own.

In terms of his amends, though, he wasn't making any more progress with stores than with his siblings. He had three years' sobriety and he was still stuck on Step Nine. Sears Roebuck, Inc. sent him to two offices before finally refusing his restitution. In the end, he wrote a letter to corporate management saying a teenager had given him two five-hundred-dollar bills mixed in with ones, for change. *Here's the difference,* he scrawled, then put the unsigned note with cash in a padded envelope. No return address. Some clown in an office would open a weekday moral test. If he was like Donnie'd been, he'd feel the prickle of chance and pocket the cash.

Without telling Julie, Donnie visited their old landlord a bunch of times until he promised to offer her the next vacancy in the building. Donnie planned to pay him separately so Julie could think it was still her old rent.

Okay, Donnie said out loud, looking at the ceiling the night of his twenty-third birthday, Sylvie at his side. He had a lot. Still, it was hard not to feel that he had all but what mattered most. Caroline wasn't in love with him. That had to be true. But sometimes it seemed she was. Or was almost.

On the freeway, driving up to LA, his mother's car overheated. While AAA towed the car to a garage, Walter picked up Donnie so they wouldn't be late for a meeting with two potential tenants and a group they were interviewing to run the outside theater in the Commons' lot. "After we do that, let's go test drive," Walter said. "We can take Jack." Susan was at a spa, to stop breastfeeding the boy, who was already talking.

Donnie preferred to repair the car. He'd driven the Chevrolet for years; his mother's plaid blanket was still in the back seat with one of Sylvie's chew-sticks, a ground rawhide bone, good for her teeth.

"Sylvie'll know a new car. You've got to get used to buying things."

Donnie drove home a new Honda Civic hatchback, with Sylvie's blanket on the seat. Caroline looked astonished.

"You really are making money."

She poured a glass of wine for herself while he fixed dinner. The kids had left that afternoon for a weeklong school wilderness training. Donnie had been looking forward to nights alone, but now the house felt too empty. He was embarrassed about the car. Donnie followed the recipe for a curry Caroline had loved the first time he made it, but tonight the sauce tasted too tomatoey. They talked less than usual while eating. After dinner, they watched an old Italian movie, *Nights of Cabiria,* and at one point her eyes closed, her head fell either on his shoulder or on the back of the couch. He felt the weight. After a while, he helped her stagger to bed. He wasn't sure if she was drunk. She'd had a little more than a glass. Their faces veered close together and he moved his lips to hers and it worked. They kissed and turned on her bed, but it wasn't what he'd imagined. He was fumbling; his arm got stuck under her side and he had to pull it out. It was like an awkward conversation. She took off her clothes, and he didn't know if he should, too. But then he did and he felt too naked in her room. He felt very awake but she seemed sleepy. He kissed her forehead and stood up, thinking that was the right thing to do, but she asked, in a small voice, Are you leaving? He fell back and that time they moved together, both their hands on each other's backs and arms and legs.

Afterwards, she shook her head. "This isn't right."

"It was a little bumpy." That didn't mean that he didn't want to try it again.

Head propped on an elbow, she said, "I can't be sleeping with a student."

"I'm not *your* student."

"But you're an undergraduate! That's what male professors do." She stood up. She was older, true, but he helped her; between them, he was the calm one. Now he was even making money. But they would never be a couple; she was making that pretty clear.

"I know," he said. "This probably only happened because the kids are gone."

"It's not the kids. You're too young. Not even only that. I want a guy who reads novels. For pleasure."

He scratched the back of his head. "I'm reading a novel," he said. "A long one." His sister had sent him a book. Middletown.

"I need a guy who would do that because he loved to."

"I might love to. I'm still just getting into it."

He couldn't help but notice that each time he spoke, she shook her head, as if to convince herself. Donnie had to summon discipline. Trish had been big on the practice of not letting yourself think about what you wanted, but, instead, concentrating on what you were giving. "What you get back is *not your business*," she liked to say. Gifts were supposed to tag you from behind. If what you wanted happened, it would only be when you'd let go of the wish for it altogether.

Of course, Trish believed in God. She prayed. Donnie did, too, but he didn't have a firm sense of to whom he was addressing his prayers. Praying, after his one night with Caroline, on the linoleum floor of his bedroom, he gave up on Step Nine for his sister and brother. He would stop making them uncomfortable with his demands for amends.

Later, he stumbled upon an amend he could do, without them even knowing. Lina and Walter had always wondered if they had the same father as Donnie. He hadn't had a name for the first months of his life. *No Name Aziz* was printed on his birth certificate. Julie had to put through an official name change on the county record. He finally received his birth certificate, with his name on it, when he was fifteen. His mom hadn't been careless; she was tortured, Julie told him. She couldn't decide between names. She liked Essem and Donnie. She finally picked Essem, but everyone else called him Donnie; so in a way she ended up having both. Thinking that made him smile. Their father had been long gone by the time he was born. And Walter and Lina were both dark—dark hair, dark eyes, dark skin. Donnie had only the eyebrows.

But Julie told him one night, during a Sunday dinner in Long Beach, that in the papers she had for Diane's divorce, there'd been an HLA blood test for him as a baby. He and his brother and sister all had type O. The divorce court considered it conclusive: the Afghan was his father. So the three of them were really the three of them. He had proof, in the form of old divorce papers, sixty pages of them, which also stipulated child support, which his mother had never received. Something felt wrong about the whole business, though, and he sat on the papers for two months, then finally sent them each a copy the week before Christmas.

They'd grown up together and she'd been their mother. What difference could different blood have made?

Donnie drove up to LA every week to walk through the renovations with Walter. He slept on the floor next to Jack's crib the night before they broke ground for the sandbox. In the morning, he and Walter watched the first minutes of excavation, with Jack on Donnie's shoulders.

The Commons wouldn't open for another six months, but Walter contracted with Delancey Street to sell Christmas trees in the parking lot, only noble firs. He and Donnie tied an eight-footer to the top of the Civic for him to take home.

The amend Donnie dreaded most was not an important one. The pudgy girl addicted to love was still mad, he was positive, for one stupid night. But you weren't supposed to be like that, *minimizing*. You had to apologize with no *but*s. The girl didn't come to their meeting anymore, but she wasn't hard to find. He took the concrete stairs to her apartment two at a time and made himself knock on the flimsy aluminum screen door. She opened thirty percent and stood there, one foot on top of the other. He couldn't have loved her if he'd tried.

That was why he wasn't a true Christian. Donnie couldn't make himself love, the way you were supposed to.

"I want to apologize," he said. He hadn't even been high. She'd asked if he wanted sex, no strings, and they'd had some facsimile of it in her car. No matter what she said, she was hoping for more. There was no more. "I'll do whatever I can to make it up to you."

"There's nothing you can do." She kept shaking her head. "You're a bad person."

He turned around, windless. He would stop. Step Nine would have to be left unfinished. Failure would remain a pillar of his life. He would need to find other doors, do extra for people he didn't know, and hope the sum evened out. He'd stay alert. Before and even now sometimes, he'd walk into a room and feel a buzz of opportunity—something he could get away with. He'd have to develop that instinct to recognize openings for restitution.

The only person who accepted his amends was his mother. She listened and murmured *Mm-hmm*. When he received his second large check from Community Commons, he kept it a week before depositing it. Then a mid-century ranch house came on the market down the street. A beauty. Walter ran the numbers. Donnie could afford it. He could make the down payment now, and when the leases kicked in, he could pay out the mortgage, Walter said. But Donnie couldn't start that conversation with Caroline. He thought even the suggestion of a change could tip her into thinking everything was a mistake. He decided to leave it alone; even forgetting that one night (which he never did), they were happy, all of them.

Then he thought of buying the house and moving his mother into it. The hospital was worse without Dr. Moss running it. He'd have to hire a nurse, Walter warned. But taking her out of 301, where she'd been so long—it was hard to know that she'd be happier. Shirley said she went every day or two and brought a bouquet of winter twigs to Dr. Moss.

Donnie started to pick her up after his classes on Wednesdays. He was planning a garden for them to work in together in the back of Caroline's rented house. He sat her in a lawn chair while he dug.

Julie's old landlord called in March. The couple with the baby was expecting again, and they'd bought a condominium in the Inland Empire. The landlord would offer Julie her old apartment, at the old price, with a 5 percent increase. Donnie said he'd eat the difference between that and market value (an opportunity for a private amend), but the landlord said no, no, she'd always been a model tenant. Sunday, Donnie drove Julie up. His chest grabbed just turning the corner at the twirled wrought-iron porch railing that he'd never liked.

But Julie decided, no. It would remind her too much of a time that was over. She said she liked where she lived now. She had a two-bedroom, with no stairs, in Long Beach. "Thinking ahead," she said. "For Diane and me."

The next Wednesday, he and his mother picked up the kids from school. Lily and Jasper were sweet with her. In the yard, she liked to sit in her chair, but they brought things out. Tea. A blanket. A peeled orange. For a while, she fell asleep, the three of them moving around her. Donnie prepared a good dinner, but she didn't eat much. Driving her back to the hospital, he asked about moving in with Julie.

No, she said. Never. She shook her head. She could still be adamant. That was a good sign.

On May 11, the day after Donnie and his mother had walked with him to the enormous bromeliad, Dr. Moss died suddenly. Heart.

Susan was breastfeeding the baby and Julie happened to be in Michigan, so Donnie and Walter attended the funeral by themselves. Patients filed into James Hall, one ward at a time. Shirley led the group from 301. Donnie and Walter were missing the ribbon cutting for the restaurant in the old fire station. They didn't see their mother. Shirley said she'd become anxious after they told her, so they'd given her a sedative and now she was sleeping. Shirley also wanted to alert them that she was leaving for vacation in three weeks. She'd started working part-time for a travel agent and with the discount they gave her, she was taking one of her daughters on an Alaskan cruise.

Caroline suggested that Donnie bring his mom to the house for the week Shirley was gone. The kids would be away at camp. They could clear out Lily's room. If it went well, then maybe they could reconfigure. She was offering that again.

Whatever Donnie had felt before dropped three stories lower.

Love didn't begin to describe it.

He spent days preparing. He took out six bags of trash. But there was more to do. He took down curtains and rods, unscrewed hooks from Lily's closet. He remembered the phrase: *danger to one-self or others*. He'd stopped the first time he'd heard it. His mother had never wanted to hurt them. She'd only been after herself. She probably didn't need these precautions anymore. Still, he thought he would close her into Lily's room at night, with a chair shoved under the knob. Just so she couldn't roam outside in the dark and trip.

Two weeks before she was coming, the next-door neighbor pounded a FOR SALE BY OWNER sign into his front lawn. It wasn't a beautiful house. The compact ranch down the street had sold; a young family lived there now. This one was right next door, though; a garden could span both yards. The house could be simplified, painted. He'd learned about that from the Commons.

A tingle.

Donnie rose early, diced vegetables for soup, then picked up his mother. There was much more bureaucracy now to get her out overnight. Shirley had packed her suitcase. But once finally home, his mother seemed disoriented. She asked where the little girl was, though she knew Lily's name from months of Wednesdays. She didn't want to eat her soup. She didn't touch the avocado either, once her favorite food. That night, she had trouble sleeping. She stayed up fretting her hands. Donnie sat with her. Shirley had handed him her medicine for each day in a ziplock and she'd carefully written out the schedule. Caroline had a sleeping pill, but they didn't think they could give it without asking a doctor. Julie was scheduled to visit the next day. Then, Donnie thought, he could rest. He'd been up more than twenty-eight hours. His mother didn't seem happy to see Julie, but Donnie excused himself for a nap with Sylvie in his room above the garage. That night, while they sat at dinner— Donnie had made risotto with fava beans, asparagus, and peas from the garden—his mother got up from the table and put her hand on the wall, saying she had to go to bed. It was five o'clock. She slept until ten. Then she was up all night again, wanting to walk outside. Donnie took her out on their quiet street. She kept turning to go the other way. She couldn't get comfortable.

Walter brought Jack the next morning. Donnie scrambled eggs, made fresh tortillas on a press he'd found at the swap meet, and added pico de gallo and thin, even slices of avocado. Jack sat on Walter's lap, making a mess. Walter surveyed the house, grudgingly approving. "I like your style. I wish Susan was here to see." It wasn't so much a style his brother admired, it was order. Donnie knew that his brother took the opportunities he could to bring Jack to his mother without Susan. The boy was active now, walking uneasily, with the risk of falling Donnie associated with their mother. Walter had already asked Donnie twice today, Didn't he think he wanted to have a kid of his own? Donnie said no, he didn't. He loved the Dauphin, but he was secretly prouder of Lily and Jasper. It bothered Walter that Caroline was older, and that she'd given birth to another man's children. Their mother liked Caroline. Maybe that bothered him, too.

Donnie herded them outside. The early summer garden was full, with the smell of tomato vines mixing with herbs. Sylvie slept in the shade.

He asked Walter what he thought of the house next door.

"Not great bones," he said.

"But think of the garden we could have."

His mother didn't show much interest in his vegetables or flowers. Maybe she no longer cared about plants. But she still liked to walk to the bromeliad at the hospital and she stopped to touch certain trees. Donnie should have planted a garden five years ago.

Walter, he could tell, thought their mother wasn't making enough of a fuss over Jack.

Donnie was afraid she was losing her taste for life.

He ended up driving her back to the hospital after her fourth night. She seemed relieved to see her clothes put back in her cubby. She patted the top of her bed. They went to the community room and she fell asleep in a chair.

Once, they'd struggled to keep the bungalow. Now he had the money to buy a house, but it might already be too late.

Donnie told Shirley about the visit when she returned from her vacation. "We all get used to our routines," she said. "And then we end up loving them."

"I'm so glad you're here," Donnie said. Shirley told him then that she'd put in her papers to retire in five months, right before Christmas. She wanted to travel with her daughters and their children.

"What should I do then? Should I try to move her again?" Donnie asked. "Maybe it just takes longer to adjust."

"You could try," she said. "I think she may be better off here." Shirley promised to work with Diane, to get her attached to someone else before she left. "Five months is a long time, every day." She told Donnie that before he died Dr. Moss had asked her to give Donnie and his brother his botanical journals. So they loaded three boxes of the *California Journal of Rare Fruit* into his Honda.

Even if the hospital was getting worse? he asked.

"Let's see."

Then, one night in August, Lina called and asked to borrow money. A place she'd wanted to buy with friends more than a year ago had sold, but just now it fell out of escrow. Donnie's cash was still all there, a pile in his checking account. He'd once bought Lina a coat and she still owned it. He was after all being given the chance for an amend.

He was nearly twenty-four years old and finally done with school. He should be having sex; he knew that. But he couldn't live without Caroline and the kids. And—and this was no small thing—Sylvie was getting older. He didn't want to disturb her routine. He could wait a little longer, he decided, as he always did. Maybe he was too willing to wait.

But then, out of nowhere, Caroline tapped his back. It was a night they were all at home, both kids, in their rooms after dinner. He and Caroline did the dishes.

"You're not a student anymore," she said. "Let's watch a movie. My bed, okay?"

This time, it didn't stop.

79.

Asking Donnie to borrow money for the down payment, Lina said that maybe she should forgo the tingle. He would be sad, she knew, for her to settle so far away.

"A house isn't a tingle," he said. He wired money the next day, with a note: *This is not a loan. Accept this please. For me.*

While Lina, Troy, and their partners were shopping for mortgages, the owners of the building received an all-cash offer. The deal looked as if it would fall through. Lina felt chastened. Another tingle forgone. One she'd badly wanted. For days, the sellers stalled and Lina felt clarified; she would live on less. She wouldn't even think, anymore, about the piece of art she'd left with Sacha. If she couldn't own anything, she would work all the time. But on the fifth day, the owners decided to honor their first commitment.

A lawyer, Martine's brother, established a ladder fee for the partners. Lina and Troy had the least money to put down, so they'd move in last. Lina didn't mind waiting. They started Sunday work afternoons to fix up the roof. Next summer, they could throw dinner parties there. This summer, Donnie had tried to move their mother in with him. "A disaster," he'd told her. And now Shirley was retiring. Donnie still drove their mother to his house. But at night, he said, she always wanted to go back.

———

The woman who'd made the best tomato soup never called Walter. But she opened a full restaurant, not just soup, jam, and pudding, three times the size of the first one. Lina and Troy ducked in on a hot August night after a movie at Symphony Space that he'd liked and she hadn't. There was a whole genre they were discovering, art that seemed to appeal more to one gender than the other, or was it just to him more than to her? "It's like our old fight over Picasso," Lina said. "Pollock."

"I'm coming around to your POV. They lived and died for art," Troy said. "Whereas Duchamp, you can know, the guy had fun."

On the small television in the back of the restaurant, black-and-white footage ran: billowing smoke from rooftops, light exploding, flames ravaging furniture inside a storefront, illuminating it for a moment, the sky rolling into an ocean of waves.

"Oh, my God. The Watts Riots," Lina said. It was a program on the twentieth anniversary. August 11.

"You must have been eight years old in 'sixty-five."

Lina felt agitated, eager to stand up and move. Troy paid for dinner. He had a gallery now, too. Lina no longer felt more successful; they'd returned to the parity they'd always had.

"Sometimes I think I should move home," she said.

They passed 110th Street, where Troy lived. He kept walking. It was still hot, after ten. "I wouldn't mind LA," he said.

They brought lawn chairs to the roof of Lina's building, where she still lived. They carried up gin and tonic and ice and bottles of tap water. One of the things Lina liked about New York was the tap water. When she climbed up, Troy was standing on the tar roof, his white shirt billowing. She gazed at him from the back. He looked tall; he'd always been tall. His arms were thin and long, his hands enormous. They'd known each other for a decade, and it had never been romantic. Now, it was, almost. Maybe she was imagining.

She tapped his shoulder, gave him a drink. Then they stood for a while, not talking. She looked down to check her clothes.

Then it started. This was new, and she didn't want to say anything to stop it. Kissing him felt rough and strange, yet gentle. He seemed to be searching her face. After a while, they were still standing, swaying, it began to rain. A summer storm. They were collecting the folding chairs, the bottles, the glasses, when the sky cracked with thunder and lightning.

In her bedroom, they ducked under her covers.

A jump off a cliff, Lina thought, because what would she do without Troy. It was the high dive, feeling the bounce of the board, and then the seconds in the air, your legs fluttering as you go up before the plunge.

I never thought I was your type, she said, after. Relieved to be talking again, back on the surface of the world.

Didn't think I had a type, Troy said.

You always liked women who weren't artists.

He laughed. Yeah, I guess I dated a few professional women.

The suits. The heels. Or the sneakers that they wore on the subway, carrying the heels. They always seemed enchanted in the beginning, Lina said.

In the beginning, he said.

Would you really move to LA?

Always wanted to live in the West.

What are we going to do now?

He shrugged. Kissed her again.

A ninety-four-year-old tenant in the Harlem building gave notice. He was moving in with his daughter, before the holidays. Lina was next in line. She'd lucked out; his apartment was on the top floor.

Only Troy was left. He slept at her place every night anyway. They hadn't talked about what they'd do with two apartments.

"You can have that one," she said, "when I move to LA."

"Don't forget, I'm coming with you."

The next time Lina bought tickets to go home, Troy came. He didn't have a license and slumped against the passenger seat as Lina drove one of Walter and Susan's cars to Norwalk.

Her mother looked down at her hands, stroking the tops of her ridged fingernails. She had once been proud of her hands. She'd told Lina, Never cut the cuticle. Just push. She had had a little metal stick with a flat end for that purpose. Now they were rough and callused from years of making arrangements with thorns.

Troy knelt down on the floor so they were at the same level. They looked into each other's eyes. Her mother smiled and patted the top of his head. She kept patting down his hair and letting it spring up.

You weren't supposed to do that, touch Black people's hair.

Troy smiled; he knew what she was thinking; they would laugh about it in the car.

I used to have hair like this, her mother said. Naturally curly.

Troy pulled her up and so her feet were on his shoes. He danced her like that until she had to sit down, out of breath from laughing.

80.

Walter awakened early, relishing the quiet of his sleeping house. He leafed through a book about company towns. He had a folder of articles about aircraft manufacture in Southern California; he wanted to get a historian to write something they could paint on a wall of Aviation Park, like the biographies of artists you saw on the walls of museums. He had a flyer, printed on rough paper, from the California Hatchery. Buff ducklings, mallards, Blue Indian Runners, and Pekins were available, three days old. They'd lost ducks from the lake in the park to migration. Walter always picked the ducklings himself. His attention meandered to a brochure showing varieties of koi. Susan had seen a koi pond at a spa and brought home pictures. They were digging a pond in the Commons where the old laundry had been. On Saturday, Walter had taken Jack to see the bulldozers. Maybe Donnie would drive to Sunland with him to pick out ducklings. Walter never liked working alone. He'd ask, but Donnie was tied up now with that sober dorm and the professor and her kids, and he still brought their mother home every week. That was pretty great of the professor. Still, Walter had a dim feeling about the relationship.

What had made the Commons work was history and restraint. They'd kept the Palisades Laundromat until the Hamel-Wongs retired. They still had the post office and the shoe repair. The barber. Walter had bought the building of the sixty-one-year-old chicken-wing place with a leaseback into perpetuity.

He'd had to resist greed.

Walter thought of Rory's pitch. But a former aircraft manufacturing plant and an old shopping center had glamour. A prison didn't. Lina had sent him pictures of a decommissioned fort in Texas where they'd once kept German prisoners of war. She'd met a sculptor once in a downtown loft where he'd eaten pasta and complained, frustrated like the rest of them. A year later, he sent a letter from Texas saying his work looked completely different in the middle of nowhere. Emptiness inspired him. He wanted young artists to come out and help him restore murals on the walls of the military base he'd bought.

I have something in me, she'd told Walter once, as the explanation of why she wouldn't move home. She believed that like a dare. You had to both pity and envy her. Walter hadn't felt that special since he was a child. Maybe for a moment when he read a plan in design class and ancient Rome sprung to life. Carrie once read him a poem about a jar in Tennessee; he pictured an empty jam jar in the dirt and leaves of People's Park and tried to draw a new city.

The closest he came to that now was a jumpy sense of *Gee, maybe I can do better than that.* But you shouldn't have to be exceptional or even lucky to live a good life. Walter remembered the scientist in the huge Berkeley hall saying look to your left, then look to your right: two of you won't get in. Why such a narrow funnel? It turned out that neither Walter nor Ken even *wanted* medicine. The scientist *himself* wasn't a doctor. And after all that trouble, Melinda worked part-time since they'd moved to the walnut farm. Cub held anesthesia contracts for two hospitals, but he sounded more excited about the mayoral campaign he was running.

"It's not about being brilliant," Walter would tell his children. "I'm just the guy who found an empty building in the middle of California." He respected architecture less than he once had. Some buildings were true art. A few more worked like machines for living.

But when he looked at most new buildings, what he saw was ego. So many people had to erect their own; it would go on until we plowed down the last trees on the planet. So Walter bought neglected structures and put thought into them. What did that make him? Not an architect, not really a developer. More like a housekeeper of commercial property. Maybe a *great* housekeeper. The kind you couldn't hire. What they used to call a wife back in the day.

Walter's driver arrived; Rory had sent a car for him. Walter had a queasy feeling about this dalliance. It was a chance for real money. He was already richer than he'd ever thought he'd be, but by now he understood there were tiers and tiers above him. This trip wasn't only for that, though. Walter wanted someone working *with* him again, not only teams working *for* him. His whole life was asleep in the house around him, but Walter felt alone. He missed Ken since Ken and Melinda had moved to Modesto. Ken was baking bread. But he was usually home and liked to talk. Walter would call him; he'd tasted an amazing dried persimmon—the chef said it was an old Japanese procedure, people strung them up. Ken's mom would know. Walter had loved having a partner. Donnie's dorm would soon be filled with living students. The professor had gotten tenure and they'd probably never return to LA.

Walter heard water running through pipes. His family waking. Susan stalked into the kitchen barefoot holding the baby, with an easy swing and smile. She picked up the five-book set of novels Lina had sent to put in the nursery.

It was time to meet Rory's prison builders. He'd said no a couple times, the way Lina did about the school. Not a forever no. He liked being asked again. An hour of research in the public library had convinced him that prisons were the future of California, the only institutions opening rather than closing. A pretty sad state of affairs. Walter had driven to Orchard Springs to walk around with the new Pakistani superintendent, who was rapidly extending the forensic side of the hospital. Walter had drawn plans to show Rory's team, based on what he'd learned from Kirkbride. He still had the old book from Em Ball.

———

Prison wasn't so different from a hospital, except that it required more security. There needed to be places for therapy, for activities, for sports, and some modest beauty.

Walter had never flown private before. The airport was the best part, rinky-dink, like an old Valley runway. Walter's driver drove right up to the metal ladder. Rory had flown down from Woodside to pick him up. Inside, there were white leather seats, white carpeting, and polished tiger maple. Rory had his shoes off. The stewardess asked Walter what he wanted to drink. They were the only two passengers on the plane.

"I'm afraid to spill," Walter said.

Rory was his old party self and ordered for the two of them. The stewardess pulled out a pocket table and set it with a white cloth and silverware. Walter found himself forming workarounds to like Rory, as he always had. He remembered his toast at the wedding about the food service cart. When he told him his ideas for correctional campuses, as Walter called them, with working gardens, animal husbandry, a library, therapy, music, and games, a blankness clouded Rory's eyes. For no reason, Walter thought of Lina. He'd sat her next to Rory at the wedding; he was glad that nothing happened there. He didn't think he'd been wrong about that place in Harlem, but she sounded happy. She'd finally moved in. Troy still didn't have his apartment. They were waiting for someone to die.

Walter hadn't taken out his plans yet. The stewardess kept bringing food. Rory was on his second drink.

When he and Rory finally sat at the conference-room table in Nashville with the investors, Walter made a case for institutions, asylums for the mentally ill, orphanages, reform schools, and true correctional campuses, which offered rehabilitation, not just warehousing. He could tell from the investors' hands, busy on the table, that they were not with him yet. He showed them his slides. When they projected their spreadsheets, Walter saw that his plans couldn't work. Their profit margin depended on housing three times more people than the current state-run facilities. There would be no leeway for bakeries or gardens, not to mention classes.

It was like the first meeting in Chicago years ago.

He'd anticipated some of this; he'd meant to argue, consider.

Then Rory ran the numbers, his numbers, what Walter would receive as compensation, and Walter experienced the dizzy sensation he'd felt that snowy afternoon long ago in Chicago, a chance to jump up an entire level to a life he couldn't even imagine.

Forget beauty, though. Maybe he could get a concession, here or there, make these complexes, as they called them (feeding troughs, he thought to himself as they showed the pictures), a little better than the next guy could, but fundamentally, the profits they were insisting on would rule out everything good. Unlike that first time in Chicago, though, now his family was settled. Donnie and Lina were living out the courses they'd chosen; even Lina, the artist, had become a nearly middle-class homeowner. His mother was as safe as she could be.

So Walter's arms flew hands-up and it was done. The forever no.

Rory was still smiling. He wanted to hit the hotel gym and meet for dinner at seven. "Knew you were a long shot," he said. They could fly back tomorrow. But Walter took a cab to the airport and bought a ticket. With the time difference, he'd get home before Susan fell asleep.

On the plane, he thought of his sister's project. She went and photographed old psychiatric hospitals, ruins most of them, and made models of those no longer standing. One or two had been converted to condominiums. In Traverse City, Michigan, they'd turned one into a shopping center. Now in California, a couple were repurposed to be prisons. Her photographs had an elegiac quality, as if emptying the institutions had been a tragedy. It wasn't just asylums, either. He wondered what had happened to all the orphanages. There was no longer such a thing as an orphanage in America. But there were still orphans.

That night, he wrote a check to Orchard Springs, mess that it was. They'd done okay by his mom. Because of her, he'd never design a prison. Rory had his own plane and he'd bought his parents a vacation house in Ireland. He was building a boat. Walter's mom couldn't use a vacation house anyway.

Walter hated that his biggest contribution to the world might be *not doing* something bad. His biggest contribution yet, anyway. He was still not dead. He smiled to himself; Rory's stewardess had slipped him her number, which he'd already thrown out.

81.

The weather had just turned to winter in Southern California, a wet black branch with pine needles against the sky. Walter walked to his polling place, a neighborhood garage, where he showed his driver's license to a teenager. He'd begun voting when Jerry Brown won for governor the first time. Despite watching nightly news and reading two newspapers, Walter always felt insufficiently prepared. People accepted inequality, most people did. They believed their place was where they belonged; what they got was what they deserved.

It hadn't been hard to get statistics about children. The department of social services was housing kids in empty office buildings downtown. But Walter couldn't just find a ruin and turn it into an orphanage; that was the easy part. There was a system of courts and social workers, the very people who'd decided to empty out the old institutions. He'd found out that the first Los Angeles orphanage once stood where Union Station was now. The Los Angeles Orphan Asylum, opened by nuns. Daughters of Charity. He wished Susan would take on something like this.

Susan called him at the Commons office to tell him the baby's poop was watery. Good she called. They'd had a fight and it still wasn't over. The mountains today looked close enough to walk to. After they hung up, he called Lina.

He'd tried to talk her into moving back for years, and in the end it was strangers who lured her, not his kids or Donnie or even their mom. She saw the Watts Riots on TV. Lina'd always taken history too personally. Maybe Troy had something to do with moving. He loved it here. She'd spent over a thousand dollars shipping back her unsold artwork. But, he supposed, that was her wealth. Two of her pieces hung in Walter's house. She'd taken the job in the school, and from what he'd heard, she was doing really well there.

He'd offered the two of them money for a down payment—they still owned that building in Harlem that they'd hardly even moved into and said they'd never sell—but they found that Gregory Ain house on their own and signed a long lease. He had to admit it looked pretty great. She had her high school English teacher's library; Troy had built shelves. She'd gotten in touch with her high school ceramics teacher and bought three or four of his sculptures. He could exactly picture the rooms where the phone was ringing, their look of marginality and New York high culture.

No one answered.

So he got out of the office and ducked into the Commons roastery, carried his cappuccino to a table by himself. He'd never had a cappuccino before Berkeley. Never heard of one. He had an hour before his doctor's appointment. He leafed through his file of proposals. Because of the Commons and Aviation Park, he was often asked to develop shopping centers. People were successful once or twice and then thought they had a magic potion. Well, he didn't. And anyway, there were no more McDonnell Douglas plants for sale.

Two guys from Stanford's business school wanted to revive Ponyland, the place divorced dads used to take their kids on Sundays in the seventies. Right next to it there'd been an amusement park. Movie stars had their pictures taken with their kids on the carousel's painted horses and then with the real ponies. The guy used to restore old carousels until Walt Disney sent him to Europe to photograph rides. He convinced Disney to build Main Street at seven-eighths scale. The Stanford guys had a site in Baldwin Hills, but, Walter thought, divorced dads got joint custody now. Since the duck pond, Walter wanted a bigger wildlife preserve in a mixed-use compound, with high-end stores, to support the birds. Maybe a firepit. Folk music at night.

Walter saw Jorge, his great parking manager, and got up to order him a coffee. Jorge liked a dry cappuccino. Walter instructed the new kid never to charge the parking guys.

He and Susan had had the Doing the Dishes fight again. Eating dinner as a family was important, Susan believed; Walter did, too, even when it wasn't fun or satisfying or even sanitary—he still hadn't quite gotten over the way his wife allowed their children to eat. He'd seen kids in Italy and Japan, even in the Midwest, eating nicely in restaurants, in little vests and ties. But after a half hour at his own family table, he felt a compulsion to flee to his desk off the family room. A thousand things happened at once in a renovation; a container of finishes from Japan was tied up in customs on the Long Beach docks. Forty-six people had left messages on the answering machine since he'd sat down, and the baby smashed sweet potato over Walter's glasses. He was *there, in the house,* he could hear the stir and patter. But he was not standing at the sink doing dishes with Susan.

She wasn't happy about that. He got her point. He would hire a person to clean up, but she didn't want someone like Lupe, hiding behind a door at her mother's house. Their one-day-a-week cleaning person was a man.

How could you live a life of ideas and productivity without people cleaning the family mess? And was that work necessarily demeaning? Mr. Wimmer said that every meal they ate his wife made with her own hands. But Susan hadn't turned out to be like that. He didn't blame her. He wanted to work, he wanted her to work if she wanted to work; mostly he just didn't want her to be mad at him.

A technician in the doctor's office held an X-ray to the light. "How long have you been smoking?"

"I never smoked," Walter said.

"Oh, grew up in LA, then?"

The firehouse chef was developing ice-cream flavors with spices, peach pits, and flowers. Saffron, cardamom, and David Austin rose petal were on his menu. Now he wanted to open a stand-alone shop in the Commons. Walter loved this guy; the first time they met, the kid told him he'd gone to the chicken-wing shed a hundred times in high school. But Walter had to crunch the numbers. He and the chef sat by a window. Everything outside was sparkling. There were no vacancies now. The chef had an idea that they could use an Airstream trailer, at the eastern corner of the parking lot, by the koi pond. He wanted a stake, he said. The kid was what—twenty-seven? Walter asked him what it would cost to gut and build out the Airstream. He relaxed; the initial outlay wouldn't be much. Might as well let him try. A girl came from the back with a hot loaf of bread on a board with a knife, butter, radishes, and salt. After this, the movie-theater people were coming; he'd formed a group to buy what was left of the 1930s palace Donald Douglas built for his engineers to watch movies on Friday nights. No one would make money on the deal. But people remembered their first kisses in the back rows.

He and the chef were sitting in the booth when a redheaded girl came running down from the office upstairs.

"Your wife needs to talk to you, right away."

And then it became the day his mom died.

She died on Election Day.

Donnie sat with his mother, in 301, as he had so many afternoons.

"You were a wonderful mother," he said. "Thank you."

"I did come," she murmured.

"I love you."

"That's all we have to worry about now. That's all that's important."

Those were the last things she said. Then she was gone. Donnie remembered something he hadn't thought about for years. His mother had once parked at the end of a dusty road lined with olive trees. This was somewhere in the Valley, long ago. A friend of hers was along, with a scarf triangled on her head, tied under her chin. Could that have been Julie? They'd parked behind a flat one-story building that turned out to be a sanatorium, and his mom was walking toward the entrance. Her friend, who now was Julie, he was sure, acted as if this were a joke, a stunt Diane had cooked up for a laugh. A nun behind the desk gave his mom a clipboard and she started to fill it out. They had her in the wheelchair already, another nun stationed behind ready to push her by those two horns down a long, empty hall.

Julie said, "Come on, Diane, let's go find a place to get ice cream." And then, at the very last minute, his mother stood up from the chair and walked outside with them, a person rising from a grave. Exhilarating. They drove around looking for ice cream and finally found a stand with strange flavors. Avocado. Date.

Donnie understood that she'd come back to life for him.

Lina had once asked Dr. Moss if her mother would get well and he'd said yes. She'd looked away then, embarrassed to be seen so happy. The only person who could redeem that promise now was dead. He'd been wrong. And it was finally over.

Lina reached her school office and closed the door, which made a sound like a sigh. She opened the desk drawer that contained her mother's wallet. She'd had this since they moved out of the bungalow, more than a decade ago. It contained her mother's driver's license, her social security card, and one Polaroid of her with Lina, their arms latched.

She would call Troy. She would go to Walter's house. But she couldn't move yet. She had had enough, she thought, in the good sense of those words. She'd had a life's worth of hope and effort and pleasure. She'd finally known love. She could stop now. She could die, too. How many times had she seen her mother put her hand to her forehead and say, "My mind isn't right." She would shake her head, disgusted with herself. In hopeful moments, she'd say, "I've got to get organized." One cold Los Angeles night, she'd asked, "Don't you hear owls?"

For years, what felt like Lina's whole life, vigilance had structured her days, no news was good news, until the piercing call would come, signaling crisis. What would her life be now? The last time Lina saw her mother, her mother's hair was tangled. Lina stood in back of her, combing it out an inch at a time. Those minutes, she left her own mind. That had been two weeks ago. Troy had been ready to drive out the day before yesterday. But she'd been tired. She'd wanted to try making a cake.

Now, as she walked out to her car, a bright guilt slammed into her, a parent who sacrificed for you had a not-good-enough life, a life not half as lucky as yours. She felt something else, too, a warmth on her hand when she stalled in the sun. The day had started cold but the temperature was near seventy now, and for once Lina had dressed right. A short-sleeved shirt, flats without socks. A breeze on her legs, sun on her hand.

Her mother must have had this, too. She must have stopped sometimes, far from the town she'd grown up in with its penitentiary and dusty orange fields, and felt amazed at the softness when pain ended. Two crossing guards, returning from break, waved. Her mother had had that, too. People liked her; they always did. She remembered her lifting face when a man at the gas station flirted with her. Even in the hospital. I've been alone most of my life, too, Lina thought, but even so, I have people. I have Troy.

But her mother had that, too, she remembered. She had us.

Susan called Walter from a pay phone, with Jack and the baby in the car. Julie was in the San Marcos Mountains with Caroline's freckled daughter, Lily. Walter and Susan had sent the two of them for a week to celebrate Julie's retirement. "I could drive down and get them tonight," Susan said, then reminded Walter that he needed a new black suit. The Princeton Shop was long closed, Mr. Barsani retired, his father back in the Ligurian town he came from. Jack, too, would apparently need a suit. This was his Susan: already thinking about clothes, for the funeral of a woman who couldn't love her. But who would even come to this funeral? Really, they should have a memorial there in the hospital.

"What about Julie?" Susan asked.

Walter liked thinking of Julie and that freckled Lily with cucumber slices on their eyes. Lily had been wildly excited about the spa; she'd done all her homework in advance for the schooldays she was missing. "We'll never get Julie there again. On the phone, Sunday, she said she'd never had a massage before and she wasn't sure she liked it."

They decided to leave them in the mountains one more night.

Walter sobbed alone in his house. How small she'd become in his life, she who'd held his hand when he was little. Lina and Julie had sent him back to Berkeley when she first went in the hospital. They had to, they'd thought, but why? Dr. Moss had told him his mother wanted a family life, not love anymore, and she'd accomplished the most important part of that. Of course, she'd hoped to finish raising Lina and Donnie. In the end, his mom spent a ton of time with Donnie. Him, most of all of them. Years now, for better or worse; it might not have been the best thing for Donnie. For the first time he could remember, Walter envied Donnie. He'd loved her, too. He remembered his idea of Yuma. He'd been an idiot.

With the windows open, roses nodded outside his study. Sunflowers tipped from the weight of their blooms. Susan's gardens looked like nature. You might not even notice their order. She'd learned to garden after they were married, Walter always thought, to win over his mom, who proved to be unwinnable for her. But now theirs was the most beautiful garden in the neighborhood. Donnie understood Susan's talent. "Better than anything I could do," Ken had said. Walter felt stirred when people saw her worth. She wasn't a noticeable beauty; some men probably compared her unfavorably to their wives. Rory would, if he ever married. But everything Susan touched was beautiful; gifts Jack brought to birthday parties were wrapped in white paper and twine, with a sprig of rosemary or a flower.

He thought of Julie at the spa. Someday he'd send her with Lily and Lulu. He pictured the three of them in white turbans. He'd given his family this life, that was not an end in itself; it was for him, but for them, it could be a beginning.

The doorbell rang. A redheaded teenager held a bowl of flowers.

Ken, the card said. Susan must have called him, too. She was running this whole thing from the pay phones at Jack's karate class.

Someday Jack would ask, Is there really such a thing as the love of your life? Walter would tell him the love of your life is the person with whom you spend your life. Susan had looked at him once, pregnant with Lulu, and asked if he'd loved Carrie. Her nose, with its small bump, made her look vulnerable, like a sheep. He said no and that was true. He'd long ago given up Carrie when he could have had her—no, he corrected himself, not *had* her but *slept* with her. Carrie wasn't even Carrie anymore. She wore Birkenstocks, she'd stopped shaving her legs. Her kid in the picture looked smart and sturdy (glasses, thick tanned legs), but she wasn't Jack or Lulu.

So much was over. He sat at his desk and mindlessly wrote down the addresses for the physical therapist, the speech therapist, the night sitter he'd hired when Shirley left. He would have the accountant send them each a year's pay and another check to the hospital. But where would it go? To the State of California? The hospital was mostly forensic now, for the criminally insane.

He took his glasses off and rubbed his brow. Ken had sent flowers that Walter had never seen before; roses with a second green blossom growing out of their centers. He dialed the number on the florist's card. A young woman on the phone thought they were called green-eyed roses. Another person in the shop said they weren't roses at all, but ranunculus. Walter wrote down both names.

He would order both, bare-root, for Susan's garden.

82.

In the hospital room at the end of Ward 301, Walter turned to Lina. "Do you want to tell our dad?"

Lina hadn't thought of him. "I'm surprised to hear you call him that. I haven't talked to him in years." When was the last time? "I don't even know if the number I have still works."

"Really?" Donnie asked. "I thought you kept in touch."

For a long time, her father hovered on the edges of her stray thoughts, but that had ended. "I doubt I'll ever talk to him again."

"So you're done with him for good?" Walter asked. "Have you forgiven him?"

"No." Forgiving her father would have been like forgiving the world for her mother's illness. It had made them who they were. Her father's crime had taken decades to complete. It was impossible to know what relationship his absence had to all that had happened. "How about you guys?"

"I'm in no position not to forgive anybody," Donnie said. "I'm still working off the harm I caused."

"Not to him."

"Not to him. But only because he wasn't around."

They laughed. It was strange to laugh with their mother in the room under a sheet.

Mr. Matthews had written to Walter after an article ran about him in Berkeley's alumni magazine, *Now that you're rich, come back and collect your degree!* Walter never had. Now, he thought, he just might. He kept in regular touch with Mr. Wimmer. Susan sent Mr. Barsani and his repatriated father Christmas baskets. When he'd first returned to LA, Walter had been taken by a visiting Sears executive to the Beverly Hills Hotel and he became entranced with its logo. He had to find out who drew that typeface. It turned out to be Paul R. Williams, another father-aged man, the only African American architect admitted to the AIA. He designed not only the Beverly Hills Hotel but also homes for Frank Sinatra, Desi Arnaz, and the first federally funded low-income housing project. When Walter finally met him, he was in his eighties. He told Walter he'd learned to draw upside down because his white clients didn't want to sit next to him; they needed the desk between. Once in a while, people asked Walter about his real father. He hated the phrase. Guy was more like a sperm donor. "One day I'll get a call and learn that he died. I'll hang up the phone and eat my lunch."

Donnie shrugged. "He never was family. Not like Julie."

Walter checked his watch. "They should be getting here soon." Troy had driven to the mountains to fetch Julie and Lily. There were no windows in the room, but it would be near dark outside. Walter volunteered to get food, but no one wanted any. The day seemed to go on forever. People came in and out of the room.

Lina told the story of her last night in New York. She'd taken a cab home and the driver was a talker. He lived in New Jersey, but his wife and son were in Yemen.

"My father is Afghani," she'd said, just to say something.

"You speak Dari?"

She answered back the few phrases she'd learned. When he pulled up to her building, he said, "You will know who I am." She looked reflexively at the name and picture on the dashboard, from the New York Taxi and Limousine Commission.

"Forget the name. Remember my face," he said, and turned around.

A short doctor huffed into the room out of breath and introduced himself to Lina and Donnie as the new superintendent. "We'll make a memorial here for her friends in 301. In James Hall, of course," he said, looking at Walter. "I wasn't here at the time of the gift, but I can assure you, James Hall is used every day. Classes. Musical performances. In another two months, there will be access from the forensic side and those patients, too, can enjoy."

It took Lina a moment to remember that Walter had given the hospital money.

The doctor looked down at the sheeted form.

"Shall I call someone to take the body? Do you have a plan?"

They wanted to wait for Julie. The doctor left, shaking their hands too hard. Donnie greeted the geri ward nurses when they each entered, hands clasped in front of them, to say goodbye. Some patients walked in. They didn't say anything, just stood there. Trish had driven over from the youth unit.

Walter volunteered again to go get food. Donnie wanted to stay. "I told Caroline I'd be here." Lina waited, too. The older professor seemed not so much older when she finally burst in with Sylvie on a leash.

Sometime before midnight, the head nurse of Geri asked if she should call someone for the body. This day seemed to have been running for longer than twenty-four hours. They were half-asleep on chairs when Troy finally arrived with Lily and Julie, red-faced from the spa—"a peel," she admitted. "Diane wanted to be cremated. That's what we always said. She wanted everything to go to you kids. There'll be something in her nurses' retirement. I have all the paperwork."

"Do you remember, Julie, when Mom wanted to check herself in to a sanatorium?" Donnie asked.

"Oh, Diane always had a sense of drama."

It was refreshing to have a memory of Julie young.

"She could have been a movie star, your mom."

They agreed. Cremation.

"And then what?" Donnie asked. Lily held her mother's hand in the corner.

"Some people bury, too. Diane did go to church growing up. I think she thought you could sprinkle some of the ashes and keep a few, for each of you. I'd like a little, too."

The head nurse finally called someone to pick up Diane's body. By the time the man arrived it was nearly two. He threw her light form over his shoulder, the sheet still wrapped around, and took her away. Then he was gone.

Donnie still didn't want to leave. Walter stood up holding his keys.

"It's too late to drive all that way," Julie said.

The head nurse had one of the janitors open Dr. Moss's old house, which was being turned into a museum. The downstairs was already set up with exhibits, but they could sleep in the old bedrooms upstairs. She'd sent someone over already with sheets. The new superintendent lived off campus.

Walter, Lina, and Troy decided to walk. Even in the dark they saw mountains, a denser black, against the small stars.

"Did I ever tell you, in Berkeley, I lived for a while in an attic. I liked the way I was then," Walter said. "Maybe I'll stop working. Go back to school."

"I'm relieved to have a job," Lina said. "That's why I came back; I saw a world going on and wanted to join it. I'm painting more now that I have a job. It's less pressure. For a long time, I thought there was something I had to pull out of myself; I didn't know if it was a huge talent or a huge rage, but if I didn't get it into the air it would be my fault for not trying hard enough. It felt like there was one conversation going on in the art world. I wanted to be in it. There seemed no other reason for me to be alive."

"There are plenty of reasons. I need you to talk to me when we're old."

"Remember once I told you I worried about getting what Mom had and you said that I was different? That did a lot for me."

"Good," he said, "'cause it's true."

Walter's benediction proved true over the following years, though there were days, sometimes two or even four, when Lina stayed in bed. She couldn't imagine what Sacha would have done with her when she was like that. She would have had to strain, as her mother had. When it happened, Troy assumed his business voice on the phone, saying the director was sick and shouldn't be expected back this week. He brought her a tray with food and a cool towel. Still, most days during the decades that followed, Lina was well. She and Troy threw their first dinner parties. On Saturdays, they liked shopping at out-of-the-way places for household things. Lina remembered her mother's and Julie's excitement once in a store with Scandinavian enamel cookware, when they were each organizing their young homes.

It's a pot, Mom, Lina had said. "I was a brat," she told Troy.

She read that Keats put on a clean white shirt in the evening, to write his poems. She and Troy both worked after dinner and all day long on Sundays. She'd kept up her research on treatment of what had once been called a female illness and collected notations from doctors, nurses, and patients during the long twentieth century. Some of her materials now were found, not made. She'd also begun to paint simple objects with no context in egg tempura. She'd always loved Morandi's flat backgrounds. It felt important that she and Troy had known each other from the beginning. They understood what the other aspired to, the risks, disappointments, and accommodations. Troy's collages became larger and larger. She loved what he made.

"The one I'm worried about now is Donnie," Walter said, walking over to the doctor's house. "He was so close to Mom. I think he could be heading for trouble."

Lina tensed. "You mean drugs?"

"No, just depression." But nothing like that happened for a long time, not until Sylvie died, and then Caroline and the kids brought him a puppy before he was ready, and did the night bathroom-training sessions until he took over.

———

The morning they awoke in the superintendent's house, Shirley climbed upstairs, thumping an umbrella. "I was just at the morgue," she said. "My Diane."

Shirley still lived in Norwalk and was working as a travel agent. In fact, she said, she was leaving for a cruise on the Yangtze River with her granddaughters in two weeks—industry perks; she was glad she was here now, to say goodbye.

Walter and Lina had been teenagers when they'd met Shirley. It had been pure luck, a slip of paper in a hat, that Shirley had been their mother's nurse. Lina had never thought of her mother as lucky during the years Lina considered the tragic period of her life. But in this place—among the falling-down buildings and poor-quality grass, the trees that had not been pruned for decades—here was Shirley, still radiant today, as her face folded in comprehending sorrow. She came to the hospital two Fridays a month now, she said, to work with another retired nurse on the archive. They'd put together the museum downstairs. She would invite them to the ribbon-cutting ceremony when it opened.

They walked through what had once been the doctor's house. In the daylight, they saw that the living room had been painted olive green, and when you pressed a button, the new round-faced superintendent delivered a speech in his lilting accent on a video monitor. He said that the hospital was changing. He said the things people say on a weekday morning in an institution that has been evidently failing for years. *Here we want to acknowledge and honor our past.* Of course, not everyone would agree to honor what had been done in hospitals like this in the past.

But this hospital had mostly done right by their mother, Lina thought, as she wandered through the room, past pictures of the hospital in its manicured prime. There were explanations of a complicated history stenciled on the walls. The hospital had been first sited for Beverly Hills.

In what had been the dining room, where she'd long ago eaten a tuna sandwich, there were portraits of old people taken by student interns. Mounted next to these color pictures were the black-and-white class photographs of the nurses, in the white uniforms and hats that they'd worn. "When we stopped wearing the uniforms, your mom asked me, 'What happened to all the little mothers?'"

You pressed a button next to a portrait and heard a voice. There was a portrait of Dr. Moss, but no button. He'd died before the oral history project.

Lina pressed a button and a thin voice came out of the speaker.

There used to be a whistle, when you came onto work and then again when your shift ended.

We used to stand at attention when the doctor walked on the ward. Most everyone that worked in the hospital lived on the grounds then. The doctors had their own residences and there were buildings for the rest of us. We had to eat our meals in the cafeteria but the doctors could order canned goods and flour from the storeroom, to cook in their residences. They also had patient help.

"We lived in those apartments when we were first married," Shirley said. "You know I met my husband working here."

A vitrine displayed the machine that administered electroshock with its old black-coated wires hanging, the clamps empty. The chairs they'd used for ECT, the bakery bowls, corsets for camisole restraint, the booties the patients wore on the wards—were all put in glass cases with typed labels.

"Remember the bread?" Shirley said.

Walter headed to the morgue to ask when they could pick up the ashes. Lina wanted to see James Hall. She would probably never come here again. Inside was a pretty auditorium, nicely finished with high windows and a modern stage, lighting, and sound equipment. It reminded Lina of the community room at her school. She'd known Walter sent a check, but he'd probably also sketched these windows, and sourced the wide-plank floors. He'd told her once that there had been a wedding here—two patients, he thought. Walter had always loved love stories. Lina asked, "Did two patients ever get married here?"

"No. Couldn't have been. We always kept them apart. Even at the dances, the female patients could only dance with doctors or staff. Patients were not allowed to dance with other patients."

They walked over to 301, where Lina collected their mother's few belongings. Shirley headed to the library, where the other retired nurse was already working. Julie said maybe today she'd join. She had an idea about making a display of some pictures she'd taken of Diane's flowers.

Donnie wanted to go to the geri unit with Sylvie to say hi. Everyone in Geri remembered Sylvie.

In the small room where Shirley and the other retired nurse worked, boxes of files covered every surface. The mountains of papers were enormous, clearly more than these women could sort if they worked every day between now and when they died.

Walter finally returned with a receipt. "They asked for Mom's maiden name. People whose mothers were murderers are still probably asked what is their mother's maiden name."

Then it was time for them to leave. This was the last time they'd ever be here. Walter asked if they'd seen the inscription on the lintel of James Hall. It was a poem Carrie had once given him.

An autumn night
Don't think your life
Didn't matter.
        —Basho

"He wrote that in 1694," Walter said. The last year of his life.

Acknowledgments

I've been amused, consoled, and inspired by daily conversations about fiction with Michelle Huneven, whose suggestions have made not only this book but also my life better. My Friday page exchanges with Yiyun Li (LMWN!) turned writing these novels into a companionable effort. A writer couldn't have a more sustaining family. Richard Appel, a treasured early reader for decades, and Gabriel Jandali-Appel offered insights from early drafts on: thank you; Grace Jandali-Appel has become my lifelong reading partner. I owe much to Elma Dayrit for beauty and order in my home life.

Randall Kennedy, a daily friend through the years of writing *Commitment*, coached me with encouragement, humor, and intellectual provocation. John Shumate saved me, time and again, from ruinous losses at the hands of Microsoft Word. I'm grateful to Christopher Bollas, not only for his important and mind-expanding work, but for our discussions about medical and spiritual varieties of despair. Thomas Helscher teaches me about resilience, layer by layer. James Rosenfield provided my education in development, decency, and neighborhood.

Rebecca McClary, Cindy Lusch, and Bin Plume at Metropolitan State Hospital spoke to me about hospital life and led me to Emily Wong, Erma Aalund, and especially Shirley Olmsted, three indefatigable women who were exceptionally generous with their memories. I'm moved by their archival work to preserve records of efforts to ameliorate the suffering of now long-forgotten patients. Any inaccuracies are mine, not theirs. Metropolitan State Hospital allowed me to visit multiple times, which helped me gain a sense of the physical grounds and their lingering past.

Binky Urban has been a friend and advocate for decades, years before I published my first book—thank you for your enduring support. I've worked with Ann Close since 1985 and have always benefited from her subtle, unerring ability to discern the inner wishes of a story. Her voice, in its distinctive accent, is by now embedded in my sensibility. This book was written in memory of my mother, our past, and what might have been and dedicated to Kevin Thomas, my future.

ALSO BY

Mona Simpson

ANYWHERE BUT HERE

A national bestseller—adapted into a movie starring Natalie Portman and Susan Sarandon—*Anywhere But Here* is the heartrending tale of a mother and a daughter. A moving, often comic, portrait of wise child Ann August and her mother, Adele, a larger-than-life American dreamer, the novel follows the two women as they travel through the landscape of their often-conflicting ambitions. A brilliant exploration of the perennial urge to keep moving, even at the risk of profound disorientation, *Anywhere But Here* is a story about the things we do for love, and a powerful study of familial bonds.

Fiction

ALSO AVAILABLE

Casebook
The Lost Father
My Hollywood
Off Keck Road
A Regular Guy

VINTAGE BOOKS
Available wherever books are sold.
vintagebooks.com